ONE
OF THE GUYS
EMMY'S STORY, Part 2

by
Kenneth Lee McGee

To Kevin and Kerry,
You Mean The World To Me

I would like to thank Denise and Stephanie again for their support and for sharing their knowledge and opinions. Without their help, this series of books would not have been possible. I would also like to thank Liz, Sue and others for reading my books. I will forever be indebted to the people of WriteOn Joliet without whose knowledge I would have never learned the skills necessary to become the writer I am today. You can't imagine how clueless I was in the beginning.

I want to thank the people from my church who have graciously allowed me to include fragments of their lives as inspirations.

Another special thanks to Sue Midlock for creating the cover. http://suesart.wixsite.com/rosewoodseries

A special thanks to Andy for his support and keeping the computers running.

I want to thank my wife Sheila for her suggestions. Several of which I have used. Some were off the wall and made me laugh, but she's getting better.

Chapter One

"I hate you! I hate you!" Emmy Colasanti raised the ice pick above her head and repeatedly stabbed down with as much force as she could muster.

Suddenly, someone from behind grabbed her wrist before she could strike again.

"Emmy, what are you doing?" Tony Bertucci asked as he held onto her arm.

"I absolutely despise this freezer. It doesn't defrost by itself, and everything I put in here turns into a cement block. I have to let the ice cream sit out for fifteen minutes before I can even get my scoop into it."

"Phew!" Tony let out his breath. "For a second I thought you were talking about me."

"I don't hate you. Sometimes I get upset with you, but I don't hate you. Now will you let go of my arm so I can kill this freezer."

Emmy enjoyed her sense of independence living in a furnished apartment in the large mid-western city of South Hampshire, Illinois. Her second floor apartment occupied the front half of what had once been the upstairs of a single family home.

"Where did you learn to defrost a freezer like that?" Tony asked as he let go of her arm.

"Grandma Sandusky taught me. She had an old refrigerator like this years ago, and I used to watch her."

"Have you told the landlord about the fridge?" Tony asked as he looked around the small kitchen. He could almost stretch his arms out and touch two walls. At six feet and two inches tall, he had long arms.

"I've mentioned it a few times, but he won't replace it. He won't buy anything new for this place." Emmy walked out of the kitchen and took a couple of steps into the living room. Tony shook his head as he followed. "Just look around. That couch has to be fifty years old. The chair doesn't match it. The end table has water stains on it. The wallpaper is ancient and disgusting. Look at it."

Tony looked at the wallpaper. "Yeah, it's pheasants and

1

quails with a bunch of hunting dogs."

"Exactly! Why can't it be flowers or something pretty? My kitchen table and chairs are old pieces of metal."

Tony turned around and looked back into the kitchen. "You do have a window in here that provides plenty of sunshine."

Emmy stared at him with the ice pick still clenched in her hand.

"The carpeting in your bedroom is new."

"Probably because the original carpeting rotted away. The floor in the bathroom is older than dirt and there isn't a shower. I hate this place."

Tony moved closer and took the ice pick from Emmy. He looked down into her sparkling blue eyes and brushed a few strands of her dark, curly hair away from her face. The rest of her hair was bunched into a ponytail held in place by a rubber band.

"If you hate this place so much, then why do you stay?"

"I stay because it's my apartment. It might be old and small, but it's mine."

"You could always move back home..."

"Don't even go there. That's not going to happen."

The date was Wednesday, July 8, 1998, which happened to be Emmy's eighteenth birthday. Tony Bertucci had stopped over at her apartment to take her out to dinner.

"Emmy, where do you wanna go to eat? Since it's your birthday, I'll take you anywhere you want to go." He asked hoping she wouldn't choose anywhere expensive.

Emmy thought about it. "You know, I think my favorite place is still either Darby's or La Cantina. How about La Cantina? It's a little bit nicer than Darby's, and since it is for my birthday, let's go there."

"Yeah, I love Mexican food. Excellent choice, Em. I love a cheap date. Yes, high-five."

"Do you want me to pay for dinner? You're so cheap."

He took her to dinner, and when they got back to her place, he had a present for her. "Open it, Em. I want to see if you like it."

She opened the box and discovered a charm bracelet inside resting on red velvet. A small heart engraved with the letters EOC

2

and APB dangled from the bracelet.

"I love it, and you had our initials engraved. That is so sweet. Thank you very much."

She leaned forward expecting him to kiss her, but instead he poked her in the side where he knew it would tickle.

"Kristen picked it out. She didn't like the football jersey I was going to buy."

It had been sixteen days since Tony's grandfather, Howard Lombardi, passed away. Tony told Emmy many different stories about him during that time. Tony talked about the diabetes that robbed his grandfather of his sight and how Grandpa refused to let that handicap dictate how he lived his life.

"I wish I had more of a chance to know him. He sounds like an amazing guy."

"He never complained about losing his sight, and he certainly never tolerated anyone feeling sorry for him," Tony said.

"I think I would have really liked him."

"Definitely. In some ways you are amazingly like him."

"What do you mean? How am I like him? He was an old man. Do I look like an old man to you?" Emmy put her hands on her hips and waited for Tony's explanation.

"Well, let's see. You are just over five feet tall and you don't weigh more than eighty pounds..."

"I do, but I'm not going to tell you how much more."

"You are the prettiest girl I have ever met."

"You're lying, but I don't care."

"You are very determined—like him."

"Yeah, okay." Emmy waited to see if Tony would stick his foot in his mouth.

"And you can be very stubborn, exactly like him."

"So you think I'm stubborn?"

"I don't mean in a negative way, Emmy."

"Stubborn, huh?" She glared at him and tried to keep from laughing.

Emmy loved Tony, but sometimes he didn't appear to share

3

her love—at least not in the same way. Tony treated her like a little sister, or like one of the guys at times, and that bugged her to death. She didn't want to be treated like that. While having lunch at Darby's a few days later, Emmy told her best friend, Kristen Keasling, how she felt.

"I've got a photo of Tony and me on the nightstand so I can see it when I go to bed."

"Oh, that's sweet," Kristen said. "These fries are really good."

Emmy took a drink of root beer. "Yeah, except sometimes I look at it and think it's a picture of me with my brother."

"I didn't know you had a brother. Is he older than you?"

"I don't have a brother, but that's how he treats me at times. I don't want to be his little sister. We were watching a game the other day, and he belched right in front of me."

Kristen laughed.

"Stop it. It's not funny. He didn't even apologize or anything. I know I'm still more like a tomboy than a prissy young lady like you, but just because I like sports, he treats me like one of his guy friends. He never opens the car door for me, and he was going to buy me a football jersey for my birthday until you talked him out of it."

"Have you ever thought about wearing dresses or skirts more often?" Kristen asked. "You always look so pretty when you dress nicely," Kristen said as she smoothed the front of her dress.

Emmy grabbed some fries. "I have to dress up for work. When I'm home I feel more comfortable in my old jeans and a sweatshirt or t-shirt. Sometimes I think he would rather play football with me than try to get me in bed. He is my boyfriend." She waved a fry at Kristen. "We've been going out for eight months now. Sometimes I want him to sweep me off my feet. I want him to try to seduce me. Not that I'm going to let him succeed, but he should still try."

"You need to be patient. I know Tony cares about you, but he teases you and treats you like a kid sister because he knows you are both too young to get physically involved."

Emmy rolled her eyes. "Oh, for crying out loud. We are

4

both old enough."

"I know you're old enough, but life can get complicated when sex is involved."

"You sound like Mama Bertucci. You are still a virgin, too."

Everyone called Tony's mother Mama even though her name was Maria Catarina.

"I know. I was trying to sound sophisticated." Kristen grinned and tilted her nose in the air.

"Boys aren't the only ones who have needs. Don't you ever want to... you know? Does that make me a bad person because I have those desires?"

"No, of course not. It just means you are human."

After graduating a semester early from Roosevelt High the previous January, Emmy interviewed, and was hired, for a full-time clerical position at Coventry Shield Healthcare. Besides working her job, Emmy enrolled in two summer night classes at Paul Frank Junior College. She wanted to earn the first college degree in her family.

Since forming four years ago, Kenny and his band, Fridays At Five, had sold over ten million copies of their first two CDs. Emmy always had one of their CDs playing. She knew all the lyrics and often sang along while doing her housework. In the bottom drawer of the bedroom dresser sat her most prized possession—the old music box that had been a gift from Grandma Mary Colasanti. Although it had been nearly nine years since her grandmother had passed away, Emmy still thought of her every time she looked at the music box.

In early August, Kristen took Emmy to see the campus of North Park College.

"I've lived in SoHam all my life, but I've never been here before, Kristen. This campus is really pretty. I love all the green, the ivy and these brick buildings." Emmy gazed in awe as she spun around looking at the buildings.

"It is charming. All the buildings are close together so it's easy to get from the dorms to the classrooms. What do you think?

Should I stay at home and commute or should I live in a dorm? If I stay at home it won't cost as much."

Emmy giggled then said, "Kristen, your parents are filthy rich. I really don't think they are going to be hurt financially if you decide to stay in a dorm room. Besides, it's lovely. I wish I could go to college here."

"You could, you know."

"Kristen!"

"Yeah, I've heard the story before. You are planning to put yourself through college without any assistance from anyone. You are so stubborn."

"So I've been told. You have to live in a dorm."

"I would get to experience more of real college life if I'm in a dorm. I could join some of the clubs. Maybe join a sorority. Studying at the library would be more convenient."

"Oh, cut the crap," Emmy said. "You mean you will have access to more college guys to date."

"I guess that would be one advantage to living on campus," Kristen said as she twirled her long wavy golden-blonde hair. "What are your plans for this fall, Em? Are you going to keep working, or are you thinking about taking some more classes?"

"I'm still planning to take two more night classes at Paul Frank. My job keeps me busy, but I want to keep going to college. I don't want to be stuck at Coventry all my life. I want to find a better job somewhere down the road—a job I can call a career. I might be able to squeeze in three classes, but that would be pushing it."

"Between your job and your night classes, do you have much time to see Tony during the week?" Kristen asked while she smiled at a couple of guys tossing a football back and forth.

The two guys noticed Kristen and Emmy. "Hey, check out those two. I wonder if they go to school here. I think the blonde in the short skirt looks like a fox."

"Yeah, but the one in the tight-fitting jeans has a cute butt."

"Maybe, but she looks like a high school kid."

Emmy answered, "We still have some time to be together. Once school starts that might change. He's already busy with

6

football practice, and when classes start, he will be even busier."

"Is he still treating you like one of the guys?"

Emmy laughed. "For the most part, yeah. I guess that's better than him trying to get me in bed all the time. As much as I complain about the way he treats me, I'm not really ready to start sleeping with him."

"You will have to make sure the time you do have together is quality time," Kristen said seriously.

"Yes, Mom!"

"You can be a real stinker sometimes, you know? I am trying to offer some sisterly advice, and you make fun of it." Kristen squealed, put her hands on her head and turned away as she saw the football flying through the air at her.

Emmy made a face at Kristen, and caught the football as it came sailing toward them.

"You're never going to grow up, are you?" Kristen asked as she looked over her shoulder at the two guys.

"Not if it means acting like a pampered princess like you," Emmy shouted as she tossed the football back to one of the guys staring at Kristen.

They kept walking, and Kristen looked back at the two guys. "Do you think those guys were cute, Em?"

"I don't know. I didn't pay them any attention because I'm just one of the guys, remember?"

Chapter Two

"Hey, Barry, would you and Linda like to come over for pizza and a movie tonight?" Emmy asked. "You've been bugging me about seeing the apartment."

Emmy was about to finish work for the day, when she decided to call her old friend Barry Newton. She had known Barry since second grade, and he still lived down the street from her parents.

"We could if you promise to behave and not attack me."

"I promise I will attack you if you tease me the way you normally do. Can you be there by seven? It's a school night, and Tony can't stay too late. You know how to get there, right?"

"I've been past the place but never been inside. I thought maybe we weren't friends anymore."

"I'm still Linda's friend. I don't know about you, though," Emmy teased Barry.

"Fine! Be that way. We'll see you guys at seven."

"I'm still at work, but I should be out of here soon. See you later."

After two years of dating, Barry and Linda Bailey recently announced their engagement, though no date had been set.

Emmy got stuck at work until six forty-five. She rushed home and found Tony stretched out on the couch watching TV. Tony, a six foot, two inch, 240 pound senior at Roosevelt High, was one of the best high school football players in the country. He already had a scholarship to play football for Notre Dame.

"Did you use the key I gave you to get in, or did I leave the place unlocked?" Emmy asked.

"I used the key. You don't have to worry about getting locked out."

"I don't worry as much since you have a key now, but I'm still kinda paranoid about it. How did practice go?"

"Coach made us run extra laps because the offense screwed up so many times."

"Oh, quit whining. Barry and Linda are coming over for pizza tonight. They should be here in a few minutes. Can you help me clean up a little?" Emmy picked up some junk mail she had angrily tossed at the garbage can yesterday but had missed.

"I will if I can have a kiss first." Tony remembered Mama's advice to treat Emmy more like his girlfriend.

"One little kiss, that's all." She kissed his cheek.

"Not exactly what I meant."

"Then you have to be more specific. Will you pick things up in here while I check the bedroom?"

Tony looked around the living room and didn't see anything out of place. He ignored the empty pop can and the bag from McDonald's sitting on the end table next to the phone. Emmy ran into the bedroom, glanced at the bed to make sure it was made and saw her dirty laundry basket. She decided to stash it in the bathroom for now since she had dirty towels to add to the pile. She made a mental note to stop at the laundromat tomorrow after work.

"Did you pick up in here? What about the kitchen?" She looked around.

"Yep, everything is all clean and organized."

"What about your stuff on the table? Is this part of the decorations?" She frowned as she picked up the trash.

"Oh, I forgot about that."

"Don't get up. I'll take care of it. I wouldn't want you to over-exert yourself."

"Relax, Em. The place looks all right. Barry won't care. Come and sit by me and tell me about your day."

"I want to make a good impression on them." Emmy tossed the trash, and then stood in front of him and asked, "Do you have any homework?"

"All finished."

"How did the offense screw up at practice?"

"They couldn't get the timing right on a new running play where the left guard pulls and is supposed to block me."

"Why not? Were you too quick for him?" Emmy teased as she pretended to be blocking Tony.

Tony tackled Emmy onto the couch and added, "We play Mansfield North on Friday. Should be a tough game. Did you have a good day?"

9

"So boring. I was getting ready to get out of there when Mr. Landburgh needed some last minute stuff done. I hate it when he does that. I think he plans it just to ruin my evenings."

"Can I have a proper kiss now?" Tony leaned in for a kiss as he reached for Emmy and pulled her close to him.

"Maybe later." She rubbed his cheek and felt his heavy five-o'clock shadow. "You need a shave." She touched the small scar on his chin and then ran a hand over the top of his head. "I know you keep it short for football, but will you let it grow out after the season's over. This is too short."

"Should I let it grow real long and pretend I'm a rock star?" Tony asked.

"Kenny's hair isn't real long," she said.

She giggled as he began to tickle her. They were about to kiss when the doorbell and her phone rang simultaneously.

"That's probably Barry and Linda," Emmy said as she jumped up. "Will you run down and let them in, so I can answer the phone and check the kitchen?"

"Yeah, but I still want a kiss sometime."

Emmy checked the caller ID. "It's Mom calling. I wonder what I did wrong now?"

"I mean it. I still want a kiss," Tony hollered as he opened the door and galloped down the stairs.

Emmy answered the phone. "Hi, Mom, I can't talk too long because I have company coming over."

"You mean Tony is there, and you don't want me to know."

"Tony's here, but Barry and Linda just arrived What's up?"

Tony answered the door. "Hey, guys. How are you? Come on up and make yourself at home. Em is on the phone with her mom. At least they aren't arguing right now."

Tony led the way up the stairs and into the apartment. Barry dropped into the recliner as if totally exhausted. Linda looked around the room, and then sat on the old tan-colored couch.

"What do you guys want to drink?" Tony asked.

"I'll take a beer," Barry answered as he removed his glasses. "I need one after the day I've had." He used his handkerchief to clean them.

"Sorry, Barry. I think there is Coke or Dr Pepper."

"Root beer, too," Emmy hollered from the kitchen.

"I'll take Dr Pepper," Linda told Tony.

"Barry?"

"I guess I'll take Dr Pepper, too."

Barry looked around and whispered to Linda, "The wallpaper reminds me of my grandmother's house."

"Hush. Don't let Emmy hear you say that."

Tony was in the kitchen getting the drinks for everyone when Emmy finished talking to her mother. He noticed and heard her empty left hand slap the wall. Though tempted, she resisted slamming the phone back in the wall-mounted base. She swore under her breath, "Get off my case, woman." She managed to smile as she joined Linda on the couch.

"I'm glad you guys could come over tonight, but I ended up getting stuck at work and just got home a few minutes ago. Linda, is that a new hairstyle?" Emmy asked.

Linda smiled and ran a hand through her layered hair. "I had my mother do it."

"It looks good on you," Emmy said. *But you look like you've gained a few pounds.*

"Thanks, Emmy. I could do something with your hair if you ever want a different style. Something more mature," Linda said.

"Well, what do you think of the place?" Emmy waved her arm.

Barry looked toward the bedroom. "We didn't see all of it."

"Follow me, guys, and I'll give you the grand tour. This is the living room, obviously."

They followed her into the bedroom, and Barry plopped down on the bed, as if he owned it.

"Seems comfortable enough to me."

Linda poked him in the leg. "Barry, get off of Emmy's bed right now."

"I was only testing it out."

"Why? Do you think Emmy is going to let you sleep on it sometime?"

"Why not? She has slept in my bed before." Barry looked

11

at Emmy, and she blushed.

"She only did that because she was homeless at the time. Now get off her bed before Tony catches you there."

"She wasn't homeless—just fighting with her parents and moved out. She crashed at my place, and I had to sleep on the couch downstairs."

Emmy showed them the kitchen but not the bathroom. "The bathroom is a mess. I threw all my dirty laundry in there."

Barry looked at her and grinned.

"Yes, Barry, my underwear is in there, so forget about going to the bathroom while you're here. You will never change or grow up."

Linda frowned at Barry. "You're right, Emmy. I have given up on him ever maturing, but I love him anyway."

They returned to the living room, and Tony passed around the drinks.

"What do you guys like on your pizza?" Emmy asked.

"Everything!" Barry answered. "And lots of it."

They ordered pizzas and some breadsticks.

"I'm gonna change clothes while we wait for the pizza. I wanna be comfortable."

"Do you need any help unzipping your dress, Em?" Tony asked.

Emmy shook her head. "No, I can manage it without your help. I'll be right out."

"I'll show Barry and Linda the movies while you change."

"We can look through them, Tony," Barry said.

Tony pointed to the TV stand. "They're under there."

Barry and Linda got up and looked at the collection of movies. Barry looked at Linda and whispered, "Is it just me, or do they act like they're married?"

"Tony sure seems comfortable here," Linda said as she looked through the few DVDs under the TV. She picked out a movie to watch. "I hope this one is all right."

"It's not a chick flick is it?" Barry asked. "Tony and I will fall asleep if we have to watch one of those."

"It's not. It's an action movie with Tommy Cruz. Will that

be okay, Tony, or have you seen it before?"

He looked to see which movie she had. "*Commando Raiders*. That's really good. I don't mind watching it again."

"Is that Emmy's or yours?" Barry asked.

"It's mine. Most of the DVDs are mine. Emmy doesn't usually buy them."

Barry looked at Linda and whispered, "See what I mean about them being married..."

"Hush." Linda poked him in the side.

Emmy came out of her bedroom wearing faded jeans with holes in the knees and a t-shirt with an old sleeveless Fridays At Five sweatshirt over it.

Barry noticed her jeans, "Now you look like the Emmy I know. You still dress like a tomboy."

"Did you guys pick out a movie yet?" Emmy frowned at Barry.

"Is this one okay, Em?"

"Sure. I like that one."

"When did you get a DVD player?" Barry asked. "I'm envious. I can't afford one. How were you able to afford that?"

"Grandma bought it for me along with the TV."

"Is your Grandma looking to adopt any other grandkids?" Barry asked.

Emmy answered, "Yeah, she is."

"Really?"

"No, you dork. Especially not one like you."

They sat in the living room and talked until the pizza arrived. Tony hurried downstairs to get it, while Emmy got paper plates out for everyone.

Emmy opened the first pizza box. "Should we start the movie and watch it while we eat, or eat first, and then start the movie?"

"We can watch the movie while we eat," Tony suggested, as he looked at the clock on the wall.

Emmy and Linda sat on the couch to eat while the movie played. Barry plopped down in the recliner across from them, and Tony took the spot on the floor in front of Emmy. The guys made

13

quick work of the first pizza, and Tony went into the kitchen to get a refill of pop. Emmy sat Indian-style on the couch.

"How can you put up with him?" Emmy nodded toward Barry.

Linda sighed then said, "He kinda grows on you after a while."

Emmy grinned. "You mean like mold grows on a wet wall?"

"You are so hilarious, Em," Barry said. "Be quiet so I can watch this movie."

Emmy stuck out her tongue and then giggled.

Tony came back and again sat on the floor in front of her. He put his hands on her knees.

"Stop it. That tickles." The phone rang, and Emmy reached for the extension next to the couch. "It's Kristen. Can I have some more pop, too, please?"

Barry held the remote. "We'll pause the movie."

Emmy took the call from Kristen. Linda went to the bathroom, and Tony got up to get some more pop for Emmy.

"Hi, Kristen."

"Hi, Emmy, what are you doing? Got a few minutes to talk?"

"Of course. Barry and Linda are here. We're having pizza and watching a movie. Tony's here, too."

"Oh, it sounds like you're busy. Maybe I should call you tomorrow. I just wanted to talk. Nothing important."

"Are you sure? Is everything okay?"

"Yeah, I'm all right. Bored, I guess."

"Okay. Bye."

Tony and Linda came back into the room.

"Who was on the phone, Em?" Tony asked.

"I told you it was Kristen," Emmy answered a bit agitated.

They restarted the movie and finished the second pizza.

As the night passed by, Emmy got sleepy and dozed off during the movie. Tony woke her up by tickling her knees. "Em, wake up. The movie's over."

"I'm sorry. I shouldn't have dozed off. What time is it?"

14

"Ten fifteen," Tony said.

"At least you weren't snoring too loud, Emmy," Barry teased.

"You're such a nerd. I don't snore."

"If you say so."

Emmy bit her lip. *No one has ever told me if I do.*

Barry stood up, and then reached out a hand to help Linda. Linda grabbed her purse from the end table. "We need to get home. We have to work in the morning."

"Thanks for coming over, guys. It was good to see you both."

"Thanks for inviting us," Linda said as she hugged Emmy.

Barry shook hands with Tony. "See ya, big guy. Take care of Emmy."

"I will. Thanks again for coming over."

Barry grinned at Emmy and made a loud noise like he was snoring.

She poked his arm. "Stop it! I don't snore, and you know it."

"See you, Em. Nice apartment."

"It's better than living at home." She glanced over her shoulder. *Anything would be better than living at home.*

On the way home Linda asked Barry, "Do you think Tony has ever spent the whole night with Emmy? Do you think he's staying tonight?"

"I'm not a hundred percent sure, but I doubt it very much. I am like ninety-nine percent sure she is still a virgin."

Linda glared at him. "And how do you know that?"

"I'm just assuming. I don't know for sure."

"You better not," Linda said.

"I know I've never had sex with her."

"You are gonna die an early death."

Tony did not spend the night with Emmy because Mama Bertucci would be extremely upset with both of them. He kissed Emmy good night and left five minutes after Barry and Linda.

Chapter Three

Tony Bertucci's senior year at Roosevelt High had begun. Though only three months younger than Emmy, the school policy at St. Andrew's Elementary School meant he was a year behind her in school. His October birthday was a month after the cutoff deadline. After football practice, he stopped over to see Emmy. He hadn't seen her for a week, and he ended up staying later than normal.

Emmy checked the clock in the kitchen and stuck her head around the door. "Hey, you better get going. It's after your curfew."

He closed his textbook. "I don't have a curfew. How late is it?"

"Almost eleven."

"Shoot!" He gathered his books and stuffed them and his homework into his battered duffel bag. "I'll talk to you tomorrow. Thanks for dinner."

"You're welcome." She opened the door and waited for a kiss.

He kissed her cheek and hustled down the stairs.

She shook her head and watched until he closed the door at the bottom of the stairs. *I might as well resign myself to being one of his football friends.*

Tony drove to his home in the Hampshire Park neighborhood, which was located west of the Raynor Park area where Emmy grew up. He parked his car in the garage and walked in the back door. "Hi, Mama, I'm home. I know it's late, but I have a good reason. Are those homemade chocolate chip cookies I smell?

Mama slapped his hand as he reached for a cookie. "Those just came out of the oven. Let them cool first." She glanced at the clock; it was after eleven. "You know I trust you completely, but I am getting a little concerned about all the time you are spending at Emmy's apartment."

"I know it's football season, but I still like to see her once or twice during the week."

"I know you do, son. Is everything all right?"

"Yeah, I had more homework than I thought. I had to finish a report for sociology." Tony grabbed a cookie and stuffed it in his mouth.

"Did Emmy help you?"

"Sure, you don't mind that she does, do you? She still manages to get her own assignments done, too. Usually she works on her assignments while I work on mine. If I get stuck, she helps me out."

"Why would I mind? She is so much smarter than me. I'm not much use anymore when it comes to your school work."

"You are smart, Mama." Tony kissed her cheek tenderly. "I know you're really concerned, but you can trust us. We don't do anything there that I wouldn't do here. I mean I just kiss her—nothing else. Well, I do tickle her sometimes."

"I know how much you care for each other and physical needs can sometimes..."

"I can always bring Emmy over here. It's just that during the week, it's easier to see her at her place."

"Please be careful, son. I'm going to bed. I love you."

"Good night, Mama. I love you, too." He grabbed four more cookies.

Emmy still wished Tony would treat her more like a girlfriend than he did. He still had a tendency to treat her like one of the guys. She didn't realize that the fault rested as much with her. She usually dressed in her jeans and old sweatshirts and talked about sports all the time.

On Wednesday Tony worked on his homework at one end of the couch while Emmy read *Montana Sky* at the other end. She glanced at him several times trying to get his attention without success. She finally put her foot against his leg. He peeked at her, but didn't say anything. She kicked his leg. That got his attention.

He closed his sociology book. "What is it, Em?"

She moved closer. "Do you remember Scott Simmons? He's that guy I met at church last summer. I saw him when we were at the mall last week."

"Yeah, vaguely." Tony grabbed some Doritos out of the

bag.

Emmy poked him in the chest. "Well, he acts more mature and grown-up than you do."

"He should. He is a few years older than either one of us. Isn't he out of college already?"

"Some people never mature even after they grow up."

"What are you getting at?" He asked as he rubbed the orange crumbs from the Doritos onto his jeans.

"Will you be more mature when you get older?"

"I promise, Em. When I turn seventy-five, I will act very maturely."

"You're hopeless!" Emmy rolled her eyes and grabbed the bag of Doritos away from him. "You ate the whole bag, you pig."

"Sorry, Em. I was hungry."

A couple of days later Scott Simmons called Emmy around ten o'clock at night.

"Emmy, I'm sorry to bother you, but I wanted to talk to you. I broke up with Meredith and wanted to know if you would go out with me?"

"What?" Emmy asked wondering if she heard him correctly. "Scott, you know I have a boyfriend. I can't go on a real date with you."

"I know you are dating Tony, but how serious can it be? I saw the way he treated you the other night. He treats you like one of the guys—not as a girlfriend. I can treat you better. I know you enjoyed it when I kissed you at Kristen's party. I could please you in ways that Tony isn't."

Scott surprised her with his offer.

She closed the textbook she had been reading. "I'm happy with Tony, and I should have never let you kiss me. I know you think he treats me differently than you would, but he has his reasons."

Scott didn't give up. "I think you are very pretty, and I would really like to get to know you better."

Emmy tilted her head and stared at the phone for a second. "I like you, Scott. I understand why girls are attracted to you, but

18

I'm not comfortable with what you're asking. If I wanted to do that, it would be with... oh, never mind. I can't talk to you about sex."

"It's just a date, Emmy."

"Maybe so, but I feel guilty just thinking about going out with you. We would never have gone to Kristen's party together if Tony hadn't been in Indiana."

"If you and Tony ever break up, will you give me a call?"

"I won't promise you anything, and I don't ever plan to break up with Tony."

"Remember that I'm interested if you ever do," Scott said.

Yeah, that's coming across loud and clear. Emmy realized. "I gotta go. Bye, Scott."

Emmy worried that Tony would not respect her if she tried to be more aggressive with him. One evening while sitting on the couch with Tony after work, she asked, "Will you rub my feet for me? They're killing me. I was on my feet all day at work."

"Should I put gloves on?" Tony joked.

"No. Just forget it. I'm not in the mood for your teasing tonight."

"I'm sorry, I was only kidding. I'll take care of your feet for you. As long as they don't smell too bad."

"Just... stuff a sock in it."

"Oh, come on. Can't you take a joke. You know I wouldn't do this for any of my guy friends."

"God, I hope not."

She put her feet on his lap, and Tony proceeded to massage them for her.

"Ow! Be careful. That hurt."

"Sorry, Em. I guess I don't know how hard to massage you. Is this better?" He used more finesse.

She closed her eyes and relaxed as Tony rubbed her feet. "Oh, that feels so good. Don't stop."

She opened her eyes a few seconds later and caught him staring at her legs. *I'm sure glad I changed clothes after work.* "Do you like staring at me?" She grinned.

"Em, I like seeing your legs, but..."

"I know you want me, and I want you, too."

"Yeah, but if I give in to those desires... I am afraid we will get carried away and do something we might both regret. What if you get pregnant, and we have a baby? I'm not ready for that. We have to wait until we are married."

"I want to wait until we're married to make love, but we can do other things without going all the way," Emmy said.

Tony finished with her feet, and she sat up. She climbed on his lap and started kissing him. She touched the front of his jeans. Her eyes opened wide and she bit her lip.

"Emmy, please stop." Tony squirmed, and then grabbed her hands. He moved her off of his lap.

"God, Tony, you don't have to get all embarrassed because I touched you." Emmy became exasperated. *I do know that guys get excited.* "Just because I am doing this does not mean I want to have sex right here on the couch. I want to kiss you, and I want you to hold me close."

"We can't because we aren't married."

"We can't kiss. Is that what you're saying?" Emmy raised her voice.

"I meant the other thing, but maybe we shouldn't even kiss. You are acting weird for some reason."

"Oh, my God! You think I'm weird because I want to kiss you." She smacked his arm. "I think you're the one who is acting freaky," Emmy said. "We can make out."

"No, we can't." Tony grabbed her hands.

"Oh, yes we can." She tried to kiss him, but he turned his head. "Oh, screw it! If you aren't even going to kiss me, you might as well go home and we don't have to see each other anymore."

"Em, if I start kissing you..."

"What? Are you afraid you won't be able to stop?" Emmy frowned and yelled even louder.

"You don't have to yell."

"You can call me when you grow up if that ever happens. On second thought, I never want to see you again. Just go." She waved in the direction of the door. "I'm not gonna wait for you to grow up, or learn how to meet my needs. I'll find someone else."

"Fine. If that's how you feel, I'll leave, and I won't be back." He stood up quickly.

"Kenny will be home from the tour soon, or maybe I'll call Scott Simmons. I know he's interested in me, and he's made it clear how he wants me. You had your chance, Tony Bertucci, and you blew it. Now it's Scott's turn."

Tony took two steps toward the door before turning back to face Emmy. "I've always thought that if I didn't try to get in your pants you would respect me more."

"Go away and leave me alone," Emmy yelled as she started crying. "And give me back my keys."

He took the keys out of his pocket and set her keys on the table. "I'm just like every other guy, Em. I want to make love to you. Now I don't know what to do." He shrugged and exhaled. "Do you really want me to pick you up and carry you into the bedroom?"

"I told you I didn't." Emmy scowled and crossed her arms over her chest.

Tony waved his hands. "I'm outta here. You've got no clue about what you really want."

"Oh, like you've got it all figured out."

Tony left upset and confused. Emmy put on her pajamas and climbed into bed. She was still so angry with Tony she couldn't get to sleep. She tossed and turned in bed for an hour. She kicked the covers off in anger. She jumped out of bed and saw his picture on the dresser. She grabbed it and started to toss it into the garbage can, but instead put it in a drawer and covered it with some clothes. She looked at the picture hanging on the wall of her on stage with Kenny and Fridays At Five.

"Oh, Kenny, when are you coming home? I miss you so much." She let the tears flow down her cheeks.

Emmy called Kristen and listen to it ring four times. "Can't you answer your phone?" When the voicemail message started, Emmy hung up without leaving a message. She sighed as she plopped on her back in bed, "Kristen, where are you? I really need to talk to you. I just broke up with Tony."

For the next week Emmy cried every time she thought about Tony. She eventually talked to Kristen and expressed her frustration and regret about what happened.

"Do you want me to talk to him?" Kristen asked.

"No way!" Emmy exclaimed. "I know you guys are close, but please don't say anything to him."

"Then you need to talk to him."

"No! I'm not talking to him until he grows up," Emmy said. "And that might take years."

Kristen rolled her eyes. "You both need to grow up."

One night after work, Emmy's phone rang. She checked the caller ID. It was Scott Simmons. She hesitated before answering. By now she had calmed down and even though she told Tony she might let Scott "have his turn," she didn't really mean it.

"Hi, Scott."

"Hey, Emmy, I want to apologize for screwing up on the phone. I hope you will forgive me. I'd like to be friends."

"I will accept your apology with one condition."

"What's that?"

"I had a big fight with Tony, and we broke up."

Scott smiled when he heard this.

"I'm still not totally over it. I'm not about to start another relationship. We can be friends, but that's it. Do you understand, Scott?"

"I understand, and I will behave like an officer and a gentleman."

"I've never seen that movie, but I trust you," Emmy joked.

Emmy talked to Scott three times over the next few evenings. He came over to see her after work one night, and they walked around the neighborhood. She didn't let him upstairs to her apartment. They saw *Rounders* at the movie theater the following night. She didn't miss Tony as much as she thought she might when she spent time with Scott.

Emmy wanted to talk to her older sister, Diane, and almost called Tony by mistake. She dialed his number out of habit, but hung up before the phone could ring. She dialed the correct number and when Diane answered, Emmy asked, "Hi, can you come over? I need someone to talk to, and I haven't seen you for so long."

"Sure, Em, I'll drop everything and rush right over," Diane answered sarcastically.

"Please, I need to talk to you about something important."

"We're talking now. Tell me what's bothering you."

"I don't want to talk about it over the phone. Please come over!"

"Em, It's Saturday night. I'm busy. Tell me over the phone," Diane said. *Why do you expect me to jump at your command?*

"I need to talk to you in person. Please!?"

Diane stared at the phone for a moment. "Oh, all right, I can be there in a while. I need to finish cleaning the kitchen first. I hadn't planned on leaving the apartment tonight. Hey, I was cleaning out the closet, and I found some dresses that I thought you might like. I'll bring them with me."

"You don't have to. I have enough clothes."

"They're not old dresses, Emmy. I'm not trying to give you hand-me-downs like when we were kids. I simply don't wear them anymore. Just take a look at them. Some of them are brand new. If you don't like any of them, give them to Goodwill or something."

Emmy sighed. "All right, but I doubt any of them will fit me. They'll be too big."

"Is everything okay, Em?" Diane made one last attempt to get Emmy to talk over the phone.

"I'll tell you when you get here. Please hurry."

You can be such a baby. Diane hung up.

Emmy paced back and forth as she waited for Diane to arrive. Thirty minutes later, the doorbell rang, and Emmy rushed downstairs.

"What took you so long? Your apartment is only five minutes away."

"It takes longer than that to get here." Diane handed Emmy the bag of clothes and followed her upstairs. *You're lucky I came over at all.* "I can't stay very long, and when is your landlord going to replace this ugly wallpaper?"

23

Emmy tossed the bag on her bed. "He won't. Do you want a Coke or something?" Emmy offered as she walked back into the living room.

"No, just tell me what's going on." Diane sat on the couch. "Sit. Talk. I don't have all night."

Emmy sat down. "I got mad at Tony, and I yelled and told him not to call me until he grows up. I said a few other things, and I might have used some words that I shouldn't have."

"Did you swear like Mom does at Dad?"

"Probably. I don't remember exactly what I said because I was so mad at him."

"What did he do, Em?"

Emmy was reluctant to tell Diane why she got upset.

"Did he get physical? Did he try something?"

"No." Emmy stared at the wall.

"Emmy! What did he do? I can't help you if you don't talk to me. Tell me, or else I'm leaving." Diane stood up.

Emmy grabbed Diane's arm and pulled her back onto the couch. "He didn't do anything. That's why I got mad and yelled at him."

"You got angry because of... nothing." Diane flipped her long hair over her shoulders. "I don't get it."

"I wanted to kiss and make out, but he wouldn't." Emmy bit her lip and looked at Diane.

"You can be a real goof sometimes, Emmy. You should be grateful that he didn't try anything with you. Would you rather have to fight him off every time you're together?"

"No, of course not. But he never tries anything."

"I don't believe that for a second."

"Well, he kisses me and hugs me."

"Does he tell you that he loves you?" Diane asked. *Craig used to tell me that all the time. At least, until I started sleeping with him.*

"Whose side are you on, Diane? Are you trying to make me feel guilty for yelling at him?"

Diane smiled. "If the shoe fits..."

"All right, I shouldn't have yelled at him. What should I

24

do?"

"Em, what is that yellow thing hanging up in the kitchen? What is it called now? I can't remember."

Emmy looked toward the kitchen and laughed. "It's a telephone. You think I should call him, huh?"

"All couples have disagreements. Craig and I fight and argue about stuff. So do Mom and Dad."

"Yeah, that's a fact." Emmy laughed. "Do you want to spend the night since it's so late?"

Diane laughed. "No, where would I sleep? You've only got one bed."

"We always shared a bed when we were kids."

"Exactly. Don't take this the wrong way, but I'd rather sleep in my own bed than share one with you."

"You mean you would miss Craig," Emmy said.

"He's at work. He's working midnights this month."

"Then you could stay and keep me company."

"Bye, Emmy." Diane stood up to leave. "Take a look at those dresses. You might find something you like."

"Night, Diane, thanks for coming over."

Emmy looked so sad that Diane asked, "Is there something else you wanted to talk about? What is it, Em? I can tell you want to ask me something. Just ask. I want to get home and go to sleep."

"Okay, do you ever regret having sex at such a young age? You were sixteen when you started sleeping with Craig. I'm eighteen now, and I'm still a virgin. Is there something wrong with me? Am I stupid for wanting to wait until I'm married?"

Diane thought about it. "There's nothing wrong with you, Em. Maybe I should have waited until I was older, but I can't change the past. Craig and I have rough times just like all couples do. The sex isn't always great—especially if he's in a hurry. I try not to spend a lot of time on things that I can't change or control."

"I feel like I'm missing out on stuff. We don't really do anything yet. We don't make out like other kids do."

"Then just do it!" Diane rolled her eyes in exasperation. "It's not like you will turn into a slut if you have sex."

"I can't just jump into bed with him..."

25

"Why not?"

"I have this sense that it's not right." She paused as she thought, *Kenny doesn't think it's right. His church doesn't condone it.*

"Lots of people do things that aren't right, Em. It's just human nature."

"That's a sorry excuse. Not everyone is like that. The kids at that church didn't act like that. They didn't use human nature as an excuse to do whatever they wanted."

"They're just religious fanatics." Diane waved a hand dismissively. "Call Tony and apologize. Tell him it was that time. Guys his age don't have a clue. He'll assume you get like that every month."

"He might not ever want to talk to me again after the way I yelled at him." Emmy looked at Diane and sighed. "I wish love wouldn't be so complicated and hard to figure out. It was never this difficult with Kenny."

"You never had sex with Kenny Colwell." Diane made a statement while asking a question at the same time.

"I know, but we kissed and I would have... done some things with him."

"If he was home now, would you have sex with him?"

"We're friends." Emmy hid the way she truly felt about him.

"Yeah, but it's better if the person you are sleeping with is also your friend."

"Is Craig your best friend?"

"Not even close." Diane smiled at her. "You have plenty of time. You don't need to be in a big hurry."

Emmy looked down at the floor. "You're right. I guess I need to stop thinking about... you know."

"It's called sex. Good night, Em. Call me sometime, and we'll do lunch or something." Diane moved toward the door.

"I went out with Scott Simmons, and he kissed me and wants to take me to bed," Emmy blurted out as fast as she could.

"What?" Diane stopped and turned back to Emmy. "When did this happen?"

26

"We went to a movie last night."

"Did you make out with him?"

"No!"

"Did you want to?"

Emmy bit her lip and rubbed her foot on a stain in the carpet. "Yeah, kinda."

"Are you seeing him just to prove a point? Are you throwing yourself at him?"

"I don't think so."

"Do you know what a rebound is?"

Emmy looked up at Diane. "Yeah, it's when the shooter misses..."

"I'm not talking about football."

"It's basketball. There are no rebounds in football."

"You are such a... I don't know. You're more into sports than any girl I know." Diane waved her hands. "I'm talking about a rebound relationship. You broke up with Tony." Diane held up one finger. "Kenny is gone." Diane held up a second finger. "Who knows how many girls he's been seeing."

"He doesn't have time for anything serious while he's on tour." Emmy stared at the floor again.

"Whatever. Look at me!"

Emmy slowly raised her head.

Diane held Emmy's shoulders. "Scott is a rebound. I know you felt attracted to him before, but you better be careful. You could get in too deep. Tony wouldn't sleep with you because of his Catholic guilt trip stuff. He'll get over that soon enough. Kenny is too nice of a guy because of his relationship with God and all. Scott might not be as reluctant to take advantage of you. So before you let him have what he wants, you better be sure you're willing to give it to him."

"I'll be careful."

"Make sure you are. I really gotta go. Call me sometime and let me know how it goes with Scott."

Emmy sighed as Diane left to head back to the apartment she shared with Craig Garrett. Emmy didn't see her sister much anymore. Their lives were going in different directions.

27

Chapter Four

"Go, Tony, go!" Emmy leaped to her feet as Tony Bertucci intercepted a pass in the fourth quarter. "Yeah! Touchdown!"

The crowd screamed and yelled with all their might.

Emmy grabbed Kristen's arm and shook it. "Did you see that, Kristen? Did you see that spin move? That was about as good as that earlier play when he sacked the quarterback and made him fumble."

On October second the undefeated Roosevelt High Rough Riders played their fifth football game of the year against the also-undefeated West Bartlett Buccaneers.

"He's got more touchdowns than anyone on offense so far," Kristen replied.

"It's about time the coach wised up and let him play on offense part of the time. He's a better tight end than anyone else on the team," Christopher Braun, Kristen's date, said and high-fived Emmy.

"He's one of the best players in the state now—maybe even the very best. He is too good of an athlete to be on the sidelines for half the game," Emmy told Christopher with pride.

"Coach McMahon wants him on the field for as many plays as possible." Christopher smiled at Emmy. "He has already caught five touchdown passes this year."

"Didn't you play football when you were at Roosevelt? I think I remember coming to a game and seeing you play. You played quarterback, right?" Emmy asked as she got pushed up against Christopher by Rudy Bregar, who she knew from her English class.

"Sorry, Emmy, I lost my balance," Rudy apologized.

Christopher yelled at him, "Be careful, will ya!"

"I'm all right. Don't yell at each other." Emmy smiled at Christopher to calm him down.

Even though she and Tony were not talking to each other now, Emmy still went to his games. She recalled the conversation she had with Kristen before the game.

"Kristen, I miss him more now than I thought I would."

"He misses you just as much."

"I'm still afraid he won't ever want to talk to me."

"There's only one way to find out," Kristen said.

After the football game, which Roosevelt won by a score of 42-7, Kristen left the bleachers and tried to talk to Tony but couldn't. She returned to Emmy and explained, "I'm sorry, Emmy. He didn't see me. There were too many people around him. I know you wanted to talk to him."

"It's okay, Kristen. Maybe another time will be better anyway."

Christopher and Kristen dropped Emmy off at her apartment. After she was already in bed, the phone rang. She answered and smiled as she heard a familiar voice.

"Hey, Emmy, how are you? I have been thinking about you and thought I should call."

"Oh, Kenny! It's so good to hear your voice..."

Emmy talked to Kenny Colwell for over an hour.

Kristen called Emmy on Thursday before Emmy left for her evening class. "Are you going to the game tomorrow? It's an away game against the Thorndale Township Falcons. They aren't real good this year, but they always play tough in their own backyard."

"How do you know that?" Emmy asked as she spread some mayonnaise on wheat bread. "You don't follow football that much."

"Tony told me. Do you want to ride with us? Christopher is driving and his brother might come with us. He would like to see you, Em."

Emmy cradled the phone on her shoulder as she opened a package of Oscar Meyer bologna. "Are you trying to set me up with Randy Braun? Just because you're dating his brother doesn't mean I want to go out with Randy."

"Randy is a good guy..."

"Ha! From what I've heard, he spends more time drinking than studying. Anyway, I wasn't planning to go to the game."

"Why not? You never miss one of Tony's games."

29

"I've got other plans."

"Do you have a date or something?" Kristen asked in surprise.

"I'm just going to be busy, that's all," Emmy answered evasively.

"Are you keeping secrets from me now?"

"No, but I kinda made other plans. I gotta run. I'm eating dinner, and I have to get to class. I'll talk to you on Saturday." Emmy hung up.

Kristen stared at her phone. *What are you up to? You better tell me on Saturday. I'm taking you to Tony's birthday party. You'll have to talk to him then.*

Kristen tried calling Emmy the next afternoon, but she didn't answer. Kristen realized Emmy would still be at work and left a message, but Emmy didn't return the call. Kristen assumed Emmy must have a date and didn't want her to know about it.

The game that night stayed closer than anyone expected. The Rough Riders trailed by seven points at the half. Even in the second half, the Falcons hung tough. Only four minutes remained in the fourth quarter when Roosevelt finally took their first lead of the game. They scored another touchdown in the final minute to win 28-14.

The following day, the tenth, was Tony's eighteenth birthday. Kristen stopped by Emmy's apartment.

"Why are you wearing those old jeans? You know today is Tony's party."

"I'm not going. I haven't taken a bath or anything today."

"Gross!" Kristen frowned. "Well, hurry up. I'll wait while you get ready."

Emmy plopped down on the couch and put her arms across her chest. "I'm not going."

"You gotta come to the party. I made a special trip over here to pick you up."

"I'm not going," Emmy answered stubbornly. "I sent him a birthday card yesterday. Is his address 2142 Crystal Drive? That's

30

how I addressed it."

"That's the right address. Why aren't you going?" Kristen stood in front of Emmy.

"I'm just not going, okay. I'm busy." Emmy bit her lip as she looked up at Kristen.

"You are being stubborn and immature. Tony won't mind if you are at his party. Why won't you come with me?" Kristen was trying not to get frustrated with Emmy. *I should tie you up and drag you to the party.*

"He'll be upset if I show up. He hasn't talked to me since we had that fight."

"If you come with me, then you guys can talk."

Emmy pulled her knees up to her chest. "No, Kristen. Please don't be mad at me. I just can't go."

"Are you seeing someone else? Did you have a date last night?"

Emmy didn't answer right away.

"Answer me before I get really pissed at you!"

Emmy shivered because Kristen had never yelled at her before. "Not really. I went out with Scott Simmons again, that's all."

"Why? You told me he was only interested in sex." Kristen's voice rose an octave. "Please tell me you..."

"He just kissed me."

"He's too old for you."

"He's only a year older than Christopher, and I know Christopher is interested in sex, so don't get on my case for seeing Scott."

"You are being a big baby. You know that?" Kristen groaned.

"I know. Please don't be mad at me, Krissy. I don't want to fight with you."

"Fine! I'll tell Mama you don't want to see her anymore." *That should put you on a guilt trip.*

Kristen left for the party without Emmy. She drove faster than normal and squealed the tires as she rounded the last corner before pulling into the Bertucci's driveway. She walked in the back

31

door and saw Mama.

"Hello, dear. Are you by yourself?"

"Yes, Mama," Kristen said. "I went to her place and begged her to come with me. I almost dragged her out the door, but she wouldn't come. I think she is really sorry for what happened that night, but she is afraid to make the first move to get back together."

"You should talk to Tony about it," Mama said as she finished frosting Tony's birthday cake.

"She won't let me," Kristen said. "She is being so stubborn."

Tony acted a bit down-in-the-dumps even though it was his birthday. The guys from the football team attempted to cheer him up and even brought a couple of infatuated cheerleaders who flirted shamelessly with him. The cheerleaders even asked him out, but he showed no interest—at least for now.

Kristen came over to Emmy's apartment on Sunday morning and Emmy apologized, "I'm sorry I missed his game. It won't happen again, I promise. I know how important they are."

"Was it worth it to miss the game to see Scott Simmons?" Kristen asked as she took off her coat and set her Burberry purse on the end table.

"I suppose not, but I did get a free meal out of it." Emmy tried to make light of the situation. She grabbed her football from the floor in front of the TV and sprawled in the recliner.

Kristen glared at her. "Not even remotely funny, Em. Can you at least sit like a lady?"

Emmy tossed her football into the air. *Jeez, Kristen, I'm wearing jeans. What's the big deal?* But she said, "Sorry. Are you going to the next game with Christopher?"

"Probably not. He's with Victoria Madison again. They get serious about each other, and then break up. This time I think they might stay together."

"She's the cheerleader from Roosevelt who had a baby and gave it up for adoption, right?"

"Yeah, and everyone assumed Matt Sullivan was the father."

"He wasn't though. Are he and Annie O'Dell still together?" Emmy asked.

"Definitely. Those two are madly in love with each other."

"I like Annie, but we don't see each other very often."

"If you come over to the dorm, you could see her. She lives in Howe Hall, too."

"That's the name of your dorm, right?" Emmy asked absentmindedly.

"Yeah, up until this year it housed only freshman girls, but they changed it and now it's open to other classes. Annie lived in Howe last year, too." Kristen looked at Emmy who lazily tossed her football in the air. "Hey, are you listening to me?"

"Yeah... what did you say?"

"You're not even paying any attention to me. I'm going home."

Emmy tossed the football to Kristen. "Don't go. Let's go grab something to eat. I'm hungry."

"I suppose you want to go to Darby's, huh?"

"What a great idea, Kristen. I never would have thought of going there," Emmy answered sarcastically.

"Why do I put up with you?" Kristen shook her head and handed the football back to Emmy.

"Because I'm your best friend, and you'd be bored without me."

Kristen frowned at Emmy. "Aren't you going to ask about Tony's party?"

"Sure. How was it? Is Mama mad at me for not coming?"

"She is disappointed, but not really mad," Kristen said and then paused. "There were some of his teammates there, and they brought some of the cheerleaders."

"Yeah, so what?"

"They flirted with Tony, and I heard a couple of them ask him for a date. I'm not sure how he answered," Kristen said.

"If you're trying to make me jealous, it's not working."

Emmy and Kristen ate at Darby's and then returned to Emmy's place.

"What should we do for the rest of the day?" Emmy asked.

33

"I have to get back. I've got reading to do that I've been putting off because I know it will be boring." Kristen grabbed her purse, coat, keys and left.

An hour after Kristen left, Scott called. "Hey, Emmy, would you be interested in dinner and maybe having some fun after that?"

"I might be interested in some fun, but I went to Darby's with Kristen."

"Would it be all right if I come over in... let's say... an hour?"

"Make it two hours. I need to clean up around here first."

The doorbell rang exactly two hours later. Emmy looked around the living room. *I guess it's clean enough.* She hurried down the stairs and let Scott inside. "Come on up. Do you want a pop or something to drink before we go wherever and have our fun?"

"Sure. A Coke would be great. Otherwise, whatever you have."

They sat on the couch and drank their pop. Emmy grinned. "So, are you gonna tell me about your plans for tonight?"

"First let me ask this. Did you like kissing me the other night?"

"You know I did." *Why would you even have to ask?*

"So did I. I liked it a lot." He moved closer and kissed her quickly. "Have you ever been to Swallow Cliff?"

"Sure, I've been there lots of times. My grandparents used to take me and Diane there for picnics."

Scott chuckled and then said, "That's not exactly what I meant."

Emmy blushed. "Oh, you're asking if I've been there with a boy to make out, aren't you?"

Scott nodded his head and grinned.

"I've never been there at night."

"Wanna check it out?" Scott lifted his eyebrows in a suggestive manner.

"Do kids still go there to... you know?"

"Let's find out. What do you say?"

I'm not sure I should. It won't be easy to stop once we get started. Emmy thought about it for a moment. "Okay, let's go for a ride. But if it's too crowded there, I want to come back here."

"Fair enough, or we could just stay here."

"No, you offered to take me out for dinner, so I want to go somewhere. Maybe we could get some ice cream." Emmy put on her old army jacket and grabbed her keys. "Let's go."

Fifteen minutes later Scott parked the car at Swallow Cliff. "There are a few cars here, Emmy. What do you think?"

Emmy bit her lip as she looked around. She saw a couple of teenagers kissing in the car closest to them. "It's still kinda light out. I can't get in back and make out until the sun goes down," Emmy teased. *Oh, God! Did that sound totally dorky, or what?*

"We could go for a walk until it gets dark."

"Okay, I remember there are some good trails in that direction."

Scott shook his head. *Geez, Emmy, do you have any experience with guys at all?*

They exited the car and Scott held her hand as they headed toward the trail. As soon as they were out of sight in the trees, Scott stopped. He put his arms on her shoulders and pulled her close. The first kiss made Emmy want another.

After the third kiss, Emmy said, "We can either keep hiking and have more privacy, or we can go back to the apartment?"

"We could walk a little farther."

They hiked another five minutes before stopping again. Emmy put her arms around his neck and kissed him. He unzipped her army jacket and put his hands on her hips.

"When I first met you, I thought you were just a kid. Now that I know you're eighteen..."

"I'm not jailbait. Is that why you never tried anything before?" Emmy asked as she put a hand on Scott's chest.

"I didn't want to take advantage of your inexperience."

"What? Do you think that's changed just because I'm a little older. It's only been four months since you kissed me for the first time."

"I didn't mean it like that, Emmy."

35

She moved his hands farther behind her. He pulled her closer. He leaned down to kiss her again, but stopped as they heard voices.

"This isn't going to work," she said. "Let's go back to my place. We can walk around the block a few times if you want."

"All right, but I won't want to walk very long." He grinned. *You seem more willing tonight. I hope that doesn't change.*

She stared out the window as Scott drove back to her place. *I should probably run in the apartment and lock the door.* She bit her lip harder than usual.

Scott parked the car in front of her apartment, and Emmy jumped out.

"Let's walk for a little while, at least," she suggested.

Scott squeezed her hand as they walked along the bumpy sidewalk.

"Watch out for the cracks. The city doesn't take good care of this part of town."

They talked about their jobs as they walked slowly away from the apartment. Emmy giggled as Scott almost tripped.

"It's not funny, Em."

"Poor baby. Did you almost fall down and get a booboo?"

"You still act like a kid at times," Scott said.

He didn't realize Emmy was laughing to cover up her nervousness about what might happen when they returned to the apartment.

Emmy looked up at him. "Should I let you kiss me again, or am I too much of a child?"

"You fill out those jeans pretty good for a child." He started to touch her butt, but she blocked his hand.

I'm not going to start anything out here. She looked up and down the street.

Ten minutes later, they sat on the couch locked in a deep kiss. Scott's hands roamed over her body. He broke off the kiss long enough to ask, "Are you on the pill?"

"No. Do you have anything?"

"I came prepared. Should we move to the bedroom?"

Emmy's heart raced. Her mind flooded with thoughts. *Oh,*

36

my God. This is really going to happen. Kenny and Tony never let it go this far. I like Scott, but do I want him to be the one?

"Emmy, are you all right? You kinda disappeared for a moment."

"I'm okay. Just thinking about something."

"You don't have to worry. I'll make sure you enjoy it." Scott kissed her. Then he stood up and pulled her up with him.

She braced herself as he took her hand and took a step toward the bedroom.

"Are you coming?" he asked.

"Should I let you go first? I mean get undressed first, or I could use the bedroom and you could get ready in the bathroom. I'm nervous about letting you see me."

"Don't be nervous."

He took her hand and led her into the bedroom. Emmy turned on the light instinctively.

"We won't need the light on." Scott grinned, as he flipped it off.

"Sorry, just a habit." Emmy bit her lip.

Scott sat on the edge of the bed and pulled her next to him.

"I really like you, Scott..."

"I like you, too, Emmy. Let me show you how much I like you."

Emmy closed her eyes. She thought about Kenny. Scott lifted her sweatshirt over her head. Her heart pounded. His hands moved to the buttons of her shirt. She held her breath.

"Sex is something special, Emmy. You will enjoy it."

Emmy's mind flashed back to a night at Kenny's church. She remembered listening to Pastor Rojas talking to the teens about sex. She could almost recall his exact words. *Sex is something very special and is a gift from God. We need to treat it as such.*

Scott unbuttoned her shirt. Tears filled her eyes, as Scott placed his hand on her stomach.

"No, wait." She pushed Scott's hand away. "I can't do this. Sex is a gift that we can't take too lightly."

He smiled. "I'm not taking sex for granted." *Far from it!*

37

"No, I mean it's a gift from God. I think we're forgetting that sex is for people who are in love."

"Okay." Scott shrugged. "I love you. Does that make it all right?"

"No, I know you don't mean that. You go to church. Hasn't Pastor Brian ever talked about this?"

"Yeah, but it's not that big a deal. People do it all the time."

"It's a big deal to me, and I almost forgot that fact. I've let my physical attraction for you cloud my judgment. We need to stop."

"That's easy for you to say, but I just can't turn it off so easily."

"You can if you think about something else for a minute." *I do know some things about guys.*

Scott tried to kiss her, but she stood up and turned on the light. "Please, Scott, if you have any feelings for me, just go." She held her shirt together.

Just be patient, he thought as he exhaled sharply. *Should I keep trying, or should I wait for another night?* He touched a pillow as he noticed a football on top of her dresser. "All right, I'll leave, but it might be a long time before I call you again."

Yeah, that's not going to work. "I'm sorry. Don't be mad at me. Will you let yourself out, please?"

Scott grabbed his coat and slammed the door as he left.

Emmy sat on the edge of her bed and fell onto her back. *God, please tell me I did the right thing. I really liked Scott. I know I don't love him, but... Oh, Kenny, I'm so sorry. I almost let you down.*

Chapter Five

Emmy bit her lip as she listened to Kristen's phone ring. "Krissy, I need to talk to you." Emmy said before Kristen could even say hello.

"What's up, Em? I just talked to you yesterday."

"After you left yesterday, Scott came over. I haven't been totally truthful about him." Emmy paced around her small living room and got tangled up in the phone cord.

Kristen sat on the edge of her bed. "I'm not gonna like this, am I?"

Emmy unwound the cord from her ankles. "It could be worse."

"What happened?"

Emmy sat on the couch and pulled her knees to her chest as she explained everything to Kristen.

"So, at the last second you remembered something that preacher told the teens at some service years ago."

"Yeah, go figure. Do you think it might have been God or something?"

"More likely your subconscious. You're still Catholic enough to have guilty feelings about sex and stuff."

"That's three times I've almost gone ahead and done it. Luckily for me Kenny and Tony didn't take advantage of my offer. Last night Scott would have. I made the choice to stop, and he kinda got mad. He said he might not call me anymore."

"He was using that as a threat," Kristen said. "Did you say a prayer after he left?"

"Yeah, kinda."

"You should stay away from Scott and older men in general. You don't have the experience to say no."

"I do now, but I'm still gonna take your advice. Except for Kenny. He's older. I thought about Kenny and felt so guilty. I can't wait till he gets home."

Kristen and Emmy attended the rest of the Roosevelt High football games together, and Emmy didn't complain when Kristen brought Randy Braun along one time. Randy had been the valedictorian of his and Derrick's graduating class, a year ahead of Kristen and Emmy.

After the game Randy asked, "Emmy, do you want to come over and have a few beers with me?"

"I think I'll pass on that." Emmy declined his offer. *If I want a beer, I can always sneak one of Daddy's. It wouldn't be the first time.*

"Oh, come on, Emmy. Just one beer."

"Not tonight, Randy. I'm not in the mood to get drunk and let you take advantage of me. You know you never had a beer in your life until Derrick's graduation party. You got drunk that day, and it changed you. Not for the good, either. Have you ever thought about seeking help for that problem?" Since Emmy's father had a problem with alcohol, she sensed a responsibility to talk to Randy. "I heard that you spend all your weekends drinking and partying."

"Not true. I drink just as much during the week. Can I kiss you?"

"Not if you want to survive the night."

Randy held his hands in the air and backed away.

Kristen apologized as she frowned at Randy. "I'm sorry I brought him, Em. I didn't know he would behave like this."

"It's all right. He needs to understand he has a problem before he can change."

Randy pointed a hand at the ground. "Hey! I'm standing right here. I can totally hear you, and I don't have a problem."

You do, Randy, but you just won't admit it, Emmy understood his reluctance. *Daddy won't admit it, either.*

The still-undefeated Rough Riders continued to play their best ball of the year as they progressed in the playoffs. They beat Wheaton North to make it to the championship game against Mount Carmel Central. Emmy and Kristen planned to attend the game on November twenty-eighth on the campus of Illinois State University in Normal. Kristen came over to the house and tried to convince Mama Bertucci to go to the game, but she refused.

"I can't bear to watch him play in person, sweetie." Mama wrung her hands as they sat at the kitchen table. "I just sit there and worry."

"You know this is his last game in high school, right?" Kristen took a bite of a warm, fresh-from-the-oven chocolate chip cookie. *This is so good. One of these days I need to learn how to turn on the oven.*

They both heard Tony tromping down the stairs.

"I'm sorry, honey, but I can't do it. If I go to a game now, it might make him so nervous that he doesn't play well. I'd rather hear about it afterward."

Tony entered the kitchen. "I could smell the cookies all the way upstairs." He grabbed two and swallowed one in two bites.

"I'm trying to convince Mama to go to the game, but she won't. Does that bother you?" Kristen swatted his hand away as he reached for a third cookie.

"Hey! I want another cookie. There's plenty left for you."

"You can have one if you answer my question." Kristen pulled the plate of cookies toward her.

"I'm used to Mama not being there, and I can understand why. Can I have another cookie, please?"

Kristen scooted the plate back to the center of the table, and Tony grabbed three more.

"Pig!" Kristen took one more.

Tony understood his mother's concern. It had never bothered him that she didn't come to his games. He talked to Mama after each game and made sure she knew he was all right. At one point as a freshman, he even thought about giving up football, but Mama wouldn't let him. She pointed out to him that football might be his ticket for a good education.

Kristen's parents bought tickets for the game and took Kristen and Emmy to Normal. They left at noon because Daniel and Karla arranged to meet up with two of his college friends, Mark and Gail Noonan. Daniel and Mark were roommates for two years and had stayed in touch. They met at the Noonan's home, and then had an early dinner at Avanti's near the ISU campus.

41

"What time does the game start? Shouldn't we be getting to the stadium?" Emmy asked.

"It doesn't start until seven, girls. Be patient. We will get there in plenty of time," Mr. Keasling assured them.

They arrived at the stadium, and five minutes later the snow began to fall. At first it was a light dusting, but as kickoff time neared, the snow began falling harder. Footing became a problem for the players as they warmed up.

Emmy grabbed Kristen's arm. "Did you see that guy? He must have slid five yards through the snow."

"I'm surprised they can even stand up. The field must be getting slippery."

"The players do have cleats on their shoes. You know that, right?" Emmy teased.

"I know that. I'm not totally ignorant about sports. I've seen Daddy's golf shoes."

"I'm pretty sure those are different, Kristen." Emmy rolled her eyes.

"Whatever! There's Tony!" Kristen stood up and waved. "Aren't you going to wave at him?"

"No, he's busy warming up. He's not even looking at us."

Emmy and Kristen sat in the student section and some of the kids threw snowballs at each other. Emmy got nailed in the back.

"Hey, who the hell threw that?" she asked as she turned around. She saw two guys laughing at her, so she threw a snowball at them.

"Don't encourage them, Em." Kristen made her turn around and sit down.

"But they started it," Emmy whined.

"Are you going to go up there and beat them up?" Kristen asked sarcastically, and then turned around as more snowballs flew at them.

Emmy threw another snowball at the guys. "Oh, shoot! I hit Mr. Culbertson." Emmy turned around and sat as low as she could in her seat. "Is he looking this way?"

"Yes, and he looks upset." Kristen grinned. "I think you're

going to get a detention, Emmy."

"But I don't even go to Roosevelt anymore. I graduated." Emmy turned to check if Mr. Culbertson was really upset. "You stinker! He's not paying any attention to me."

The Roosevelt High Rough Riders won the coin toss and elected to kick-off. It proved to be a wise choice. On the second play of scrimmage, Tony tackled the ball carrier and caused him to fumble. The ball scooted through the snow until finally a Roosevelt player recovered it. Three plays later, Tony caught a pass in the end zone for a touchdown. The Maroons from Mount Carmel Central had no luck moving the ball on their next three possessions. They went three-and-out each time and had to punt the ball away. The Rough Riders scored touchdowns on their first four possessions to blow the game wide open. By the start of the second half, the snow turned into a blizzard. Emmy and Kristen enjoyed every minute of the game as the Rough Riders kept pouring on the pressure.

"Oooh, did you see that, Kristen? Tony hit that runner so hard he slid backwards for ten yards."

Emmy ducked as another snowball flew toward her way. It hit Kristen instead.

"Hey, what was that?" Kristen brushed the snow away.

"Those two guys are throwing snowballs at me again. I ducked, and it hit you."

Kristen looked at the two guys. "Do you know them, Em?"

"Just by sight. I don't know their names."

"I think they're flirting with you."

"Get out. They're just having fun." Emmy turned to look at the guys and was pelted in the chest by two snowballs.

"What the..."

"Oh, yeah. That's definitely flirting," Kristen teased.

Some of the adults had trouble coping with the cold and snow. They sought shelter under the stands since the game had turned into a blowout. Kristen's mom called her cell phone to let her know where they were. "We'll meet you under the stands after the game."

"Okay, Mom. I'll call if we don't see you."

Emmy looked at Kristen's cell phone, envying her friend's material advantages. She felt another snowball hit her in the back and turned around. She noticed the same two guys smiling at her.

"Emmy, don't encourage them. Watch the game," Kristen said.

"I'm watching the game, but we're going to win. I want to have some fun." Emmy threw snowballs back at the guys.

Kristen glanced over her shoulder at the two kids. "Em, they're sophomores. Don't flirt with them."

"I don't care how old they are." *They won't try anything like Scott did.*

The Rough Riders scored on their third possession of the second half to make it 35-0. The Maroons still had no success moving the ball against Tony and the tough defense. The third quarter ended and Roosevelt pulled all the starters at the beginning of the fourth quarter. Only in the last couple of minutes did Mount Carmel Central even come close to scoring. They moved the ball to the five yard line when a Rough Riders cornerback slipped on the slick field and allowed the Maroons to complete a long pass.

Tony stood next to Coach McMahon, "Do you want us to go back in the game?"

Coach thought about it before he answered, "No, let the kids see if they can hold them. I'd rather they get some game experience than send you guys back in just to preserve a shutout."

"I understand, Coach," Tony said. "I guess no one will remember the score, only the fact that we won."

The second string tried valiantly, but on fourth-and-goal the Maroons scored from the two on a play-action pass. The tight end got behind the defense and made a catch at the back of the end zone.

The clock wound down to zero and Roosevelt High won the seventh Illinois state championship in the school's history.

Emmy hugged Kristen as they jumped up and down. "Tony will be so happy. He was so disappointed when they lost the championship game last year."

Kristen smiled as she looked at Emmy's hair, which was wet from the snow. "Why aren't you wearing your stocking cap?

You're going to catch a cold."

"No, I won't." Emmy remembered playing in the snow with Tony on their second date. She turned around, smiled at the two sophomores and tossed a snowball at them.

Tony peered into the stands and saw Kristen waving at him. He noticed Emmy throwing snowballs at some of the kids.

Kristen nudged Emmy. "Stop that. Tony is waving at us."

Emmy took a snowball to the chest. She threw one more, and then turned around, but Tony had begun celebrating with his teammates.

"You missed it," Kristen said. "Let's find my parents."

As they made their way under the stands, Kristen searched through the crowd. "There they are, Em." She and Emmy ran over to them.

"Wasn't that exciting?" Emmy asked.

"Tony played great. I think this game proves he's the best player in the state," Kristen's father said, and then added, "I think we should head home right away. I checked with the state police, and this snow stops north of Lexington. We should be able to make it home all right."

"That's all right, Daddy. We won't be able to see Tony tonight anyway, and besides, neither Emmy or I brought any clothes for tomorrow."

They said goodbye to the Noonans and hit the road. They arrived home safe and sound shortly before midnight.

"Do you want to spend the night here, Em?"

"If it's okay with your parents, I will."

"Oh, no, they don't want you to stay," Kristen teased. "Do you really think they would mind if you spend the night? You can be a real goof sometimes."

Chapter Six

For all of 1997 and much of 1998, Kenneth Travis Robert Colwell and the band, Fridays At Five, toured the world in support of their multi-platinum selling CDs. Andy Walker, the band's manager, kept the band as busy as he possibly could. This year Kenny arrived home on the Sunday before Christmas, the twentieth. He called Emmy as soon as he set foot inside his parents' house. Emmy heard the phone and answered without checking the caller ID.

"Hello," she answered as she kicked the refrigerator door. "I absolutely hate you!"

"Merry Christmas! How are you?" Kenny laughed, "Are you talking to your refrigerator, or do you really hate me?"

"Oh, Kenny, I've been waiting for your call. Can you stop by and pick me up?" Emmy asked. "And I don't hate you."

"I think I might be able to squeeze a short visit with you into my busy schedule. Let me see... I can squeeze you in for ten minutes on Thursday around three."

"Darn it! That won't work. I have an appointment to have my toenails done then. Too bad. Maybe I can see you the next time you are in town," Emmy teased him right back.

Kenny laughed and asked, knowing that she never had her toenails painted, "What color are you painting your toenails these days?" She normally didn't even bother with fingernail polish.

"Purple! That's my favorite color. Please come over and take me away from this tiny apartment. I'm getting cabin fever."

"How do I get there again?" Kenny had never been to her apartment.

"Remember where Cooper's Drugstore is on the corner of Center and Midland?"

"Yeah, I think so."

"My apartment is next to the building next to the building next to the store."

Kenny laughed. "Oh, yeah, I totally understand you. I'll be there in about a half hour."

"I'll be ready. Hurry!" Emmy hung up and dashed to the

bathroom. *I wonder if I can do my toenails before he arrives?*

Emmy squealed for joy. Her oldest friend, and the person who knew her better than anyone else in the world, came home for the holidays. She was on break from school and on vacation for two weeks since the office closed completely this year.

Almost exactly thirty minutes later, her doorbell rang. She took a final look around the apartment to make sure it was tidy and ran downstairs.

"Welcome to my castle, my lord." She let him in the door, then jumped into his arms and hugged him.

"Does this mean you are happy to see me?"

She stopped hugging him and pointed to her feet. "Look. I painted my toes."

Kenny looked at her bare feet and indeed her toes were painted purple.

"When did you start doing that?"

"Thirty minutes ago. Kristen gave me some polish. Do you like how they look?"

"They look... they look... purple. What made you decide to do this? As far as I know you've never worn nail polish and certainly not toenail polish."

"It was a spur of the moment thing. I wanted to surprise you and show you that I'm not a total tomboy anymore. I use nail polish occasionally, and, get ready for a shock, I've even started wearing some makeup. Not all the time, but when I want to look more mature."

"I'm glad you said 'to look mature' and not to look pretty." *You do look more grown up than when I saw you in May.*

Emmy took Kenny upstairs and gave him a tour of the apartment. She fixed two glasses of pop, and they talked on the couch.

"It feels so good to be home. The guys and I talked it over, and we are never going to be on tour during the holidays again."

"I really missed you last Christmas," she said as she rubbed his cheek. He hadn't shaved for a couple of days, and she liked the look.

"I missed being home."

47

They talked about everything and everyone with one exception—Tony Bertucci. Finally, Kenny asked, "Are you going to tell me what happened between you and Tony? When I saw you in February and May, you seemed to be so happy together."

Emmy stared down at her lap and didn't look at Kenny.

"Emmy," Kenny said slowly, "are you going to tell me, or should I go home?"

"We had a little disagreement about something." She knew how silly it would sound to Kenny. "You might think it's frivolous, but I wanted him to... I wanted him to treat me more like a girlfriend. Sometimes he treated me just like Kristen, or one of the guys. I wanted him to kiss me and... maybe a bit more."

"Were you ready to sleep with him if he wanted?"

She poked him in the arm. "No, but I would have done some things." She blushed. "You think I'm childish, don't you?"

"Not at all, Em. I totally understand."

"You do? You are on my side?" She sat up on her knees.

"I'm always on your side."

She pouted. "You're teasing me."

"There are usually two sides to every story, and you are both partially right and both partially to blame. You will have to decide how much your relationship means to you." He tilted his head as he gazed into her eyes. *I'm kinda hoping it doesn't mean all that much.*

She sat back down and pulled her knees up to her chest. "Well, right now it doesn't mean squat. I mean we don't have a relationship. We don't talk or anything. We're not even friends because friends at least talk to each other."

After a few more minutes of discussion, Kenny said, "Let's go somewhere. I need to do some shopping, and I'm hungry."

"Can we go to Darby's?"

"I was going to suggest that very place. You must have read my mind."

"I want a chili cheese dog and fries and a root beer."

Kenny smiled at her and remembered the first time he took her to Darby's; she was probably eight, and she ordered the exact same thing. Although fast food chains dominated virtually every

48

corner in South Hampshire now, the locally-owned, one-of-a-kind Darby's still thrived.

Emmy walked in and saw Mr. Darby behind the counter.

"Hi, Mr. Darby. Look who finally decided to come home."

Mr. Darby looked up as he heard Emmy's voice. "Well, I'll be, if it isn't SoHam's very own famous rock star. I suppose you want to order something that's not on the menu." He reached out a hand and shook Kenny's.

"I would like a chili cheese dog, fries and a root beer, please," Emmy said.

It reminded Mr. Darby of how she would place an order as a kid.

"And for you, Mr. Rockstar?"

"I'd like a beef sandwich with red sauce, large fries and a Coke."

"Hey, Danny, do we have any red sauce back there?" Mr. Darby hollered to his son. He chuckled because the red sauce Kenny asked for was merely a simple family recipe of ketchup, vinegar and a couple of secret ingredients. Only his favored customers knew he made it.

"We don't carry red sauce," Danny hollered. "Is Kenny Colwell back in town?"

"Yeah, and he's asking for red sauce."

Danny walked out of the back, wiped his hands on his white apron and shook hands with Kenny. "It's good to see you, man. It's been a while."

"It's good to be home." Kenny felt so comfortable coming here because Mr. Darby treated him exactly the same way he did before he became a celebrity.

"I suppose I can find some red sauce around here somewhere. I'll bring your order out. It's break time anyway."

Kenny and Emmy claimed seats in their favorite booth in the back next to the wall of photographs. Kenny smiled as he slid onto the red vinyl bench. Kenny imagined the stainless steel table looked as shiny as the day the place opened twenty-five years ago.

Emmy reviewed the pictures on the wall. Right above them hung a photograph of Fridays At Five with a young female singer.

49

"I think this is my favorite shot of the band," Kenny said.

"Is that because of that gorgeous singer on the stage with you?" Emmy teased as she placed her elbows on the table, put her chin in her hands and gazed into his eyes.

"Yeah, I wish I could remember her name."

"It's me, you silly boy." Emmy stuck out her tongue as she asked, "That shot was taken at Larry's Uptown Grill, right?"

Kenny kept his eyes on the photo and sighed. *You were so young then, Em. If you only knew how difficult it's been for me knowing you were here in SoHam, and I was on the road. I couldn't wait for you to grow up.*

Emmy touched his hand. "Hey, are you gonna answer me? You look like your mind is a million miles away."

"Yep, and we used it in the liner notes of the first CD." Kenny smiled as he gazed into her eyes.

Danny Darby brought their order and sat next to Emmy.

"Scoot over. How have you been, Emmy? We don't get to see you as often anymore."

"I know. I'm doing all right. Going to Paul Frank and working full-time."

"Dad wanted me to ask if you are old enough to apply for a job yet. Are you?" Danny was teasing because her first job happened to be at Darby's—the perfect job for her because of the location only a couple of blocks from her parents' house.

"If I work here, do I get free food?"

Danny hooked his thumb at Kenny. "You can have free food, as long as he pays for it."

Kenny had a mouthful of fries, but he managed to say between bites, "I've been to fancy restaurants all over the world, but I still love coming here to eat."

"Hey, Danny, are you on the clock, or are you on vacation?" Mr. Darby hollered.

"Gotta go, the old man is helpless without me."

"See ya, Danny." Emmy grinned.

After they left Darby's, Kenny took Emmy through some of the neighborhoods to see the Christmas lights.

"Kenny, look at that house. It looks like the Griswold house

50

from *Christmas Vacation*. I'd hate to have to pay their electric bill."

Kenny laughed. "At least they don't have Cousin Eddie's motorhome in the driveway."

They went back to her apartment, and Kenny stayed until nine o'clock.

"I should get home so I can visit with Mom and Dad. I didn't have much of a chance to talk to them before I came over."

"Will you come back tomorrow?" Emmy asked hopefully.

"Sure, maybe we can do some shopping and grab lunch somewhere."

She walked downstairs with Kenny and kissed him goodbye, giddy with happiness because he was home. With Kenny she felt free to be herself, and she acted more like a child than she did around anyone else. They had been friends since she was seven and he was ten. They basically grew up together. His family lived three doors down from Emmy's parents.

In the morning they went Christmas shopping, ate lunch together and decided to see a movie in the afternoon.

"I want to see *You've Got Mail*." Emmy bounced on her toes.

"I'd like to see *Star Trek: Insurrection*."

"But I want to see Meg Ryan and Tom Hanks together again."

"How about this?" Kenny offered a compromise. "We can see the Tom Hanks movie today if you promise we can see *Star Trek* tomorrow."

"Deal!" Emmy promised—she wanted to see the Star Trek movie as much as Kenny.

After the movie, Kenny was hungry again. "Since we are already out, why don't we have an early dinner?"

"Okay, then can we go back to my place?" Emmy hoped to have a chance to kiss him again.

"I don't see why not. Where do you wanna go for dinner?" Kenny asked while checking out the movie posters.

"Would you like pizza? We could go to Kerry Lynn's Pizza and Pasta."

"Yeah, good idea. I love the sauce they use. Should we order it and take it to your place, or eat there?"

"Why don't we eat it at the restaurant? Would you mind?"

"It should be all right," he said without a lot of enthusiasm.

"Oh, I forgot that sometimes you get bothered by your fans. Maybe we should take it to my apartment. I forget that you are a famous rock star now."

"I'm not usually treated as a celebrity, except by the paparazzi, and especially not here in SoHam. Mr. Darby has always treated me the same as when we were kids."

"I noticed that at lunch. He gave you a hard time about wanting red sauce on your sandwich."

"He always does, but he makes it the way I like it anyway."

They decided to eat at the restaurant. Several fans approached Kenny and asked for his autograph, he didn't mind. The owners' redheaded son, Kevin Kennedy, stopped at their table to talk to Kenny. They graduated the same year from Roosevelt High.

"Hey, Kenny, how's the band doing? Silly question. I know you guys have sold like twenty million CDs. Are you guys on vacation now?"

"Yeah, we're taking a break this holiday."

Kevin looked at Emmy and recognized her. "You're Diane Colasanti's little sister, right?"

"Yes, I'm Emmy."

"How is Diane? I haven't seen her since high school. We dated a few times, but it never got real serious."

"She's doing okay. She still lives in SoHam."

"Is she still together with... what is his name?" Kevin asked while glancing around the dining area.

"Craig, yeah, they're still together."

"I'll let you guys get back to your pizza. Please say hello to Diane for me if you think of it."

"It was good to see you, Kevin," Kenny told him, and then looked at Emmy. "Maybe we can have dinner at your apartment the next couple of nights." He thought it would be a way to avoid being recognized by fans.

"That would be all right with me." Emmy grinned. *That means I can spend more time with you in private.*

On Tuesday morning, they did some more Christmas shopping and saw *Star Trek: Insurrection* in the afternoon.

"Can we stop at the store on the way home?" Emmy asked as they walked out to his car. "I want to make a taco salad tonight, and I need to pick up a few groceries."

"We can stop if you let me buy the groceries." Kenny opened the door for her.

"No way! You know better than to ask that."

"Just thought I would offer. I don't mean to brag, but I do have a little bit of money in the bank."

"That's your money. I have my own money."

He smiled. *You're still as stubborn as ever.*

They spent an hour grocery shopping, and, to the other shoppers, they behaved like any other young couple. Emmy made Kenny push the cart and sent him running all over the store for items.

Emmy made a taco salad for dinner as Kenny listened to a U2 CD.

"It's ready. Come and get it if you want any." Emmy waited a few seconds. "Did you hear me?" She looked out to the living room and noticed Kenny sitting on the floor wearing her headphones.

Emmy walked over to him and knelt behind him. She wrapped her arms around him and kissed his cheek. He removed the headphones and unplugged them.

"The taco salad is ready if you want some."

"Good! I'm starving." Kenny stood up and faced Emmy. She put her arms on his shoulders and they began to dance. She moved closer until their bodies touched.

"What about the taco salad, Em?"

"It will be okay if we wait a few minutes."

He leaned closer, pulled her close until their bodies pressed together and kissed her.

She sighed. "I have missed doing this so much."

53

"Me, too, Em." He remembered dancing with her in the carriage house when she was fifteen and wishing she was older.

Thirty minutes later, they still sat on the couch eating the taco salad.

"This is really good, Em."

"Do you really like it, or are you just saying that?"

"It's really good. Do you think I would have eaten three bowls if I didn't like it?"

"There's enough left for lunch tomorrow. We will need to finish it then, or else it goes bad. What would you like for dinner tomorrow night?"

Kenny thought about it. "Have you made mostaccioli lately?"

"It's been a while, but I think I could manage it."

"Can you make it with Italian sausage and mozzarella cheese and bake it? I could put together a salad, and we could have garlic bread."

"I think I've got everything I need. Oh, I don't have any garlic bread. I might need to go to the store to get a few things I didn't pick up today."

"I could stop by, and we could go together."

"Sounds good to me."

After dinner they sat on the couch together and watched TV, but mostly they just talked. Emmy leaned against him on the couch, and he put his arm around her shoulders.

"Did you meet anyone special on the tour?" Emmy asked.

"We did meet the guys from R.E.M."

"That's not what I meant." She elbowed him in the ribs.

He smiled as he rubbed his side. "I didn't meet any females that interested me."

"Thank you for being such a good liar."

"Are you going to tell me about Tony and this Scott character you mentioned on the phone?"

She bit her lip but told Kenny about Scott.

"Thank God you remembered what Pastor Ronnie talked about."

"I feel so stupid now." She blinked away a tear. "I'm not

54

like Diane. Sex has always been so casual for her."

"You're not like Diane, Em. I've known that since we first met." *Remember? I chose to be your friend even though you were so much younger.*

"It's not easy to be good."

Tell me about it. "Have you talked to Tony since that night?" Kenny asked.

"Not really," she said but then crossed her arms over her chest. "Can we not talk about him?"

You must have some feelings for him, Em. "Dad told me Roosevelt won another football championship."

"I went to the game with Kristen and her parents." She told Kenny about the blizzard and throwing snowballs. "It was a blast."

They didn't leave the couch until after eleven o'clock.

"Em, I should get going," Kenny said.

"It's kinda late. Do you want to crash here tonight?" Emmy asked as she gazed admiringly at Kenny and bit her lower lip. *Please say yes. I don't want to let you out of my sight.*

Kenny knew why she was asking. "Are you sure you want me to stay, Em?"

She nodded her head. "I'm older now, Kenny."

"I know you are." Kenny peered into her eyes—very tempted to stay—but he told her, "I didn't bring any clothes or a toothbrush or anything."

Emmy sighed. "You're saying no. You could stay tomorrow night. You could bring an overnight bag."

He looked at her and thought about how much he would like to stay. The choice of whether to be just her close friend, or being so much more than a friend, tore him apart.

He decided to answer like a politician and not make any strong commitment. "I've slept in worse places than this couch. Okay, I'll do that, and we can see how things go. You might be tired of me by tomorrow night."

"True, but we'll see how I feel." Emmy hid her disappointment by teasing him. She knew very well that she would still want him to stay even if he slept on the couch.

Chapter Seven

"What are we gonna do today?" Emmy asked as she ran up the stairs after letting Kenny inside.

"Why don't we get the grocery shopping out of the way first. Then see what we want to do."

"Okay, I made a list. Did you have breakfast yet?"

"No, you?" He stood on the landing outside her apartment.

She pulled him inside. "Not yet. Should I make something here or do you wanna go out?"

I don't want a repeat of what happened at the pizza place. He thought about it. "It's early. I think it will be all right. Let's go out. There's a place in the plaza by the Sainsbury's. I haven't been there for a while, but they used to have good food."

"Is it cheap?" Emmy asked as she turned off the music.

"Yes, Emmy, it's cheap. It's usually full of senior citizens, and they like to eat cheaply. Does this mean you are buying?"

"I can buy breakfast if you buy the groceries today," Emmy told him, even though it hurt her pride.

"I can buy the groceries." He knew she had to live within her budget, and it didn't include feeding and entertaining him.

They ate breakfast, did the grocery shopping and were back at her apartment by eleven. Kenny bought her enough groceries to last a month, despite her protests.

"Where do you want me to set these bags?" Kenny asked Emmy with his hands full.

"Just drop them on the table or on the floor. I'll put the cold stuff in the fridge, and then you can help me decide where to put everything else." She kissed him quickly while he still had his hands full. "You know you didn't have to buy so much."

"You can count it as part of your Christmas present," Kenny said.

They put the groceries away, and Emmy asked, "Do you want to finish up the taco salad now? Silly question, I know."

They sat on the couch and watched TV as they ate the last of the taco salad. After finishing lunch, Kenny helped with the dishes: he dried as she washed. They kept bumping hips in a

56

playful way.

"What do you want to do this afternoon? Got any ideas?"

She grinned as she looked at him. "We could stay here and..."

Kenny snapped the dishtowel at her bottom. "Don't even think about it. I know what you are thinking."

"What? What exactly do you think I'm thinking about, huh?" Emmy asked, pretending to be annoyed.

"You want... never mind. Maybe I was thinking about it, too."

"What? I want to know exactly what you think I am thinking about." Emmy wouldn't let it pass.

Kenny grinned. "Sex! You are thinking about sex."

"You're only partly right. I thought it would be nice to kiss and hold each other, but I wasn't going to jump into bed with you."

Emmy knew Kenny had an overnight bag in his car because she had seen it in the backseat when they went shopping. She hadn't mentioned it, or asked whether he planned to spend the night. She didn't want to think about that yet. She did want him to spend the night, but hoped he would sleep on the couch.

"We've been to two movies... our Christmas shopping is done... I don't need more groceries. What else can we do together?" she asked as she put her hands together behind her back and twisted back and forth.

"We could go to Windsor Park and go sledding," Kenny said, although he would rather take her to bed. He knew he wouldn't though.

"Duh! Have you looked outside lately? It's over fifty degrees. We haven't had any snow to speak of, and I think it would be rather difficult to go sledding without snow."

"We could call Diane and see what she and Craig are doing," Kenny suggested. *Though I'd rather go to the dentist and have all my teeth pulled.*

"They are working. Diane told me Christmas is the only day they have off. That would suck. I'm glad our office is closed."

"Do you want to call Kristen and see what she's doing?" he asked.

57

Emmy shook her head as she plopped down on the couch. "I talked to her this morning before you got here. She and her mother were going to be busy helping Mama Bertucci wrap gifts."

"I know it might be boring, but I have two books I want to read while I'm home."

"I have some library books I need to finish." She glanced at the books on top of the TV.

"What would you say to an afternoon of reading and relaxing and not going anywhere?"

"I need to do some laundry," she remembered.

"How about we take your laundry to my parents' house, and do it there. We can read in the carriage house and listen to tunes. What do you say?"

She thought about the old couch where he first kissed her. "I like that idea."

"I did buy a new futon, and you haven't seen that yet."

"Did you get rid of the couch?" Emmy asked with a trace of disappointment in her voice.

Kenny smiled and said, "No way. It's still there, Em. You know I won't ever get rid of that couch until it totally falls apart."

"Just reading, huh?" Emmy asked.

"And listening to tunes," he said.

"We are still coming back here for dinner though, right?"

"If you're still willing to cook, we are."

"Okay, let's go to your place so we can read." Emmy grinned devilishly.

She grabbed her library books, and he carried her laundry. They snatched their coats off the wall rack and headed out the door. She looked at Kenny's car, a red 1993 Honda Civic which originally belonged to his mother, and shook her head. "What kind of rock star drives a Honda Civic? Are you ever going to get a new car? How many miles does this thing have on it, anyway?"

"If you must know, I've been thinking I would buy a new car while I'm home. Mom used the car the other day and noticed it had over 100,000 miles. She told Dad I should get a new one."

"You never get rid of anything, do you?"

"As long as it runs, why should I? I don't get rid of my

58

guitars because they're old. Actually the guitars are more valuable because they are old."

They drove to Kenny's place. He pulled into the alley and opened one of the garage doors. He parked his trusty Civic next to his father's '97 silver Accord. In another part of the large garage was a '96 Honda Odyssey minivan that Mr. Colwell bought for the band to use. They used it to travel for part of their first year before purchasing a bus. His parents used it now when they went to estate sales, auctions and garage sales.

Emmy looked at all the vehicles. "Do you guys ever buy anything besides Hondas?"

"Dad likes them because they are reliable."

"Don't you want a fancy sports car, or a big truck or something?" Emmy teased.

"Why? I would hardly have a chance to ever drive it. It would just sit in the garage and get covered in dust," Kenny replied, and then had a thought. *You need a car, Em.* He didn't say anything, but a plan took shape in his mind.

"I want to see your new futon. Did you get anything else since I was last up here?" Emmy ran up the stairs to Kenny's apartment. He heard her shout, "Hey! There's a door here now. When did this happen?"

Kenny made his way up the stairs. "I had Dad make some improvements while I was gone. He suggested this door for security reasons." Kenny used his key to open the door. "I've got a spare key you can have if you want."

They stepped inside, and Kenny flipped on a light. Emmy looked around.

"Do you remember the first time you came up here? You were about eight, and I was eleven. The place was full of discarded furniture and junk that had been collecting dust for fifty years. There were cobwebs everywhere. You were scared and held onto my hand for dear life."

"I wasn't scared."

"Yes, you were. It frightened me to come up here," Kenny said.

"Look at it now. It's nicer than my apartment. It's huge

compared to my place."

"I've never really measured it, but Dad said it's over a 1000 square feet. Dad and I cleared it out when I got to high school, and I used it as my music studio."

Emmy added with pride, "I remember that. This is the place where the world famous Fridays At Five originated."

"You were here at the beginning, Em. You and I would practice together. You would sing, and I would play the guitar. Those were some good times."

She looked at the old couch and sighed.

Kenny put his hands on her shoulders and whispered, "I remember the first time I kissed you."

Her heart fluttered. "I won't ever forget it." She turned and faced him. "I've always felt so loved by your parents... and you. I don't know how I would have survived if you weren't here. My parents would fight, and I would get scared and run away."

"You would run over here and tell me about it."

"I used to wish your parents would adopt me." She bit her lip. "I'm so glad that they didn't." She kissed him for a moment, and their bodies melted into each other.

His heart raced after the kiss. For a moment they were both quiet and tempted to forget about reading their books. She waited for him to make a move.

Kenny broke the silence. "Dad had one of his friends remodel the bathroom, too. There's a shower and new tile and stuff." Kenny opened the door to the bathroom to let Emmy see.

"Oh, wow! A new bathroom. How exciting." She feigned interest. "You know there's enough room up here that you could make an actual bedroom if you wanted. A really big one. With a real bed."

"Yeah, I know, but I don't mind crashing on the futon. I do have my bedroom in the house."

Yeah, you have your pick of bedrooms. Must be nice to have extra space. Emmy thought about the Colwell home. The two and a half story brick house had been in the Colwell family for over a hundred years.

"Let's take your laundry to the house and get it going."

He carried her laundry into the house. Emmy managed to get everything into the washer in one load.

"Where are your parents?"

"They're spending the day in Galena with friends. They won't be home until tomorrow."

"So we have total privacy, huh?"

"Yes, no one but God would know if we did anything."

"That's no fair."

They headed back to the carriage house, and Emmy mentioned, "Too bad you still have to take laundry to the house. Did you ever think about putting a washer and dryer out here?"

"I suppose if we had a tenant living in the apartment, we could do that, but I don't mind."

Kenny turned on some music, and they settled down for a quiet afternoon of reading. Despite there being a new futon and a recliner to choose from, both Kenny and Emmy sat on the old couch to do their reading. She giggled as she read and occasionally put her feet on his legs. After an hour, they went back to the house, and she threw her laundry into the dryer. Kenny searched through the pantry until he found a bag of mesquite barbecue chips. They headed back to the carriage house, and, in another hour, Emmy had finished her book.

"I'm done. What's taking you so long?" She moved closer to Kenny on the couch.

"This is an adult book. It takes longer to read because it's more complicated and deep. It's not like those teen romance books that you read." Kenny set his book down and grabbed her around her waist. He pulled her onto his lap as they looked into each other's eyes. She folded her arms around his neck as he kissed her.

"Do you still like to kiss me, Kenny?"

"No, not really. I'd rather be doing laundry or taking out the trash," he teased.

"I feel the same. I'd rather be cleaning my bathroom or living room than sitting on your lap and having to kiss you."

"I could dump you on the floor..."

"Don't you dare," Emmy shouted as she clutched Kenny tighter. "I suppose I can put up with kissing you for a few

61

seconds."

They kissed again, but stopped before they got carried away. She slid off of his lap.

She looked at him. "I'm sorry I'm such a tease. I know you want to have sex, but..."

"It's okay. I realize it's not easy for either of us to deny what our bodies are telling us to do."

"I guess I kiss you and tease you about sex because I know you love me and aren't going to take advantage of me like most guys would."

"I know we would enjoy it if we went ahead, but I would feel guilty afterward. It's because of how I've been brought up."

"You mean because your church thinks premarital sex is wrong, right?"

"Right, it's wrong." They looked at each other and laughed. "Oh, Emmy, I do love you."

I know you do, and I love you, too. She bit her lip. "I look at girls from school and most of them are sleeping with their boyfriends. Sometimes I feel weird because I haven't done it yet."

"Don't feel that way, Em."

"I broke up with Tony because he wouldn't... sleep with me is kinda how I told him, but that wasn't the whole truth." She paused and took a deep breath. "I know now that I wouldn't have slept with him, but I wanted him to try. I know I used that as an excuse because I was afraid." She put her hands under her knees.

"What were you afraid of?"

"I was afraid I would become like my mother, and Tony would be like my dad. You know how they always fight. I thought that would be me and Tony in a few years."

"Do you feel that way about us?"

"No, because your parents don't fight. God! Are all teenage girls as screwed up as me?"

"Probably, but I don't love any other teenage girls. I love you."

"Can you hold me for a moment? I need to cuddle."

By five o'clock, Emmy's laundry was dry and folded. They were ready to go back to her apartment. Once home, Emmy put her clean clothes away, and then started dinner.

"I'll get the mostaccioli going if you put together a salad."

"Okay, where is your salad bowl?"

Emmy bumped into Kenny as she pointed to the cabinet next to the fridge. "It's under there."

Kenny stooped over to grab the bowl. Emmy bent over to grab a pot for the water. As they both backed up, their bottoms touched. They stood up and turned around.

"Hey, watch it there, bud."

"Sorry, Em, I didn't mean to back into you."

Emmy giggled before saying, "I'm not complaining. You can touch me there if you want."

"This kitchen is too small for two people, Em."

"I know. If I can ever afford a better place, I want a bigger kitchen. I've never lived anywhere that had a big kitchen."

Emmy placed the mostaccioli into the oven, and they sat on the couch to wait while it baked. Emmy sat cross-legged and looked at Kenny as though she was upset about something.

"What is it, Em? Why are you looking at me like that? Did I say something to hurt your feelings?"

Emmy shrugged her shoulders, but didn't answer.

"Something is bothering you. Spill it," Kenny insisted.

"Do you really think all I read are silly teenage romance novels?"

"Is that what's bothering you?" Kenny moved closer to her and put his hands on her knees. "I know you read other books, too. Besides, why shouldn't you read teen novels? You are still a teenager, Em."

"I don't want you to think I'm just a kid with no brains."

Kenny looked Emmy in the eyes, "I know how intelligent you are. Just because you look like a fifteen-year-old girl doesn't mean I think of you that way." Kenny didn't know if he should kiss her or not, so he asked, "How soon do we need to put the garlic bread in the oven?"

"In about fifteen minutes. Are you hungry again?"

"You know I'm always hungry."

Emmy took the dinner out of the oven, and they sat at the

table in the kitchen to eat instead of in the living room.

Emmy asked, "Do you like it? You had two helpings."

"It's very good, Em. I like sausage with a little kick to it. Did you like the salad?"

"Yes, you put more stuff in the salad than I ever do. I usually just chop some lettuce and maybe a tomato," Emmy teased.

They cleaned up the kitchen, and then sat on the couch again. Emmy didn't turn on the TV. She had other things on her mind.

"Are you going to spend the night?"

Her question did not surprise Kenny because she had never been afraid to speak her mind about anything with him. He had thought about how he would answer this question last night as he lay in bed. He responded quickly, "Yes, I will spend the night."

Emmy bit her lip.

"I will stay with you on one condition."

"What's that?"

"I have two sleeping bags in the car. I can use them..."

"You mean we're going camping like we did when we were kids? Are we going to sleep outside in a tent?" Emmy remembered how she used to go camping with Kenny—in his backyard.

"It might be a little too cold outside, Em. I thought I could use the sleeping bags out here on the couch."

"Oh, right, on the couch—good idea." Emmy realized that even though she wanted Kenny to stay, now that it came down to it, she knew she wasn't ready to sleep with him. "Can we stay up all night talking like we used to?"

"I guess so. Are you disappointed that I won't..."

"A little, but I'll get over it. I know you love me, and I love you, too, but I can wait. After all, you only do it the first time once." She bit her lip. *Oh, God! He must think I'm the biggest dork in the world.*

"You are amazing, Em. One of the negatives of being on the road so much is being away from you. I realize that's my choice. Right now you may think it doesn't matter, but down the road, it might."

"I know. I wish I was through with school so I could go

with you. Or would you not want me with you because you have different girls everywhere you go?" Emmy teased.

"Oh, yeah! You know me—a different girl every night. I have to maintain my image as a decadent rock star," Kenny teased back. After a pause he reminded her, "It's not always easy to be on the road. The thrill wears off real quick. You have to live out of a suitcase and sometimes it's hard to even remember where you are. There is a lot of down time and that gets boring. At least I like to get out and run. That helps me stay in shape."

They talked until midnight, by then Emmy was ready to fall asleep.

"I'm going to bed now..."

"I need to run out to the car and get the sleeping bags. They've been behind the rear seat and are probably frozen. I'll be right back."

Kenny ran outside, grabbed the sleeping bags and dashed upstairs. He closed and locked the door but didn't see Emmy.

"Where are you?"

"In the bedroom."

"Are you decent?"

"I'm in my jammies in bed. You can come in," she said.

Kenny stepped into her bedroom. He could barely see her face in the dim light. He brushed her hair off her face, kissed her cheek. and whispered, "Pleasant dreams, my sweet girl."

"Night, Kenny. Would you leave that little light on in the hall outside the bathroom?"

"Are you afraid of the dark now?" Kenny teased.

"No, but I like to leave it on so I can see if I have to get up at night."

"See you in the morning." He got ready for bed and adjusted the sleeping bags. He stared at the ceiling. *Em, you might think you're all grown up, but you're still more of a kid than you realize. It's one of the things I love about you. I'm willing to wait.*

Chapter Eight

It's a good thing you have a large bed, Emmy, Kenny stood in the doorway of the bedroom and looked at her. She was still asleep—almost sideways on the bed with the covers twisted up. He moved to the edge of the bed and grinned at her.

"Are you gonna sleep all day, Em?" he asked as she began to stir.

She opened her eyes and smiled. "What time is it?"

"Just after eight. Did you sleep all right?"

"Yeah, have you been up long?"

"Just a few minutes. Do you want me to fix breakfast?"

"Yes, please. Can you make pancakes with blueberries?"

"Can I get dressed first?"

"If you insist. Don't take too long. I want to take a bath."

They ate breakfast together, and then spent most of Christmas Eve hanging out at her apartment.

"Are you going to stay again tonight?"

"I need to go home tonight, Em," he said. *If I stay again, I might not be satisfied with the couch and that would be wrong.*

After dinner, Emmy took him to see Kristen and Derrick. Emmy and Kristen exchanged gifts upstairs in Kristen's bedroom, while Kenny talked to Derrick and his girlfriend Amber in the family room downstairs.

Kristen sat on the edge of her bed as Emmy rummaged through Kristen's walk-in closet. "Did I mention that Tony is stopping over tomorrow? If you had waited until then to come over, you could have seen him."

Emmy held one of Kristen's dresses up and looked in the mirror. "You did mention it, but I thought it would be better if we came over tonight. We're going to spend tomorrow morning at Kenny's house after we see my parents. I like this color. It's too pink for me to wear, but it would look good on you."

"Are you and Kenny more than just friends now, Em?" Kristen asked as she stood up. "I know you've been spending a lot of time together."

Emmy blushed as she looked at Kristen. She didn't respond,

and Kristen didn't press her for an answer.

"Let's go downstairs, Emmy. Amber is here with Derrick, and some friends from North Park are supposed to stop by."

Amber Quinlan, flew home with Derrick for the holidays and Kenny talked to her about college. Amber shared her goal of becoming a doctor. Some of Kristen's friends from North Park College dropped by. Kristen watched as Emmy and Kenny held hands and noticed the sparkle in Emmy's eyes whenever she looked at Kenny.

"What are you thinking, Kristen?" Derrick asked as he sipped some wine.

Kristen took the wineglass from Derrick, took a sip and then said, "I'm glad that I didn't call Tony and invite him to come over tonight. It would have been an awkward situation."

"Emmy does seem to be smitten by Kenny," Derrick said as Kristen handed him back the wineglass.

Kenny took her back to her apartment but didn't come upstairs. "I'll see you in the morning, Em."

"Night, Kenny. I had a good time tonight." She stood inside the door and watched him drive away. *It's too bad your religion frowns on premarital sex, but it's probably better that way.*

Emmy got up early on Christmas Day. When the doorbell rang at nine, she was dressed but still drying her hair. She flew down the stairs and opened the door for Kenny.

"Merry Christmas, Em," he said as he kissed her.

"Same to you. My hair's still wet," she informed him as they ran upstairs. "Should I change and wear something nicer than these old jeans?"

"Maybe you should. I know you have a newer pair. These do have a few worn spots."

"Okay, give me a couple minutes. We need to take that bag of gifts on the couch. There are some for my parents and yours, too." Emmy changed clothes, dried her hair and was ready in fifteen minutes.

It only took a few minutes to get to the Raynor Park neighborhood where Kenny and Emmy grew up and both sets of parents still lived. Kenny parked in the alley by the Colasanti's garage.

"Are you ready for this, Kenny?" Emmy asked wondering how her parents would greet them. "I haven't been in the house since I got my apartment."

"Be positive, Em. It is Christmas after all. Are Diane and Craig coming over?"

"They're supposed to stop by for a few minutes, but I'm not sure if they will. Diane and Mom don't even talk to each other anymore." They climbed the back porch steps and Emmy knocked on the door. "Let's get this over with."

"Merry Christmas, Mom," Emmy said quietly as her mother opened the door.

"Hello, Kenny. It's good to see you. How are your parents doing?"

"They are both doing well, Mrs. Colasanti. Thanks for asking."

"Merry Christmas, Mom." Emmy repeated after her mother ignored her for a moment.

"Merry Christmas, Emmy. Didn't I say that already?"

"No, but it doesn't matter. Where's Daddy?"

"In his recliner, of course. Do you think he could be bothered to move out of his chair to help with Christmas? No, all he does is drink beer and watch TV."

Emmy looked at Kenny, and he squeezed her hand. Kenny hung up their coats and followed as Emmy walked into the living room and saw her father.

"Hello, Daddy, Merry Christmas."

"Hello, sweetheart, how are you? Hi, Kenny, I didn't know you were coming over."

"Merry Christmas, Mr. Colasanti. It's good to see you." Kenny shook his hand. Then he and Emmy sat on the couch.

Directly in front of the large picture window was the radiator where Emmy used to sit as a child. Emmy sat on the couch, reached back and could feel the heat from the radiator.

Mom walked into the room and sat in her recliner. Her father's recliner angled toward the TV, while her mother's recliner faced the couch and the front windows.

Mom peered at Emmy. *Where is Tony? I thought you would bring him.*

I wonder if she knows Kenny stayed overnight? Emmy avoided her mother's stare. *Please don't make a scene.*

Kenny glanced around the room. *No Christmas tree again.*

Mom broke the silence, "Are you still fighting with Tony?"

"No, Mom, we aren't fighting. We don't even talk to each other."

"Are you and Kenny a couple again? Are you going to keep switching back and forth like your sister did?"

"That's enough, Patricia!" Emmy's father smacked a hand against his recliner. "Can't you leave well enough alone for just today."

"I was asking a simple question about our daughter and her... lovers," Mom yelled back.

Emmy was sitting close enough to Kenny that he could feel her trembling.

Dad yelled louder, "It's her life. If she wants to have more than one boyfriend, let her."

"I want her to settle down and choose one or the other." Mom slapped the arm of her recliner.

"You want to run her life," Dad yelled. "You always have."

Kenny held onto Emmy's hand as she listened to her parents arguing. *Oh, Kenny, why do you even like me? I might end up like my mother.*

Kenny let go of her hand and held up the gifts. "We brought a couple gifts for you. Would you like to open them now?"

At that moment the front doorbell rang. Emmy twisted on the couch, looked out the window and saw Diane and Craig. "I'll get the door. It's Diane."

Emmy opened the door for her sister and her boyfriend and whispered a warning, "We've only been here five minutes, and they are already at it. Just beware and please try not to argue with Mom."

Diane and Craig walked into the room, and Diane handed her father a gift without glancing at her mother. "This is for both of

69

you. We can't stay long."

Dad opened the envelope. "Thank you, Diane. We like going to Olive Garden. We will use this soon."

Kenny lifted the gifts he and Emmy brought out of the bag and handed one to each of her parents.

Mom opened the gift from Emmy. "Is it really from Marshall Field's? That's an expensive department store." Mom held up the top and looked at the size. "Thank you, dear, it's my size and very pretty."

Dad opened his gift. Emmy wasn't sure what to get her father. He would never give her any ideas other than a gift certificate to his favorite bar. "Thank you, Emmy. I can always use flannel shirts."

"I hope you can really use it, Daddy. I know you'd rather have a case of beer," she joked weakly.

Mom held up two envelopes. "We didn't know what to get you girls so here is some money. You can get whatever you want that way."

"Thanks, Mom," Emmy said.

Diane nodded her head and mumbled something under her breath about not even taking the time to go shopping.

"It's time for my eggnog." Dad stood up, went out to the kitchen and returned with his eggnog, rum and several glasses on a tray. "Since you are on your own, you are old enough to have some, Emmy."

She glanced at Kenny. "I think we'll pass on the rum, Daddy, but thanks."

Everyone else drank up. Kenny and Emmy drank the eggnog without adding any of the Bacardi Gold rum.

Five minutes later, Diane announced, "We gotta run. Have a nice holiday, everyone. See you next year." She and Craig got up to leave. Craig hadn't uttered a word to either of her parents the whole time, though he did talk to Kenny briefly.

Emmy let Craig out the front door, grabbed Diane's arm whispered, "Thanks for at least dropping by. Have a good rest of the day and holiday season."

"Some holiday! We've both got to work tomorrow, but at

least we have Sunday off," Diane answered bitterly.

Emmy hugged her sister. *Oh, Diane, I wish I knew of something to say to get you to change your attitude. You're too young to be so bitter.* She watched them get into the car and drive away like they were in a race. She sat next to Kenny, and he patted her hand.

She and Kenny stayed until her mother mentioned, "We are supposed to meet your Aunt Betty and her husband. I can't remember his name. She's been married so many times."

"His name is Clifford Rochon, and she's only been married twice," Dad yelled.

"Well, she's had a lot of friends lately. I can't keep track."

"She is your sister, not mine," Dad reminded her.

"I know she's my sister. Sometimes I think you wish you'd married her instead of me."

Emmy stood up and tugged on Kenny's arm. "We'll go then. It was good to see you both. Have a Happy New Year."

Her parents didn't acknowledge her as they continued to argue. Kenny buttoned Emmy's coat for her as she looked up at him.

"I'm sorry my parents are so horrible," she said as her lip quivered.

"It's all right, little one."

Emmy hurried out the back door and sprinted toward the alley. Kenny struggled to catch up to her.

He grabbed her shoulder and spun her around. He noticed tears flowing down her face. "It will be all right, Em. You don't have to be sad."

"I'm not crying because I'm sad." She stomped her feet. "I am just so... mad at them." Emmy wiped her eyes. "They can't even try to get along for Christmas. I have such a screwed up family, Kenny. I don't know why you even put up with me. I can never get married because they will chase away anyone I care for." She brushed his hand away and took off running.

"Emmy!" He shook his head and ran after her. *It's a good thing I keep in shape.*

"Leave me alone. I'm not worth the trouble."

71

"Don't you ever think like that." Kenny caught her, and, this time, he grabbed her by both shoulders. He said adamantly, "I am still here, and I've known your parents for... what... eleven years."

"You're lucky. You're gone most of the time." Emmy looked at Kenny, and he was smiling. She stopped crying and though she tried not to, she began to smile, too. "I hate you! You can always make me laugh and smile even when I so desperately want to be mad at someone, usually Mom and Dad. Do you know how infuriating that can be?"

"Yes, I know. I'm trying to learn how to become less infuriating, but I'm just so charming and good-looking," Kenny joked.

"I should smack you." Emmy took his hand and whispered, "I don't really hate you."

He looked at her and whispered, "I know, and I love you, too."

Emmy knocked an icicle off the neighbor's garage as they walked through the alley. "Your parents get along so much better than mine."

"I've never heard them argue or raise their voices in anger. I know they don't always agree, but they have a way of working out their differences," he explained.

"So do my parents. They yell and scream and throw things at each other."

As she walked in the back door with Kenny, Mrs. Colwell greeted her with a big hug. "Emmy, it is so good to see you. How have you been?"

"Merry Christmas, Mrs. Colwell, I'm doing great. It has been so good to have Kenny home this year. I missed him so much last Christmas."

"I know how you feel. We were able to see him in England for a few days, but it's better to have him home."

Mr. Colwell, wearing a gawd-awful Christmas sweater, walked into the room and also greeted Emmy warmly with a hug. Emmy looked at Kenny and closed her eyes to prevent the tears that were welling up from escaping. It didn't work. Her lip

72

quivered. She sobbed and her tears burst forth and rolled down her cheek. Kenny smiled at her and winked because he understood her feelings.

"Let me have your coat, sweetheart," Mrs. Colwell said.

Kenny unbuttoned her coat and handed it to his mother.

"I still hate you," Emmy whispered as she brushed her tears away and stuck out her tongue.

He swatted her bottom lightly and answered back, "Not as much as I hate you."

She bit her lip. "Your parents must think I'm such a loser."

"Not at all, Em." Kenny shook his head. He glanced at his father, chuckled and said, "I thought you threw that sweater away. It's hideous."

"What? You don't like this. I think it's very fashionable." Mr. Colwell proudly displayed his sweater to Emmy. "What do you think, Emmy?"

"It is quite unique." She laughed as she touched the fabric. *It's got one red sleeve and one green sleeve, and that is the ugliest representation of a Christmas tree I have ever seen.*

"My mother gave me this three years ago. I think she gave one to your uncles, too," Mr. Colwell told Kenny.

"Your mother won't be here today, Carter. You don't have to wear that... that..." Mrs. Colwell waved one hand and pressed her other hand to her forehead. "Please, take it off before I become ill."

"You're sure Mother won't be here?"

Mrs. Colwell nodded.

"Thank God! The thought of being photographed while wearing this sours my stomach." He immediately removed the sweater. "I can shove this to the bottom of the cedar chest until next year."

Emmy laughed and forgot about her parents.

They gathered in the living room, and Emmy noticed the many presents under the tree. Kenny passed out the presents and took photographs constantly. His mother took photos of Kenny as he opened his gifts.

"This one is for you, Emmy. It's pretty big and heavy. Do you want some help opening it?" Kenny teased.

73

Emmy teased back, "I think I can handle it." She was still enough of a child to be excited by the large size of the box. She opened it and saw a picture of a Yamaha LP3 on the box—a stand for an electric piano.

"Is this really what's inside?"

"Yes, Dad and I will put it together for you."

"Thank you, Kenny."

Kenny chuckled as he looked at her. "Will you help me for a second, Dad?"

Kenny and his father left the room for a moment. Mrs. Colwell talked to Emmy and kept her attention away from Kenny. She had her camera ready as Kenny and his father carried a new Yamaha P200 digital piano into the room. They set it on the coffee table.

"Since you now have a stand, I thought you might need something to put on it," Kenny said with a straight face.

She looked at the piano, and then at Kenny and his parents. Kenny knew she was going to lose it. She bit her lip, and her eyes filled with tears again. She couldn't say anything as the tears started flowing.

"Now you can practice all you want. You can use headphones so the landlord won't complain about the loud music," Kenny said as Emmy stood up. She held out her arms. Kenny held her close as she cried softly on his chest. Mrs. Colwell took several pictures and did manage to get one of Emmy's reaction when she first saw the piano. Emmy stopped crying, and Kenny dried her face.

"You are too good to me, Kenny. I don't deserve this."

"I think you do. You can use this to play and write songs in your apartment. There is enough room in the living room if you move the recliner a bit."

"Will you show me how it works?"

"We can use it tonight. There is a case for it in the minivan. The cords and everything are already in the case. I can put the stand together when we get to your place."

Emmy turned to Mr. and Mrs. Colwell. "Thank you for everything. I really appreciate it."

Mrs. Colwell hugged her again, "I know you do, sweetheart." Mrs. Colwell knew Emmy was not talking about the piano, or the stand. Emmy was talking about the love she had always experienced in this home.

Kenny and Emmy ate lunch with his parents and stayed until two in the afternoon. Kenny and his father loaded the piano and stand into the Odyssey.

Kenny winked at his mother. "I might not be home until late. I'll stay in the carriage house, so I don't disturb you."

"I'll see you when you get back. Whenever that might be." Mom's eyes twinkled.

As Emmy and Kenny drove up Fifth Street toward her apartment, she asked, "Do we have time to stop at Grandma's house?"

"I think we might be able to swing by there. Is she here or in Florida?"

"I talked to her a couple days ago, and she said she wasn't leaving until after Christmas this year."

I wish we were in Florida, Kenny thought.

Emmy stared out the passenger window but glanced at Kenny several times.

Eventually, he noticed. "Is there something wrong? Do you want to tell me about it?"

"Yeah, kinda. I didn't mention it before, but there were three people who got laid off from work. The boss told them right before Christmas."

"What terrible timing."

"I know. Everyone in the office got really pissed at him. I heard a rumor there might be more layoffs in a few months."

"Is business slow? People still get sick."

"The tech guys have installed some new programs."

"Don't you just love technology, Em."

Kenny drove to Grandma Isabel's house; Emmy got out and ran up to the door and rang the bell. It took a few seconds for the door to open.

"I didn't expect you to come and see me, Emily. I figured everyone had better things to do than stop over here," Grandma

75

replied without sounding bitter or disappointed that her family would not visit her on Christmas.

Emmy smiled because Grandma always called her by her full name. "I know I talked to you already, but I wanted to see you, Grandma."

"Well, come on in before I freeze." Grandma saw Kenny and chided him, "It's a good thing you are home this Christmas, Mr. Famous Rockstar. You really disappointed Emily by not seeing her last year."

"I'm sorry about that, and it won't happen again."

Emmy and Kenny spent two hours visiting with Grandma Isabel. No one else from the family bothered to even call.

When they got back to Emmy's apartment, they struggled getting the piano up the stairs but finally managed it. Kenny put the stand together, and they spent a couple of hours figuring out how to use the different features. They even forgot to eat—something that Kenny rarely did.

When it was time to go to bed, Emmy looked at Kenny.

"I should go home, Em."

"You can't. I want you to stay. You can sleep on the couch if you must, but please stay."

Kenny didn't want to disappoint her. "Okay, baby, I'll stay."

Emmy grinned mischievously. "I put your overnight bag in the van when you weren't looking."

"You are a stinker sometimes."

"I know. Do you still love me anyway?"

"I suppose so," he replied as he kissed her.

Chapter Nine

Emmy woke up early the next morning, Saturday, and walked out to the living room, wearing her warm flannel pajamas. Kenny was still asleep on the couch, so she tried not to wake him. She prepped the Mr. Coffee machine, went back to her bedroom and threw on some clothes. When she returned to the living room, she sat on the edge of the couch and whispered, "It's time to get up, sleepyhead. I started the coffee already."

Kenny opened his eyes and looked at her. Then he grinned and pulled her on top of him.

"Hey! What are you doing?"

"I was having a pleasant dream until you woke me up."

"Really?" Emmy grinned at him wickedly.

"It wasn't that kind of dream. We were on stage singing in front of a large crowd."

"Oh, too bad." She put her hands on his chest. "Did you survive sleeping on the couch, or are you all stiff and sore?"

"Its not the worst place I've ever slept. What time is it?"

"It's almost eight. Are you gonna stay in bed all day?"

Kenny grinned, and then kissed her. "That is a very tempting idea, but I should get up." He tapped her hip, moved out from under her and stood up. "Do you have anything for breakfast?"

"Like what?" She sat up on the couch. "I've got bacon, eggs, sausage. Just about anything you might want. Oatmeal?"

"Did we buy potatoes the other day?"

"Yes, I've got six of them. Why?"

"How about a fry-up?"

"What's that?" She reached out and Kenny pulled her up.

"I'll slice up some potatoes, onions, peppers." He made a chopping motion. "Add either sausage or bacon—or both. Fry it all up. Add some hot sauce and voila. Breakfast."

"Sounds delicious. Do you need my help?"

"No, I'll take care of everything, m'lady. You stay out of my kitchen." He tenderly tapped her nose.

"Good. Then I'm going to take a bath."

77

"Let me use the bathroom first, and then it's all yours."

Kenny worked on getting everything ready for breakfast while Emmy took a bath. Fifteen minutes later the fry-up was almost ready, but Emmy remained in the bathroom.

Kenny knocked on the door. "Are you still alive in there or did you drown?"

"Why? Is breakfast ready?"

"In about five more minutes. Are you still in the tub?"

"Yes, so don't come in."

Kenny went back to the kitchen, and Emmy got out of the tub. She dressed, and then paused by the kitchen doorway.

"That smells good. Is it ready?"

"Almost," Kenny answered as he turned around and saw her. "You might have to dry your hair after we eat."

"Okay, but it will be a mess if I do. You might have to brush it out for me."

"I can do that," he said. "I can remember Mom brushing your hair in the kitchen after we played Cowboys and Indians in the backyard. It was all tangled up, and you cried."

"I didn't cry!" She made a face at him. *I remember it, too, and I did cry. But I'm not going to admit it now.*

Kenny fixed a plate for each of them while Emmy covered her wet hair with a towel, and they sat on the couch to eat.

"This is delicious," she said with her mouth full.

"The trick is to time it just right. The potatoes take longer to cook, so I start them first. Then I add the onions and peppers," he explained very seriously.

"Duh." She stared blankly at him.

"Stop that." He stabbed some potatoes. "I know you can cook."

"I can feel my arteries clogging as I eat it. Do you make this often?"

"Maybe once a month. I try to eat healthy most of the time, but sometimes I like to go nuts."

"I've been eating too much crap," she said over her shoulder as she walked into the kitchen and helped herself to seconds.

78

"I'll tell that to Mr. Darby the next time I see him."

"Don't you dare! And I wasn't thinking about Darby's." She stood in the doorway and frowned.

After filling their stomachs, Emmy sat on a kitchen chair as Kenny brushed out her hair.

"Ow! That hurt," she yelled as he pulled on a tangle.

"Sorry, Em. I'll be more careful."

"Do you think I should get my hair cut short?"

"How short? You've had long hair since I've known you."

"Short enough so I don't have to spend a lot of time drying it. A hairstyle where I could just wash it and let it dry on its own."

"It would be easier to take care of, that's for sure."

"I'll think about it. Mom always insisted I keep my hair long. What are we gonna do today?"

"For one thing, we can practice on your keyboard. I can show you all the different features."

They spent the day at her apartment playing songs on the new keyboard and actually wrote a couple of new tunes. They ordered Chinese for dinner and watched a movie on TV as they ate.

After dinner they sat on the couch. Kenny placed an arm around her shoulder as she rested her head on his chest.

"What will you do if you get laid off from work?" he asked.

"I'll have to find another job real quick. I have enough money in my savings for about a month, but that's it."

"I might be able to help you out." Right away Kenny knew that was a mistake because she sat straight up, moved away from him and frowned.

"I'm not going to take your money."

"I meant I might be able to find you a position with the band. You could help in the office. That way you could still go to school."

"I don't want to think about it right now. If it ever happens, I'll deal with it then."

They spent a few more minutes talking, and then Kenny mentioned, "I should head home, Em." He stood up, walked over and grabbed his jacket from the doorknob.

"Can't you stay again tonight? Please stay."

"Maybe I can stay tomorrow. I need a shower, and I want to sleep in my own bed."

"If you stay tomorrow, I'll let you have the bed, and I'll take the couch." She grinned coquettishly as she stood before him.

He put on his jacket and zipped it up. "Are you trying to bribe me, young lady?"

"No, I don't get to see you that often, so when you're home, I don't like to let you out of my sight."

"Would you like to go to church with me in the morning? I'm not singing or playing my guitar, but I would like for you to come with us. Mom and Dad are going. Tom and Sherry will probably be there."

"You're talking about Mr. Hanna, right?"

"Yes, I forgot that you always call him that."

"I haven't seen them since their wedding. What time should I be ready? Do I have to wear a dress? Please say I don't."

"You don't have to wear a dress, but please don't wear those jeans with all the holes in them."

"What? Why can't I wear my holy jeans to church?" Emmy asked with a straight face but then giggled.

"You are just too funny." He kissed her quickly. "Mom is going to make dinner for everyone. Do you wanna eat with us?"

"Sure, should I bring anything?"

"No need. There will be plenty. I'll pick you up at ten."

"I will be ready and waiting, sir." Emmy stood at attention and saluted him.

Kenny shook his head. *You never cease to amaze me.*

A few minutes before ten, Kenny parked the car in the street, ran up the sidewalk, took the steps two at a time and rang the bell to Emmy's apartment. She grabbed her coat and purse and hustled downstairs.

"I'm ready to go. Do I look all right?" she asked.

He checked out her jeans and sweater.

She turned around. "I put a ribbon in my hair."

"You look adorable." He helped her on with her coat. *Em,*

you look so sexy in those jeans. It's a good thing I didn't spend the night.

They met Kenny's parents in the foyer of Faith Bible Church and Kenny hung up their coats. A few minutes later Tom Hanna and his wife Sherry arrived. Kenny and Emmy walked over to talk to them. Sherry took off her coat and handed it to Tom.

"Hey, Tom. Hi, Sherry. How's married life treating you?" Kenny asked.

"Fantastic," Tom answered as he shook Kenny's hand. "Hello, Emmy, Kenny told me you might be coming today. How have you been? How's college going?"

"Hello, Mr. Hanna, it's good to see you again," she replied quietly.

Kenny grinned because Emmy was acting shy in front of his cousin.

"Sherry, have you tried that recipe I gave you for potato and leek soup?" Mrs. Colwell asked.

"Yes, it was delicious. Thank you, Aunt Elly. I found a recipe for a corn souffle that I want to try. Have you ever made that before?"

Emmy heard Sherry mention corn souffle. "I made that once. Mama Bertucci showed me how. Mine didn't turn out as good as hers."

"It's not easy to make. You have to..." Sherry looked at Emmy and suddenly remembered her. "Emmy, I almost didn't recognize you. I'm sorry for not saying hello. How have you been? I haven't seen you since our wedding."

"It's good to see you again, Mrs. Hanna."

"Oh, no you don't." Sherry grinned as she shook a finger at Emmy. "You can call Tom 'Mr. Hanna' but no way am I letting you call me Mrs. Hanna. You have to call me Sherry."

"Okay, Sherry."

"Let's go find a pew before all the good ones are taken." Sherry took Emmy's arm, and they walked into the sanctuary.

After the service Ronnie Rojas, the youth pastor, saw Emmy and headed over to talk to her.

"Hello, Emmy, are you here with Kenny and his family? If

81

I remember correctly, you are neighbors. It's a pleasure to see you again. Are you still singing and writing songs?"

"Once in a while, but Kenny is gone so much of the time. I didn't see him for over a year. It sure is good to be able to spend time with him now."

"Have a happy New Year, Emmy. You're always welcome to join us on Wednesday evenings and on Sundays."

"Thank you," she said quietly as Kenny walked up behind her and put his hands on her shoulders. She looked at him and smiled.

"Hello, Kenny, I mentioned to Emmy that she is welcome to join the teen group whenever she has the opportunity. There are even more high school kids than before. You wouldn't be free on Wednesday by any chance?" Ronnie asked Kenny.

"I'm sorry, Pastor Ronnie, we are going to be rather busy getting ready for the tour."

He shrugged his shoulders. "Just thought I would ask."

"Maybe the next time I'm home I could stop by and play guitar while Emmy sings."

Emmy looked at Kenny and bit her lip nervously as Kenny grinned at her.

"The kids would love to hear both you guys," Pastor Ronnie said.

On the way to the Colwell home, Emmy asked Kenny, "Why did you say that? You know how nervous I am when I get up in front of strangers. Pastor Ronnie must think I'm still in high school and still live next to you. I didn't tell him differently."

"You should think about singing for the teens. It will help you with the stage fright."

She stared out the car window. *I could avoid stage fright all together by not singing at all.*

When they arrived at the Colwell house, Emmy offered to help in the kitchen.

"Thanks, dear, but everything is almost ready. I just have to warm up the potatoes and the roast. Why don't you talk to the kids. Kenny wants to show them the latest changes in the apartment. I'll send Carter out to get you when everything is ready."

"Okay, Mrs. Colwell." Emmy sounded disappointed.

"Emmy, Kenny told me you are becoming a good cook." Mrs. Colwell smiled and squeezed Emmy's shoulders. "I would gladly let you help me if there was something to do."

Emmy smiled and headed out to the carriage house with Kenny, Tom and Sherry. She held Kenny's hand as they walked along. Sherry noticed and looked at her husband. He shrugged.

Kenny led them all upstairs. Tom saw the door and commented, "You should have done this a long time ago. You had all that gear up here."

"I know. We always put it off. Now I feel better about having stuff up here. If you ever need, or want, to get up here, there is a spare key in the house somewhere. I have my key and Em has hers, but no one else has one."

Sherry looked at Tom again. *Why does Emmy have a key to the apartment?* She pulled Tom to the side so Emmy couldn't hear. "I never saw them apart at the wedding. They danced together all night like they were joined at the hip. Even when we took our bridal party pictures, she was waiting right there. How old is she again?"

"I think Kenny told me she is eighteen, so she's only three years younger than him."

"She sure doesn't look a day over fifteen, if that," Sherry said.

"I know, but she is older. Kenny has known her since they were kids. They've been friends for a long time. Are you jealous that she looks so young?"

"Are you telling me I look old?"

"No, dear. You look absolutely adorable... for your age."

"You will pay for that remark later, Mr. Hanna." Sherry grinned as she kissed him.

Kenny showed Tom and Sherry all the changes while Emmy took some dishes out of the sink and put them in the cabinet. Sherry noticed and thought that Emmy must be very familiar with the apartment if she knew where Kenny kept his dishes.

A few minutes later, Mr. Colwell hollered up the stairs,

83

"Elly said that dinner is ready, and if anyone wants to eat, they had better get in the house before she eats it all."

Kenny laughed because his mother ate like a bird. "We better get back." He took Emmy's hand, and she smiled at him.

They gathered in the dining room; Emmy sat next to Kenny across the table from Tom and Sherry. His parents were at the ends. Emmy listened quietly to the conversation. Tom remembered her as being rather quiet in school but very intelligent. He smiled at her and asked, "Where are you planning to finish your degree after you graduate from Paul Frank?"

"Hopefully," she said as she crossed her fingers. "I will be able to finish at North Park. That way I can live at home—at my apartment, I mean."

"How are your grades?" Tom asked, remembering that she never settled for anything less than perfect.

"I usually get A's," she answered.

Kenny told everyone, "The last time Emmy got a B in a class was in ninth grade when she got one in Spanish class."

"Did you have Mrs. Vidales for Spanish?" Tom asked.

"Yes, and she gave me a C. Did you have her for a teacher?" Emmy shuddered as she asked.

"Yes, and she was mean. Some teachers are strict, like Mr. Culbertson, but Mrs. Vidales was just plain old mean."

Emmy laughed as she agreed with Tom.

Kenny asked Tom, "Are you guys going to start a family soon, or are you gonna wait a while?"

Sherry answered right away. "We want to wait a couple of years until we buy a house. Are you and Emmy going to wait, or do you want kids right away?"

The room was suddenly as quiet as a library as everyone looked at Sherry.

She noticed and asked, "Did I say something wrong?"

Emmy looked at Kenny, and then at his parents.

"We haven't thought about kids yet, Sherry. We are not at the place in our relationship yet where kids are even a possibility." Kenny frowned as he answered.

Tom glared at his wife for trying to embarrass Emmy.

84

Emmy answered, "I would like to have a family when I grow up, but I'm still a kid myself, Sherry. It would be unwise of me to start a family this young."

Sherry looked away with a sudden interest in the China cabinet until Emmy said, "I think you and Mr. Hanna will make perfect parents. Maybe Kenny and I can be like an aunt and uncle when you have kids. I would like that."

"You would make a great aunt, Emmy. I'm sorry if I embarrassed you," Sherry apologized.

Emmy smiled. "It's all right. Who knows? Maybe someday Kenny and I will have a whole bunch of kids."

After dinner Mrs. Colwell asked, "Sherry, would you mind if I leave the cleanup for you and Emmy? I'm feeling rather tired, and I should lie down for a rest." She used that excuse so Sherry and Emmy would have some time together.

"We will take care of everything, Aunt Elly. You should rest. Dinner was delicious, by the way."

"Thank you, dear. I'm sure the men will want to go in the living room to watch football." Mrs. Colwell looked at her husband, who didn't care about football in the least, and nodded toward the living room.

"How about it guys? Up for some football?"

"Sure, Dad. Come on, Tom. Let's see who is playing first."

Emmy hollered, "The Bears are playing the Packers at home. It's the last game of the season for the Bears. They suck this year, but the Packers are in the playoffs."

The guys laughed because Emmy knew more about the NFL than they did.

"Thanks, Em. Do you want to watch with us?"

"After I help Sherry in the kitchen I might."

The guys turned on the football game and within twenty minutes were sound asleep. Emmy helped Sherry with the dishes, and they talked.

"I should apologize again."

"It's okay, Sherry."

"No, it was a mean thing to do, and I'm sorry. Are you and Kenny just friends?"

85

"We're more than friends, but we aren't doing that... yet," Emmy said and then giggled.

After cleaning the kitchen, Emmy and Sherry checked on the guys.

"Look at the poor babies. They must be so tired," Sherry said as she and Emmy laughed together. Sherry sat beside Tom on the couch. Mr. Colwell snored loudly in his favorite recliner. Kenny sat in his mother's recliner. Emmy sat on his lap with her feet over the arm of the recliner. He opened his eyes as she kissed his cheek.

"If you are so sleepy, then maybe you should go to bed."

Kenny grinned. "Are you trying to be naughty because of what Sherry said?"

Emmy giggled and replied, "Not at all. Like I said, I'm still just a kid."

Emmy sat with Kenny as they watched the Bears lose to the Packers on a fourth quarter field goal. They watched the second game until halftime when Emmy wanted to go home. By this time everyone was awake and in the living room.

"Thank you for dinner, Mrs. Colwell. I had a good time seeing you again, Mr. Hanna, and you, too, Sherry."

"You are never going to call me Tom, huh?" Tom asked as he smiled at Emmy.

She shook her head, "I'm sorry, but I can't. I will always think of you as Mr. Hanna because you were my teacher."

There were hugs all around as Kenny and Emmy left. He took her home, and they sat on the couch and watched the rest of the game. The game ended and Emmy looked at Kenny and grinned.

"I know that look means you are up to something, Em. What are you planning?"

"Nothing," she tried to convince him.

Kenny grabbed her around her waist and pulled her onto his lap.

"Please, sir, I am an innocent child. I've never kissed a boy before," she said.

"You are the prettiest liar I've ever seen, and I'm going to kiss you."

"Are you going to use your tongue when you kiss me?"

"I thought you were innocent. How does a never-been-kissed girl know about that?"

"I saw it in a movie once." Emmy laughed until she got stitches in her side.

"You are a regular laugh riot, Em. As soon as you stop laughing, I'm gonna kiss you for real."

They kissed and a few seconds later she pushed Kenny onto his side and lay next to him.

"Are you acting so weird because of what Sherry said?"

"Maybe."

After about ten minutes Kenny stopped and sat up on the edge of the couch. "We have to stop, Em."

"Okay, but it was fun."

"Now you can't say you've never been kissed," he teased.

"I know. I'll behave now. Are you hungry? Let's see what we can have for a snack."

They made some nachos and watched TV as they ate. Kenny glanced at the clock. *It's only eight, but if I stay much longer, I won't want to leave.* He stood up.

Emmy knew he was thinking about leaving. "Don't leave."

"I really should go."

"I don't suppose I can convince you to stay," Emmy said as she put her hands on his hips.

"Definitely not tonight, Em. It would be too dangerous." He tucked some loose strands of hair behind her ear. "I'll be back in the morning. I want to go to the Honda dealer tomorrow. I might pick out a new Civic."

"About time you bought a new car. Are you sure you don't want a Corvette, or maybe a Ferrari?"

"You want me to buy something like that so you can drive it when I'm on tour."

"Oh, I never thought of that," she replied with a grin.

He kissed her good night. "I'll be back around nine. We can do breakfast, and then go car shopping."

"Are we gonna go out for breakfast, or eat here?" Emmy

asked.

"We can go out if you want. Night, Em."

"Night, Kenny. I love you." She thought about what they were doing on the couch and sighed. *I never realized a tongue could be so useful.*

As Kenny drove home he wondered, *Em, if we keep this up, I don't know how much longer I can wait before I make love to you. I know it's wrong, but I can't resist. And cold showers are just not working anymore.* He parked his car in the garage and headed inside.

"Aw, you came home. I wasn't sure if you would," Mom Colwell said as she sat on one of the barstool drinking tea. "Have a seat."

"Mom," he said as he sat down.

"Don't Mom me. I need to talk to you."

"Are you mad at me?" he asked.

"Should I be?"

He took a deep breath then shook his head.

"I know you want to spend time with Emmy while you're home. I understand that, but..."

"Mom! Yeah, I've spent the night at her apartment, but I slept on the couch," he said.

She took another sip of tea, looked at him and said, "How long do you think that will last?"

He shrugged and then sighed.

"Not long I would guess."

"You're probably right, Mom," he admitted.

"I love you, son, and we all love Emmy. That won't change no matter what happens, but."

"You're saying I should know better, huh?"

"I'm concerned. I realize you are an adult and make your own decisions. Staying overnight maybe is not the wisest choice. That's all I have to say. Good night and I'll see you in the morning." Mom patted his arm and left.

Kenny sat and thought about Emmy. *Lord, it's not always easy to do the right thing.*

Chapter Ten

"Morning, Em. Where do you want to go for breakfast?" Kenny asked as he arrived back at Emmy's apartment the next morning as promised.

"Morning, my famous handsome wealthy rock star, wherever you want to take me is okay. I am all yours today." She met him downstairs with a kiss.

He shook his head. "I'm not buying a Corvette."

"Fine. Then take me to Southern Belles. If you won't buy a fancy sports car, you can at least buy me an expensive breakfast."

They were seated in a booth by the windows facing the street. Emmy didn't even look through the menu. When she ordered blueberry pancakes, Kenny gave her a hard time: "Don't you ever order anything different? Why don't you try an Irish skillet or biscuits and gravy?"

"I like blueberry pancakes." She remembered the first time she ever had blueberry pancakes. It was Christmas Day, 1995. She was at the Colwell's because her parents had been fighting. She would always remember that Christmas because for one of the first times in her life, she felt truly loved by a family. "What are you gonna get?"

Kenny smiled at the waitress. "An Irish skillet, please, with scrambled eggs and wheat toast."

"Have you already decided what color and model car you want?" Emmy asked as she watched the traffic pass by.

"Yes, I want a red Civic EX four-door sedan. I called and they have one on the lot. I would settle for a blue one, but my first choice is red."

"Some rock star you are. Haven't you ever seen *Lifestyles of the Rich and Famous*? You need to buy an expensive car and a huge house," Emmy teased.

"What? Just one car and house? Shouldn't I have several?"

"Sounds good to me. If you have your heart set on a Honda, you could wait. I read one of those car magazines. Honda is coming out with the S2000. That's a sports car."

"I heard about that. It's a two-seater. Not very practical."

"That's enough for us."

After breakfast, Kenny drove them over to the dealership.

"What are you gonna do with this car?" Emmy asked. "Are you gonna trade it in?"

"Mom wants to keep it as a spare car. I don't know why. She always drives the Accord even though it's supposedly Dad's."

Three eager salesmen approached Kenny and Emmy as soon as they entered the showroom. They were all pleasantly surprised that anyone would be looking for a car three days after Christmas. Kenny asked for Davonte Valadez, and he appeared in a flash. Kenny told him what he wanted; within thirty minutes the deal was done. Kenny paid $17,000, out the door—tax, registration, everything. It took an hour to do all the paperwork and prepare the car for delivery.

Kenny handed Emmy the keys to his old car. "Will you follow me home?"

"What? Aren't you going to let me drive the new one?" Emmy teased.

"Can't I drive it first?"

"I'm kidding. I'll follow you."

Kenny parked his new car along the side of the house. Emmy drove the old car and parked it outside the carriage house. His parents came outside to look.

Mom walked around the car. "I like that shade of red. Did you get a good deal?"

"I think so. I checked the Kelley Blue Book."

"I thought you planned to trade in the other car, but you didn't take the title with you. Did you change your mind for some reason?" Dad asked.

Emmy looked at Kenny. "You said your mother wanted to keep this car. What gives?"

Kenny looked at Emmy. He knew she would be mad, but he went ahead. "I thought that you might need a car, and this one still runs great. It could last another five years, or even longer."

"I don't have any money to buy a car..."

"Exactly my point." He gently placed his hands on her shoulders. "This one is paid for already."

Emmy pushed his hands away, put her hands on her hips and planted her feet. "I'm not taking your car. I will buy one on my own when I have enough money."

"But, Em, this car will just sit in the garage. It needs to be driven, or else it will start falling apart from neglect. I'm not saying you have to drive it all the time, but there are times when you need a car. Why not use this one?"

Emmy shook her head and frowned.

"You can be so stubborn sometimes, Emily Colasanti." Kenny scolded her, but then he grinned.

Emmy tried to stay mad, but she couldn't.

"You are so bad, Kenneth Travis Robert Colwell. I hate you with all my heart." Emmy started to cry.

"I know you do, and I hate you, too." He hugged her and let her cry on his chest. "Will you use the car part of the time?"

Emmy nodded. "All right, but I want to pay for insurance and gas and stuff."

"You can pay for gas and oil changes maybe, but not the insurance. Dad will cover that."

After lunch with Kenny's parents, Kenny mentioned, "Since it's such a pleasant day, I want to take my new car for a drive. Should we go see if Kristen is home?"

Emmy giggled.

"What's so funny?" Kenny asked.

"Do you think Kristen will be impressed by a new Civic?"

"I don't know. Does she have a car?"

"She drives a 1996 Acura CL. I think that's what it is. I know it's an Acura. It used to be Derrick's car, but now Kristen uses it. Derrick bought a new Integra Type-R. It's more of a sports car. You could buy one of those."

"Acuras are like Hondas. Honda owns Acura."

"I didn't know that," Emmy said.

"I guess a new Civic will not impress her."

"She will be happy that you have a new car and would never make fun of you for buying it, but Derrick would probably tease you."

"Like you do?"

"Not that much," Emmy said.

"Then let's go see Jeff. He will appreciate my new ride."

Jeff Rawlings played bass guitar for Fridays At Five. He and his wife, Frances, lived in South Hampshire and were restoring an old three-story house in the Timberline Heights neighborhood where Frances grew up.

Kenny drove Emmy over to Jeff's house. They parked in the driveway, which must have been over a hundred feet long. Kenny knocked on the back door and Frances let them in.

"Hi, guys. Jeff is upstairs painting a bedroom. Go on up. He will be glad to see you. Tell him I said he could take a break."

Kenny laughed. "Thanks, Frances, I'll tell him. Did you guys have a good Christmas?"

"Yes, we visited both sets of parents and had a pleasant time."

Kenny ran upstairs to get Jeff while Emmy talked to Frances. The guys came running downstairs and headed outside. Jeff checked out the car. "It looks nice. Hondas last forever."

"Emmy got on my case about buying it. She tried to talk me into a Corvette or a Ferrari."

"Really?" Jeff asked. "That doesn't sound like Emmy."

"She was teasing. She's going to use my old car since she doesn't have one."

Kenny and Emmy hung around until dinnertime. Frances wanted them to stay and finally convinced them. Kenny and Emmy got back to his parents' house a few minutes after eight.

"You are coming over, right?" Emmy asked.

"Yes, I will stay. Let's drive the old car over to your place, and tomorrow you can bring me home. I need to go to the Steward Music office and work on the details of the tour. We have to leave January third."

Emmy drove them to her apartment in Kenny's old car. They stayed up until after midnight talking.

"I'm ready for bed. Are you tired yet, Kenny?"

"Yeah, I should call it a night. I'll sleep on the couch again."

Emmy looked at him and bit her lip, "You don't have to,

92

you know?"

"You shouldn't have to sleep on the couch. It's your apartment, after all," Kenny teased.

Emmy's bright blue eyes twinkled. "I wasn't going to sleep on the couch."

"Em, we can't..."

"I know, but that doesn't mean we can't share the bed. We have slept together before..."

"We fell asleep for a couple of hours on the old couch. We were still dressed. There's a big difference."

"We shared a tent in your backyard," Emmy said.

"We were kids, Em."

"My bed is even bigger than your old couch."

"I know I will regret this, but all right, what is your plan?"

"You have to sleep in the sleeping bag." She pointed to where the two sleeping bags were on the floor next to the dresser. "That way we can be sure that nothing will happen."

Kenny looked at her and had to make a choice. His libido screamed at him to sleep with her, but his heart told him it wouldn't be right. "I know you broke up with Tony because of this... sex thing, but..."

"There were also other reasons. I'm not going to break up with you just because you won't make love with me. At least you treat me like a girlfriend, and if I have to wait until the time is right, I will."

"Emmy, I love you and believe me, I want to share your bed so much."

"It's okay if you use the couch again. Are you sure you will be able to sleep?"

"Yes, and your virtue will be safe, even if you don't want it to be."

"Okay, but the bedroom door will be open in case you can't sleep."

Emmy got ready for bed in her bedroom while Kenny used the bathroom.

She was already in bed as he stood in the door to the bedroom and asked, "Are you ready for me to turn off the light?"

93

"Yes, did you leave that light on in the hall outside the bathroom?" Emmy asked rather softly.

"Yes, I did, Em. Are you afraid of the dark now?"

"No, but I like to leave it on so I can see if I have to get up at night. I told you that before. Stop teasing me or else you will have to sleep out on the landing," Emmy said in a whisper-like voice that was both innocent and sexy.

"Night, baby."

"Don't I even get a good night kiss?"

"One little kiss. That's all!" Kenny kissed her quickly.

Emmy sighed and whispered, "Night, Kenny. Thank you for the car. I love you."

"I love you, too, little one." Kenny called her by an old nickname. Then he turned off the light and went back to the living room. As he arranged the sleeping bags, he thought, *I know that nothing has happened when I sleep over, but am I setting a bad example for people? If I was home all the time, I could see Emmy as often as I wanted, and I wouldn't have to spend the night.* He slipped into the top sleeping bag and chuckled. *Oh, Em, you can be so contradictory at times. You look so sexy without even realizing it, but yet you want a nightlight on. You keep a football on top of your dresser, and I bet you still have that stuffed teddy bear I gave you for Christmas when you were twelve. I know I have wished you were all grown up before, but I still love that you can be so innocent and childlike with me.*

Emmy was still sleeping when Kenny woke up. He got dressed and was checking his pockets for his car keys when he remembered, *Shoot, Emmy is supposed to give me a ride home.*

Just then she walked out of the bedroom. "What time is it? Where are you going?"

Kenny looked at her and smiled. "Emmy, your hair is a mess. You look so tired. And I think you are the most beautiful girl in the world."

"You're making fun of me."

"No, but I really need to get to the office, Em. It's almost nine thirty."

"Why did you let me sleep so long? I'm supposed to give you a ride home. Give me five minutes to get dressed, and I'll take you home."

On the way to his house, Kenny said, "I'm really going to be busy for the next couple of days. We've got to go over details of the tour and practice a little. I might not have much time to see you."

"Oh, that's all right. I guess I will survive for a couple days. I've got stuff I need to take care of, too. Are we still going to Kristen's New Year's Eve party on Thursday?"

"I would like to. You do still want to go, right?"

"Absolutely!"

"How about I call you tomorrow night. We can figure out something to do during the day, and then go to her party."

"Will you stay with me that night?" Emmy asked.

Kenny looked at her, and she bit her lip. He smiled because he loved the way she looked when she did that.

"Yes, we can have another sleepover, Em."

"Good! I know you think I'm nuts because I want you to stay overnight, but I won't sleep with you."

"I know, baby. One of these days that will change."

She giggled and then asked, "So, you will sleep with me eventually, huh?"

He felt his face turn red. "I meant that I won't always be on the road most of the year."

She checked her mirror. *I've often wondered what it would be like to have a normal relationship with you.*

She stopped in front of the Colwell home, and Kenny kissed her. "I'll call you tomorrow night. If we get finished early enough, maybe we can grab dinner. I'll call you one way or another. See ya, Em."

"Say hi to the guys, and tell Mr. Walker that I expect him to make sure you're always home for the holidays."

"I'll pass that along to Andy." Kenny laughed as he opened the car door.

Chapter Eleven

It sure is convenient to have a car. Beats walking and carrying my dirty clothes. Emmy thought after having been to the laundromat three blocks away. She was humming Kenny's song about her "Sweet Girl" when the phone rang.

"What are you doing, Em? Are you real busy?"

"I'm doing something I look forward to every Wednesday. Oh, Kenny, this is so exciting. I'm having the time of my life."

"So, you're either sorting dirty clothes or folding clean clothes. Which is it?"

"Folding clean ones. How are you? Are you finished and ready to come and see me?"

"Not exactly finished. Would you like to come and meet us for practice? We're going to run through a set, and then have dinner. I was hoping you could join us."

"Normally I would love to, but I do enjoy folding clothes. It sometimes takes me hours to get them folded just perfect."

"I totally understand. Maybe I can see you another time." He laughed.

"Oh, all right," Emmy rolled her eyes as she pretended to be disgusted. "I suppose I could tear myself away from my greatest pleasure and hang out with you for a little while."

Kenny chuckled and asked, "Do you remember where the warehouse is?"

"Do you mean the one you guys have used for years now, or is there a new one you haven't told me about?" Emmy asked.

"You are just too funny."

"What time?"

"Can you get here by four? Do you remember the code to get in?"

"I can make four. Is it still..."

"Don't say it over the phone. This line might not be secure. There are spies everywhere."

"Oh, sorry, 007, I wasn't thinking. I'll see you at four." Emmy grinned as she thought about the security code.

Emmy drove to the warehouse the band had used for

rehearsals and storage for a couple of years. The band bought the building from Jeff's father and used it to store their gear between tours. They had a stage complete with sound, lighting and pyrotechnics set up at one end of the 55,000 square foot building. Emmy parked the car and hurried over to the side door. She punched in the code, 0-7-0-8-8-0, her birthday, and opened the steel door. She could see the stage lights flashing as one of the tech guys ran through cues. She saw Kenny talking to Andy Walker and hurried over to join them. Andy saw her first because Kenny had his back to her.

Andy gave Emmy a big hug. "Good afternoon, Miss Colasanti, I'm glad you are here. All right, everyone," Andy hollered to the guys. "The princess is here. We can get started." He looked back at Emmy and laughed. "I'm teasing you."

"Who knows? Maybe someday I will be a singer, and you can help me set up my cross-country tours." She turned to Kenny and gave him a kiss as he hugged her.

They walked to the front of the stage, and Emmy hollered up at the guys—Jeff Rawlings, Jeremy Lenhart and Dave Persching, the other members of Fridays At Five—"Hi, guys. Happy New Year! I mean happy almost New Year."

Dave hollered back, "Happy almost New Year, Emmy. Come up here so we can see you and give you a hug."

Emmy ran up the stairs and over to Dave.

"It's been a while since I've seen you. You are getting prettier and look more grown-up every time I see you. You must be twelve now, right?" Dave teased.

"I'm thirteen now, Dave. A real teenager," Emmy teased back in her most child-like voice.

Jeff and Jeremy walked over and gave Emmy hugs and talked to her.

Andy and Kenny joined the others on the stage. Andy announced, "Let's get this show on the road. I'm hungry, and I don't want to starve to death while you guys are standing around wasting time."

Ninety minutes later, the guys were satisfied they had gotten the rust off. They let Emmy sing along and even made her sing a couple of solos. She and Kenny sang a duet on the song she helped write "I Will Be True To You." She had fun being on stage with the guys as she danced and thoroughly enjoyed herself. She even joined Jeremy on the keyboards when they did the song "Too Bad," the band's first hit.

"All right!" Andy hollered as the guys shut down their gear. "Let's go eat."

"Where are we going?" Dave asked Andy.

"I got us a room at The Hungry Lion. I'm taking the whole crew out."

"Is this coming out of our earnings?" Jeff asked.

"Do you think we can afford this?" Jeremy teased.

"Maybe just this one time, but you better not get used to being treated like rock stars."

Andy picked up the check for the dinner.

Two hours later, Kenny and Emmy were on their way to his house. He grabbed some clothes, an acoustic guitar, his overnight bag, and they continued to her apartment. He looked at her and a thought popped into his head. He understood they were like children playing with matches. Just as children who play with matches might start a fire that they can't put out, Kenny realized that if he spent another night with her, it was likely their passion would spark a flame that would engulf them both. A flame they would not be able to control once it got started. He slept on the couch again that night.

They both slept late on New Year's Eve morning. Kenny didn't wake up until after ten. He stretched his arms above his head, stood up and touched his toes to stretch out his back. He didn't hear Emmy so he checked her bedroom. He grinned as he saw her sprawled out on the bed with the sheet and blanket all twisted and only covering her below her knees. He walked over and kissed her cheek. She stirred. Then she opened her eyes and smiled.

"Good morning, sunshine. Are you gonna sleep all day?"

"No, wake me up at six so I can get ready for the party," she said. "What time is it, anyway?"

"Five-thirty," Kenny answered.

Emmy opened her eyes wide. "Are you kidding? Did I sleep all day?"

Kenny grinned, and Emmy knew he was joking.

"I hate you. What time is it really?"

"A few minutes after ten. I'm hungry. I want breakfast," Kenny whined, sounding exactly like a kid.

She grinned. "So do I. I want blueberry pancakes and some bacon. Coffee would be good, too. How soon can you have it ready?"

"If you get up, I'll make something, but you are gonna owe me big time."

They ate breakfast, and then listened to tunes and even finished the lyrics to a new song. Emmy turned off her keyboard, and Kenny set his acoustic guitar back in the case. She flipped the switch to her practice amp. Kenny frowned.

"Ooops! Sorry. I forgot. I'm supposed to turn off the amp first."

"It's all right." Kenny got a real serious look on his face. "Do you think you could be happy in a relationship where I'm gone so much?"

"Whoa! Where did that come from?" She gathered up their music and put it in Kenny's folder.

"Just been on my mind."

"Let me think." She put a finger to her mouth and rubbed her lower lip. "When I finish school, maybe I could be a part of the crew. I could do something to help the band."

He looked at her and knew she would probably get angry if he said what he was thinking, but he barged ahead. "You could quit working and go to school full-time..."

"No," Emmy interrupted.

"Just listen, Em, and please don't bite my finger," he said as he put his finger on her mouth.

"Don't even bring up money. You know how I feel."

"I know you want to put yourself through school on your own, but if you let me help you financially, you could finish quicker and have your degree. You could concentrate on school

99

and take extra classes." He continued as Emmy shook her head. "You could be done in two years."

"Are you finished?" she asked coldly.

"Yes."

"Good. Now we can get back to reality."

"But, Em..."

"No, absolutely not! I won't take your money."

"Then marry me. It would be *our* money if we get married."

She was stunned and neither of them spoke for a moment.

"Great! We are having an argument and you propose to me. How romantic," Emmy said sarcastically as she moved back a step.

"You are the most stubborn person I have ever met." Kenny sat on the couch, and then pulled her onto his lap. "And I love you so much."

She looked at him and couldn't stay mad—not even now. "I know you do, and I love you, too, but you know how I feel."

She put her arms around his neck, and he held her close. As if they would fly away if they were to let go. They were both lost in their thoughts until Kenny asked, "Are we still going to the party?"

Emmy giggled and answered, "Yes, and I need to get ready pretty soon. We are going out to eat first, right?"

"Yes, is it all right if I pay for dinner?" Kenny asked knowing he would get a reaction.

"You can pay as long as you never bring up that subject again."

"Okay, I'll never ask you to marry me again..."

"I meant the college thing. You can ask the other question again when you really mean it," she answered as she kissed him. "You can ask again if you're serious. I know you didn't mean it now." She got up from his lap.

"Maybe it was a one-time-only offer," he teased.

"Too bad if it was. You will never get to make love to me."

They ended up going to Darby's for dinner. Emmy insisted on paying for her chili dog and fries. Kenny didn't argue with her.

After they got back from Darby's, Kenny used his old car to

run home to get ready for the Keasling's New Year's Eve party. Emmy wanted the apartment to herself so she could get ready. She had a new black dress and wanted to surprise Kenny. The dress had a scoop neckline, short sleeves, the flared skirt hit three inches above the knee, and she had a necklace of white beads as an accent. She decided to wear her charm bracelet even though it was a gift from Tony.

He returned at seven thirty with his new Civic and used the key Emmy had given him.

"Em, I'm back. Are you decent? Where are you?"

"In the bedroom. Give me a minute or two, and I'll be out," she answered.

Kenny sat on the couch and read a magazine. Emmy came out five minutes later, and Kenny glanced at her, and then back at the magazine. He did a double take, dropped the magazine and stood up. "Holy cow! You look great. Is that a new dress?"

"Yes, do you like it?" Emmy asked as she spun around.

"Oh my God, Em. It looks perfect on you and I like the way you fixed your hair. I like that necklace." He saw the charm bracelet on her wrist. "Is that the one Tony gave you?"

"Yes, is it all right if I wear it? I don't have any other jewelry to wear. I never buy any for myself."

"I don't mind if you wear it. You look amazing."

"I don't look like I'm twelve, do I? Diane always tells me I look twelve just to piss me off."

"Not at all. You look at least fifteen."

Emmy stuck out her tongue and made a face at him.

They made it to the Keasling house shortly after eight thirty—the first couple to arrive. Emmy rang the front doorbell, and Mr. Keasling opened the door.

"Hi, Mr. Keasling, I know we're a little early, but I couldn't wait any longer to get here."

"Come on in, Emmy. It's good to see you, too, Kenny. How have you been?" He took their coats and hung them in the closet.

"I've been doing great. It's so good to be home for the holidays. How are you, Mr. Keasling?"

"We are doing all right. Kristen is in the kitchen with her

101

mother."

Emmy looked around the room and noticed all the Christmas decorations. "Thanks, Mr. Keasling. The house looks so festive."

Emmy took Kenny's hand and pulled him along as she headed to the kitchen.

"Festive?" Kenny looked at her and grinned.

"Be quiet. I wanted to sound like an adult." Emmy made a face at Kenny, and then yelled, "Kristen, we're here!" as she let go of Kenny's hand and ran toward the kitchen.

Kenny watched and shook his head. *You're still a tomboy, Em, even if you're wearing a sexy new dress.*

"I'm in here, Em. Just helping Mom and Mama finish these appetizer things."

Emmy ran into the kitchen and right into Mama Bertucci.

"Emmy, dear, it's so good to see you. How have you been? You didn't come to see me at Christmas."

"Hi, Mama, I'm sorry I didn't stop by. I sent a card." Emmy couldn't look Mama in the eyes as she shifted her weight back and forth, but Mama treated her just the same as always. She gave Emmy a hug, and put her to work helping Kristen.

"Emmy, you finally bought a dress that makes you look like a grownup," Kristen said. "Does Kenny like it?"

"You should have seen his jaw drop when first he saw it," Emmy said and then giggled.

Kristen saw the necklace around Emmy's neck. "I have a pearl necklace that I'm not going to wear tonight. You wanna borrow it?"

"Is it real pearls? If it is, I would be afraid to wear it."

"Don't be silly. When I have a free moment," Kristen turned and scowled at her mother, "I'll run upstairs and get it for you."

Kenny walked into the kitchen. "Hello, Happy New Year!"

"The same to you, Kenny. Would you carry these trays to the dining room for me?" Mama gave him a hug and a job to do. It didn't faze her that Emmy was here with him and not Tony.

When Emmy and Kristen had a chance, they disappeared

upstairs for a couple of minutes. Kristen dug the pearl necklace out of her jewelry box.

"You can wear this. Kenny will love it."

"Are you sure? What if I break them?"

"I don't think you can break pearls, Em. I think they are as hard as diamonds."

"Thanks, Krissy."

"Do you have an evening bag? I have one that would look great with your dress."

"I stuffed my little purse in my coat. I don't want to carry it around all night."

Kristen laughed with her nose in the air. "I suppose I can't expect you to change from a tomboy into a refined lady like me just because you're wearing a fancy dress."

Emmy made a face, and then asked, "Is Tony gonna be here?"

"Yes, and he's bringing a date. His teammate, Terry, talked him into bringing a girl to the party. You will have to talk to him at some point."

"Do you know who he's bringing?"

"Nikki Foster. Do you know her?"

"I think so. Isn't she a cheerleader?"

"Yes, and her father is a doctor... and... she's really pretty, Em."

"I know. She's probably a better choice for a girlfriend than me. She's more his size," Emmy said.

Nikki was blonde and about five feet, six inches tall with fashionably-styled shoulder-length hair.

"Are you and Kenny a couple now?"

Emmy looked at Kristen and didn't want to answer, but she finally said, "Probably just while he's home. He'll most likely tell me to date other guys while he's gone."

"Do you want to, Em?"

"No," she said softly, "I don't."

An hour later the house was crowded with party guests. The younger crowd stayed in the large family room and finished basement, for the most part. The adults congregated in the kitchen,

103

living room and dining room. Emmy and Kenny were talking to Derrick and Amber when Tony and Nikki arrived.

Kristen saw him and poked Emmy's arm. "Tony just got here. Do you want to say hi?"

"Not yet."

"Too bad! He and Nikki are coming this way."

Emmy turned around and saw Tony and Nikki, but Tony didn't see her. Derrick and Amber intercepted Tony and Nikki and the guys introduced their dates to each other. When Derrick and Amber stepped aside. Emmy was holding Kenny's hand. Tony saw them.

"Hello, Kenny, it's good to see you again."

Tony and Kenny shook hands as Emmy let go.

"Hi, Tony, Emmy mentioned that you guys won the state title in football. Congratulations."

"Thanks. Oh, this is Nikki Foster. Nikki, this is..."

"Hi, Kenny, I love your music."

"Kenny Colwell from Fridays At Five," Tony finished. *Great! I hope you don't pester Kenny all night and forget about me.*

Emmy was still standing close to Kenny when Tony looked at her. "Hi, Emmy. I hope you had a good Christmas. Mama said you sent a card."

"Thanks, Tony, I did have a very nice Christmas."

The conversation dwindled. Tony shuffled his feet and shifted his attention to the picture of the Colosseum in Rome on the wall. Emmy cast her eyes downward, bit her lip and turned to the side.

At last Kenny spoke. "Tony, I hear you are going to play football for Notre Dame."

"Yes, I made up my mind and committed to them at the beginning of last year. I guess it's always been my dream to go there. Heather is still living in South Bend."

Soon Tony and Kenny were deep in conversation, without any tension in the air at all.

Kristen stood next to Emmy as they listened to Tony and Kenny talking. "That wasn't too terrible, was it, Em?"

104

"It was a little awkward, but Kenny knows how to handle any situation."

"Nikki looks very attractive in that dress," Kristen mentioned.

"You can say it, Krissy. They look good as a couple."

"I don't think Tony realizes that Nikki has already hooked him, and she's just taking her time reeling him in." Kristen and Emmy both giggled.

Tony and Emmy met unintentionally in the kitchen an hour later.

"I need some more pop. Can I refill your glass, Em?"

"Thanks, Tony." She pointed to the Dr Pepper.

He opened the two liter of Dr Pepper and poured.

"You look nice in that dress, Emmy. I hope you don't mind me saying that." He recognized the charm bracelet on Emmy's wrist as the one he gave her for her birthday.

"I don't mind. Thank you. Nikki is very pretty."

"Thanks," Tony replied.

"That's full enough."

Tony spun the cap back on the plastic bottle, then looked at Emmy. Neither one spoke. They didn't have anything else to say to each other. Emmy smiled weakly, but then turned and walked away. Tony watched her for a second before rejoining Nikki.

The countdown had started and everyone was ready for the new year to begin. The couples were getting ready to kiss as the countdown reached... three-two-one. Kenny held Emmy in his arms as they shared a passionate kiss. She closed her eyes and put her arms around his neck as her body melted into his. After the kiss, Emmy opened her eyes, looked into his eyes and whispered, "I really loved that kiss. Do you have any more of them for later when we are home?"

"I might have one or two left, Em," Kenny said as he quickly kissed her again.

As the countdown reached zero, Nikki kissed Tony, but he didn't really kiss her back. He watched Emmy and Kenny as they kissed and hugged. He didn't know if he should be jealous or happy for them. He knew they had been friends for such a long time. He decided he was happy for Emmy. He kissed Nikki back as Emmy watched. Emmy saw him kiss her and had the same thought as Tony. She decided to be happy for him, too. After the kissing had stopped, Tony and Emmy ended up close to each other. Emmy looked up at him as he looked down into her eyes. She lifted her arms, and they hugged.

"Happy New Year, Em."

"Happy New Year to you, Tony."

He whispered in her ear, "I hope he makes you happy."

"He does, Tony. He really does."

"I guess you have found the love of your life," Tony whispered so softly that Emmy couldn't hear him.

Emmy and Kenny arrived back in her apartment shortly after one-thirty. She looked at him and grinned. He knew why.

"I only have one of those kisses left, Em. Should we save it for another time?"

"Let's use it now before it reaches its expiration date," Emmy teased.

They moved close, and Emmy reached out her arms. She didn't have to reach up as high to hug Kenny as she did with Tony. They kissed and held each other tightly.

"That was the last of my kisses, Em. What are we gonna do now?"

"It's lucky for you that I stopped at the store and bought a dozen passionate kisses in the floral department. I want to use one of them now." She kissed him again as passionately as before.

After they had stopped kissing, Kenny asked, "How did it feel to see Tony again? A bit awkward?"

"I felt a little nervous at first. Then it got really awkward," she said and then giggled. "I didn't know how he would react to seeing me."

"Seeing you with me, or just 'seeing you' at all?"

"Both. I saw him kiss Nikki, and I think he saw us kissing."

"Do you still have feelings for him?"

"Certainly. I mean he's still a nice guy, and I hope we can be friends in the future. Maybe tonight we took the first step in that direction."

"I got the sense that he still cares about you, Em."

"You aren't going to be jealous, are you?"

"No, I didn't mean to imply that. It might be more difficult for you and Tony to just be friends than you realize, that's all."

"I'm tired. Where are you gonna sleep?" Emmy asked as she bit her lip.

"I know where I want to sleep, but since I'm here instead of my own room..."

"You stinker. You can always go back home if you want. I know where I am sleeping, and I'm going there now." She turned her back to Kenny and asked, "Would you please unzip my dress for me?"

He unzipped her dress, put his hands on her shoulders, took a deep breath, and then released it very slowly. "You looked so wonderful tonight, Em. Just like the song by Eric Clapton."

"I have a CD with that song on it. Should I put it on so we can dance?"

He turned her around and gazed into her sparkling blue eyes. "Maybe we shouldn't."

"Oh, right. The landlord's wife would get upset. She is forever complaining about me playing music."

"I was thinking of something else. A different reason for not dancing right now."

"I think I understand. Good night, Kenny," she whispered softly.

"Night, m'lady. I'll see you in the morning."

She bit her lip. He hadn't called her by that childhood nickname for several years. It brought back the memory of the day they first met.

Kenny waited a few minutes until he heard her get into bed. Then he got ready for bed. He grabbed the sleeping bags, laid them on the couch and slipped into the top bag.

"Kenny," he heard Emmy whisper.

"Yes, Em. What is it?" *Maybe tonight will be the night.* He thought.

"Will you turn on the night light, please?"

"Sure, baby. I'm sorry I forgot."

Chapter Twelve

On New Year's Day Emmy and Kenny slept until ten and didn't eat breakfast. They got dressed and hung out at the apartment.

"Hey, Em, listen to this."

She walked out of the kitchen as Kenny played a new melody on her keyboard.

"That's pretty cool. Did you just make it up?"

"I was playing it on my guitar the other day. Maybe we can turn it into a song."

"Will I get a share of the credit if I help you?"

"I always make sure you get credit for the songs you help write."

I know and one of these days I'll use some of that money, but not yet. She asked, "Can we watch football? The bowl games start at noon, I think."

"Sure, we can do whatever you want."

The games started. They sat on the couch, watched football, ate snacks and drank pop.

"Are you bored with simply hanging out with me? Do you want to go somewhere and do something exciting?" Emmy leaned up against him.

"I'm perfectly content to just hang out, Em. I don't often get to do that. I need times like this to recharge and stay grounded. Being on the road isn't very conducive to a normal life."

"You're still the dorkiest rock star ever." She kissed his cheek. "And I'm so thankful for that."

After the Rose Bowl ended, Kenny told her, "I need to go home tonight, Em. If I stay, I might not want to sleep on the couch."

"I wasn't going to make you sleep out there last night, but it's best that you did. It would have been messy." She remembered telling him about the first time she had her period. She blabbed about it like talking about a skinned knee. It didn't embarrass her at all back then, but now it did.

"Are you hungry, Kenny? I could make some spaghetti real

108

quick."

"Sounds good to me. You need any help?"

"Nah, I can handle it."

They ate dinner and watched one more game. Then Kenny kissed her and headed home.

"I was starting to wonder if you had already left on tour," Dad Colwell said as he sat in his recliner in the living room.

"Hi, Dad," Kenny said and then looked at his mother.

She looked up at him from her recliner. "It's good to see you."

"Sorry, Mom."

"It's all right," she said.

"I need to sleep in my bed tonight. The couch is hurting my back."

Mom smiled. Dad tilted his head. Kenny headed upstairs.

"Is he talking about that new futon thing, Elly?" Dad asked.

"Yes, Carter," she answered and then smiled.

On Saturday morning Kenny got everything he needed for the tour packed and ready to go. Emmy needed to take care of grocery shopping and paying her bills. They planned to get together to watch football in the afternoon. The NFL playoffs were underway, and Emmy wanted to see the games. Kenny came over in the afternoon. Emmy could never sit still while she watched football. She got excited and yelled at the TV. She screamed at the officials whenever she thought they made a bad call. She was so animated she almost ended up in Kenny's lap at times.

"Em, do you realize that every time the running back carries the ball, you wrap your arms over your football, too?"

"What do you mean?" Emmy looked at the football cradled in her arms.

Kenny tried to take the football away, but she held on tight.

"See what I mean? It's like you're willing the player not to fumble."

After the games were over, Kenny asked, "Are you interested in pizza for dinner?"

"I guess so. Do you want to have it delivered or what?"

"I'd rather have it delivered than go out."

"That's fine. Can we get pepperoni and some veggies on it?"

"Sounds good to me." Kenny made the call.

Since the games had ended, Emmy came down off her adrenaline high and became rather uncommunicative as they ate the pizza and drank their pop. They both knew tonight would be their last time together for several months.

Kenny eyed the last piece of pizza in the box. "I'm stuffed. Do you want it, Em?"

"I can't eat another bite. I'll have to buy a larger size of jeans if I keep eating like this."

Kenny laughed and held up his hand with two fingers raised. "You had two slices of pizza, Em."

"Yeah, but they were big slices." Emmy held her arms out wide as she sat cross-legged at her end of the couch facing Kenny. She didn't say a word as Kenny eyed the last slice of pie. When he turned to look at her, he saw tears streaming down her face. He moved close to her. She reached out her arms, and they held each other close.

"Don't cry, Em. It will be all right. I'll be back sooner than you know."

Emmy cried quietly for a minute, but then sat up. "Take me with you. I don't want to let you go. Take me with you. I can't stay here without you. We can live together. I don't care what anyone else might think."

"Em, those are lyrics to one of our songs," he reminded her.

"I know, but they fit the situation."

"We can't make a decision like that on the spur of the moment, or just because we let our physical needs control our choices. We can't let our desire for each other compromise our judgment." *Oh, God! Did I actually say that out loud? I wish I could take you with me.*

"Why not? No one else loves me. I'm all alone here. I want to be with you."

"You have people here who love you..."

"If you say my parents, then I will hate you for real."

Kenny held his tongue for a moment before continuing, "I know your parents are... difficult... to say the least, but they love you in the only way they understand. Kristen loves you. My parents love you. Mama Bertucci loves you."

Emmy crossed her arms over her chest and asked, "Do you love me?"

"Yes, baby, I love you. You know I do. I love you enough to say no. Sometimes when we pray and ask God for something, the answer is no. He knows what is best for us."

"You're not God!" Emmy yelled as she threw a small pillow across the room.

"Of course not. I'm far from being the person I should be, but I can't use that excuse to do something that we both know isn't the right choice to make at this time."

"What if I was older and out of school? Could I go with you then?"

"In that situation I would take you with me tomorrow."

Emmy stretched out her arms, and they held each other silently. After a couple of minutes, she let go and moved back to her end of the couch.

"I hate that you are always right."

"It's a cross I have to bear," Kenny said and then grinned.

Emmy laughed, and then tumbled onto her back hitting her head on the couch's arm. "Ow." She rubbed her head. Then she stretched out her arms and looked up at the ceiling. "Why can't I be like Diane? It would be so much easier if I didn't have any sense of right or wrong, or any morals. I could live as guiltless as a bird in the sky. Do whatever I want. Sleep with whoever I want. Oh, Kenny, why do I feel like there's someone watching over me and keeping me from making stupid mistakes and out of danger?"

"That's because there is, Em. God is watching over us. I know he has a plan for your life. That's why you feel the way you do. You know what is right and wrong."

"Are we going to church in the morning?"

"Yes, we can go to church, and have dinner with my parents. Tom and Sherry will probably stop by."

Emmy sat up and smiled. "I love you, and I understand

111

why you have to go home tonight. I know I can't go with you on tour, and it's all right, but if you tell me to go out with other boys while you are gone, I will break all your guitars, or something equally rotten."

"How about if you date just one boy while I'm gone?" Kenny teased.

Emmy knocked him on his back on the couch and climbed on top of him. "I suppose you have someone in mind." She rested her head on his chest.

"No, but I'm sure there must be someone you could spend time with that you don't detest."

"If you're saying that because you want to date other girls on the road, then you are in big trouble, mister."

"I'm sure you will keep tabs on me somehow."

"That's right. I'm going to make sure Mr. Walker keeps his eyes on you." She looked at Kenny and smiled. "Do you really think God has a plan for my life? What could it be? How am I supposed to know what it is? It's not like he's going to call me on the phone and tell me."

"Well, you have a beautiful voice, and you can write songs. Maybe He wants you to be a singer."

"Then why am I scared to sing with you at church?"

"That's normal. Almost everyone suffers from a bit of stage fright."

"You don't. You never get nervous about performing in front of thousands of screaming fans."

"I'm weird that way. I feed off the energy of a crowd. The more they yell and scream, the more energized I feel."

"Will you pick me up in the morning?"

"Of course. A little before ten, okay?"

"I'll be ready." She paused before continuing. "I feel better now, Kenny. I hope you're right about God watching over me. I'm sure I will need His guidance in the future."

"Jesus loves all of us, Em. You just need to accept Him. And you know what?"

"What?"

"It's free! It doesn't cost an arm or a leg or anything. He

paid the entire price for us. Isn't that great?"

"You're talking about when He was killed, then rose again, right?"

"Yes, that was the reason He came to earth. He knew it and He still did it."

Emmy looked at Kenny and asked, "How could anyone do that?"

"I don't know, Em. I can't understand it, but I have faith and believe that He did."

Emmy walked him downstairs, and he drove home. She went to bed and lay on her back, thinking about what Kenny had told her about God and Jesus. She fell asleep without understanding everything but sensed that people never do understand it all.

Kenny picked her up for church in the morning. She was ready to go when her doorbell rang.

"Morning, Em, did you sleep okay?"

"Yes, I did. You?"

"Slept like a baby."

"You mean you woke up every hour crying for your mommy?" Emmy teased.

"I didn't mean it like that. I meant that I fell asleep and had a good night's sleep without any worries on my mind."

"So did I. I remember laying in bed and thinking about us and about God. Then I just kinda fell asleep knowing that somehow everything would work out, and I would be all right."

After the church service, Emmy ate dinner with Kenny, his parents, and Tom and Sherry. She and Sherry were becoming friends after getting off to a rough start. Both Kenny and Emmy knew that the minutes were counting down, and he would soon have to leave. Yesterday morning Emmy wasn't sure she would be able to survive Kenny leaving without her, but now she knew she would make it through until he returned.

"Will you help me carry my bags out to the porch?" Kenny asked Emmy while they were upstairs in his room.

"Do you really need all this stuff?"

"I can't wear the same thing every day like you do," he teased.

"I don't wear the same clothes every day. I change my underwear..."

"You do know I'm joking, right?" Kenny asked.

"So am I. I wear the same underwear all week."

"Not even the guys on the crew are that bad and they are pretty gross at times."

At 2:35 Kenny's tour bus pulled up in front of the house. The driver hopped out and loaded Kenny's bags onto the bus.

"It was good to see you, Tom. Take care of Sherry."

"I will. Have a good tour."

Kenny turned to his mother and smiled.

"You be safe out there on the road and don't be checking out the girls," Mrs. Colwell said.

"I'll be good, and I have the two best girls in the world right here."

He hugged and kissed his mother, and then shook hands with his father. Then he and his father hugged for a moment.

"Take care of Mom. I'll be in touch. I love you, Dad."

"We love you, son. Be safe and we'll see you when you get back."

Kenny turned and took Emmy's hand. They walked toward the waiting bus.

"I will call as often as I can, Em."

"I know you will. You should go before the guys get mad at you," Emmy told him though she meant before she started to cry. "I love you!"

Kenny kissed her once, and they held each other as he lifted her off the ground. He whispered in her ear, "I love you, too. I'll see you soon." He stepped onto the bus and was gone.

Kenny and the band left to start another tour in California. The tour would take the band through Arizona, New Mexico and Texas for the months of January and February. Then they planned to take a break from touring to work on songs for the next project, which they would be recording in Los Angeles.

"He will be back before you know it, sweetie," Mrs.

114

Colwell whispered as she put her hands on Emmy's shoulders.

"Come back inside with me, and we can check out the info for this tour. I can show you..."

"Oh, for heaven's sake, Carter. Don't bore her with all that trivia." Mrs. Colwell cautioned her husband.

"I don't mind. I like to hear about the band."

Emmy walked back into the house between Kenny's parents. His mother ran her hand through Emmy's hair.

"The time will pass quickly, sweetheart. You can always come over to see us if you get lonely."

Emmy slipped her arm around Mrs. Colwell's waist. "I will. I promise, Mom."

They looked at each other.

Emmy bit her lip. "I mean, Mrs. Colwell."

Chapter Thirteen

The second semester at Paul Frank Junior College started on January eleventh. Emmy looked around the classroom and saw a few new faces. By the end of the first week, a couple of the guys asked Emmy for dates, but she didn't have the time or desire to go out with them. Since Kenny was on the road again, she didn't want to go out with anyone.

Kristen came over to see Emmy on Saturday. She glanced out the kitchen window of Emmy's apartment and saw the next-door neighbor lady working in her apartment. *You need more privacy, Emmy.* Kristen pulled down the window shade and turned to Emmy. "I know how you feel about Tony. You did talk to him a little at the New Year's Eve party. Why won't you let me talk to him, and see if you guys can get together and at least be friends."

"No, Kristen! Please don't say anything to him. He probably hates me after the way I yelled at him. I'm sure he doesn't want to be my friend."

"Emily Colasanti! How can I make you understand? Tony doesn't hate you. He likes you, and you like him."

Emmy shrugged.

"Sometimes you infuriate me to no end, but I still love you anyway."

Tony eventually gave in to one of his teammates, Terry Pagonis, and went on a double date. Terry and his girlfriend Belinda took Tony and Natalie Givens, who was at Tony's birthday party, out to eat, and then to a movie. Tony thought Natalie was attractive, but he was not really interested in her romantically. Terry got on Tony's case at school one afternoon.

"You really need to forget about Emily Colasanti, big guy. It's obvious that she has moved on so you need to do the same. I heard she's got a thing goin' on with Kenny Colwell now. If you get my drift."

"Be careful what you say about her, Terry," Tony warned.

"Hey, I'm just sayin', man." Terry held his hands up as if surrendering. "Nikki really likes you, and so does Natalie—she's

116

just as pretty. They both have better bodies than Emmy. You can take my word for that." Terry grinned smugly. "Why don't you ask Nikki to go to a movie or something? Give it a chance. You told me you had a good time at Kristen's party. What harm can it do? Who knows? You you might even have fun. You do remember what fun is, right?"

"I don't know," Tony said as he watched some other students heading to class. "I know Nikki is really popular and she's pretty. Anyone can see that. I don't think I want to go out with Natalie again."

"Why not? She can show you a good time."

"That's just it. She acted a little too eager to show me a good time." He thought about what he heard at school. *I've heard rumors about her, and I think they're true.*

"You say that like you think it's a bad thing. What's wrong with you?" Terry punched Tony's arm. "You turning into a priest?"

"Nothing's wrong with me. It's the way I was brought up, all right. Will ya get off my back already? Maybe I will talk to Nikki after English class."

"Make sure you do," Terry said.

Later that day, Tony saw Nikki after class. He hesitated but then decided to talk to her. "Hey, Nikki!" he hollered as he walked up to her. "Can I talk to you?"

"Hi, Tony, how are you? I had a good time at Kristen's party. I told you that already, but I wanted to tell you again."

Tony shifted his weight back and forth but then asked, "Would you like to go out again? Just by ourselves."

"I would like that very much. When?"

"How about dinner and maybe a movie on Friday?"

"Oh, Tony, I can't. We have a basketball game that night."

Tony sighed and stared at the floor.

Nikki quickly added, "I'm free on Saturday."

"Okay, Saturday will work," Tony said. "Did you finish your paper for sociology?"

"Not yet. I'm still working on it."

"Me, too! Maybe we can work on our papers together," Tony suggested.

"Yeah, I'd like that. I need someone to read my paper and critique it for me."

Tony picked Nikki up on Saturday, and they went out for dinner and a movie. During the movie Nikki sat close to Tony and slipped her arm through his. He could feel her body's warmth as she snuggled close to him.

He thought about Nikki and Emmy. *I suppose most people would say that you and I are a better fit as a couple. Emmy is tiny compared to you.*

Nikki waited for Tony to kiss her, but he was too shy even though they had kissed on New Year's Eve.

Tony took Nikki home after the movie and walked her to the front door. "I enjoyed tonight, Nikki."

"As did I. Would you like to come in? My parents have seen you play ball, and they would like to meet you."

"Sure, I can come in for a while."

Nikki saw her father reading a medical journal in the living room. Her father was a doctor—a surgeon actually.

"Daddy, this is Tony Bertucci from school."

Dr. Foster stood up and shook hands with Tony. "It's a pleasure to meet you, Tony. I have watched you play for three years, and you improved every year."

"Thanks, Dr. Foster. I appreciate it." Tony glanced around the room and noticed the large stone fireplace.

"Have a seat," Dr. Foster pointed to the couch. "Nikki informed me you are going to Notre Dame to play for the Irish."

Tony nodded.

"Did she mention I'm a Notre Dame alumnus?" Dr. Foster asked.

"No, sir, she didn't mention it."

Dr. Foster really enjoyed talking to Tony; they talked until Nikki told her father, "Daddy, I would like to have Tony back now. We want to be together."

"Oh, sorry, honey. I didn't mean to monopolize him."

Nikki took Tony into the family room, and they talked on the couch until Tony needed to leave.

118

"I had a good time, Nikki. Maybe we can go out again sometime," he said as Nikki walked with him to the front door.

Nikki smiled and answered, "Anytime is okay with me." She wanted Tony to kiss her like he did at Kristen's party, but he didn't.

Tony looked at Nikki, *You are very pretty. Almost as pretty as Kristen or Emmy.* He kissed her cheek before he left.

At school on Monday Nikki convinced all her girlfriends that she and Tony were now a couple. When Tony heard what Nikki was telling people, he got upset and denied it. He told his friends, "We went out twice, but we aren't exclusive yet."

Terry chuckled and then said, "You had better talk to Nikki then. The whole school will think you are engaged by the end of the day."

Tony took a deep breath and then looked at his friend. "What should I do?"

Terry shrugged. "Don't worry about it too much. Nikki is just excited because the best football player in the state is going out with her."

Tony and Nikki talked about their relationship after school that day.

"Nikki, I didn't appreciate it when I found out you told all your friends we are a couple. We went on two dates, but that's it. You made it sound like we are engaged or something."

"I'm sorry. I guess I got ahead of myself. I wanted everyone to know that we went out. Will you forgive me?"

"I'll forgive you." He rubbed his jaw. *We did have fun, and you are really pretty.* "Maybe we can get together once a week to go out or something. Would that interest you?"

"That would be great. My dad really likes you, and he doesn't usually like the guys I bring home."

"That's good to know," he replied. *I wonder how many guys you've dated. I guess it doesn't matter.* "Maybe we can go to my house tonight and study. We could have dinner with my mother and watch a movie or something." Tony noticed two of his friends approaching. He turned Nikki and they hustled away.

119

"I would like that a lot," Nikki answered.

Tony took Nikki to her house so she could change clothes, then brought her home with him. They walked in the back door and found Mama busy cooking.

"Mama, I want you to meet Nikki Foster. Nikki, this is my mother. Everyone calls her Mama."

"It's nice to meet you, Mrs. Bertucci."

Mama was surprised that Tony had brought a girl home, but she didn't let it show. "It's a pleasure to meet you, too, Nikki. Please call me Mama, or else I won't know you are talking to me."

Nikki smiled and looked up at Tony.

"I hope it's okay, but I invited Nikki to stay for dinner."

"It's okay, son. We will have plenty of food."

Tony kissed Mama on the cheek. "We're going to study in the dining room. If you need any help, let me know, okay?"

"I can handle it in here. You kids finish your studies."

After a time Mama called out, "Dinner is ready. Come and eat while it's hot."

Tony brought Nikki into the kitchen, and they sat at the table with Mama.

"How do you like school, Nikki?" Mama asked.

"I enjoy school. I'm a cheerleader."

"That's nice, dear, but how are your grades?"

"I'm in the top twenty of my class, so far." Nikki immediately perceived that being intelligent was more important to Mama than simply being pretty. "My dad is a doctor, and I plan to go to med school, also. I would like to become a pediatrician because I love kids so much. I have three nieces and four nephews that I love to spoil."

Mama smiled. *I should have known Tony would not be interested in just a pretty face.*

After dinner Mama asked Tony and Nikki to help with the cleanup. Nikki did, but it was obvious that she didn't help in the kitchen on a regular basis. Tony and Nikki watched *There's Something About Mary*, and then he took her home.

"I had a good time, Tony. I really think your mother is special."

Nikki waited for a kiss, but Tony told her, "Yeah, I had a good time. I'll see you in class tomorrow."

Nikki grabbed his arm before he could leave. "Hey! Is something wrong? Do I have bad breath? It's all right if you kiss me."

"Sorry, Nikki," Tony said as he stared at his feet. "I'm not real good at knowing what girls want."

Nikki smiled. "I would like a goodbye kiss, and if I have to be more specific, I would like it on my lips."

Tony leaned forward and kissed her quickly.

"Thank you. That wasn't so difficult now, was it?" Nikki smiled again.

Kristen enjoyed living in the dorm even though her bedroom at home would dwarf three dorm rooms put together. While at the North Park library one night, Kristen met a guy named Ryan Gresham from Winnetka, Illinois. He started a conversation with Kristen, and they began dating.

Kristen picked Emmy up for the Roosevelt High basketball game on February fifth.

"Thanks for driving. Where's Ryan tonight? When do I get to meet him? What does he look like?" Emmy asked while getting in the car.

"He's working tonight, and I promise to introduce you soon."

Emmy rolled her eyes and said slowly, "Can you at least tell me what he looks like?"

"Fine! He's almost six feet tall. Maybe just a bit taller than Derrick. He has green eyes," Kristen said but then didn't say anything more.

"Is he skinny? Fat? Does he weigh three hundred pounds?" Emmy asked and then giggled.

"Do you honestly... never mind. He's skinnier than Derrick."

"So, maybe the same kinda build as Kenny, huh?" Emmy asked.

"He's taller than Kenny and his hair is shorter," Kristen said as she raced through a yellow light.

"Does he have any tattoos?" Emmy asked and then giggled again.

"You are going to get it, Emmy. No! He does not have any obvious tattoos."

When they got to the gym, Emmy saw Tony talking to Nikki Foster. "There's Tony with Nikki. Are they dating regularly?"

"Yeah, but I don't think it's real serious. Do you want to go talk to them?" Kristen asked.

"No! I don't want him to see me. Let's just grab our seats and watch the game."

At halftime Kristen was fed up and decided to get Emmy and Tony together to at least talk to one another.

"Come on, Em. Let's get some popcorn and something to drink." Kristen took Emmy by the hand and dragged her along to concession stand in the hallway.

"We'll take two large bags of popcorn and one large Coke, please, Millie. Have you seen Tony Bertucci lately?" Kristen asked.

Millie got Kristen her order and pointed. "I saw Tony over by the trophy case a minute ago. He's still there. Look!"

"Thanks, Millie, talk to you later. Say hi to your brother for me, okay? Tell him to call me if he wants to go out again."

Kristen handed Emmy one of the bags of popcorn. "Follow me, Em."

"Where are we going?"

"Just follow me, I want to talk to someone."

Emmy followed Kristen through the crowd.

"Hi, Tony!" Kristen called to Tony when she got close to him.

"Hey, Kristen. How's it going? Are you here by yourself?" He glanced to his right where Nikki was talking to some of her friends.

"No, I'm here with Emmy, and you need to talk to her. Emmy, at least tell Tony hello." Kristen turned around, but Emmy

122

was not in sight. "Oh, crap!" Kristen said as she spilled some of her popcorn. "Tony, she was right behind me. Now I don't know where she is. Do you still want to be friends with her even if you aren't going out?"

"Yes, I do, Kristen. I really miss talking to her. She knows a lot about football. She's like one of the guys."

"I'll pretend I didn't hear that."

"Come on. I know she's not a guy."

"I'll tell her when I find her. She will be so pleased to know she's a girl." Kristen's voice oozed with sarcasm. "See you later. Oh, are you staying for the dance?"

"Yeah, I'm planning to stick around for a while, but I'll be with Nikki if that makes a difference."

"It doesn't matter. Look for us. I'll try to make Emmy stay. Later." Kristen waved, turned around and saw Nikki out of the corner of her eye. *You may think you've got him wrapped up, but I'm not giving up. He and Emmy belong together.*

Kristen found Emmy back in her seat. "Why did you run off? I wanted you to talk to Tony. He told me that he still wants to be your friend. I know he still cares for you."

"I just couldn't talk to him with all those kids around listening."

"Well, I told Tony I would get you to stay for the dance. You can talk to him then."

"I can't stay for the dance, Kristen. I'm not in high school anymore. Besides, I need to get home."

"Why do you have to get home? You don't have to work tomorrow. It's Saturday. You should stay. It will be fun. We can get in with Tony. Coach McMahon is checking for IDs, and he won't care if Tony brings us in."

"No, I can't! Tony probably doesn't want to see me. He will be with Nikki. Why does it matter so much to you that I'm friends with Tony?"

"It matters because you're my best friend, and Tony is my friend, and cousin," Kristen said.

"I know he's your cousin. You don't have to mention it all the time."

"If we do things together, and Tony is around, I want you guys to be able to be friends, that's all. You know, you can be so frustrating sometimes! How many times do I have to tell you that he isn't mad at you? He still likes you. God, you are so stubborn!"

Try as Kristen would, she couldn't get Emmy to stay for the dance.

"Well, I'm going to stay for the dance, and since you rode with me, you have to stay unless you want to walk home. So there."

Emmy zipped up her army jacket and crossed her arms over her chest. "I'll call my dad and have him pick me up."

"You would bother your father rather than stay for the dance. Why?"

"I just don't want to stay."

Kristen shook her head and waved a hand dismissively. "Do what you want then. I'm staying. I want to have some fun. Maybe I'll call you tomorrow if I'm over being mad at you."

"I'll see you, Kristen. Please don't be upset with me. I'll get a ride home from my dad."

Emmy called her father. He picked her up and on the way to her apartment, he asked, "Didn't you want to stay for the dance, honey?"

"Not really, Daddy. Tony and Kristen were staying, but I didn't want to face him. He's going out with one of the cheerleaders now anyway."

Her father didn't ask her any more questions until he got to her apartment.

"Emily, you shouldn't underestimate Tony. He probably misses you just as much as you miss him."

I'm really getting tired of hearing about Tony. Tony this and Tony that. It's over and done with. Emmy sighed. "Good night, Daddy. Thanks for the ride."

Meanwhile, back at the dance, Kristen danced with Tony. "I tried to make her stay, but she wouldn't. I don't know what's wrong with her. She seems different for some reason. I don't know how many times I've told her you aren't mad at her anymore."

Tony thought he knew why Emmy behaved differently. He

124

thought Emmy and Kenny had become more than just friends. His heart ached whenever he thought about her being with another boy. If he was totally honest with himself, he knew he still had some feelings for Emmy that would make it difficult for them to be merely friends. Tony danced most of the night with Nikki Foster, much to Kristen's chagrin.

Kenny had a new cell phone, so Emmy talked to him three or four times a week and he updated her about the tour.

"Why don't you let me buy you a cell phone? I'll pay for the plan and everything."

"Okay, you can buy me a phone, and I want a new car and a house and I want to take expensive trips to Italy..."

"Em! It's just a phone. They're not that expensive, and you should have one with you since you are driving by yourself at night. What would you do if the car broke down?"

"I'd catch the bus like I always have. The school isn't that far away. I could walk it easily. I should probably jog home. I would get a good workout by doing that."

"With a backpack?"

"I promise I'll look into getting a cell phone, but I won't get one unless I can afford it on my own."

"No! I'm not letting you get away with that. I'm buying you a cell phone whether you like it or not."

"No!"

"Yes, I am! Now stop arguing with me."

"Fine." She rolled her eyes. "Can I have a purple one?"

Kristen and Ryan had been dating for nearly a month when Kristen called Emmy one night with some important news.

"Emmy, how are you? Got a minute to talk?"

"Sure, what's up?" Emmy put her hand over her mouth, "Oh, Krissy, I forgot that yesterday was your birthday. I'm so sorry. Work kept me going all day, and then I had class. Happy birthday!"

"It's all right. I don't like to make a big deal out of my birthday, but I kinda did last night. You know I've been going out with Ryan and, well, last night we spent the night together."

"Krissy!" Emmy exclaimed and then thought about it. " Ah, you're teasing me."

"No, I'm not, but let me rephrase that. He didn't spend the whole night with me. I decided that I wanted to find out what the big deal was about sex, so I did. I found out. I gave myself to Ryan as a birthday present to myself."

"You're serious!?"

"As a heart attack," Kristen said.

"Why? You aren't in love with him, are you?"

"No, I'm not in love with him, but I really like him. I hope you're not mad at me."

"I'm not mad at you. You're still my best friend. Are you okay with what happened?"

"Yeah, I guess so. I mean I'm not going to start jumping into bed with every guy I like or anything, and I might not even stay with Ryan, but what's done is done."

Two days later, Kristen called Emmy again. "I broke up with Ryan."

"Why? I thought you really liked him."

"I did, but we had a fight because he wanted to sleep with me again, and I wouldn't. He assumed that because I did it once, I would sleep with him whenever he wanted."

Emmy was quiet for a moment. *I wonder if all guys are like that.* "Are you okay? Are you sad about breaking up with Ryan?"

"I'm fine. I'm not sorry I broke up with him. I'll find another boyfriend sometime, and I don't regret sleeping with him, if that's what you really want to know. I know you feel differently about sex and that's all right. I respect you for sticking to your guns. I hope you don't think I'm a slut."

"Oh, Kristen, I would never think of judging you like that. You're my best friend, and I love you, no matter what." Emmy paused, then asked, "Are you going to..." she paused again.

"What is it, Em?" Kristen asked.

"Will you tell me what the first time is like?"

"Sure, Emmy, what do you want to know?"

"Did it hurt? Was it real messy? Are you still sore? I've

never been close enough to a girlfriend to talk about this before. When Diane told me about her first time, I was fourteen and not real interested in boys yet."

"You can be such a darling goof at times, Emmy. Okay, let me see. I'm supposed to be so sophisticated and all, but it kinda surprised me. It did hurt a little, but kinda like getting your ears pierced. It only hurt for a moment."

"My ears aren't pierced, Krissy. Did it feel good after it stopped hurting?"

"Yeah, but it only lasted about three minutes."

"Is it supposed to take longer?"

"Geez, Emmy. Don't you know anything?"

"Never mind."

"I'm sorry. I think it takes women longer to get... warmed up. I know Ryan has been with other women, but I kinda got the feeling it had been a while."

"Did it make a mess in the bed?" Emmy asked.

"Yeah, there was a little mess. I changed the sheets before I went to bed."

Emmy suddenly remembered. "Please tell me your roommate..."

"No," Kristen said and then chuckled. "Marnie stayed with a friend. Do you really think... never mind. Anyway, I think I surprised Ryan by saying yes."

"Has he wanted to sleep with you before?"

"Duh. He's a guy, Em. All guys want to have sex if they possibly can. After it was over, Ryan cuddled with me for a few minutes, but then got dressed and left."

Emmy asked Kristen a few more questions, and Kristen answered and shared the details about her night with Ryan. After Emmy was satisfied, she asked, "Would you ever live with your boyfriend before you were married?"

"If we were married, he wouldn't be my boyfriend," Kristen teased.

"I'm serious! Would you?"

"I've never given it much thought. Why? Are you planning to move in with Kenny?"

127

"Maybe... I don't know."

"But I always thought you wanted to wait until you're married. Have you changed your mind?"

"Almost everyone I know is living together before they get married. I don't think Diane and Craig ever talk about getting married. Scott Simmons is living with a girl. I don't know what's going on with Barry and Linda anymore."

"Has Kenny ever asked you to move in with him?"

"No, not in so many words." Emmy almost told Kristen about the day Kenny asked her to marry him, but she didn't. "I know his parents would let me live in the carriage house, but I'm not sure I would want to live that close to my parents. My mother would be after me everyday to get married."

"You're too young to get married! I mean you're legally old enough, but..."

"But I'm not mature enough. Is that what you're telling me?"

Kristen tried not to, but she couldn't help but laugh, "Emmy, you still sleep with a light on and you have a teddy bear on top of your dresser."

"I do not have a teddy bear on my dresser. I have a football. I put Teddy in the closet, and Kenny gave that bear to me for my birthday."

"See what I mean? You're still a tomboy."

"What's wrong with liking football? I like to cook and clean the apartment."

"You don't 'like' to clean your apartment. You clean it because you are an obsessive neat freak."

Emmy didn't say anything for several seconds.

"Are you still there, Em"

"I have to go now. I've got to dust the apartment and clean the kitchen and whatever else obsessive neat freaks like me do."

"I'm sorry, Em. I didn't mean anything negative."

"Bye! I'll call you after I stop being a tomboy." Emmy hung up.

"Oh, for crying out loud, Emmy!" Kristen muttered even though she knew Emmy couldn't hear.

128

Chapter Fourteen

"The trees that fell damaged the roof, and the windows in your bedroom and the living room blew in. The rain has ruined the carpets, part of the ceiling and walls need to be replaced... in other words, you can't stay here," Bob Didirosi, the landlord, said as he showed the damaged apartment to Emmy.

"What am I gonna do?" Emmy bit her lip.

On the morning of March seventeenth, Mother Nature pounded the Chicagoland area with a freak winter thunderstorm. Several inches of rain fell in South Hampshire in a five-hour period and winds of fifty miles-per-hour were reported. Emmy worked until noon and came home to a real mess.

"I'm sorry, Emmy. Do you have someone you could stay with? Your folks maybe?" Mr. Didirosi asked as he removed his baseball cap and scratched the top of his bald head. "I've got a company coming to board up the windows as soon as they can get here."

Emmy looked around the apartment. "I'll be okay. I have a place I could stay for a few days. Does the phone still work?" she asked.

"It might. You can try it, but be careful. I don't want you to get hurt."

She picked up the phone and got a dial tone. *Who should I call?* she thought. *Kenny's parents are in Florida, so I don't want to stay in the carriage house apartment. I refuse to go back to my parents' house. None of my other friends can help.* She looked around the room and shook her head. The rain still came through the broken windows. She looked at her TV and piano. *I need to cover them somehow.* Emmy hung up the phone. *I could call Kristen, but she's at school. I might have to stay in the carriage house.* She was near tears until she thought about Tony. Desperation forced her to make an unusual decision. She decided to ask Mama Bertucci if she could stay with them for a couple of days, even though she and Tony had not spoken to each other since the New Year's Eve party. She picked up the phone and dialed the number she knew from memory. Mama answered after two rings.

"Hello."

"Hi, Mama, it's Emmy."

"Emmy, dear, how are you? I miss you! When are you coming to see me?"

"Maybe soon. My apartment suffered some serious damage in the storm today, and I need a place to stay. Would you mind putting up with me for a day?"

"Of course you can stay here, dear," Mama assured Emmy. "You can stay as long as you want or need."

"Thank you so much! I didn't know where I was going to stay tonight. I'll be there in about an hour."

She looked at her TV and piano again. An idea popped into her head. She carefully made her way to the dresser in her bedroom and took out her spare set of sheets. She used them to cover the TV and her Bose music system. She packed a suitcase with enough clothes for a few days, grabbed her music box and left.

When Tony got home from school, he was surprised to see Emmy in the kitchen with Mama. He stood in the doorway and looked at his mother and then back at Emmy. "Hi, Emmy. I didn't know you would be here. How are you doing?"

Emmy stayed close to Mama. "I'm all right, but the storm damaged my apartment today. I needed a place to stay, and Mama told me I could stay here. I know we haven't been talking to each other, and if you want me to leave, I will. I'll find somewhere else to stay."

"No, Emmy, don't leave. You can stay here. I don't mind."

She walked up to him and looked up at his face with such sad eyes. Tony picked her up and hugged her tightly. Emmy had her arms around Tony's neck and her face on his chest as she cried.

"My apartment is ruined. I'm not sure I'll be able to live there anymore."

Tony rubbed her back. "You can stay with us until things are settled."

"Thank you, Tony. I'm so sorry I yelled at you that night. Can you forgive me? I know I said some horrible things to you."

Tony set her down. "You don't have anything to be sorry

130

about. I'm really sorry things didn't work out better for us."

"I'll try not to get in your way, and you won't even know I'm here. How are you and Nikki getting along? She's very pretty. You are so lucky to be going out with her."

Tony was embarrassed that Emmy mentioned Nikki.

"Yeah, Nikki is pretty, and I met her parents, but we aren't engaged or anything."

After dinner Emmy asked Mama, "Would it be all right if I call Kenny to let him know where I am? He'll be worried if he calls, and I don't answer."

"Certainly, dear. Use the phone in the den so you can have some privacy." Mama steered Emmy toward the den.

Emmy called and reached Kenny. "Are you all right, Em? I heard about the storm and tried calling."

"I'm okay, but the apartment is a wreck. I won't be able to stay there until it's fixed. Right now I'm at Tony's house. Mama said I could stay here."

"You know you can stay in the carriage house, Emmy. You have your key, right?"

"I've got the key, but I don't feel right staying there with your parents in Florida."

"It's all right if you do. They won't mind," Kenny said and then asked, "Are you afraid to stay there by yourself?"

"Maybe a little, but I would have gone there if I couldn't stay with Mama Bertucci."

"Is the car all right?"

"Yeah, it wasn't in the street so it's okay."

"You know there are three cars in the carriage house you can use if you ever need to."

"I would if one of them was a Corvette," Emmy said, so Kenny knew she was doing all right. "I'll try to call you if I stay somewhere else so you know where I am."

"I should have bought you a cell phone before I left."

"I'll buy one this weekend..."

"And I will pay for it and don't argue. Did you let your folks know you are okay? Or at least let Diane know."

"I'll call Diane."

131

"She won't call your parents. You should call your mother."

"All right. Mama will make me anyway."

Emmy left the den and walked back into the kitchen. "I talked to Kenny."

Tony and Mama stopped their conversation and turned to look at her.

"Are you sure you don't mind if I stay here? I could go somewhere else," she said.

"Nonsense!" Mama said as she moved closer and opened her arms. "Let me hug you again, dear." Mama squeezed her as Emmy looked up at Tony. "Now you have to let your parents know you are safe. I'm assuming you are unwilling to stay there."

Emmy nodded and called home.

Emmy returned to Mama's house after work the next day. "Something smells delicious." Emmy checked the stove.

"I'm making rigatoni and sausage with homemade sauce," Mama said. "It should be ready soon. This is Thursday, and Tony said you have a class tonight. What time do you need to leave?"

"It starts at six thirty. I need to leave in forty-five minutes."

Emmy and Tony ate with Mama, but she left for Paul Frank after helping clear the table.

Tony was in the kitchen drinking a glass of water later that night when he glanced out the window and saw Emmy pull up to the garage. He opened the back door and waited for her. "How did it go tonight?"

She shrugged. "All right. Nothing too exciting." She scooted past him as he set his glass in the sink. "I'll talk to you tomorrow."

"See ya, Emmy." *I wasn't going to hug you again if that's why you ran out of here so fast.* He walked out of the kitchen and heard her dash up the stairs.

On Friday evening Nikki came over to study with Tony. Emmy had been at the library reading for one of her classes. She walked in the back door and opened the fridge, looking for something to drink.

"Mama, is there more bottled water somewhere? I don't see any in the fridge," Emmy hollered because she thought Mama was in the living room.

"There's some behind the pop on the bottom shelf, Em," Tony answered from the dining room.

"Oh, thanks, Tony. I see it now." Emmy grabbed a bottle of water and walked into the dining room. "What are you doing..." Emmy stopped before finishing her question. "I'm sorry, Tony. I didn't know you had company. I'll go upstairs."

Emmy turned to leave, but Tony reached out his hand and stopped her.

"You don't have to, Emmy. We're just studying. You remember Nikki, right?"

"Hi, Nikki. How's school going?"

"Fine, but I am struggling with this math. Tony is helping me a lot." Nikki remembered that Emmy was in the top twenty of her class and graduated early. "How is college going for you?"

"It's going well. I have straight A's so far."

"Oh, wow, I heard that North Park is tough academically."

Emmy's face turned red as she explained, "I'm taking classes at Paul Frank and working full-time."

"Oh, I thought you were at North Park College with Kristen Keasling."

Emmy didn't want to admit that she couldn't afford to go there.

Tony came to her rescue. "Emmy is paying her own way through college without any financial help from anyone."

Emmy silently thanked Tony. Nikki thought about how she often took her family's money for granted.

"Emmy is staying here while her place is being repaired," Tony said. He then covered the basic details of the storm damage to Emmy's place.

So why is she staying here? Nikki wondered but didn't ask. *I remember now. You guys dated a few times.* Nikki narrowed her eyes and stared at Tony. *Are you dating other girls, Tony Bertucci? I will be upset if I learn that you and Emmy are still going out.*

"I should go upstairs and let you guys finish studying.

133

Good to see you again, Nikki."

"It's good to see you, too, Emmy."

Emmy ran upstairs to Heather's room. She lay on the bed on her back and fought back tears. She heard a soft knock on the door, and then Mama walked in. "Are you all right, honey?"

"I'm okay, Mama. It just surprised me to see Nikki. I'm all right."

Mama walked over and sat on the edge of the bed. Emmy looked up at Mama.

"They are just friends, dear. You still have his heart even if he doesn't realize it right now."

Emmy called her landlord the next day. "Anything new about my apartment?"

"I'm afraid I have some bad news. The apartment won't be ready as soon as I originally thought. I'm having some cosmetic work done since the insurance is covering it."

"How long will it take?"

"It will probably be until the end of next month before you can move back in. I will refund part of the rent you paid this month. I guess I should tell you now that I'm raising the rent by a hundred dollars after your lease is up."

"I don't have a lease, remember?" Emmy reminded him.

"Right." He scratched his head. "We originally planned to do that after the last tenant left, but my wife told your mother we would let you stay here at the cheaper rent for a year. You've been very good about paying your rent on time, but can you afford to pay more?"

"I'm not sure," Emmy answered.

"You could find a cheaper apartment if you get one that's not furnished," he suggested.

"Thanks. Can I at least get in to pick up some more of my clothes?"

"I will let you in, but we will have to be careful. The place is a mess right now."

When Emmy discovered the sad shape of her apartment, she wondered if it wouldn't be even longer before she could move back—especially since no one appeared to be working on it now. At least her TV, DVD player and her Yamaha piano were undamaged and still covered. She decided to start looking for a new apartment because she really didn't want to pay the higher rent. Besides, the landlord's wife always told Emmy's mother when she had company over, and Emmy knew it.

On Tuesday after her night class, Emmy talked to the woman sitting next to her and mentioned her apartment and the storm damage.

"That was a dangerous storm. It knocked down two trees in our backyard."

Emmy nodded. "I need to find a new place because I can't afford the higher rent."

"My son and his wife are moving out of their place at the end of the month." She described the apartment; when she mentioned that the landlords name—the O'Briens—Emmy remembered the place.

"Is it above a garage?" Emmy asked.

"Yes, I should have mentioned that."

"I've been there before! The O'Brien's are really friendly. They are Irish and have three sons."

"If you are interested, I'll have my son tell Mr. O'Brien. Maybe you can check it out sometime. It would be a longer drive to school."

"And to work. But I'm not going back to the apartment I have now."

Later that night after her shower, Emmy met Tony in the hallway outside the bathroom door wearing a towel over her underwear. Tony moved to the side to let her pass. Emmy moved in the same direction. They looked each other in the eyes, and Tony looked down at her towel. She covered her chest with her arms.

"Sorry, this hallway should have been built wider," he said.

"It's all right."

For a second Emmy remembered a time when she would have wanted Tony to take the towel away and carry her off to his bedroom. The same thought crossed Tony's mind. They faced each

135

other for a few seconds without saying a word. Finally Tony moved to the side and let her pass.

Mama sat down in the living room with both of them the next night. "Please let me say my piece without interruption, then I'll get out of your hair. I've been watching you two, and I can't keep my mouth shut any longer. You have feelings for each other, but you are acting like two total strangers. I don't know if it's your pride or what that's keeping you apart. You're polite to each other and make small talk at the dinner table, but I haven't heard you say a word about your relationship and what happened to it. You don't make any effort to discuss anything important. I'm letting you know that if you don't stop treating each other like this, you will lose your friendship and destroy any possible chance for a future together of any sort. I want you two to sit on the couch and talk to each other, and I don't mean about the weather or the last movie you saw. Talk about what you mean to each other. I'm going upstairs to bed, but before I do I am going to say a prayer for both of you. Now good night!"

"Good night, Mama." They looked at each other as they sat on the couch. They each waited for the other to say something.

"Man! How about that wind today, huh?" Tony finally broke the silence.

Emmy grinned. "You know Mama ordered us not to talk about the weather, right?"

"I know. I thought that would break the ice. Did I ever tell you what I want to do after college?"

"What do you want to do? I always thought you wanted to play in the NFL."

"I would like to give that a try, but after that I want to start my own business."

"What kind of business? You could always work for your Dad and your Uncle Daniel's construction company."

"I know, but I want to start one that I can call my own. I'm just not sure what yet."

They spent time together talking but didn't get anything substantial accomplished. Before Emmy headed off to bed, Tony asked her, "How is Kenny doing on his tour? I know you talk to him almost every day."

"He's doing great. They played in Houston last night."

"Do you miss him?"

Emmy looked at Tony and whispered, "Of course I miss him."

"I will miss you when I go to school in the fall, Emmy."

"I will miss you, too. I'm really sorry I screwed everything up. It's like we can't even be friends anymore. I'm sorry for that."

Emmy took Tony and Kristen with her to her old apartment after breakfast Saturday morning. She informed the landlord that she would be moving. She and Kristen packed up her clothes and personal items. They filled a couple of boxes with her kitchen stuff. Tony carried the boxes and her TV and electric piano out to his car. They drove over to the Colwell's house.

"Kenny's parents are still in Florida," Emmy said.

"Will they mind if you leave stuff here?" Tony asked. "How will you get in?"

Emmy showed him her key. "They won't mind. I told Kenny what I planned to do."

"I'm surprised you aren't staying here, Emmy," Kristen said.

"I'll probably stay here if I can't find another apartment real quick," Emmy said as Tony started unloading the car.

"This would be cheaper," Kristen said. *I doubt if Kenny's parents would make you pay rent.*

"I want to leave the big stuff here for now," Emmy said. "I only need to keep some clothes at your house, Tony."

Tony carried everything up to the apartment. "This place is pretty big." Tony checked it out.

"Thanks, Tony. I appreciate it." Emmy stood by the old couch.

"No problem, Em. Do you really know how to play that keyboard?"

"Yeah, I can play a little."

"She can play better than she's letting on. She's good

137

enough to play in Kenny's band," Kristen said.

Emmy shook her head. "Don't believe her. I'm not nearly good enough to do that."

"So what are you gonna do?" Tony asked.

"Your mother told me I could stay at the house, but I feel like I've already imposed on her hospitality for too long."

"No you haven't. Mama doesn't mind having you there," Tony insisted. *And I've kinda gotten used to you being there.*

"I think it upsets her that we don't get along like we used to." Emmy sat on the old couch. "I really need a place of my own."

"Did Kenny ask you to move in here?" Kristen waved her hand around. "You know this would be a perfect place with just a little work."

Emmy recalled her last conversation with Kenny. "He kinda wants me to move in here."

"Really?" Tony raised his eyebrows.

"Not like that!" Emmy frowned. "He doesn't like the idea of me paying rent. I'm not sure if I want to live this close to my mother."

"Are you afraid she would make your life miserable again?" Kristen asked.

"Yeah, but I am thinking about it."

Chapter Fifteen

Before Emmy had left work on Friday, she talked to two of her coworkers, Lynn Aylesbury and Eva Hill. "I know you guys have been looking for an apartment. I'm looking, too."

"We're going out tomorrow afternoon to do some apartment hunting. We've been living in studio apartments, but thought we might try to find a two-bedroom to share. It would be cheaper. Wanna come with us?" Eva asked.

"Would you mind? I know about this apartment in Crest Ridge that I want to check out."

"That's rather far from work. We were thinking about the Raynor Park area." Lynn glanced at Eva to gauge her reaction.

I don't want to move back to my parents' neighborhood unless it's into the carriage house. Emmy thought and then said, "The apartment in Crest Ridge is supposed to be pretty big and the rent would be reasonable if we split it."

"I suppose we could see it at least," Eva offered.

They made plans to meet the next afternoon.

The last Saturday in March was sunny with temperatures in the sixties. Emmy met Lynn and Eva at the McDonald's in Crest Ridge for lunch; afterward they followed Emmy to the O'Brien's.

Mrs. O'Brien opened up the apartment and informed her, "You can take all the time you need to look around, Emmy."

"Thank you, Mrs. O'Brien. I appreciate it. I can't wait to see the apartment."

"It's good to see you again, dear." Mrs. O'Brien headed back inside the house.

"Hey, you guys! Check this out. There's ivy on the front." Emmy pointed at the front of the garage.

"Yeah, but it covers part of the windows. That's not good," Lynn mentioned.

"The entrance is on the side. Look. There's a porch with windows and those stairs go into the apartment." Emmy pointed them out to her coworkers.

"Girl, you know this is farther from work and school,

139

right?" Eva put her hands on her wide hips.

"Yeah, I know, but it's got to be bigger than where I was living. Come on, let's at least check it out!" Emmy tried to be positive, but the other women expressed a lot of negativity about the apartment even before they got inside. Emmy originally hoped one of them would share the apartment with her because there were two bedrooms. Already doubts of that happening crept into her mind. They spent a few minutes walking around the apartment.

"The living room is pretty big and so is this bedroom!" Emmy liked the apartment more and more, but Lynn and Eva were still not convinced.

"Emmy, I don't know if I could live here. This bathroom is way too small. I'm skinny, but I don't think both of us can even fit in here at the same time, and you know that would happen every morning when we have to get ready for work," Lynn said.

Eva complained, "The whole place needs to be painted and what is that smell? The place smells like cats peed everywhere. Can't you smell that, Emmy?"

"You know we could clean the place up and paint the walls. I bet the O'Briens might replace the carpet and even offer to paint the place. I've met them before and they are really nice. They would make better landlords than the couple where I was living."

"I don't know, Emmy. We are going to keep looking. I really don't want to live in Crest Ridge. I know it's just on the edge of SoHam, but it's too far away from work and our old neighborhood." Lynn looked at Eva for confirmation.

"Yeah, I don't think I want to go in on this place with you. I'm sorry." Eva couldn't wait to get out of the apartment.

"It's okay. I thought it would be better than where I'm at."

Emmy liked the apartment because of the larger size and the fact that the O'Briens would be her landlords, but she didn't know if she could afford the rent without a roommate. She would have to pay her own utilities, also.

"We're gonna take off, Emmy. We know of a two-bedroom place in Raynor Park that's a lot closer to work."

Emmy's shoulders sagged. "I grew up in Raynor Park. My parents still live there."

"We saw an ad for a place on Sixth Street and we want to check it out."

I definitely don't want to live on Sixth Street. That's just a block over from my parents' house. Emmy's face displayed her obvious disappointment. "Thanks for at least looking at this place. I'm sorry you had to waste your time. I'm gonna stay here and talk to Mrs. O'Brien some more." She now believed the carriage house might be her only option.

"We'll see you on Monday, Emmy."

Lynn and Eva left, and Emmy spent a few minutes talking to Mrs. O'Brien about the utilities and the monthly rent.

"Did your friends leave, Emmy? What did they think about the apartment?"

"They thought it... was too far from work." Emmy didn't want to mention what they really said.

"You think about it and let us know. We won't rent it out until we hear from you."

"Thank you, Mrs. O'Brien. That's very kind."

Scott Simmons came over to see two of the O'Brien boys, Ronan and Patrick, who were on spring break from Illinois State University. They were about the same age as Scott and had been friends for a long time. Emmy finished talking to Mrs. O'Brien and ended up playing basketball with the guys.

"None of you guys can shoot worth a darn," Emmy said.

"We're not pros, Emmy, but I blocked two of your shots," Ronan said.

"Only because you're half a foot taller than me, and you fouled me all the time." *You're such a klutz. You remind me of Barry Newton with those weird glasses.*

Scott laughed. "I didn't try to block your shots even though I easily could have."

"If you were playing against Tony, he would cream you guys."

None of them bothered to ask about Tony.

When Ronan and Scott went into the house to find something to drink, Patrick asked, "Emmy, are you still going out with Scott and is that why he's here?"

141

The question surprised her. "No, Patrick, we're not going out—we went on a couple dates a few months ago, but that's all. I'm not sure if we are even friends at this point. I'm not sure I even want to be his friend, to tell you the truth. I know he's living with his girlfriend, and I don't think that's right."

"I didn't know that." Patrick ran a hand through his sweaty, short-cropped reddish hair. "I'm surprised that he would do that. He certainly knows better and his parents probably aren't happy about it if they even know."

"Do you know his parents? He never talks about them."

"His parents are missionaries in Africa. They are supported by our church. You've been there before."

"Do you mean the church on Canton Lane?" Emmy asked as she dribbled the basketball between her legs.

"Yeah, Scott hasn't been coming to church for a while. I guess he must feel guilty about the way he is behaving."

Scott and Ronan came back outside and shot hoops again.

Later, Mrs. O'Brien hollered out the back door, "Ronan, will you run to the store for me? I need some groceries, and I'm in the middle of making a pie. Be a dear and help me out, love."

"Sure, Mom."

Ronan took Scott with him, but Patrick stayed home. Patrick and Emmy kept shooting baskets in the driveway while they waited for the guys to get back from the store. Patrick opened the side service door to the garage and turned on the lights.

"I know you were checking out the apartment, so I thought I would show you the garage. The tenant gets that parking space and this is the furnace and water heater over here. Any questions?"

Emmy giggled then said, "No, I don't think so. Thanks for showing me around, Patrick."

"Sure, Emmy, no problem, anytime."

She heard a car pull into the driveway, and one of the overhead garage doors creaked and groaned as it opened. The guys had returned from the store.

After the guys carried the groceries inside, they played ball again. Sean, the youngest O'Brien brother, had arrived home from work, so he joined them. Emmy stood next to the garage and

142

watched the guys. *I can tell Ronan and Patrick are brothers. They both have reddish hair, but Sean is kinda blonde and taller. Ronan looks like a bear with that beard.*

Patrick took a shot and the ball landed at her feet. She bent over to pick it up. When she straightened up, Scott stood in front of her with a stupid smile on his face.

"Thanks, Emmy."

She handed him the basketball, but didn't say anything.

"Do you wanna get something to eat after we finish?"

"No, thanks. I'm not interested," she answered coldly.

"Suit yourself," Scott replied.

She watched the guys for a few more minutes. "I'll see you guys later. I need to get back."

"See ya, Emmy," Sean hollered. His attraction to her appeared obvious to the other guys.

"Hey, little brother, are you hoping she moves in?" Ronan teased.

"Yeah, maybe. Why not? She's pretty and close to my age. When are you gonna stop calling me little brother? I'm only fifteen months younger than Patrick and three years younger than you."

"Like I said, little brother." Ronan and Patrick laughed.

Sean grabbed the basketball, threw it at Ronan and nailed him in the back.

When Emmy talked to Kenny later that day, she mentioned the apartment and her concern about the rent and utilities.

"I'm using Mama's phone, so I can't talk too long." Emmy sat in Mama's chair in the sewing room.

"I know we've talked about this before, and you always say no, but what about the carriage house? It would be closer to work, and you know my parents wouldn't charge you any rent."

"And what would we do when you're home? You know we can't share the apartment."

"I do have a room in the house."

"But you wouldn't stay in the house."

"Okay, you're probably right about that," Kenny admitted.

"I really appreciate the offer, and I would love living there with you," Emmy said. "Wait! That didn't sound right. I didn't

143

mean living together with you."

"I know what you meant, Em."

"Your parents have always been so good to me..."

"You're worried that your mother will bother you since you would be so close."

"Yeah. I'm sure she would be coming over every day to make sure you weren't staying with me."

"Unfortunately, I think you're right. What about this new place? Can you afford the rent by yourself?"

"I talked to Mrs. O'Brien, and she told me what the previous tenants were paying. It would be tight, but I could probably manage... and don't even say what I know you're going to. I won't take your money. It's bad enough you gave me a car."

Kenny shook his head and muttered, "So stubborn. Are you using the new car once in a while to make sure it starts?"

"Yes, I have been using it on the weekends to make sure your 'baby' is okay."

"Please think about the carriage house before you make up your mind. Maybe you could talk to your parents and come to some kind of arrangement so your mother won't be bothering you."

"I still have the same mother that you've known for all these years. She hasn't changed, and she never will."

"I suppose you're right, and I doubt she would ever believe we weren't living together in the carriage house."

"She wouldn't believe it because it wouldn't be true. You know if I stay there, we will be living together. How would your parents and your church feel about that?" Emmy raised her voice.

"Okay, I understand your point."

"The girls from work didn't like the apartment at all. They complained about everything. They are the same way at work. In a way, I'm glad they didn't like it. I can't see myself sharing a place with either of them. They would drive me up the wall."

Emmy decided to take a couple of days to make a decision about her options—she could live in the O'Brien's apartment or the Colwell's carriage house. She did look at three other places on Sunday but did not care for any of them.

She decided to talk to her mother about the carriage house. She drove over and they sat at the kitchen table to talk later Sunday evening.

"Where's Daddy?"

"Where do you think?" Mom said. "Would you like some coffee, Emmy?"

"No, I'm good. You know about what happened to my apartment, right?" Emmy asked.

Mom smirked. "Yes, dear. I know about everything that went on in that apartment."

Emmy let that slide. "Mr. Didirosi is raising the rent, so I told him I'm leaving. I've got two options. One is an apartment in Crest Ridge, and the other is Kenny's carriage house apartment."

"I didn't know there was a real apartment up there." Mom didn't mention an obvious third option. Emmy could move back home.

"Kenny and his dad are gonna make some improvements. I can stay in the main house until it's ready."

"So you're planning to move in with him, huh?"

"Mom! It's not like that."

"You can't fool me." Mom banged her hand on the table. "I know how things are in the real world, little Missy. I guess both of my daughters are gonna be living with their boyfriends." She didn't think about how hypocritical she was being. "You can go ahead and move in with him, but your father will be so disappointed. He still thinks you are his innocent little girl. Ha! What a laugh! I won't spoil that for him, but I will keep a close eye on you. You can count on that!" Mom pointed her finger at Emmy.

"Oh, believe me, I know. You've been in my business ever since I moved out," Emmy shouted.

"If you think I was interfering in your life before, just try living with your boyfriend." Mom spat out the words as she banged on the table again. "I will make your life miserable. I thought you might be different from your sister, but you're not. You're just like her—a real slut!"

Emmy wanted to slap her mother, but she couldn't move her arm. She sat still. She didn't cry. She didn't breath. She didn't

145

blink an eye.

Mom closed her eyes. "I'm sorry. I didn't mean that."

Emmy regained her composure. "Fine. If that's what you think, so be it. Goodbye, Mother. Say goodbye to Daddy for me."

"I'm sorry, Emmy. I don't think you're like that," Mom said.

Emmy got up and walked out the back door. *I'm never coming here again. Now I totally understand why Diane doesn't talk to her.*

Emmy returned to Mama's house, called Kenny and informed him of her decision, "I'm going to move into the O'Brien's apartment. They will let me have a six-month lease to make sure I can handle the rent."

"If that's your decision, I will go along with it, but you know I wish you would choose the carriage house."

Emmy didn't tell Kenny about the threat her mother made. "I understand. If things don't work out, I will move into your place."

"I like that idea."

Emmy bit her lip. "If I move into the carriage house, will you make a real bedroom?"

"Yes, Dad and I have already talked about doing some more remodeling."

"You mentioned that before."

"We will remodel the place so there will be an actual bedroom for us."

"I would like that better than sleeping on the futon."

"Yeah, the futon isn't like a real bed. It won't take too long to get the carriage house in move-in condition. I'll talk to you later, Em."

She hung up and thought about what he said. *You said us. I like the fact that you think of us as a couple. Maybe I should move into the carriage house. Mom is going to believe what she wants no matter what I do. But I can't take the chance that she will cause trouble for your parents. That settles it. I'll try the O'Brien's apartment for now.*

Chapter Sixteen

On Easter Sunday Emmy began the move into the O'Brien's apartment. The O'Briens had replaced the carpet and even had the place painted after Mrs. O'Brien kindly informed her husband that he needed to do that. After he hesitated, she ordered him to do it like a general would issue an order to a private.

Emmy's parents agreed to let her take the bedroom set from her room, since her mother planned to turn the now empty space into a sewing room even though she didn't own a sewing machine. Emmy asked Tony to help retrieve the bedroom set. He talked his friend Terry into helping and using his truck. Emmy didn't speak to her mother, who sat in the living room and didn't acknowledge Emmy's presence.

"Oh, Mrs. O'Brien, I'm so thrilled to have a bigger place." Emmy gushed as she and Mrs. O'Brien stood in the wide concrete driveway and watched Tony and Terry carry the bedroom set into the apartment.

Mrs. O'Brien hugged her. "We're pleased you have chosen to be our tenant."

"I'm going to need to find some used furniture. My other apartment was furnished."

"You know, we could help you out." Mrs. O'Brien turned and pointed to the top of the stone house. The roof angled steeply toward the sky. "There is a huge attic under the roof. I know we have a kitchen table and chairs and even a couch up there. You could take a look at them and see if they are okay."

"That would be too kind of you. I couldn't bother..."

"Nonsense, love! The stuff is being wasted." Mrs. O'Brien waved at her son. "Sean, would you take Emmy up to the attic and move whatever she might need?"

"Sure, Ma."

Emmy gratefully used the furniture from the O'Briens' attic. Sean, Tony and Terry helped her move everything into the apartment. Kristen helped organize the kitchen. After everything had been moved into her apartment, Emmy and Kristen drove back to the Bertucci home for Easter dinner.

"We're back, Mama. Everything smells so delicious." Emmy walked around the kitchen checking out the food.

"Did you get everything unpacked?" Mama asked as she walked into the kitchen.

"Most of it. Kristen helped with my clothes and the kitchen, and the guys moved all the big stuff. I still need to find a few things. How soon is dinner going to be ready?"

"Probably ten minutes or so. Will you and Kristen make sure the dining room table is set?"

"How many people are going to be here?"

"Six, unless Terry is staying for dinner."

Tony entered through the back door. "He already went home, so I guess it will just be six."

After dinner, Emmy and Kristen helped Mama clean up the dining room and kitchen.

"Thank you for all your help. You can go bug Tony now if you want. I think he went downstairs."

Kristen ran out of the kitchen and headed downstairs while Emmy remained behind.

"Mama..." Emmy started to say something but then paused as her lip quivered and one tear escaped down her cheek.

"What is it, dear?" Mama took her in her arms and hugged her.

"I want to thank you for everything you've done for me. You have always treated me like part of the family, and I appreciate it so much."

"You are a part of the family as far as I'm concerned. Now run along and let me talk to Karla and Daniel."

Emmy headed to the basement where Tony and Kristen were watching a movie. The movie ended and Tony teased Emmy.

"Since you have a bigger apartment now, and you're farther away from your parents, are you gonna have parties all the time? Will you let your boyfriends spend the night?" *I know Kenny has spent the night. Kristen told me.*

"Oh, sure all the time," Emmy answered. "I'm going to have wild parties and invite lots of guys over."

"Why did you say that, Tony?" Kristen asked. "That wasn't

very appropriate." *I should have never told you that Kenny spent the night.*

"Because she got mad at me for not treating her more like a girlfriend and not trying to sleep with her." *Just bad timing, I guess.*

"That's not the only reason I got mad at you. You make it sound like I was going to let you do whatever you wanted... whenever you wanted." Emmy raised her voice as she got excited.

"Isn't that the way it was?" Tony raised his voice in return. "You made it rather obvious that you wanted to have sex."

"No! I wanted you to treat me more romantically. That didn't mean you could have sex with me every time you saw me."

"Are you going to sleep with Kenny whenever he's home?" Tony put his arms across his chest. "He probably has lots of women on the road."

"Hey, you guys, knock it off." Kristen tried to intervene. *What is going on?*

"If I do, it's none of your business!" Emmy yelled as she stood up in front of Tony and poked him in the chest.

Tony snorted, "You're gonna end up like your sister."

"You can go to hell, Tony Bertucci! I never want to see you again!" Emmy's heart pounded.

"Fine! The feeling is mutual!"

Emmy left the house in tears because she was so mad at him. Kristen ran outside with Emmy to try to talk with her, but Emmy left without a word. Kristen headed back downstairs.

"You are a complete idiot! How can we even be related? Why on earth did you say that to her? Were you intentionally trying to start a fight, or are you just a complete moron?" Kristen pushed him onto the couch.

"No..."

"Well, you certainly made a mess of things." Kristen smacked his arm. "God, why can't the two of you get along anymore?"

"Because I'm an idiot at times." Tony smacked the couch with his fist.

149

Tony vented his frustrations and released his emotions in the weight room at school. He worked out harder than ever and pushed himself to get in the best possible shape.

"Hey, big guy, what's with you? You're attacking those weights like you want to hurt them." Terry wiped his arms with a towel. "How are things going with Nikki?"

"We're getting along all right." Tony dropped the barbell on the floor. "Have you heard something?"

"She told Natalie what you guys did last week. Way to go!" Terry high-fived Tony.

"Keep your mouth shut. We didn't do all that much."

"I guess you've finally gotten over Colasanti," Terry said as he grinned. "I heard that she's shacking up with her rock star boyfriend. Don't know what he sees in her."

"Don't talk about her like that," Tony warned. "She's a sweet kid."

Tony found that he missed having Emmy staying in the house. He regretted the fight and couldn't believe he said what he did.

After work the next day, Emmy talked to Kenny and described the new apartment to him. "It's above a four-car garage. Not as large as the carriage house, but it's bigger than my old apartment. There is ivy on the front windows, and the entrance is on the side. You go into a porch and then up some stairs," Emmy said.

"What's the outside made from?" he asked.

"Oh, it's all brick. Kinda like the carriage house but not the same. There's another door at the top of the stairs. There are three doors to unlock before I get inside."

"Sounds pretty secure," Kenny said and then chuckled.

"I'll probably leave the top one unlocked. Anyway, once you get inside there's a small area kinda like the landing at my other place. From that area you can go into either the kitchen, bathroom or the living room. The living room is huge, and the main bedroom is almost as big."

"How will you fill up the space, Em?"

150

She explained about the furniture she moved into the apartment.

"That sounds like a start, Em," Kenny said.

"The second bedroom is really small. It's maybe ten by eight. The bathroom is kinda small, but it does have a shower in the tub. That's a big plus."

"I thought you liked taking baths better."

"I like to take bubble baths, but showers are quicker for getting ready for work."

"What about the kitchen?"

"The kitchen is bigger than the old place, but it's not real big. The table in there is bigger and the fridge and stove are full-size and the freezer doesn't freeze the ice cream so hard that it takes twenty minutes to be able to spoon it out. I hated the fridge at the other apartment. Oh, I gotta tell ya. Kristen and I were shopping at a used furniture place, and I bought a nightstand for the bedroom, a cabinet for the Bose and a recliner and guess what? I only paid $212 for everything."

"I can't wait to see it, Em. We're in Florida now. We have dates in Miami, Tampa, Jacksonville and Tallahassee. Then we head up the coast. I can't remember all the places we're going to play, but I do know I'll be home for a week in May."

"It will so exciting to see you again. It's one thing to be able to talk on the phone, but I miss holding you in my arms."

"I miss you, too. I gotta run. I'll call you tomorrow."

"Okay, I'm going to go for a run around the neighborhood. The streets in this neighborhood aren't as busy, so I'll feel safer."

Mrs. O'Brien saw Emmy outside just as Emmy returned from her run. "It's a beautiful evening. Did you go far?"

"Yes, just perfect for a run." Emmy stretched her legs. "Just over a mile."

"You are welcome to come to church with us, Emmy. There is still a large group of kids your age. You might remember some of them."

"Thanks, Mrs. O'Brien. I'll let you know." *I probably should go back.*

Scott Simmons broke up with his girlfriend, Erica, moved out of her apartment and moved in with the O'Briens temporarily. He saw Emmy one day as she arrived home from work.

"Hi, Emmy. How was work?"

"Okay. How have you been, Scott?" *I know your girlfriend kicked you out. Sean told me.*

"All right. I'm looking for a new place to stay. Can I come up and talk to you?"

"I don't know, Scott."

"Emmy, I just want to be friends, promise." He used his charming smile to set her mind at ease.

"Okay, Scott, you can come up, but you better behave." She recalled the day they met and how she thought he reminded her of a taller version of Tommy Cruz.

"If I must," he laughed.

"You must," she said sternly.

"Do you like this place better than your other apartment?" He followed her up the stairs and into the kitchen. "It's bigger than I thought."

"Would you like something to drink?" She opened the fridge. "I've got Coke."

"Sounds good."

She opened two cans of pop, handed one to him and he followed her into the living room. She closed the door to her bedroom. "It's bigger than my last one." *I'm not even going to let you see it. I remember what happened before.*

"I'll take your word for it, Emmy."

They sat on the couch and talked.

"I want to get married someday, Emmy. I am ready to settle down and find the right girl and have a family. Maybe you are the right girl for me. We'll never know if we don't give it a chance."

She let the bubbles go up her nose and coughed. "I can tell you right now that I'm not the right girl for you."

"Come on, Emmy, how will we know if we are right for each other if we don't try?" He quickly finished his Coke. "I want to kiss you, and we can see where it leads."

"Scott, I'm not stupid. I know where you want it to lead and that's not gonna happen." *Geez! You just can't stand to be on your own, huh? Are you afraid you might not have sex for a few days?*

"It's not that big a deal. People do it all the time." He moved a bit closer and touched her thigh.

"I don't!" She stood up and put her hands on her hips. "Why are you treating me like this, Scott? Patrick told me that you were raised to know better. Why don't you go to church anymore?"

"I don't feel like it right now, okay."

"You need to leave." She pointed to the door.

"Fine! Be like that." *You need to grow up.* Scott grew disgruntled with her and left.

He returned the next night with a dozen red roses in his hand. This time Emmy didn't let him upstairs.

"I'm sorry about last night, Emmy. I got upset, and I shouldn't have. Will you forgive me?"

Emmy held the roses up to her nose. "Thanks for the roses, Scott, and I will forgive you, but I'm still not giving in to you. It would probably be best if you didn't call me or come over here anymore."

"But I'm staying with the O'Briens. I'll see you around."

Not if I can help it! She turned on her heels and went back inside.

One Sunday morning Emmy went to church with the O'Briens. She met Senior Pastor Ausland and looked for Lynette Rosas, the young woman who first took her to the church, but didn't see her anywhere. She did see some kids that looked familiar but couldn't remember their names. They talked to her and invited her to come back again. She agreed to try.

Later that afternoon Emmy drove over to see Mama. She knocked on the front door and waited for Mama to open it.

"Emmy, come in. You know you can come right in don't you, honey? You don't have to knock."

"Thanks, Mama, but I would feel funny just walking in. Especially since Tony and I aren't on the best of terms right now."

"Well, maybe we can work on that."

153

Before Emmy could object Mama called upstairs, "Tony, can you come down here please? There is someone here to see you."

Mama smiled at Emmy, "I'll be in the kitchen if you need anything."

Emmy walked into the living room. *Shoot! I shouldn't have come over here. We'll probably just fight again.*

Tony came downstairs and saw Emmy. He walked over to where she stood looking out the window. "Hi, Emmy. I didn't know you were coming over."

"I'm sorry I dropped in without calling first. If you're busy, I'll go home."

"No, please don't go. I wasn't doing anything too important."

Emmy looked up at Tony. *Don't you dare try to hug or kiss me. I'm still kinda mad at you.*

He didn't try to do either. He shifted his weight back and forth as he looked around the room.

Emmy stared at the family photos on the fireplace mantel. She finally looked at him. "I still like you and don't want to fight with you anymore. I want us to be friends and get along and not argue, okay? I'm tired of fighting."

"Okay, Emmy, I'll be your friend. Maybe that way we won't argue so much. I'm really sorry about what I said. I'm an idiot. Kristen really let me have after you left and she was right. It was totally my fault we got into a fight. I think I was feeling a little jealous of Kenny and finally let it erupt.

They talked and Mama insisted that Emmy stay for dinner. After eating, Tony and Emmy sat on the couch in the living room and watched TV. They were laughing and teasing each other.

Mama watched. *You're acting more like brother and sister than two kids who, not all that long ago, loved each other.* "I'm going to go read," Mama said as she left the room.

Emmy looked at Tony and asked, "Are you still seeing Nikki Foster?"

"I see her at school everyday."

"That's not what I mean, and you know it."

154

Tony grinned at her and didn't answer.

She poked his arm. "Well, are you?"

"We still study together, but we aren't romantically involved."

"That's a bunch of bull." She laughed. "Have you kissed her much lately? I know you kissed her at Kristen's party." *How many other times have you kissed her?*

"Maybe. Why do you care?" *I'm not telling you about our relationship.*

"I don't. I was just wondering. Is she a good kisser? I know her body is better than mine."

Tony grinned. "Really? I never pay much attention to her body."

"You are such a liar, Anthony Bertucci." Emmy pretended to be upset with him. "How can you not notice her body. Are you blind? She is so much better built than me. You should go after her."

"How can you say that, Em? You have a nice body... for your size!"

Emmy smacked his arm again. "Ow!" she cried. "That hurt me and you didn't even feel it."

"Serves you right for hitting me," Tony said.

Emmy stared at him.

"What?"

"Well, have you kissed her or not?" *Why am I even asking? I don't want to know it if they've made out or something.*

"Okay, maybe I kissed her once or twice but only because she made me."

"She made you kiss her. That's rich. Did she threaten you or something?"

"Emmy, it's not like we were making out or anything. We just kissed." He blushed. "We haven't done as much as you and Kenny."

Don't go there! She frowned, but kept quiet.

Shoot! I need to keep my big mouth shut and not say anything about Kenny. Tony grabbed her ankles, stood up and was about to hang Emmy from the ceiling when Mama walked back

155

into the room. Emmy squirmed, trying to get away and hollered at Tony, "Put me down, you big ape!"

Mama shook her head. "Are you kids fighting again? Tony, you better be nice to Emmy."

Tony put her down on the couch, and she punched his arm again.

"We aren't fighting, Mama. I was teasing Tony about Nikki. That's all."

"I was just going to see if I could still lift her."

"Why? Do you think I've gained fifty pounds? Have you gotten weaker?" Emmy teased.

"I think I can still hang you from the ceiling." Tony grabbed her ankles again.

"Stop it, you goof." Emmy laughed. "I know you are strong enough to lift me over you head, but if you want to hang anyone from the ceiling, it should be Nikki! She's your girlfriend—not me."

"I would never think of doing that with her. You know I would never drop you, right?"

"I know, but maybe we're too grown up to do it anymore."

"I'm more mature now, but I don't know about you," he said.

She proved his point by sticking out her tongue and making a face at him.

Chapter Seventeen

Emmy pulled into the driveway and saw Sean O'Brien shooting baskets. She had become friends with Sean since she had been living in the O'Brien apartment. She parked the car and watched him take a few shots.

"Hey, Emmy, how are you? You're home early." He walked toward her. "Is everything all right?"

"Yeah, I got out of there two hours early today. Why?"

"No reason. Just thought you usually got home later. Wanna shoot some hoops?"

Sean passed the ball to Emmy, and she took a shot. It clanged off the front of the rim. She and Sean talked as they took turns shooting the ball.

A few minutes later, she caught him staring at her legs. "I need to go upstairs and change." She tossed the ball back to him.

"Can I come up? I would like to see what you've done with the place if you don't mind."

If you think you can try anything like Scott did, you've got it all wrong. She was leery but decided to trust him. "Okay. Would you like some Dr Pepper?"

"Sure," Sean answered.

Emmy led him up the stairs and into the apartment. *I hope I didn't leave a mess in the bathroom.*

"Come on in." She closed the bathroom door before he could peek inside. She showed Sean around the apartment.

"It looks nice. You must really like Fridays At Five."

"Thanks, Sean. Did your father ask you to check to see if I had a pet like the last tenants?"

Sean grinned sheepishly. "Yeah, he expressed some concern about that. He doesn't want to have to replace the carpet every time someone moves out."

"Well, I don't have any pets, and I don't anticipate getting one."

She fixed two glasses of Dr Pepper. They sat on the couch and drank the pop.

"I want to ask you something, Emmy, but I don't want you

157

to get mad at me, okay?"

"Okay, I won't get mad. What is it?" Emmy answered wondering what Sean was thinking. *I hope you aren't going to ask me out for a date. I don't want to hurt your feelings.*

"Have you really been with Scott as many times as he claims?"

Emmy blushed at his frank question. "What?"

He repeated the question.

She jumped to her feet and angrily informed him, "I don't know what Scott has been telling you, but I can assure you that I have never been with Scott, not even once! And that is a rather personal question to be asking me, Sean O'Brien." *I can't believe it. You're asking about my sex life. I let Barry Newton get away with that, but I've known him almost as long as I've known Kenny.*

"I'm surprised because Scott talked about being in the apartment with you and how good a kisser you are." *I guess maybe I assumed he did more than kiss you, but he sure made it seem like that.*

"That really bugs me that he would lie to you. I need to use the phone for a minute. I'll be right back. Stay right here, Sean. I need to talk to you some more."

She stomped into her bedroom and called Scott's cell phone. He didn't answer, so Emmy left him a "message." She blasted him with some coarse, strong language about lying to Sean. Sean could hear her and was surprised by her language. He laughed as Emmy used some words that good girls don't normally use. Emmy changed clothes and came back out in shorts and a sleeveless sweatshirt.

"I would appreciate it if, when you see him again, you tell him I don't ever want to see him or talk to him or anything because he is such an ass and a liar. Oh, I'm so freakin' mad at him!" She stood in front of the couch and pointed a finger at Sean. "I don't know what it is with you O'Brien boys, but it is very impolite to ask a girl the question you did. Way too personal. I know we are friends, but please try to think of my feelings before you ask me stuff like that."

"I'm really sorry, Emmy." Sean stood up and grabbed her

hand. "I wasn't thinking straight and opened my big mouth too soon. I was surprised when Scott told me that, and I guess I didn't want to believe him, so I wanted to hear it from you."

She pulled her hand away. *If you try to kiss me, I swear I will punch you so hard. I'll move out and live with Kenny if you or any of your brothers tries anything.*

"I won't do it again." Sean lifted his hands in surrender. "And I'll give Scott your message and one of my own if I see him. He moved out, and I'm not sure where he's staying."

"You better not." Emmy turned her back to Sean and headed for the door. "Come on. Let's go back outside."

Sean followed as they headed back out to the driveway and shot baskets.

"Nice shot, Emmy. You know you're pretty good for a girl."

"Thanks, Sean. You're pretty bad for a boy."

"Thanks a lot. So, Emmy, do you think you'll shoot Scott when you see him?"

"I'll think of something to do. Since you were asking me about my love life, do you have a girlfriend?"

"Not right now. The last girl I dated broke up with me last week." He grinned at her. "Are you applying for the position?"

"No, but thanks for asking, and quit looking at my legs."

"I wasn't looking at your legs. I was checking out your shoes."

"Oh, yeah, right. These ratty old tennis shoes are so interesting. I know you were looking and probably thinking about something other than basketball," Emmy said. *You're never coming back up to the apartment, Sean O'Brien.*

"Maybe I wouldn't be looking at your legs if you weren't wearing shorts that showed so much of them. Boys do like to look at pretty girls, you know. Especially when they're wearing shorts and getting beat at one-on-one." Sean made a layup. "I win."

"No fair. I thought you were taking a time out, so I stopped guarding you."

Mrs. O'Brien opened the back door. "Sean, dinner's ready! Emmy, come in and have dinner with us. I made enough potatoes for an army."

159

"Be right there, Mom. Come and eat with us, Emmy." Sean flipped the basketball over his shoulder at the basket.

Emmy watched as the ball landed five feet short of the hoop. "Nice try." She shook her head.

Emmy knew that Mrs. O'Brien wouldn't take no for an answer, so she went in to eat. She sat across the dining room table from Sean. His parents sat at opposite ends.

"Sean, would you pass the salt, and why do you have such a silly grin on your face?" Mrs. O'Brien asked.

"I was thinking about something I heard."

"Do you want to share it with us?" Mr. O'Brien set down his fork.

"No biggie. Just heard a rumor about a girl I know."

Emmy gave him a dirty look and tried to kick him under the table, but she missed. She stuck her tongue out at him.

After finishing dinner Emmy thanked Mrs. O'Brien, and then she and Sean rushed out the door. They sat on a bench by the side of the house.

"You are a creep, and don't you ever do that to me again. I'm not that kind of girl, and I never slept with Scott."

"I didn't think good girls used the language you did when you were leaving Scott that message."

"You weren't supposed to be listening."

"I couldn't help but hear. You were yelling pretty loud."

"I don't usually swear like that, but I was really mad."

Sean smiled as she pretended to be mad at him. With her hair in braids and her baby-faced smile, she looked like an innocent young schoolgirl, despite the language she had used. They sat on the bench talking and laughing for a while. She tucked her legs underneath her and sat facing him. Sean kept looking at her legs.

"Stop it, Sean. You're still looking at my legs." She tugged her shorts down to cover her legs a bit more.

"I'm looking at your shoes again, Emmy."

"Liar! My shoes are under me. You can't even see them."

She kept her eyes on his face and eyes. At that moment she thought about Tony. *I kinda miss the way Tony used to tease me.*

160

Sean teases me, but it's different.

Sean's mom opened the back door and called to them. "Sean! Sean! Where did you guys go?"

"We're over here, Mom. What's up? Kinda busy right now."

Mrs. O'Brien leaned over the iron railing but couldn't see Sean and Emmy. "You've got a call. They say it's important."

"Be right there, Mom." He placed his hands just above Emmy's knees. "I'll be back in a minute. Don't leave, okay?"

"Where would I go? I live here, remember?" she said.

He took the call and came back outside. "I've got to go talk to someone. It's important, and I need to run. See ya, Emmy."

"See you later. I want a rematch," Emmy shouted as Sean ran to his car parked on the street and squealed the tires as he drove away. *What was that all about?* She sat on the bench, looked up at her apartment and let her mind roam. *I like how Sean is playful like Tony, but I don't have the same feelings for Sean that I once did for Tony. Sean is a friend and kinda like a brother. No, I take that back. The way he was looking at my legs was definitely not like a brother. It was kinda creepy.* She shuddered but then smiled. *I could never think of Kenny as a brother.* Her smile faded as her thoughts focused on Tony. *I'm not sure how I feel about Tony. It changes every time I see him. Sometimes I just want to be his friend, but then I think about how sweet and charming he treated me on our dates. I wish I could make up my mind. I wouldn't have to even think about this if I was on tour with Kenny. Maybe I should have moved into the carriage house.* She sighed and then headed back to her apartment. She slapped the ivy covered bricks as she walked past.

The next evening Emmy saw Sean waiting outside as she got home from work. *Are you going to explain why you ran off so fast last night? Did you find another girlfriend? Not that I care if you did.*

"Emmy, can I talk to you for a minute?" Sean asked as he walked toward her.

"Sure. What's up?"

"Well... uh... I'm leaving for the Army in a couple of days, and I would like to see you again before I leave, if you have time."

"What? The Army?" She dropped her keys and purse. "Sean, when did you decide to do this? You never mentioned a word about it to me before. How long have you known you were going away?"

He bent over and picked up her purse and keys. "I've known for several weeks, but I just found out last night when I have to report. Can I talk to you later?"

"Sure, we can talk." She emphasized the word talk. *Please don't ruin our friendship by trying something.*

"Mom's making pot roast. Wanna come over for dinner?"

Emmy bit her lip. "I've got some leftover spaghetti I need to eat."

Sean grinned. "I know you like pot roast."

"I really do, but I can't tonight." She grabbed her keys and purse. "Come over after dinner. We can do something then."

"Sounds like a plan." Sean smiled and watched Emmy walk around the corner.

She met him outside the house after dinner, and they walked to the elementary school down the street.

"Why are you joining the army now?"

"I'm not interested in going to college now—maybe never—so my friend Jay and I decided to enlist and see what happens."

"What do you mean?" She poked his side. "You could get hurt or even worse. That's what could happen."

When they got to the school, Emmy played on the swings, the slides and other playground equipment as Sean watched.

"This is fun! I haven't been on a slide in years."

"Do you want to play tag?" Sean asked.

She slapped his hand. "You're it!"

They chased each other around the playground—all very innocently on her part. Sean wanted to kiss her, but she didn't realize it. She ran over to a slide and climbed up as Sean waited at the bottom. When she came to a stop at the bottom of the slide, Sean looked at her, not so innocently this time. His eyes roamed over her body. His heart raced. He put his hands on her hips. *I don't care if you and Scott did anything. I think you're really sexy.*

Emmy bit her lip as she looked into his eyes. *Uh-oh! I've seen that look before.*

"Can I kiss you, Emmy?" He leaned down.

She put a hand to his chest. "Please don't, Sean. I don't have those kind of feelings for you."

"I think you do, Emmy. I know how I feel about you." He leaned down even closer.

She had to put both hands to his chest to push him away.

"I just want to be your friend," she said. *Why did I let down my guard? I completely thought we were just having fun.*

"We can still be friends. Really close friends."

She turned her face away. "No, Sean! Let me go." She got ready to kick him if it came to that.

After a few seconds, Sean stood up without kissing her. "I'm sorry, Emmy. I got carried away."

"It's all right." Emmy remained on the slide as her heart raced.

"I misread your signals. It's all my fault." He turned and kicked at the ground.

Emmy got up. *What signals? What did I ever do to make you think I wanted you to kiss me?*

They talked as they walked home.

"How long will you be gone?"

"Three years unless I re-enlist."

"Do you know where you will be stationed yet?"

"I only know where I will be for boot camp. Mom will have my address if you want to write."

She stood on the steps to her apartment. "We've haven't known each other all that long, but I consider you a good friend. I will write you as often as I can. I promise."

"I'd like that, Emmy. I'll try to write you a note when I write to Mom."

Two days later, Sean reported to the Army while Emmy was at work. She went to church with the O'Briens again and prayed for Sean's safety.

Chapter Eighteen

"We sold out both shows at the Garden and probably could have sold out a whole week of shows!" Kenny called Emmy on Friday, May fourteenth, with good news. "After the show tomorrow night, we will be heading home. Andy is letting us fly home from Boston. We've got a charter leaving from Hanscom Field in Bedford after the show. I'll be home on Sunday morning. Will you be happy to see me?"

"Who is this again? I think I recognize the voice, but I'm not sure," Emmy teased.

"Oh, sorry! I guess I must have a wrong number. I'll hang up now..."

"Don't you dare! What time will you land? Do you need a ride home?"

"Not sure what time we'll get into Chicago, but I don't need a ride. Andy made arrangements to have a couple of limos bring us home."

"Now that sounds more like my favorite rock star! Are you gonna have groupies on the plane with you?"

"I suppose I could arrange that." He laughed. "Oh, Em, it will be so good to see you. If we took the bus home, it would take sixteen hours or more. That would waste a whole day."

"Call me as soon as you get home. I don't care if it's the middle of the night. I want you to come over right away."

"It might be easier for you to come to my parents' since I've never been to your new apartment."

"I can do that. I might even stay in the carriage house Saturday night. That way I will be there when the limo drops you off." Emmy bit her lip as she thought about what might happen.

"I like that idea. I know Mom and Dad would love to see you again."

Kristen called Emmy later and announced, "Woo hoo! I have finished my first year of college. I had my last final today, and I'm through until the end of August."

"I'm happy for you. Did you do all right on your finals?"

"I think so, but I won't know for sure until the end of next

164

week. How did yours go?"

"Okay. They were easier than I expected, and I decided not to take any classes this summer. I need a break." Emmy sighed. "I still have to work, and that's enough to keep me busy. Though, there were more rumors of layoffs. In some ways, I hope I get let go. I want to have some time to enjoy the outdoors this summer." *I want to have lots of time to spend with Kenny.*

Kenny talked to his mother on Saturday before the show. "I'll see you and Dad in the morning. It will be the middle of the night, or very early in the morning, when I get home, so I'll let you guys sleep."

"Okay, son. Emmy wants to have dinner with us this evening. She will be as nervous as a long-tailed cat..."

"Yeah, I know. A long-tailed cat in a room full of rocking chairs."

"She probably won't get a minute of sleep until you get here."

"Tell her to go to bed like she normally would. It will be probably close to six before I get home."

Emmy had dinner with Mr. and Mrs. Colwell. She brought her dirty laundry and a book to occupy her time. After dinner, Emmy helped Mrs. Colwell clean up the kitchen. Around eight Tom and Sherry Hanna arrived for a visit.

"Emmy, why are you so nervous?" Tom asked even though he knew the reason. "You're looking at the clock every five minutes."

Sherry got after her husband. "Don't tease her like that! You know why she is so anxious."

"I'm not anxious for him to get home," Emmy insisted as she peered at the clock again.

"Of course not." Tom smiled at her.

After Tom and Sherry left, Emmy headed out to the carriage house to read and wait for Kenny. By one o'clock she had finished her book and decided to try to go to sleep. She tossed and turned on the futon until three.

When the show in Boston ended, Andy Walker and the guys took off for the airport with a police escort. They departed without any problems or delays. Just over two and a half hours later, they touched down in Chicago. Two limos met them at the airport. Exhaustion had almost caused Kenny to fall asleep on the ride home from the airport. He arrived home at 5:07 and headed to the carriage house. He entered his apartment as quietly as he could. He dropped his bags by the door and turned on a light. He could see Emmy sprawled almost sideways across the futon under the covers. Kenny chuckled softly and took off his shoes. He stood by the futon and gazed longingly at Emmy. He didn't want to wake her from a sound sleep, so he decided to sleep on the old couch.

Emmy woke up and peered at the clock. It was only minutes after eight. She looked across the room and smiled. She got up and quietly walked over to the old couch, kissed Kenny's cheek and said, "Good morning, sleepyhead."

He opened his eyes and smiled at her.

"What time did you get home?"

"Just a little after five. What time is it now?"

"8:06. Are we going to go to church, or should I let you sleep?"

"I should get up. I feel like I'm jet lagged."

"I brought clothes for church. Should I shower and get ready first so you can have a few more minutes to sleep?"

"Okay, but don't let me sleep past nine."

Emmy got ready and woke Kenny up at nine. He showered and dressed in fifteen minutes, and they headed over to the house.

"Morning, Mom, how are you? I could smell breakfast as soon as I opened the door. Where's Dad?"

Just then his father walked in the kitchen. "Hello, son. I see you made it home in one piece. Morning, Emmy, did you get any sleep, or did you stay up all night?"

"I think it was after two before I could fall asleep, Mr. Colwell."

"I've been updating my band files. Did you guys really play 'Dirty Water' as an encore last night?"

Kenny chuckled as he nodded. "Yeah, we thought it was

166

fitting." He turned to Emmy. "Dad is our official band historian. He keeps track of all our gigs, what songs we play, attendance—any facts he can gather really. He has it all on his computer."

"And backed up on discs!" Mr. Colwell pointed out. "Just in case someone wants to write a book someday."

"The song 'Dirty Water' Dad mentioned is about Boston, so that's why we used it last night. It's a garage band kinda song. You've probably never heard it."

Emmy shook her head. "You'll have to play it for me sometime."

After breakfast they headed to church. Kenny and Emmy saw youth pastor Ronnie Rojas and walked over to talk to him.

"Hello, Kenny. Hi, Emmy. It's good to see you guys. I hate to even ask, but I will. John Roberts called a few minutes ago to let me know he wouldn't be here because he is sick. He was supposed to sing a special today. I understand if you can't..."

"We can do a song if you need. Do you know what song John planned to sing?"

"He planned to do that Rich Mullins song 'Awesome God.' Do you know it?"

"Sure, I know it, and I think Emmy does, too. Would you be willing to sing this morning, Em?"

She bit her lip, but nodded her head. "Can we go over it?"

Ronnie nodded his head. "The worship band is back in the music room if you want to go over the song. Thanks so much, guys. I'm in your debt."

Kenny took Emmy back to the music room, and they practiced that song and a couple of others. Emmy kept switching the microphone back and forth from one hand to the other. She twirled her hair around a finger and Kenny grinned. He knew she did that because of nervousness.

After the service Ronnie thanked them again. "I appreciate you helping us out at the last minute. Is there any chance..."

Kenny laughed and asked, "What time do you want us here on Wednesday?"

"Service starts at six thirty. The worship band will be here, but if you want to do two or three songs... or four or five. That would be great."

Mrs. Colwell made a pot roast for Sunday dinner. Emmy helped set the table while the guys were watching TV. Over dinner Kenny updated his parents and Emmy about the current tour.

"Almost every show sold out. I think the biggest crowd might have been Rupp Arena in Kentucky. We sold over 22,000 tickets for that show. Andy keeps track of all that stuff."

Dad mentioned, "I see that you guys are doing some of your new material."

"We are doing some of the cuts from the new CD to see how they go over. We cut down on some of the cover songs, too."

After dinner Kenny asked Emmy, "Would you mind if I crashed for an hour or so? I'm kinda wiped out."

"That's all right. I'm kinda sleepy myself. Can I take a nap with you?"

"As long as you promise to behave."

"I am going to go upstairs and use your room. You can go out to your apartment," Emmy teased.

"Oh, no, you're not. You're coming with me, young lady." Kenny took Emmy's hand. "Thanks for dinner, Mom. The roast was great. It's so good to be home and have some home-cooked meals."

"You're welcome. It's good to have you home. Are you kids gonna be around tonight?"

"I think so. I really don't want to go anywhere."

"I need to go home tonight. I have to work, you know," Emmy reminded him.

"If you get hungry, there are leftovers in the fridge," Mom said.

Emmy bit her lip and looked back at Mr. and Mrs. Colwell as Kenny pulled her toward the back door. Mrs. Colwell smiled. Mr. Colwell scratched his chin.

"Are they... uh... you know?" Mr. Colwell asked after Kenny and Emmy were outside.

Mrs. Colwell poked his side. "Not yet, but it could happen soon."

She has really grown up from the first time she came over here. Mr. Colwell kept staring at the door even though Kenny and Emmy were long gone. "Did they elope or something, and no one has bothered to tell me?"

"No, now come with me. I need an afternoon nap."

"Are you sure they're not, uh?"

"I trust our son to make the right choices." Mrs. Colwell led her husband up the stairs. *At least I hope he's making the right decisions.*

Kenny and Emmy headed out to the carriage house.

Emmy grinned. "Did you see the look on your father's face? He must think we're gonna be naughty."

"Maybe we will." Kenny raised his eyebrows.

Once they were in the apartment they took off their shoes. Suddenly Kenny picked her up.

"If you think you are carrying me across the threshold like married couples did in ancient times, you're supposed to do it before we get inside."

Kenny kissed her and carried her to the futon where he unceremoniously dumped her. "What was that about married couples?"

"Nothing. Lay down next to me and tell me about the tour."

They lay side by side and talked until they fell asleep. They slept for forty-five minutes, and then woke up simultaneously. Emmy noticed he had a hand on her breast.

He noticed and moved it. "I'm sorry, Em. I didn't mean..."

"I know. It's all right. Nothing happened. We're still dressed except for our shoes." Emmy looked over at the couch and reminded Kenny, "The first time we took a 'nap' together, it was over there. I like the futon better. There's more room."

"Are you hungry yet?" Kenny asked even though he knew she wouldn't be hungry for a few more hours.

"No, but I know you are. You haven't eaten for a couple hours. Poor baby."

"Come on. Let's go raid Mom's fridge. She and Dad are probably taking their afternoon naps."

The nap fully recharged Kenny. He and Emmy got up and

169

ran to the house. Kenny opened the fridge and stood in front of it.

Emmy bumped his hip. "Hey, let me have some room." She squeezed in front of him and giggled as he touched her side. "I know what I want." She reached for the homemade apple pie.

Kenny searched through the fridge, made his choice and pulled out the pot roast, potatoes and gravy.

The afternoon sun warmed the breakfast nook as it shone through the uncovered windows. Kenny and Emmy were sitting on the barstools at the breakfast counter eating when his mother walked into the kitchen.

She saw what Kenny had on his plate and shook her head. "I knew I should have made more potatoes. Is there anything left for your father?"

"Not much, Mom, sorry, but Emmy ate it all."

Emmy smacked his arm and looked at Mrs. Colwell. "I didn't eat anything except for another piece of apple pie. He ate everything else." She stuck out her tongue at Kenny and he tried to grab it. She giggled as he tried to tickle her ribs.

"Stop it! You'll make me fall off the stool."

Mrs. Colwell watched as Kenny and Emmy acted like a couple of kids. *You guys used to sit on those same stools and tease each other like that when you were younger. You still behave like kids most of the time. I don't think you've changed too much.*

He stopped tickling her, and she kissed him.

"Are you going to behave now? Your mother will think we are acting like children."

"Would you like for me to order a pizza? I know you will need something later. What time do you need to get home, Emmy? Can you stay for awhile, or do you need to go now?" Mrs. Colwell asked.

"I can stay until about eight or nine, Mrs. Colwell. Is that all right?"

"You can stay as long as you like, dear. It's always a pleasure to have you here. I know Mr. Colwell likes to talk to you about Kenny's band. You are the only person who will listen to his rambling about the set lists and other stuff."

"I have always felt right at home here." She gestured to

170

indicate the spacious kitchen, but she meant the entire house. "Thank you." Emmy smiled at Mrs. Colwell.

Later, Mrs. Colwell ordered a large pizza to alleviate Kenny's hunger.

"I should go, Kenny. I have to make sure the apartment is clean, and I have to put my clean clothes away. Will you carry my laundry out to the car for me?"

"Sure, where is it?"

"In the laundry room, I think."

"It's on the counter in there, Emmy. I folded it for you," Mrs. Colwell said.

"Oh, you didn't need to do that, Mrs. Colwell, but thank you."

Kenny and Emmy headed out to her car.

"Are we gonna get together after work tomorrow?" Emmy asked.

"Yes, but I can't on Tuesday. I have to meet the guys at the studio to listen to some tracks. I would invite you, but it's easier if we don't have anybody there but us."

"That's okay. I understand. I'll find something to do. Are we going to sing for the teens on Wednesday?"

"Do you mind?"

"Not at all. I like it at your church. I gotta go. I'll call you tomorrow after work."

Mondays at the office were chaotic for Emmy. This Monday the commotion kept everyone in a frenzy. Emmy tried to avoid the furor caused by the latest gossip about impending job cuts. She kept on the move all day, and by five she was mentally and physically drained. She drove home, stopping for gas. She arrived at her apartment and struggled to open her door.

"Why won't this darn key work?" She looked closely at the key. "Duh! This is for the carriage house. No wonder it won't work."

She inserted the correct key, opened the door and dragged herself up the stairs. She used another key to open the door at the top. She stepped inside the apartment, took off her jacket and hung it on the hook on the back of the door. She kicked off her shoes as she limped into the living room. She collapsed into her recliner and closed her eyes. Just then her cell phone rang. She knew it was Kenny by the ringtone. She struggled out of the recliner and managed to retrieve her phone from the pocket of her jacket.

"Hey, Kenny."

"Hi, Em. How did your day go?"

"I just got home, and I'm wiped. Are we doing anything tonight?"

"I could pick up some Chinese and bring it over there. That way you won't have to leave the apartment. Plus, I can at least see the place."

"Do you know how to get here?"

"I've got the address. Anything special you want for dinner?"

"Fried rice, for sure... and... just surprise me. I'm too tired to think of anything right now. I'll leave the door unlocked in case I fall asleep."

"See you soon, Em."

She changed clothes and ran around the apartment making sure everything was dust-free and spotless. She had just sat down when the phone rang again. She answered without looking at the caller ID.

"It's your mother. I am extremely upset with you, young lady!"

"Why? What did I do now?"

"I heard that you slept with Kenny Colwell again. I hope you are being careful."

"Mom! Where did you hear this?"

"I'm not going to divulge my sources."

For the next ten minutes Emmy listened to her mother rant and rave at her. She would hang up but knew that would only make matters worse. Occasionally her mother paused for breath, and Emmy had a chance to try to explain, but her mother didn't want to hear the truth. She was still on the phone when Kenny pulled into the driveway. She saw his car and opened the door at the top of the stairs. He walked into her apartment, and she motioned for him to

172

be still.

"It's Mom, and she's on a rampage," she whispered.

"Is he with you now? Is he going to spend the night?" Emmy's mother asked.

"Yes, he's here. He brought dinner over, but he's not spending the night. I gotta go, Mom. I wish you would believe me, but I know you won't."

Kenny couldn't hear what her mother said to her, but she started to cry as soon as she hung up. He set the Chinese food on the kitchen counter and held her. He didn't say anything until she stopped crying.

"Are you all right now?"

"I don't know why I let her upset me so much. Let's eat."

"Aren't you gonna show me your apartment first?"

"Oh, sorry, I guess I should."

Two minutes later with the tour completed, they opened up the carryout.

"What did you get me?"

"I got some house fried rice, an order of crab rangoon, sweet and sour pork and empress chicken. If you want dessert, I thought we could go out for ice cream."

They sat at the kitchen table and ate. Kenny listened as Emmy told him what her mother said.

"She thinks we're sleeping together."

"Did you tell her the truth?" He added more fried rice to his plate.

"Of course, but she just won't believe me. What can I do?"

"I don't know if there's anything you can do. I suppose we should not stay overnight with each other. That gives her the wrong impression."

"But we aren't doing anything wrong, are we?" Emmy asked as she ate the last piece of crab rangoon.

"We know that, but other people might get the wrong idea." He mentally chastised himself, *I never should have spent the night at her apartment. It doesn't matter that we didn't do anything. It gave the appearance that we were sleeping together. I know better.*

"Do you think she's spying on me, or us?" Emmy asked.

173

"I know she talked to my mom."

"Your mother wouldn't say anything to hurt us."

"She would be honest, and if your mother asked the right questions..."

"I see what you're getting at. My mom already assumes the wrong thing and will twist anything your mother says around to fit what she wants to believe."

After finishing their dinner, Emmy put the leftovers in the fridge. Kenny turned on some music, and they sat on the couch and talked. Time passed quickly, and Kenny looked at his watch.

"I should go, Em. You have to be at work early. Could you call me on your lunch break? We may not see each other tomorrow, but we can still talk."

"Okay, you can let me know what songs you want to do Wednesday."

Emmy walked him out to his car. He gave her a quick kiss and headed home. He didn't notice a car parked at the end of the block.

Emmy's mother had rushed over to the apartment as soon as she hung up the phone. "Well, at least he's not spending the night tonight. I hope you're being careful, Emily. You're too young to have a baby," Mom muttered as she started the car and drove away.

Chapter Nineteen

Emmy got home from work on Tuesday, spotted Mrs. O'Brien working in her flower bed, waved and walked over to talk to her.

"Emmy, how are you doing, dear?"

"I'm fine, Mrs. O'Brien."

"Isn't this a lovely spring day!" Mrs. O'Brien removed her large floppy hat and wiped her brow.

"I love it when everything turns green. Would you mind if I help you?" Emmy asked.

"That would be lovely. You can help anytime you want."

Emmy held a peony in her hand to smell it. "If I ever get a house, I want to have flowers everywhere."

As Emmy and Mrs. O'Brien were talking in the yard, Scott Simmons drove up and parked in the driveway. Emmy hadn't seen or talked to him for over a month.

"Hello, Mrs. O'Brien. Hi, Emmy."

"Hello, Scott. How are you doing? I saw you at church Sunday, but I didn't have a chance to talk to you."

"I'm doing fine now, Mrs. O'Brien. I wanted to stop by and talk to you."

"What's on your mind?" Mrs. O'Brien asked.

"I should go and let you talk," Emmy told Scott and Mrs. O'Brien as she turned to walk away.

Scott looked at Emmy. "I also wanted to talk to you, Emmy. Can I have a little of your time?"

Emmy stared at him for a few seconds. "Okay, come on over and ring the bell when you are finished. You can't come upstairs, but I will come down and talk to you."

Emmy went into her apartment and changed clothes. Scott talked to Mrs. O'Brien for a few minutes, and Emmy saw Mrs. O'Brien hug him as Scott finished talking to her. Scott looked up at her apartment, walked over and rang the bell. Emmy came downstairs, and they sat on the steps. She made sure she kept some elbow room between them.

"Emmy, I know you probably hate me, and I don't blame

175

you for that. I deserve it for what I told Sean about us."

"That was a rotten thing to do," Emmy said.

"I am truly sorry for that and for my behavior the last year. You heard Mrs. O'Brien say she saw me at church Sunday. It finally dawned on me what a mess I was making of my life, and I knew I had to do something about it. I went to church and asked God to forgive me. I have been such a fool."

"Scott, I don't hate you. You pissed me off with what you told Sean and how you treated me, but I don't hate you."

Scott looked at her, "Emmy, I accepted Jesus as my Savior, and I needed to tell you that. I grew up in the church, and I thought I could get by with merely acting like everyone else. I don't think I ever had a real relationship with Jesus until now. I need to tell you how sorry I am for how I treated you. I hope that you can find it in your heart to forgive me. I don't expect you to forget, but can you forgive me?"

Emmy stared at him for ten seconds as she tried to decide what to say.

To Scott it felt like ten minutes.

"Yes, Scott, I can. I'm happy for you. I think you are sincere, and you seem different."

"Thanks, Emmy. That means a lot to me. I have more news to tell you. You might not care, but I am moving to Texas. I got a new job in Dallas, and it's a chance to make a clean start of my life. I flew to Dallas for an interview, and I found another church while I was there, too."

"When are you leaving, Scott?"

"This weekend. I start work on Monday."

"What kind of job is it?"

"I will be working for Gilbert Publishing. That's what I went to college for, so I'm happy. You are such a good person, Emmy. I don't mean that because you are pretty or anything. I mean on the inside. You are sweet and honest and all the good qualities that a guy should look for in a wife."

Emmy stared at Scott. *If this is another come on, I'm going to make you pay.* He didn't move closer to her or try to touch her. She decided to give him some leeway. "Thank you, Scott. I

176

appreciate that. I wish you well in Texas. I hear they have a lot of gorgeous women there."

"Who knows? Maybe I can find the right one for me."

Emmy looked at Scott as her stomach growled.

He grinned. "I heard that, Emmy."

"I'm hungry. Would you have time to take me to dinner?"

"I would love to take you to dinner... as a friend."

"I would like to go to dinner with you... as a friend. If you give me a minute, I'll be ready to go."

They decided to go out for Mexican. Scott drove, and he behaved like a gentleman, like when they first met. Emmy relaxed with him and tried not to think about the hurtful aspects of their past. After dinner, Scott drove her back to her apartment.

"It's such a pleasant evening. I like to go for walks around the neighborhood. Would you like to join me?" Emmy asked.

"Sure. It's a real shame. I feel as if we are just getting to be friends, and I will be gone soon. I sure wasted my time with you, Emmy."

"I hear that some parts of Texas have phone service now and even post offices that deliver the mail on a weekly basis," she teased. "Of course, cows still outnumber people."

Scott laughed. "Would you mind if I emailed you occasionally, Emmy? I won't bother you by calling, but I can try to email."

"I would like that, Scott. We can keep in touch and who knows? Maybe one day we will see each other again."

They finished their walk and returned to her apartment. He found a piece of paper and pen in his car and they exchanged email addresses.

"I had a good time, Scott. I hope you don't forget to email."

"I did, too. I'm truly sorry about how I treated you."

"Yeah, that's in the past. Nothing we can do about it now. I hope you treat any women you meet in Texas the way you treated me in the beginning."

They looked into each others eyes for a moment. Emmy clenched her fist. She intended to use it if she needed.

"God bless you, Emmy. Maybe you can remember me in a

better light now."

Emmy relaxed her fist.

Scott put his hands tenderly on Emmy's shoulders and gave them a gentle squeeze, as her friend.

The next evening Emmy drove straight to Kenny's house after work. She changed clothes, and they went to the church to rehearse with the band. They practiced four songs, including one Emmy wrote and sang for the teens before. Over fifty teens crowded into the room in the basement for the service that evening. Pastor Rojas wondered where the church would fit all the kids if the group continued to grow. There would have been even more teens present if they had known Kenny was going to be there. The worship band played a couple of songs before Ronnie Rojas led the teens in prayer. Then he brought Kenny and Emmy up to the small stage. They sang four songs, and then Ronnie gave a devotional message taken from the book of Acts. After the service, Kenny talked to the kids; a few even asked for autographs.

Emmy stayed in the background and watched. She suppressed a giggle. *If you kids knew how much of a dork he is, you wouldn't be asking for his autograph. He's an anti-rock-star. He still has the same values as he grew up with. That must be why I love him so much.*

Kenny took her to Darby's afterward.

"I think the teens really enjoyed your song, Em."

"Really? Are you sure they weren't listening because of you?"

"I don't think that's it at all. Most of the teens have met me before and are kinda used to me. There are a bunch of them who have known me for years, so they don't think of me as anyone special."

Emmy smiled at him. "I've known you for a long time, and I still think you're special."

"Are you making fun of me? I know you think I'm the dorkiest rock star in history."

"That's true, but I still love you."

Emmy dropped Kenny off, but didn't get out of the car.

"I need to get home. Is it all right if I don't come in?"

"Sure. Are you worried that your mother might find out and get on your case again?"

"I suppose in a way, but I'm kinda tired. I'm going to go home and crash."

"I'll see you after work tomorrow. Get some rest so we can do something." Kenny kissed her good night, and she headed home.

On Thursday Emmy and Kenny ate dinner at her apartment. He had stopped at the store and picked up two filet mignons. Emmy made two baked potatoes and put together a garden salad. They sat at the kitchen table to eat.

"If you ever move again, will you at least try to find someplace closer to Raynor Park?" Kenny asked. "Please don't stay in Crest Ridge. It takes too long to get here. The carriage house is a lot closer."

"You could always move."

He shook his head. "I'm not home enough to have an apartment somewhere in the city."

"So you're always going to live at your parents house, huh?" Emmy asked as she cut off a small piece of her steak.

"You know it's not just my parents' house. Our family has been living there for over a hundred years."

"And since you are an only child..."

"It will be mine someday, but my parents could live another forty or fifty years. One of these days I will build a house for myself."

Emmy grinned. "And your wife?"

"She has to build her own house." Kenny grabbed Emmy's hand so she wouldn't throw something at him.

She made a face at him and responded, "I'll try to find a place closer to our neighborhood, but it has to be far enough away that my parents aren't always coming over."

"You mean your Mom. Has your father ever been in either one of your apartments?" Kenny cut another piece off his steak.

"He didn't come inside, but he dropped me off once at my

179

first place."

Kenny shook his head in in bewilderment. "I can't imagine my parents never coming to visit me if I lived somewhere else."

"As far as I know, Mom and Dad have never been inside Diane and Craig's place."

"The carriage house is close."

Emmy read between the lines and shook her head. "I can't. Not yet at least." She still wouldn't tell him about her mother's threats.

They continued eating without much conversation.

"I suppose you will not accept any help with the rent?"

"Nope! Grandma Isabel is going to help me for a while." Emmy stood up and took her plate to the white-enameled sink.

"Why do you let her help and not me?"

"She's family. We've been over this before."

"We could charge you rent for the carriage house."

Kenny took his plate to the sink. He turned and put his hands on her shoulders. She smiled at him.

"Yeah, your father informed me he would charge me a dollar a month and not a penny more."

"Five dollars a month?" Kenny asked.

Emmy shook her head.

"You are so... determined to be independent."

"And I will be as soon as I stop accepting money from Grandma."

"What if you and Kristen find a place together? Have you considered that?"

"She likes living in the dorm."

Kenny remained silent as he washed the dishes. Emmy dried them and put them away.

"Are you going to stay with me Saturday night? The limo will be there Sunday morning at seven to take me to the airport."

"I'm not sure yet. Do you think I should after what happened the other day when we were taking a nap?"

"Oh, come on, Em. Nothing happened. If you want to stay, I will sleep on the couch, or in the house, if that would make you feel better."

"I'll think about it. If I stay, you can sleep on the couch. It wouldn't make any sense for me to stay if you're in the house."

"You mean you are afraid to sleep in the carriage house alone!" Kenny teased.

She snapped her dish towel at him. "I am not afraid to sleep out there by myself."

Saturday morning Kristen met Emmy at her apartment.

"Can we take your car to get Kenny, please?" Emmy asked.

"Sure, I figured we would. Why are you so anxious to take my car?"

"Because I want him to see how nice your car is compared to the old Civic. Your Acura is even nicer than his new Civic."

Kristen laughed. "He's not going to buy another car, Em."

When they got to his place, Emmy made sure he noticed all the features of Kristen's car.

"I'm not buying a sports car just for you to drive when I'm on tour, Em."

"Some rock star you are," Emmy teased by sticking out her bottom lip and pouting. "Won't even buy your favorite groupie a fancy car."

Even Kristen giggled.

They did a bit of shopping for Emmy's apartment and ended up at Darby's again for lunch. After lunch, they drove back to Emmy's apartment and spent the afternoon hanging up pictures and cleaning the apartment.

"How would it be if we moved the couch over here in front of the windows?" Emmy asked Kenny, as she surveyed the living room.

"Are you going to leave the TV on this wall by the bedroom?"

"I could move it over there with the stereo. It would fit on top of the cabinet."

Kristen imagined the new setup. "You could get another recliner and put it where the couch is now."

"What about your keyboard, Em? Are you going to leave it in the bedroom?"

"No, I want to bring the keyboard out here. If we move the TV, I could put the keyboard here." Emmy stood where she wanted the Yamaha piano to stand.

"Let's try and see how it looks. You can always move everything back," Kenny said. Then he stretched out his back.

"Does that mean if I don't like it, I have to move everything back by myself?"

"No, sweetie, I'm sure Kristen will help," he teased.

Thirty minutes later the living room was rearranged to Emmy's satisfaction.

"Do you want to go to dinner with us, Kristen? I'll buy since you helped me this afternoon." Emmy glanced at Kenny to see if he minded.

"Are you sure you want me along? I know Kenny is leaving in the morning."

"We will have time together later." Emmy bit her lip as she thought about how that must sound to Kristen.

"I'll go if Derrick will go with me."

"When did he get home?" Emmy asked as she straightened a photo of Fridays At Five on the wall.

"Supposedly this morning. I'll call, and see if he'll go. Will you buy dinner for him, too, Em?"

"I'll buy Derrick's dinner and no argument from you, young lady," Kenny stated firmly.

"Fine. I'll buy for the girls, and you can take care of the guys," Emmy said.

Derrick readily agreed to go, even though his "dinner date" was Kristen. He wouldn't admit it to her, but he missed his sister.

"Where should we go?" Emmy asked.

"I'll call Mr. Sabatino and make a reservation for eight o'clock at Ciao Bella. Is that enough time for you girls to get ready?"

"I don't know. It's already after five, and I need a couple hours to do my hair." Emmy removed the rubber band holding her hair in a ponytail.

"I need three hours to do my hair and make-up. How about dinner at ten?" Kristen asked sarcastically.

Kenny laughed. "Emmy and I will pick you and Derrick up at seven whether you're ready or not."

"We could meet you guys there. That would save you a trip out to our house," Kristen suggested.

"Okay, we'll meet you guys at Ciao Bella at eight. I hope we can find a place to park."

Kristen headed home. Emmy took a quick shower and got dressed. She packed an overnight bag, and they drove to Kenny's place.

"Does Kristen know you are spending the night at the carriage house?"

"No, I didn't tell her."

"Does she know you have spent the night..."

"She knows I have crashed there before."

Kenny got the sense that Emmy didn't want to talk about this, so he changed the subject. "I like that dress."

"Thanks," Emmy responded but then remained silent until they got to his house. "Do you mind if I run in and talk to your parents while you get ready?"

"Go ahead, Em. I'll come in when I'm ready. We don't have to leave until seven forty. That will give us plenty of time to get there."

When Kenny walked into the main house, Emmy was in the kitchen with his mother. Mrs. Colwell saw Kenny and commented, "You both look very dressed up tonight. I really like your dress, Emmy."

"Thank you, Mrs. Colwell. This is what I wore to the New Year's Eve party."

"I hope you don't freeze if it gets cooler later."

"I have a sweater in the car. I'll be all right."

Kenny and Emmy left on time and got to The Hill neighborhood. After driving around for ten minutes, they found a parking space only four blocks from Caio Bella—not bad for a Saturday night.

Derrick and Kristen had arrived earlier and huddled inside the jam-packed waiting area.

"I love the aroma in this place. I think I gain weight just

183

inhaling the smell of the fresh baked bread." Kristen sighed as a waiter walked past with a loaf of homemade Focaccia bread.

Derrick looked at his watch a couple of times.

"They'll be here soon. They're probably trying to find a parking spot closer than two miles away," Kristen said.

Derrick glanced at his sister. "Sometimes I wonder why I miss you at all."

"You could have gone to college somewhere closer than Arizona."

"What, and have to put up with you all the time. No thanks."

Mr. Sabatino greeted Kenny and Emmy as they arrived. He escorted the group to their table in a back corner—Kenny had asked for a table with privacy.

"Enjoy your meal." Mr. Sabatino smiled at Kenny and nodded his head.

They ordered two appetizers—Maryland blue crab-cakes and Caprese salad—and bottled water to drink. The special that night was Rotollo Florentine which Kenny, Emmy and Kristen ordered. Derrick ordered a New York strip steak, Tuscany style. An hour later they were talking about the great food they always enjoyed at Ciao Bella. Their waiter asked if they were ready for dessert. Emmy wondered if she would have enough money to pay for her and Kristen's share of the bill.

Kristen asked Derrick, "Will you split some tiramasu with me? I want dessert, but I can't eat a whole one."

"Okay, I'll split it with you."

"Want to split some strawberry cheesecake?" Kenny asked Emmy.

Emmy nodded. "You will have to eat most of it. I'm still stuffed."

The desserts arrived, and Kristen gawked as Emmy and Kenny fed each other. She daydreamed about having a boyfriend feed her. While Kristen daydreamed, Derrick ate most of the tiramasu. Kristen finally noticed and smacked Derrick's arm. "Hey, I wanted some of it."

"You snooze, you lose."

At ten o'clock, Kenny mentioned, "I'm ready to go."

Emmy asked, "Did we get a check yet?"

Derrick knew that Kenny had given the waiter $300 and told him to keep the change.

Kenny smiled at Emmy and answered, "I took care of it while you and Kristen used the ladies room."

"How much was my share?" Emmy asked.

"Ten bucks should cover it."

"Come on, Kenny, I told you I would pay for the girls tonight. Do I have to ask Mr. Sabatino?"

"Are you going to make a scene?"

She made a face. "I will if you don't tell me how much I owe you."

Just then Mr. Sabatino walked over. "I hope everything met with your approval."

Emmy asked, "Mr. Sabatino, I am supposed to pay for Kristen's and my share, but Kenny won't tell me how much I owe. Do you know?"

"I know exactly. All pretty girls are being charged ten dollars tonight." He managed to keep a straight face. "And girls as pretty as you and Miss Keasling are allowed to eat for free. It is such a pleasure for me to have you in my restaurant. I feel that I should pay you for the privilege of gazing upon your beautiful faces."

Emmy giggled and then said, "You are so full of it, Mr. Sabatino, but thank you for the compliment. I'll make sure Kenny suffers later. By the way, everything tasted fantastic tonight. It always does, but tonight everything was simply divine."

"I will tell Mrs. Sabatino that you were pleased."

As they walked to their cars, Kristen asked Emmy, "Is Kenny taking you home?"

"Actually, no."

Emmy didn't elaborate, and Kristen didn't pry.

"Thanks for dinner, Kenny. I'm glad we had a chance to go out even if I had to eat with Kristen. Have a great tour." Derrick shook Kenny's hand.

"You're welcome for the dinner. We should do this again

when I get back."

Emmy hugged Kristen when they reached Kristen's car. "Thanks for all your help today, Krissy."

"I'll talk to you tomorrow, Em." *Be careful. It only takes one time to get pregnant.*

Derrick and Kristen got in her car.

"I think she's spending the night with him," Kristen said as Kenny and Emmy held hands as they walked along.

"And why does that bother you? She is free to date who she wishes."

"Spending the night," Kristen repeated. "Understand?"

"It's not her birthday, is it?" Derrick smirked.

"You're a creep. I never should have told you." Kristen smacked his arm with enough force to hurt her hand. "Ow! That hurt."

"Serves you right for hitting me."

"She was in love with Tony not too long ago."

"Yes, but they broke up. It happens, Miss Matchmaker. You broke up with Ryan, remember?"

"Please don't remind me about him." Kristen sighed, and then added, "Maybe she and Kenny are still just friends. After all they have known each other since she was a little girl."

Derrick looked at his sister and smiled. "If you want to believe in fairy-tales, it's okay with me."

"I just hope she doesn't get hurt."

"Hey, Kenny is not like Ryan."

Kristen glared at Derrick. "How do you know? You never met him."

"True. I assumed he wasn't all that bright since he... "

Kristen made a fist.

"Ruined his relationship with you," Derrick finished.

"That's almost sweet coming from you."

When Kenny and Emmy got to his car, he opened the door for her, but she didn't get in. She grabbed his shirt and kissed him—a long, passionate kiss.

"I don't care who knows I'm spending the night with you. Tonight is the last time I will see you for... when will you be home

186

again?"

"In August. I think it's the week starting on the eighth."

"Will you kiss me when we get to your place?"

"No way! Your mother might have hidden cameras in the place. I'm sure it's bugged, and she probably listens to every word we say."

"Then I'll give her some choice words to listen to."

Once inside the carriage house apartment, Emmy walked around saying naughty things in case the place was bugged. Kenny could barely hold his laughter as Emmy pretended to be doing things she knew her mother would not like.

"I think your mother gets the picture, Em. Do you really want me to do those things?"

Emmy blushed, "God, no! It's embarrassing just thinking about... that."

She helped him get packed as they listened to some tunes. Afterward they sat on the couch. She looked at him and smiled.

"Are you going to cry in the morning, Em?"

"Why on earth would I do that? You'll be gone, so I can do whatever I want. I might start dating a different guy every weekend. Maybe a different one on Friday and Saturday."

He pulled her onto his lap. She closed her eyes in anticipation of a kiss. His lips brushed gently on hers. Her heart raced. She opened her mouth to receive his tongue. But he stopped. He moved her off of his lap and stood up.

Emmy looked at him and knew why. "I'm glad you have self-control."

"If we even kiss, I won't want to stop."

"I understand what you mean. I feel the same way," Emmy whispered. "I might not like it, but you are doing the right thing." *Sometimes I hate it when you act all admirably.*

Around midnight Kenny looked once more at Emmy as she slept soundly on the futon. He turned off the lights and lay down on the old couch that still had sentimental value for him. He remembered the first time he kissed her.

Kenny had his alarm set for six. He woke up five minutes

187

before it buzzed. He turned it off so it wouldn't wake up Emmy. He got ready and was about to wake her up but stopped. *You look so peaceful. Maybe I won't even wake you.*

Jeff called. "Hey, we're about ten minutes away. Are you ready?"

"Yeah, I'm ready to go," Kenny whispered.

Kenny again looked at Emmy as she slept. He needed to choose between letting her get some needed rest and waking her up to say goodbye. He knew she would be disappointed if he left while she slept. He sat on the edge of the futon and watched as she slept peacefully. He couldn't leave without saying goodbye, so he gently touched her shoulder.

"Em, I have to leave in a few minutes."

She opened her eyes and smiled.

"Did you hear what I said? I have to leave in a few minutes."

She reached out and pulled him next to her on the futon.

"Just hold me for a minute before you go."

Kenny held her as she cried. "It's all right, Em. I'll be back before you know it."

His phone rang—Jeff again. "The limo is a couple of minutes away."

"I'll meet you out front." Kenny snapped his cell phone closed, looked at Emmy and whispered, "I gotta go. I'll call you as often as I can. I love you."

"I love you, too. Be safe and stay away from the girls."

"Not a problem. I've got the best girl in the world waiting for me."

Chapter Twenty

After Kenny left on Sunday morning, Emmy went to church with his parents and stayed for lunch. She had just walked into her apartment when her cell phone rang.

"Hey, Kristen, what's up?" Emmy asked.

"Nothing, what are you doing?"

"I just got back from Kenny's house. I need to do some grocery shopping. Want to help me?"

"Oh, golly gee!" Kristen answered in an exaggerated high-pitched voice. "That sounds exciting. How can I possibly pass up an opportunity to spend my afternoon in a grocery store."

"Well, I suppose I could do it after work tomorrow. Why don't you come over, and we can do something."

"Okay, I'll be there soon."

Kristen hung up and headed over to see Emmy. She wanted to ask her about last night.

Emmy was outside shooting baskets when Kristen arrived. "Hey, Kristen, want to play ball?"

"What are you doing, Em?" Kristen walked toward Emmy.

"Just getting some fresh air. It's such a beautiful day and life is so good!"

Kristen stopped and stared at Emmy. *Why are you so happy, Em? Kenny just left on tour. Could it be because you spend the night with him?*

Emmy tossed the basketball to Kristen. "Take a shot."

Kristen threw the basketball toward the basket—like a girl. It missed by several feet.

"I'm not very good at basketball, but I like to play tennis. Is there a place around here to play?"

"I think the closest place is at the high school, and that's about a mile away."

"That's too far. I'll shoot baskets with you for now."

Emmy shot baskets while Kristen watched. Every so often Emmy threw the ball to her, and Kristen took a shot. She finally made a basket.

"All right, I'm done. I made a basket. Can we go inside

now?"

"Okay, but I want to see if I can make a basket from over here first."

Emmy shot from the far corner of the driveway and missed everything. She ran after the ball, returned to the spot, tried again and got closer. On the third try she swished it. She lifted her hands in the air as if signaling for a touchdown. "Yes, that was a three-pointer for sure."

"Hooray!" Kristen yelled and waved her hands like a cheerleader. "Now are you finished? Are you going to try out for the team at school?" Kristen asked sarcastically.

"I was just having fun, Kristen. Why are you acting like this?"

"I'm sorry. Can we go inside and talk, please?"

"Yeah, sure."

They went inside and up to Emmy's apartment.

"Do you want something to drink? I'm gonna have water."

"Water is all right."

Emmy fixed two glasses of ice water and brought them out to the living room where Kristen sat on the couch.

"Thanks, Em."

"What do you want to ask me? I know there is something on your mind. So go ahead and ask."

"Where did you sleep last night?" Kristen asked abruptly. "Did you spend the night with Kenny?"

What Kristen implied upset Emmy so she answered, "Yes, I did spend the night with him, and he showed me how much he loves me. So there."

"It's all right, Em. Were you careful? Are you feeling okay now? It took a couple of days for my soreness to go away."

"I'm not going to talk about it anymore. You are just like my mother."

"I'm not like your mother. You're my best friend, and I love you."

"Good! Then we can move on to another subject." Emmy intentionally gave Kristen the wrong impression but didn't care.

Kristen stared at Emmy for a few seconds. *Are you going to*

tell me about it? I told you intimate details of my night with Ryan.
But Emmy didn't volunteer any information.

"When will he be back?"

"On August eighth. He'll be home for a week," Emmy answered but didn't say anything more.

Kristen set her glass of water down on the carpet, stood up and walked into the second bedroom. "Are you gonna put anything in here?"

"I'd like to pick up a used bed and a dresser. I thought about putting that old exercise bike in there, but I won't use it if it's not out here. I want to be able to watch TV if I'm gonna be working out."

"I know where you can get a bedroom set that will fit in here."

"Where? I can't afford to pay much."

"We have one in the storage room above the garage. Mom would probably let you have it for free. Before you get all stubborn and refuse it, I would give it to you as an apartment-warming present."

Emmy looked at Kristen and thought about refusing the offer, but she didn't.

"I would love it. That would be so generous of you, Krissy. Or rather your Mom."

"I'll talk to her about it this week. If she agrees maybe we can get Derrick to help us move it."

Emmy looked at Kristen with guilt about what she said about last night. "Krissy..."

"Yeah, what?"

"I spent the night at Kenny's, but we didn't sleep together. He slept on the couch. I'm sorry if I was a little short with you earlier."

Kristen smiled and replied, "You're always a little short, Em."

When Kristen returned home later that day, she saw her mother sitting in the family room. "Mom, Emmy needs a bed for her spare room. Do we have anything she can borrow for a while?"

"I don't know if there's anything she can borrow, but she

191

can have the bed and dresser in the storage room above the garage. There's a mattress and box spring, too. Have Derrick or Tony load it up. I don't want you or Emmy to hurt yourselves trying to carry that dresser."

"Thanks, Mom! I'll see if the guys can help me move it tomorrow. It's too late to do it today."

Kristen ran up to Derrick's room and asked, "Will you help me move a bedroom set from the storage area and take it to Emmy's tomorrow?"

"I suppose so."

Kristen didn't expect him to agree so readily. "What, no smart remark?"

"No, I'm not doing anything tomorrow, and I like Emmy."

"So, if I was asking you to help me move it into my room, you would refuse?"

"You got that right."

"Men! They are all impossible, and brothers are the absolute worst."

Kristen called Tony; he also agreed to help.

Tony met Kristen and Derrick at four o'clock the next day. The guys loaded up Mr. Keasling's van. Tony followed Derrick and Kristen over to Emmy's apartment; twenty minutes later Emmy had a bed and a dresser in the spare bedroom. Mrs. Keasling had also sent along two lamps.

"Will you guys let me take you out for dinner?" Emmy asked.

"You don't have to do that, Em."

"I've got a pizza I could throw in the oven. Would that be all right?"

"Yeah, that would be okay, but how about playing some basketball first while it's still light?" Tony suggested.

"Okay by me," Derrick answered.

Kristen decided to join them, also. Emmy was goofing around, trying to block Tony's shots. She couldn't get close. Kristen took a shot. It missed everything and rolled over to the four-foot-high fence that separated the O'Brien's yard from their neighbors.

Emmy ran over to get the ball and saw a young man in the yard. She smiled at him, and he smiled back.

"Hi, we're playing some ball. Wanna join us?"

He looked at Emmy, and then saw Tony and Derrick. "Sure, don't mind if I do." He put a hand on top of the fence and hopped it with ease.

"I'm Emmy." She pointed to the upper floor of the garage. "I moved into the apartment a while back."

"I'm LaRon Robinson."

Tony walked over and offered his hand, "Hi, LaRon. I'm Tony, and these are my cousins, Derrick and Kristen Keasling."

LaRon looked at Tony and smiled. "I know you. I played wide receiver for Crest Ridge, and we met in the third quarter of our game this year."

Tony tilted his head and wrinkled his brow as he looked at LaRon.

"I caught a short pass over the middle and ran right into you. You hit me and knocked me almost to the sideline. Man, I was woozy for a week after that hit," LaRon explained.

Tony grinned. "I think I remember that play. You held onto the ball. I thought for sure I hit you hard enough to knock it loose. I remember reaching out a hand to help you up."

"I don't remember anything except being hit by a truck." LaRon laughed. Emmy flipped him the ball and he took a shot.

"Do you play basketball, too?" Tony asked. "I can tell you have some talent."

"I've been on the varsity team since my freshman year. Not that that's a big deal because we suck at basketball. You guys won the state championship during my freshman year. I remember when we played you, I had to guard that guy who was so good."

"Mace Franklin," Emmy said. "He plays at North Park now. Tony's football team won the state championship this year, and he was voted player of the year!"

"I think I read that in the paper. Congratulations. I saw that game. I bet you had a blast playing in a blizzard. You guys kicked Mount Carmel's butt."

They shot around for a time, but then Emmy wanted to

choose sides and play a game of two-on-two. Kristen didn't want any part of that, so she stood by the garage door and watched.

Emmy threw the ball at Derrick. "I want to be on LaRon's team. I think we can beat you guys."

"Wanna put something on that, Em? Make it interesting?" Derrick asked as he tossed the ball back to her.

"Like what?"

"You can think of something, I'm sure."

Emmy smiled at Derrick and informed him, "If LaRon and I win, then you have to take us to dinner at Darby's. If you guys win, then I will make you dinner next weekend, or whenever you're home again."

Derrick grinned. "I don't know about that. You might try to poison me."

Emmy stuck out her tongue at Derrick. "I might."

The game began. Tony guarded LaRon and was quick enough to stay with him. LaRon sacrificed two inches of height to Tony, but could jump higher. Tony could have played on the basketball team had he so chosen, so the guys were pretty evenly matched. Derrick played tennis on the University of Arizona team and kept himself in good shape. Emmy lacked the size and strength to guard Derrick, but LaRon kept the game close. Emmy knew enough about basketball to move to the rim when Tony and Derrick double-teamed LaRon. He managed to get her the ball, and she made a couple of easy layups.

She pointed a finger at Tony and Derrick after making one shot. "Yeah! Take that! You can't guard me because I'm so good."

Tony shook his head. "Check the score, Em. I think we're winning."

"Not for long. I was just letting you score," Emmy teased.

"Big talk from a little girl." Derrick picked her up and held her over his shoulder. "What should I do with her, Tony?"

Tony laughed. "I think you should smack her butt for taunting you like that."

"Don't you dare, Derrick Keasling!" Emmy screamed. "I'll tell Kenny if you do."

LaRon doubled over with laughter as he watched.

194

Kristen asked him, "Have you ever heard of Fridays At Five?"

"If you mean the band, sure. I've got their CDs."

"Yeah, the band. Emmy is Kenny Colwell's girlfriend."

"Get out. Are you putting me on?" LaRon looked over his shoulder as Emmy yelled.

"Put me down before I hurt you," Emmy warned Tony.

Kristen laughed. "No, they've been friends since she was a little girl and now they're... you know."

LaRon nodded his head as he read between the lines of Kristen's statement. *I guess he likes young girls.* "Do all you guys know him?" LaRon kept watching Emmy.

"Yeah," Kristen answered with pride.

"I read that he went to Roosevelt High, and everyone knows they are from SoHam."

While Kristen and LaRon talked, Derrick and Tony took turns carrying Emmy around and teasing her. Finally Tony set Emmy down so they could finish the game.

Tony took a pass from Derrick and hit a a shot from the free throw line. "Yeah! That's game. We win."

Tony and Derrick high-fived and then shook hands with LaRon.

Tony grinned at Emmy. "What were you saying before?"

She responded by sticking out her tongue at the guys and then turning to LaRon. "I'm sorry we lost. You deserve a better teammate than me."

"It's all right. I nearly busted my gut watching those guys carry you around. Hey, Kristen told me that you're dating Kenny Colwell. Is that for real?"

"Yeah, but he's on tour a lot of the time. I might be able to join him after I graduate."

"Are you going to Crest Ridge now, and I just haven't seen you?"

"No, I meant from college. I'm older than I look. I graduated from Roosevelt, and I work full-time and take classes at Paul Frank."

Emmy didn't say anything about living alone, and LaRon

195

assumed that Kristen must be her roommate in the apartment.

"Are you gonna make that pizza now?" Derrick asked as he dribbled the ball.

"I'll go throw it in the oven," Kristen said.

Everyone else stood around and shot baskets as they talked. LaRon listened for a time, but needed to get home so he told everyone goodbye and hopped the fence. Emmy and the guys went into the apartment. Emmy wanted to check on the pizza.

"Did you remember to turn the oven on and let it warm up, Kristen?"

Kristen gave Emmy a dirty look. "I may be blonde, but I'm not illiterate. The pizza will be ready in five more minutes."

Emmy opened her arms wide. "This is the first time I've had a kitchen big enough for two people to work in it at the same time."

The pizza disappeared only seconds after it came out of the oven. Emmy and Kristen each managed to grab a slice before Tony and Derrick inhaled the rest of it.

"Thanks for helping today, Tony. It was fun playing ball, too."

"You're welcome, Em. Say hi to Kenny for me, okay?" He glanced at the clock on the kitchen wall. "I gotta run."

"You don't have to leave," Emmy said.

"Yeah, I do. Thanks for the pizza, Em. See you guys later," he said to Derrick and Kristen as he ran down the stairs.

"Where's he going? I thought we could hang out and maybe play a board game." Emmy closed the door. "Does he have a hot date or something?"

"He's going to see Nikki," Kristen revealed. "He told me they had an argument about her seeing other guys."

"No wonder he was in such a hurry to leave."

Kristen leaned against the counter. "He told me since they will be going to different colleges, she wants to date other guys. That upset Tony so he's going to try to talk her out of it."

"Maybe Tony should let her go and start going out with friends. Just casual dates." Emmy washed the pizza cutter and set it on the counter to dry. "Face it. When he gets to Notre Dame, he won't have much time for socializing. He'll be busy with football."

"You're probably right," Kristen agreed.

Derrick and Kristen hung around. Derrick made himself at home by turning on some music and plopping down on the couch while Emmy and Kristen talked in the kitchen.

"Hey, Emmy," he hollered.

She stepped out of the kitchen. "Yeah, what? If you want something to drink, you have to get it yourself. I'm not waiting on you."

"Nah, it's not that. I just wanted to make sure you aren't mad at me for carrying you around."

"Oh, you would know if I was upset with you. At least your hand didn't end up on my butt." Emmy grinned. "At least not all of the time."

"I wonder what LaRon thought about the way Tony and I teased you. Do you think you'll see him again?"

"I suppose so since he lives next door." Emmy turned up the Bose system. "I love this song."

"What's the name?" Derrick asked as he stood up and began dancing with Emmy.

"It's 'In a Moment' and it's great for slow dancing." Emmy allowed Derrick to hold her close.

"What are you guys doing?" Kristen stood in the doorway with her hands on her hips.

Derrick grinned. "Just showing Emmy how good I am at dancing."

"Well, stop it. You're all sweaty from playing ball." *And you shouldn't be dancing that close to Emmy.*

"It's all right, Krissy. I don't get many chances to dance with Kenny gone."

Hmmm. I think you might have an opportunity real quick. Kristen smiled.

Chapter Twenty-One

Kristen saw Tony at his house on Tuesday evening. "Thank you for helping Emmy move her stuff."

"No problem. I actually had a good time."

"I think Emmy was happy to see you."

"Did she say anything about me after I left?" Tony asked as he searched through the pantry for something to eat.

"Maybe I shouldn't tell you, but she let it slip that since Kenny is gone, she might be willing to hang out with you as a friend. Are you and Nikki still dating? Were you able to patch up your differences?"

"Not really. She broke up with me. I didn't want her to see other guys. At least not until the fall. Now we're not going out at all. She's going to the prom with Randy Braun."

"So I heard."

"Then why did you ask?" He frowned at her as he opened a jar of honey roasted peanuts.

"Christopher called me at lunch today. He told me about Randy and Nikki. I'm sorry. I know you really liked her."

"Are you and Christopher seeing each other again?" Tony asked while chewing a mouthful of peanuts.

"Gross! Do you have to talk with your mouth full?"

"Sorry." He took a few seconds to chew before continuing, "Kristen, I know you have something on your mind. I know how devious you can be. What are you thinking about?"

"You haven't said anything about a new date for the prom, and I know you have your tux. Why don't you see if Emmy is busy Saturday night? She might be willing to go with you again."

They sat down at the kitchen table.

We were dating last year. I don't think she would go with me now. "I'll think about it."

"Are you thinking of asking someone else?" Kristen held out her hands, and Tony dumped some peanuts into them.

"I know two girls that don't have dates, and I was thinking I might ask one of them."

"Why not both? You could handle two dates, right?"

Kristen teased. "Are they cute?"

"I never thought of that," he teased right back. "I could handle both of them."

"You're a dork." She popped another peanut into her mouth. "Why isn't the school having the prom at The Regency Hotel like the year we went together?" Kristen asked.

"Probably because of the fire that gutted the place a week later. That's my guess, anyway."

"I forgot about that." Kristen smacked Tony's arm for being sarcastic to her.

"Ow!" Tony winced as he pretended Kristen hurt his arm. "Well, Mr. Barclay offered the use of the country club for free. Does that explain it?"

"Give Emmy a call. Do you have her number?"

"No. She never gave me the number to her new place."

"Write this down." Kristen gave Tony the new number.

"Okay, if she doesn't want to go, will you? I did you a favor and took you to the prom."

Kristen shook her head. "No, I'm busy that night."

"No, you're not. I'll call Emmy and ask her, but if she refuses, which she probably will, then you have to go with me. It's too late to find anyone else."

"The only reason I asked you to take me to the prom was because the guys who asked me included a certain expectation."

"Yeah, I remember." He laughed. "They all wanted you to spend the night with them."

"Well, do you blame me for not accepting their offers?" Kristen popped more peanuts into her mouth. "It's not like I wanted to go to prom with my least favorite cousin. You should have taken Emmy that year."

"I thought she wanted Derrick to take her. Wasn't that around the time they dated?"

"They weren't 'dating' like you're thinking," Kristen reminded him. "They did things together as friends. He brought her to a football game with all the rest of us and they went hiking."

"Those sound like fun dates to me." Tony crunched on more peanuts.

"Yeah, but you're a jock. You don't have a romantic bone in your body."

"So I've been told."

"What did Nikki say?" Kristen put her elbows on the table and leaned closer to Tony. *I want to hear all about it.*

"She complained that I'm more interested in football than her."

"True. Did she want you to promise her something special after the prom?" Kristen grinned.

Tony stared at her for a few seconds. "She sorta mentioned something like that."

"And you turned her down. Most guys would jump at the chance."

"I'm not most guys," Tony asserted.

"Mama would be proud of you."

"So what about Emmy and Derrick?" Tony walked over to the fridge and grabbed two Cokes.

"Yeah, she kinda did want to go with Derrick, but he and Clarissa Morgan went together. They actually dated that year—romantic dates."

"So, will you go with me or not?"

"Fine. But she will say yes. I just know it. Call her right away. That's an order."

"Yes, sir, General Keasling!" Tony stood at attention and saluted.

"Don't be such a doofus."

Within twenty minutes, Tony had worked up the courage to call.

"All right! I'll call her, Kristen. Quit buggin' me." Tony walked into Mama's sewing room to make the call in private.

Emmy answered even though the caller ID showed the call came from Tony's house.

"Hello, Mama. Are you all right?"

"Hi, Emmy, it's me."

"Hey, Tony, how are you? Thanks again for all your help yesterday. Is Mama okay?"

"I had fun helping you, and Mama's fine." He waited a few

seconds and then asked, "Would you be interested in dressing up and hanging out with a bunch of high school kids this Saturday?"

"Why on earth would I want to do that?" She laughed. "You know I'm too busy to be hanging out with immature high school kids... except for you, I mean. You're the only immature high school kid I would consider hanging out with."

"That's kinda what I thought you'd say."

She thought about his request. "Wait a minute. Tony Bertucci, are you asking me to the prom?"

"Yeah, would you be interested in going with me?"

"When is it?"

"This Saturday."

"This coming Saturday?" Emmy's voice rose in pitch. "Like four days from now?"

"Yeah! How about it?"

"I would love to go, but I've already got plans for that night. Sorry, Tony."

He glared at Kristen. *Yeah, I'm gonna shoot you for even suggesting this.* "What are you doing that night, Em?"

"Well, I bought a bunch of new underwear and socks and pantyhose and stuff, and I need to rearrange my underwear drawer and toss some old stuff," Emmy said without giggling.

Kristen stood in the doorway and eavesdropped. She whispered, "Did she use that excuse about her underwear drawer again? She's such a stinker."

"Oh, I guess that has to be done." He started to hang up until Emmy started laughing. "I guess I will have to take Kristen, after all."

"What? You weren't buying the underwear drawer excuse at all, were you?" Emmy asked.

"Not for a second. Do I look blonde to you?" He waved at Kristen and whispered, "Go away."

Emmy bit her lip. "Maybe I could go with you."

"Does that mean you'll put off rearranging your underwear for one night?"

"I suppose I'll have to just to keep Kristen away from you. Why aren't you going with Nikki?"

201

"We had a fight, and now she's going with Randy Braun."

"Aren't you going to tell her more than that?" Kristen sat in Mama's rocking chair. She could hear Emmy's side of the conversation now.

"I already rented a tux, and Mama told me she would pay for your dress."

"That's very kind of Mama, but I don't need a dress."

"Why? Do you already have a prom dress? Did you keep the one you wore last year?"

"No, I mean yes I kept it, but I'm going to wear my old jeans and a t-shirt. You still think I'm a tomboy anyway, so I'll dress like one."

"I must be blonde after all," Tony said. "Is that a yes?"

"Okay, I'll go with you as a friend as long as Kenny doesn't mind," she said and then giggled, "Are we gonna go somewhere afterward and fool around?"

Kristen glared at the phone and then at Tony. *Don't even think about it.*

He almost dropped the phone. "I didn't think about that..."

"I'm kidding! Do you really think... Oh, never mind. It might be fun, and you are a pretty good dancer... for a jock," she teased. "I'm going to hang up so I can call Kenny. Later."

"Later, Em." Tony hung up and stood in front of Kristen. "If you weren't my favorite cousin, I would think very seriously about never talking to you again. Couldn't you let me talk to her in private?"

"Why? You would tell me what she said anyway. Or she would. Regardless, I would know everything." Kristen grinned, stood up and kissed Tony's cheek.

As soon as Emmy hung up, she called Kenny, hoping to catch him before he and the band went on stage.

He answered after two rings and said, "Hey, Em, I've been thinking about you. How are you?"

"I'm fine, but I miss you already. I have a couple things to tell you. Do you have time?"

"I always have time for you. Did you have a fight with your parents about spending the night in the carriage house?"

"No, not them, but I caught some grief from Kristen about it. She knew I spent the night with you, and I sorta gave her the impression that we slept together."

"Why did you do that?" Kenny asked as he scratched his two-day-old beard.

"I'm not sure. I think because I was kinda upset that she asked."

"But you guys tell each other everything. She told you about Ryan and expects you to tell her about us."

"I know, and I felt rotten about it and told her the truth later."

"Good. What's the other thing, Em?"

"Tony called and asked me to the prom this Saturday, I guess his other date had a fight with him and blew him off. Would you mind if I went with him, as a favor for a friend?"

"Of course not. You need to get out and have fun." *I wonder if he still has feelings for you?*

"Are you sure you don't mind?" *Why can't you act all jealous and tell me that I can't go?*

"Emmy, if you don't want to go, just say so. You can't use me for an excuse."

"It's not that I don't want to go. I don't want anyone to think that Tony and I are back together."

"I don't expect you to stay home by yourself every night while I'm gone. You should go out once in a while." Kenny checked the time. *I really can't talk about this now, Em.*

"I'll go with Tony to the prom, but I'm not gonna start dating guys every week. I have enough stuff to keep me busy."

"That's good to know. I love you, Em. I'll talk to you later. Call me and tell me about the prom when you have a chance."

"I will, and I love you, too. Come home soon."

Emmy scrambled and, with help from Kristen, managed to find a dress. Mama even helped alter the dress to make it fit better, but Emmy wouldn't let Mama pay one red cent to help her with the purchase. Kristen was with Emmy when Tony arrived to pick her up on Saturday.

203

"Come on in, Tony. Emmy will be ready in a few minutes."

"I know I'm a little early. I brought some clothes for tomorrow, like you told me to, in case I have to stay here tonight. Here's the corsage thing."

"Hang on to the corsage. I'll put your clothes in the spare room. Have a seat, young man. I need to have a serious talk with you. I'll be right back."

"What?" Tony tilted his head. *Why are you acting like Emmy's mom or something?*

Kristen returned and pointed a finger at him. "Just because you are taking my little Emmy to the prom does not mean you can stay out all night, and it certainly does not give you the right to take advantage of her innocence either tonight or tomorrow. I know how a high school jock's mind works. You think you're hot stuff. Well, I know all your tricks and believe me, buster, you will pay dearly if you even lay a hand on her. Do you understand me or is your brain totally drained?"

Tony looked at Kristen with a dazed and confused expression.

"Well? Do you have anything to say for yourself, Mister Big Shot High School Jock?"

"Well... since I can't take advantage of Emmy, can I with you?" Tony ducked as Kristen threw one magazine at him and picked up another one. "I'm just kidding, Krissy. Don't throw anything else." He stood up ready to dodge out of the way.

"How could you ask such a thing, Tony, even if you're kidding?" Kristen moved closer to him.

"I figured as long as you were teasing me, I would tease you back."

"Who says I'm kidding? I am dead serious. You had better not try to fool around with Emmy. I know you guys broke up because you wouldn't do anything, but now is not the time to change that." Kristen poked Tony in the chest hard enough for him to lose his balance.

"All right! Geez, Kristen."

Just then Emmy walked out to the living room. "What are you guys arguing about?"

Kristen turned to look at Emmy. Tony's mouth opened. Kristen stopped breathing. Tony took a step forward as Kristen dropped the other magazine. Tony slipped on the magazine. The corsage flew into the air, and Emmy caught it.

"What's the matter with you guys? Never seen a girl in a dress before?"

"Emmy! You look... you look..."

Tony managed to speak. "Yeah. You sure do look..."

"Will you two knock it off. It's just a dress and you had better not try to look down it, mister. I feel half-naked in this thing. And this new bra doesn't feel right. Now put this corsage thing on me and don't stick the pin in me."

Kristen recovered and took the corsage from Emmy. "Nice catch, Em."

Tony was still staring at Emmy as Kristen pinned the corsage on Emmy. "I guess you guys are ready to go."

In the car on the way to the country club, Emmy asked Tony, "What was Kristen telling you? I heard something about taking advantage of me."

"She told me to behave."

"Tony! Tell me, please," Emmy said more authoritatively than normal as she glared at him.

Tony glanced over at her, then turned his eyes back to the road. "Kristen wanted to make sure I knew we couldn't have sex just because we're going to the prom."

"Darn it! Kristen is always spoiling my fun." Emmy grinned. "I figured we would spend a little time at the prom, then leave and..."

"I'm not blonde, Em. I know you're kidding. You already teased me about that."

They had a fantastic time dancing and socializing with friends at the prom. Tony treated her like a "girl" and not one of the guys. He brought her punch to drink and a small plate of appetizers when she got hungry. He even brought her dessert. He spent some of his time eating, too.

Tony didn't mention to Emmy that he had been nominated for prom king, or that Nikki had been nominated for prom queen.

205

The voting took place the previous week and the results kept secret.

Shortly after ten o'clock, the DJ stopped the music. Mr. Culbertson, the senior class faculty sponsor, walked out onto the stage.

"It is my job to announce this year's king and queen."

"Go for it, Mr. Culbertson!" someone yelled.

"I have the results here." He held up an envelope. "This year's prom king is... Tony Bertucci."

Emmy squealed as she heard Tony's name announced. He smiled at her, then turned to walk toward the stage. Several of his football buddies whistled and those close enough slapped him on the back. Tony walked up the steps and received his crown.

Mr. Culbertson smiled at Tony. "Now for the important announcement."

Tony shuffled his weight from one foot to the other as he waited.

"Your prom queen is... Miss Nikki Foster!" Mr. Culbertson shouted into the microphone. The DJ played some music as Nikki walked onto the stage. She sat on her throne as she received her crown and a bouquet of red roses. A photographer took several pictures of Tony and Nikki, before their dance. Tony held Nikki's hand as they walked down the steps and into the center of the dance floor.

"Congratulations, Nikki," Tony said.

Nikki managed to smile for the camera. "Thanks, Tony. I'm sorry if this feels awkward to you."

After thirty minutes, Tony returned to Emmy.

"I'm so happy for you, Tony."

"Thanks, Em. I hope it didn't bother you."

"Not at all. She looks beautiful in that dress. I could never wear one without some kind of straps to hold it up, but she's built differently." Emmy adjusted the thin spaghetti straps of her dress as Tony watched. "Stop looking at me like that."

"Sorry, Em, I didn't see anything."

Emmy grinned. *Compared to Nikki, I don't have anything to see.*

When Tony and Emmy got back to her apartment, Kristen was asleep on the couch. She woke up when Emmy touched her shoulder.

"Wake up, Kristen. We're home. You'll never guess who was elected king and queen."

Kristen opened her eyes slowly. "What time is it?"

"It's a little after two."

This woke Kristen up instantly. "Two o'clock! Where have you been with my little Emmy? You better not have tried anything or else I'll... I'll... I'll do something and you won't like it."

They laughed. Emmy sat next to Kristen. "The kids elected Tony and Nikki king and queen. I've got pictures of them dancing together. Tony, tell Kristen about prom while I get out of this dress. Will you unzip it for me?"

She directed the question at Kristen, but Tony unzipped her dress and Emmy ran into her bedroom. Tony sat beside Kristen and gave her a running account of the prom, as best he could remember. Emmy came back in a few minutes in a t-shirt and a pair of old shorts from gym class.

Kristen grinned and said, "Now you look like the Emmy we know and love."

"Can I change, too?" Tony asked.

"Go ahead, your stuff is in the spare bedroom." Kristen pointed in that direction as Emmy stared at her. "I told him to bring extra clothes in case you got home real late. Like you did."

Emmy sat down with Kristen, and they talked about everything that happened from Emmy's perspective this time. Tony came back into the living room after he changed out of his tux. They talked for another hour until they got too sleepy to stay awake. Now Emmy wondered if this was why Kristen made sure she had a bed for the spare room right away—so Tony could sleep there tonight.

Tony told Kristen, "I need to go to bed, or else I will fall asleep right here."

"Okay. Thanks for taking Em tonight. She needed to have some fun."

Kristen kissed his cheek. He looked at Emmy not sure if he

should kiss her or not.

She settled the matter by saying, "Thanks for thinking of me. I had a good time tonight. I'll see you in the morning," and then headed to her room.

Tony went into the other bedroom a couple of minutes later. Kristen sat on the couch and thought about how to get Tony and Emmy back together. She said out loud to the picture of Emmy and Kenny on the end table next to the couch, "I introduced them, so it's my responsibility to find a way to get them back together. Sorry, Kenny, but that's how I feel."

Tony's graduation ceremony from Roosevelt High was in the morning on Saturday, June fifth. He finished in the top ten of his class academically and won several awards, including the one for the best athlete. Emmy attended the ceremony with Mama, Heather and Kristen. Mama threw a "small" party for Tony at home that afternoon. Emmy helped Mama prepare enough food to feed a small nation's army.

Later, Emmy told Mama, "None of the food has gone to waste."

"Emmy, dear, you're wrong, all of it has gone to waist. W-A-I-S-T that is."

Emmy laughed with Mama at her joke. "That was weak, Mama. I mean w-e-a-k."

Mama pretended to scold Emmy. "Are you critiquing my jokes now, little one?"

"No, Mama. I'll take these sandwiches out back." Emmy scooted out of the kitchen.

Tony was going to have some free time this summer, and he planned to take advantage of that. He sat beside her in the backyard. "Mama, where do you want to go for a vacation? I will take you anywhere you want to go, as long as we can drive because I can't afford plane tickets for four people."

"Four people? Are Heather and Marco coming along?" Mama asked as she watched some of the kids, including Emmy, playing catch with a football.

"Actually, I thought Emmy and Kristen could go with us."

"Let me think about it, and we will figure something out."

Later, Tony talked to Emmy and said, "I have some time off this summer until football practice starts, and I thought about going on vacation somewhere with Mama. Would you and Kristen like to come with me?"

Emmy set her plate of food down and looked up at him. "I can't go on vacation with you. What would Kenny think if I did that? You should definitely take Mama on vacation though. She works hard all year long. She deserves a vacation. You could take Kristen if you want, but they've probably got plans already."

Tony mentally castigated himself for getting his hopes up because of taking Emmy to the prom.

"It's about time you got here. What have you been doing lately?" Kristen asked as Emmy walked into the living room at the Bertucci home on Friday after work.

"Working like a dog. It's been a rough week. I spend all day at the office, and I never have time to see my friends except for you guys."

"We wouldn't see you either if Mama hadn't convinced you to come over for dinner."

Emmy paused, but then joined Kristen on the couch. Tony had been trying to read a book but now gave up and set it down.

"Hey, Em. How's Kenny doing?"

"He's doing great. We email each other every day, and, since he bought me a cell phone, I can talk to him more often. Have you been seeing anyone?"

"Just you two. Are things really going great between you guys?"

"As good as it can be considering he's away on tour. I know it's never going to be easy to maintain our relationship, but we're working at it."

Tony smiled at Emmy. "Did I mention how much fun I had dancing with you at the prom?"

"You have reminded me a few times."

"You didn't let me kiss you though."

"And I'm not going to let you now, either. You need to find

209

a girlfriend because you're horny all the time."

Just then Mama Bertucci walked into the room. "I heard that. Dinner is about ready. I hope you are hungry because I made lots of spaghetti."

"Yes, Mama, we know. It smells delicious," Kristen said.

"It's so good to see you, Emmy. You should come over more often. Tony would like that."

Emmy was embarrassed and answered, "Mama, we're not really dating. We're just friends. I'm certainly not thinking about anyone except Kenny—especially not him." She poked Tony in the chest. Then she ran out of the room and into the kitchen.

Tony followed. "You look very pretty in that dress."

"Thank you, Tony. I came straight from work."

He surprised her with a quick kiss. Kristen happened to see the kiss.

"Stop that! Why did you kiss me? I told you not to." Emmy pushed him away.

"Sorry, I lost my head for a second."

She left the kitchen totally embarrassed and walked to the living room. Kristen grinned at Tony. "I think she liked that kiss."

"No, I think I embarrassed her and ticked her off. She loves Kenny, and you aren't going to change that."

"Maybe, but he's not here, and you are. You should ask her out sometime. Take her to dinner."

Tony shook his head. "I don't want to do anything to hurt her relationship with Kenny. I think they are really serious about each other."

"I sure hope they are after she spent the night with him again," Kristen said and then covered her mouth. She looked at Tony with wide eyes after divulging that information.

"It's okay, Kristen."

"I shouldn't have said anything. Please don't tell her I did."

"I won't ever mention it if you don't ever tell her anything you know about Nikki and me."

"I promise I won't ever tell anyone." *Emmy would be so disappointed if she knew.*

Chapter Twenty-Two

"I made a cold spaghetti salad for dinner. I had one chicken breast leftover from last night, so I added that. I hope it's enough." Emmy opened the fridge and pulled out a large bowl as she and Kristen were ready to eat after work on Friday the eighteenth of June.

"Sounds good to me. I'm not real hungry," Kristen said as she searched the fridge looking for something to drink. "Why did you have an extra chicken breast?" She wondered if maybe Emmy had invited Tony over for dinner.

"There were two in the package, so I cooked them both." Emmy looked at Kristen and added, "I didn't have anyone over in case that's what you're thinking."

"You could ask Tony over for dinner sometime."

"Yeah, maybe."

They had dinner, and then went for a walk around the neighborhood. Emmy asked, "What is Derrick up to these days? Is he going to be here all summer, or is he going on vacation somewhere exciting?"

"He's not going back to Arizona until classes start. He's still going out with Amber. Do you remember her from the party?"

"I remember her. She's very pretty, but I don't think she liked me being friends with Derrick."

"Oh, yeah, she's pretty all right."

"What do you mean by that?" Emmy asked.

"You'll understand if you get to know her better."

They were walking past the elementary school down the street when Kristen stopped.

"Emmy, how many other boyfriends do you have right now beside your lovers Kenny and Tony? Three, four, five? Tell me, how many?"

Where did that come from? Emmy turned around to face Kristen. "Kristen Lynn Keasling, you know very well that I am in love with Kenny and don't have any other boyfriends. And FYI, Tony and I are not lovers."

"I'm teasing you about the other boyfriends, but didn't

211

know if you and Tony have been getting serious about each other again. I guess I've been wondering if you had... you know... and you were afraid to tell me."

"You know I would tell you if Tony and I did that, don't you? I mean Kenny."

Kristen wondered. *Would you really? I'm beginning to believe that you wouldn't, and if you aren't going to share, then I won't either.*

Emmy wanted to steer the conversation in a different direction, so she asked Kristen, "Do you like that boy you talked to at Darby's the last time we ate there? He was cute."

"Uhhh, so-so," Kristen motioned back and forth with her hands, "but my new boyfriend is even better looking." *Oh, I shouldn't have let that slip.*

"What new boyfriend?" Emmy asked as she grabbed Kristen's shoulders. "Just when were you going to mention this? Are you keeping secrets from me now, Krissy?"

"I met him at the end of last semester, and we hit it off right away."

"You haven't said a word about that. Does he have a name or is that classified?"

"Harrison. His name is Harrison Stewart and don't ever call him Harry. I called him that once, and he let me know that he did not tolerate being called that—not even as a kid."

"He sounds kinda... never mind. I'm happy for you. Now give me all the juicy details." Emmy suppressed a giggle. *If I ever meet him, I'm going to call him Harry.*

"We met in the library. I dropped a book. He happened to be standing there, and he picked it up for me."

"Are you kidding me, Kristen? That never happens in real life, just in those old movies."

"Would it sound better if I tell you we met at a bar, and he bought me enough drinks to get me drunk?"

Emmy thought about it. "That's more believable, but stick with the library story."

Kristen laughed. "Well, that's how it really happened. He picked up my book, noticed what I was studying, and we started talking. He is a graduate student working on his master's degree in education."

"How old is he?"

"He's fifty-six or fifty-seven. I can't remember for sure," Kristen said.

"It's about time he finished his masters. Does he have any grandsons I could date?" Emmy asked with a straight face.

"Okay, so he's not in his fifties. He's twenty-two, and he lives in an apartment off-campus with two other guys. Before you even ask, we have not slept together. You know *I* would tell you if *I* had done that." Kristen tapped her chest with her thumb.

"I wasn't going to ask that." Emmy looked hurt that Kristen would even think such a thing, even though Kristen was exactly right.

"Don't even give me that look. I know you too well, Emily Colasanti. I know how your mind works."

Emmy smiled at Kristen, "What else is going on? I can tell you've got something else you want to tell me."

"Maybe later."

"You can tell me."

"I really do have something on my mind and want to talk to you about it, but not right now. Maybe later. Derrick asked about you."

They kept walking. Kristen's attention wandered to another place. She was not listening, so Emmy said, "Kenny and I decided not to wait until we get married. In fact I'm pregnant already."

This didn't get a reaction from Kristen.

"I've been having sex with Kenny, and I'm pregnant," Emmy repeated.

Kristen muttered, "That's nice."

Emmy grabbed Kristen's shoulders. "Okay, spill it! What's bothering you, Kristen."

"Huh? What? I didn't hear you."

"What's bothering you?" Emmy said slowly.

"I'm sorry, but I have been thinking of ways to get you and Tony back together. I know how much you like Kenny, but he's always gone."

213

Emmy grabbed Kristen's arm. "I love Kenny."

Kristen looked into Emmy's eyes for a moment before she looked away. "I know, and I shouldn't interfere. I'm sorry. I don't want to run your life like your mother does."

"I won't hate on you for that."

They headed back to her apartment.

"What else do you want to do? You are gonna spend the night, right?" Emmy asked. "Wanna spend the whole weekend? We could do something else."

"I brought an overnight bag. I wanna do something together, Em."

When they got back to Emmy's apartment, they sat outside on the front steps and talked until they both got sleepy.

"I'm tired. Let's get ready for bed, and we can talk until we fall asleep."

"I'm ready to fall asleep now, Emmy."

"Just stay awake a little longer, please."

"I'll try."

"I haven't told anyone, but I checked into some scholarships at North Park. I haven't heard back, but if I receive enough scholarship money, maybe I can go there next semester."

"I'd love it if you could. Maybe we could be roomies. I'm not rooming with Marnie Karras again. She turned out to be a slut."

"Please don't say anything yet. I might not qualify."

"There's always..."

Emmy poked Kristen's arm. "I'm not using Kenny's money."

"If he was my boyfriend, I think I would."

"He's not your boyfriend, and I'm not letting him pay for my education."

They headed upstairs and eventually fell asleep on Emmy's bed still dressed in their jeans and t-shirts. Emmy woke up during the night and undressed. She put on one of Tony's football jerseys that he gave her when they were dating and slept in the spare room for the rest of the night. Kristen slept throughout the night without waking up at all.

214

Saturday morning arrived; Emmy woke up before Kristen. She still had on Tony's long navy blue jersey. It looked like a dress on her because of its length. Emmy walked out to the kitchen, turned on the coffee machine and dropped two slices of bread into the toaster. She opened up the living room curtains to look outside at the beautiful sunny day and raised some windows to let in the fresh air. She turned on the radio to listen to her favorite morning show, "The Marty and Kerry Morning Drive." Kristen woke up after she smelled the coffee.

"Kristen, I made some coffee. Do you want some? I'm gonna make some scrambled eggs and bacon. I'm hungry this morning."

"I'll take some, too."

Emmy and Kristen were sitting at the kitchen table, laughing about a joke they heard on the radio, when Barry Newton pulled into her driveway in his newest old car. Emmy couldn't see Barry's car from the kitchen and didn't realize he was there until she heard the doorbell buzz. She walked out to the living room and saw his car.

"Oh, shoot! I forgot that Barry and Linda were coming over today. We're supposed to go hiking. He wants to check out Josh Delane State Park. I'll be right back."

"Hey! At least put on some shorts," Kristen yelled. "Where is it? I never heard of it."

"Not sure, but Barry knows." Emmy ran into her bedroom. Kristen heard her open a drawer, then slam it shut. A few seconds later Emmy returned hopping on one foot as she struggled with a pair of old gym shorts. She managed to get them on before she opened the door and flew down the stairs. She opened the porch door. "Hey, guys, come on in."

They followed her up the stairs.

Barry asked, "Where's Tony? Isn't he going with us? I hoped we could use his car. You did remember to ask him, didn't you, Emmy?"

Kristen looked at Emmy with a puzzled expression. "Did you ask Tony for a date?"

"It's not like that, Kristen. I know he likes to go hiking, so I

215

thought he might like to get some fresh air. It wasn't going to be a date."

"Yeah, right. I totally understand," Kristen teased as she smiled.

Emmy gave Kristen a dirty look and stuck out her tongue. "Tony is taking Mama to visit family today, so he can't go. Uncle Vincent is in the hospital, and they're going to see him."

"Mom didn't tell me Uncle Vincent was in the hospital," Kristen said. "I hope it's not his heart again."

"Then Mama was going to his house to cook enough food to last a month, as usual. Tony said he might stop over this evening if he can." She looked at Barry. "I'm sorry, but I totally forgot you guys were coming over this morning. It's a good thing you didn't get here sooner, or you would have caught us in bed."

Barry looked at Emmy with surprise.

"I didn't mean like that, Barry. You've got a dirty mind. I meant that we just got up a few minutes ago." Emmy smacked his elbow. "Sit down and have some breakfast with us."

Barry and Linda ate breakfast with them as she and Kristen had some more coffee.

"Kristen, would you like to come along? I know it will be hard to spend the whole day with Barry, but he will be pestering Linda most of the time."

"That sounds like fun even with Barry along, but I need to shower first before we go."

"I do, too," Emmy replied.

Kristen wanted to shower first, so Emmy grabbed a clean towel for her. Emmy waited with Barry and Linda while Kristen showered and got ready. When it was her turn, Emmy spent too much time in the shower, so Barry knocked on the door.

"Hurry up. What are you doing in there anyway?"

"I'm almost done. Keep your pants on," Emmy hollered through the door.

"Barry! You should never ask a lady what she is doing in the bathroom. It's not cool," Linda scolded.

"I wasn't asking a lady, I was asking Emmy." He made sure he said it loud enough for her to hear.

216

Emmy finished getting dry and wrapped her towel around her. Her wet hair dripped down her back as she opened the door to find Barry standing in front of her.

"So I'm not a lady, huh?" She kicked him in the shin.

"Ow!" he exclaimed as he moved out of her way. "I've been waiting to use the bathroom. What took you so long?"

"I've been doing my makeup. If you have to go so bad, go outside and use a tree." Emmy laughed as she headed to her room.

Kristen slammed the door closed. "Emmy, I'm still getting dressed. Couldn't you have closed the door?"

"Sorry, Krissy, I forgot. I don't usually close it."

I hope you close it if Kenny is here, Kristen thought, and then added, "Why did you tell Barry you were putting on makeup? You hardly ever wear any makeup."

"He doesn't know that."

Barry returned to the living room. "Hurry and get dressed. I want to get there before dark."

"We won't take too long to get ready. Probably an hour or so."

Barry groaned loud enough for Emmy and Kristen to hear. They both giggled. Emmy found a tank top to wear, then grabbed a t-shirt to put over that.

"You're going to be too warm if you wear both layers, Em."

"I'll be all right."

It only took Emmy and Kristen fifteen minutes to get ready, but Barry complained the whole time.

"About time you're ready. It doesn't take Linda that long to get ready."

"Stuff a sock in it, Barry. It doesn't take Linda as long because her hair is styled differently. She's got short hair that dries instantly. We have long hair and it takes time to dry."

"Yeah, whatever. Can we go now?"

They piled into Barry's car for the trip to the state park. Barry and Linda sat in front; Emmy and Kristen squeezed into the backseat.

"This car is better than the first one you had, Barry, but could you buy one with a larger backseat next time?" She flicked her finger at the back of his head.

"Ow! Stop that. It runs a lot better, too. I still keep jumper cables in the back though, just in case."

Linda asked Emmy and Kristen about their relationship. "Have you guys been friends all your life? It seems that way. You're so close."

"We haven't really known each other all that long. Emmy has known Barry for a lot longer than she has known me—poor girl."

"What did you guys talk about all night?" Barry asked. "Sex, most likely."

"Quit being a pervert, Barry," Emmy warned.

"I'm sorry, Emmy. You know I like to tease you."

Linda frowned as her eyes narrowed. "Will you quit teasing Emmy about sex? Sometimes I think you like her better than me."

"Linda, you know I love you." Barry stopped suddenly as the light turned yellow.

"Yeah, but you also love Emmy," Linda said. "And you don't have to stop at yellow lights. You could get rear-ended."

"I don't love her the same way I love you, baby, and I knew there wasn't anyone behind me."

"You better not. You're lucky Tony knows you are harmless. If he thought you were serious about the way you talk to Emmy, he would flatten you like a tortilla shell." Linda assumed Emmy and Tony were still together.

They arrived at the state park. Barry parked next to a pickup truck, and he and Linda got out.

"Barry, there are only two cars in the entire parking lot and you had to park next to them. Why?" Linda waved her hands at the empty spaces.

"Sorry, just a habit. I like to park next to a vehicle in case I need a jump. Should I move the car?"

Linda walked away without answering.

Emmy jumped out of the back seat, threw her hands up and twirled around. "It's going to be such a sunny day. This is going to be such a blast."

"We're just going for a hike, Emmy. Chill out already."

Kristen laughed. "You get so excited about the simplest things sometimes."

Everybody was wearing shorts and t-shirts except for Emmy.

"Emmy, aren't you hot with that t-shirt over your tank top?" Barry asked.

"Not yet, but if it gets too hot later, I can take the t-shirt off to get cooler."

"Wouldn't you be cooler if you only had the tank top on?"

Linda gave Barry a dirty look.

"What?" Barry shrugged.

"Don't worry about whether or not Emmy is hot, okay."

"I love you, Linda."

"Knock it off. I'm still mad at you for last night."

Emmy and Kristen looked at each other and snickered.

"I guess Barry didn't get any last night," Emmy whispered.

"Emmy! I'm surprised at you."

"What? I know they have sex. They're living together."

They stuck together and hiked a couple of miles until they found a bench to stop and take a break. Barry and Emmy listened as the conversation between Kristen and Linda turned to the topic of men.

"I have never been with anyone other than Barry," Linda mentioned as she watched a squirrel scramble up the tree across from the bench.

Kristen said, "Oh, Linda, I'm so sorry. That must be awful."

The expression on Barry's face betrayed the fact that his pride and feelings were hurt.

"Kristen, what a terrible thing to say about Barry. He can't help it if he's the world's worst lover," Emmy teased. She hid behind a tree for a moment before returning to stand behind the bench.

Barry looked at Emmy and Kristen, "Ha! Ha! You guys are too funny."

Emmy tapped him on the arm. "You know we wouldn't tease you like this if we didn't love you, Barry."

"Yeah, I guess so."

Kristen teased Barry even more. "You really believe that? Barry, we don't even like you. We just keep you around because you have a car, and we don't have to pay for gas."

Emmy bit her lip. "I kissed Kenny when I was a kid and we..."

"What do you mean when you were a kid? You're still just a kid, Emmy," Barry teased back.

Emmy stuck out her tongue and made a face at Barry.

"Proves my point, I would say." He looked at Linda and Kristen and said, "Just a kid."

"You're gonna get it!" Emmy shook her fist at Barry, and he took off running. She chased him and caught him. They were both laughing and fell to the ground. She punched Barry lightly on his arm.

"Still a kid, huh? I'll show you." Emmy pushed Barry onto his back and straddled him. Barry laughed until his side hurt as Emmy pinned his arms to the ground and smiled at him.

"Are you gonna punch me in the stomach like you did when we were ten?"

"I probably should. You deserved it then and you do now."

Linda and Kristen strolled over to check on Barry.

"What are you doing to him, Emmy?" Kristen frowned.

"Help! Linda, save me," Barry hollered. "I'm being attacked by a crazy girl."

Linda smiled. "Do whatever you feel is right to punish him, Emmy. He certainly deserves it for teasing you."

Barry looked up at Linda. "Help me get away from her. I'm afraid she will hurt me."

"Serves you right if she does." Linda turned around and marched away.

Emmy and Barry got up and continued hiking—Linda and Kristen fell behind. Emmy and Barry could hear Linda and Kristen talking and giggling about something at first, but couldn't hear anything after another minute. After a while Emmy and Barry stopped and looked back up the trail.

"Maybe we should turn back because I don't see Kristen or Linda anywhere," Emmy said.

"Okay, we can head back, but first I want to give you a kiss. You never let me kiss you the first time I tried." Barry remembered Emmy's reaction when he tried to kiss her almost ten years ago.

"Yuck! No way!" Emmy grinned. "I remember that day, too."

Barry moved toward her. Emmy squealed and ran away. He chased her and caught her.

"We are so lucky to have found the perfect people to spend the rest of our lives with, Emmy."

"For once, I agree with you, Barry." She knew Barry loved Linda, but she didn't know whether he meant Kenny or Tony for her. "We should keep hiking."

They found Linda and Kristen after a couple of minutes. Linda ran up to Barry and kissed him.

"Oh, Barry, I love you. Where did you go?"

"I was talking to Emmy, and I love you, too, honey."

Kristen smiled at Emmy as they watched and listened to Barry and Linda.

Suddenly, Barry saw something out of the corner of his eye. "I'm hungry enough to eat a bear. Just like the one over there on the trail." He pointed to a large dog coming toward them.

"Barry, make it go away. You know I don't like big dogs like that." Linda hid behind him.

Barry waved his arms and yelled at the dog. "Shoo! Go away big bad bear."

The dog tilted it's head, as if trying to figure out what Barry was doing, and then turned around and trotted away.

"Oh, Barry, you are so brave. You're our hero," Emmy and Kristen teased. "We're hungry, too. Where should we go?"

"There's a Burrito King on the way back."

"Yeah, let's stop there. Is that all right with you, Linda?" Emmy asked.

"Sounds okay to me."

They stopped for a late lunch, and then headed back to town. Barry dropped Emmy and Kristen off at Emmy's apartment.

"See you guys later. We had fun today," Emmy said.

221

"Take care, Emmy. You might not see Barry for a while because I'm going to murder him for teasing you so much."

"Oh, please, don't do that. I would hate for you to get in trouble. I'm used to his teasing. He's been doing it for as long as I've known him."

"Thank you, Emmy." Barry sounded grateful.

Emmy giggled and then added, "On second thought... go ahead and murder him."

Barry and Linda left. Emmy and Kristen sat on the couch and talked while they waited for Tony.

"We have to do this again soon, Kristen. I told you it would be a blast. Do you want to stay for dinner?"

"Sure. What are you making?"

"I could make tuna noodle casserole or maybe some chicken breasts."

"How about the tuna casserole. I haven't had that lately."

"Have you ever had it? I can't picture your mother making it."

"Maybe not, but I want to try it. My hair is such a mess. The wind really tangled it up."

Emmy grabbed her ponytail. "That's why I did this."

Tony showed up around five.

"Tony's here. I'll let him in," Kristen told Emmy, who was busy in the kitchen.

"Hey, Kristen. How are you?" Tony asked as he hugged her. "Hi, Em." She didn't get a hug.

"How is Uncle Vincent doing?" Kristen asked.

"He's a lot better now. The doctor told him he could go home tomorrow. Did you guys have fun at the park today? I wish I could have gone with you, but Mama really needed to see her brother."

Kristen rang her fingers through her tangled hair. "It was fun even with Barry along. We teased him about sex and really embarrassed him. You should have seen how red he got. Even his freckles turned red. We teased Linda about how sorry we felt for her. Then we embarrassed Emmy by asking her about her love life."

222

"I told them I haven't done anything more than kiss, and they didn't want to believe me."

Tony smiled and didn't say a word. Kristen looked at him, and then back at Emmy. Kristen could tell that Emmy was blushing. Kristen frowned at them.

"Fine! If you don't want to tell me what you guys have been doing, that's just fine. I'm never telling you anything else about any boyfriend I might have, Emily Colasanti."

Kristen looked at Tony and smacked him on the arm.

"What was that for?"

"Just for being here, and whatever you did with Emmy that she's too embarrassed to talk about."

Tony and Emmy looked at each other. Tony knew he and Emmy hadn't done anything serious enough to make her blush. *What have you and Kenny been doing, Em?*

Chapter Twenty-Three

A few days later, Kristen called Emmy with an invitation. "My parents have rented a house outside of Aspen, Colorado, for practically the whole month of July. You gotta come with me. It will be boring if you aren't there."

"Oh, Kristen, I would love to go with you, but I'm pretty sure I'm gonna get laid off at work." Emmy opened the warm oven, slid in a Tombstone pizza and set the timer. "I won't have any money to spend on a trip to Colorado."

"Don't worry about the money. My parents will help you out," Kristen said.

"I know your parents have lots of money, but I don't want to take charity from them. I wouldn't feel right doing that." Emmy plopped down on a kitchen chair.

"You're just being stubborn. Derrick and Amber will be there." Kristen hoped the chance to see Derrick with his gorgeous girlfriend would entice her to come.

Emmy laughed. "I don't think Derrick will even notice I'm there if Amber is with him."

That didn't work like I thought, but you might be right. "I'm going to ask Barry and Linda and some other friends to join us."

"What about Harrison? Is he going?"

"I'm not sure about him. We had another fight, and I'm mad at him. Is Kenny going to be home in July at all?"

"Not in July, but he will be home in August for a week."

"Oh, too bad," Kristen said. *I have to get Emmy to come. I can pair her and Tony up again. I just know it.*

"Kristen, I can tell you are pleased Kenny won't be home," Emmy said. "You're still trying to get me and Tony back together."

"No, I'm not."

"Yes you are and don't bother trying to deny it. I can hear it in your voice."

"I'm sorry, Em. Tony might be coming. He has some free time this summer, but might not have any after he starts at Notre Dame. Might be your last chance to spend some quality time with him."

"You're still playing the matchmaker role. Is he bringing Nikki or another girl with him?"

"I'm not sure." *He better not be bringing a girlfriend with him.*

"How is everybody getting to Colorado?"

"Duh! We're flying. Why would we drive all that way?"

"I'll ask my parents." She glanced at the timer on the stove.

"Uh, Emmy, dear, you don't live with your parents or did you forget. You can make your own decisions."

"I know that." She opened the oven to check on the pizza. "But I might need them to watch the apartment for me while I'm gone. The O'Briens are going on vacation in the summer."

"Does that mean you'll go?"

"I'll let you know, Kristen."

"Seriously, you would ask your parents to keep an eye on your apartment?"

"No, I guess not. I know I wouldn't let my mother have my spare key."

After she finished talking to Kristen, Emmy waited for the timer to ding. She opened a Coke, checked the pizza and pulled it out. She rummaged through the utensil drawer and grabbed her pizza cutter. She cut the pizza, tossed two slices on a plate and sat down. She took a bite.

"Wow! That's hot." She took a drink of the cold pop, and then called Kenny.

"Hey, Em. It's good to hear from you."

"Kristen just called. Her parents have rented a place in Colorado for a whole month, and she asked me to go with her. I know you won't be home, but..." she paused.

"Wow! Colorado! You've never been there. Are you thinking about going? Can you get the time off work? Maybe a couple of weeks even?"

"I think I'm going to be laid off, so the time isn't the problem. I don't know if I can afford to go." She took another bite of pizza.

"Em..."

"No, don't even say anything about that." She talked with

225

her mouth full. "You know how I feel about taking money from you."

"Yes, and you know how I feel. I have enough money to last a lifetime. I can certainly afford to help you go on vacation."

She paused long enough to swallow her pizza. "Maybe I won't go to Colorado, and we can go somewhere in August when you're home."

He responded, "We can still do that even if you go to Colorado—especially if you are laid off."

"Kristen mentioned that Tony might be going. Would that bother you?"

"I don't think so. Should it?"

"Not really. We're friends now, and I think Barry and Linda are going. Derrick and his girlfriend are going. Tony might be bringing someone, too, so it's not like it would be just me and Tony."

"I wish you would let me help you, but I understand. I miss you, Em."

"I miss you, too. How have the shows been going?"

Kenny and Emmy talked for over an hour before he had to go. After she hung up with Kenny, she wrapped the leftover pizza in foil, stuck it in the fridge, and then called Tony.

"Hey, it's Emmy."

"Hi, Em. What's up?"

"Kristen invited me to go to Colorado with her. Have you heard anything about this trip?"

"Hang on a second, and I'll ask Mama." Tony asked Mama about the trip.

"I'm going," Mama quickly replied.

Tony looked quizzically at his mother. "You knew about this before, didn't you? Is that why you didn't want to make any other plans when I offered to take you on vacation?"

Mama smiled at Tony.

"You know you have to fly, don't you?"

"I'm not afraid of flying. Your Aunt Karla told me about the trip several weeks ago, and I agreed to go. I didn't want to say anything until I knew your summer schedule."

Tony got back on the phone with Emmy. "Mama has known about it for a few weeks. She's going, so I guess that means I'll be going, too. Do you think you can go, Em? I know you're worried about getting laid off."

"I have some money saved up, so I might be able to go if I can get some help from Grandma with the plane ticket. I'll talk to you later. I need to call Kristen back."

Emmy called Kristen and said, "I'll go if I get laid off and can get a plane ticket somehow."

"Mom and Dad are paying for all the plane tickets, so you are coming. I won't let you stay home because of your stubbornness. I need you to be there."

"But..." Emmy started to argue, but Kristen stopped her.

"Don't even think about arguing about it. Barry and Linda are coming for two weeks, and it's going to be such fun for all of us to be on vacation together."

"How big is this house your parents rented?" Emmy finished her Coke and grabbed another can from the fridge.

"The main house has two floors and six bedrooms and a whole bunch of bathrooms. There is another smaller house on the property where my parents and Mama will stay."

Emmy couldn't believe the Keaslings would be so generous but then remembered how they usually traveled to Europe in the summer, so Colorado must be cheaper for them.

As her shift was ending on Friday, Emmy got called into the office and laid off for at least six weeks, so she had the time to go to Colorado.

The phone rang as soon as Emmy stepped in the door. She thought it might be Kenny and answered. "Hey, Kenny, guess what?"

"This is your mother. What were you going to tell Kenny?"

"Oh, hi, Mom. It's nothing." She walked into the living room and plopped down on the couch. *This should teach me to screen my calls.*

"You made it sound like it was important. Why can't you tell your own mother?"

"Fine. I got laid off today." She held the phone away from her ear expecting her mother to yell.

"That's a shame. Do you know for how long? Do you think they'll ever call you back?"

"It's kinda hard to tell. I'm going to start looking for another job."

"Your father and I would help you if we could."

"I'm not taking any money from you, Mom."

Mom grunted. "I know that my mother is giving you money."

"And I'm keeping track of how much. I will pay her back one of these days," Emmy said with determination.

"Since you won't have to go to work, what are you planning to do? Are you gonna join Kenny wherever he is?"

"No, but Kristen invited me on vacation." Emmy explained everything. *I know you're going to tell me that I can't go.*

Mom shocked Emmy. "That sounds like a great time. You should go with her."

"Really?" Emmy's mouth opened wide. "You think I should go to Colorado?"

"It would be a chance to see the mountains. Your father and I have never been out there."

"I'll think about it," Emmy replied. *I wonder what you have up your sleeve. This is not at all what I thought you would say.*

Chapter Twenty-Four

July finally arrived, and Emmy packed for the trip to Aspen. There were eleven people in the group flying out to Denver. Mr. Keasling thought about renting cars in Denver and driving to Aspen but discovered it would make more sense to get a commuter flight right into Aspen and rent cars as needed.

Kristen fastened her seatbelt and looked at Emmy. "Is this your first time on a plane? You keep biting your lip."

"Does it show that much? Is it stamped on my forehead?"

"Don't worry, Em. I'll be with you all the way."

"That's good news. I was hoping you wouldn't parachute out somewhere over the mountains." Emmy tried to be funny to hide her nervousness.

Emmy closed her eyes and held onto Kristen during takeoff.

"You can let go now, Em. We're in the air."

"That's the scary part," Emmy said.

The two flights went smoothly, and they arrived in Aspen late Friday evening on the second of July. Mr. Keasling signed for the rental vehicles. As they drove to the property, Emmy gawked at the breathtaking beauty all around her.

"The mountains are amazing. I can even see snow on some of them."

Kristen teased, "Em, close your mouth and quit acting like a tourist. They are just mountains."

"I don't care if everyone knows I am a tourist." Emmy continued to stare out the window.

Kristen explained to Emmy, "Mom made arrangements for a part-time cook and maid while we're here. She doesn't want to have to cook or clean up after everybody while she is on vacation, but Mama told me she thinks it is a waste of money and that she can take care of everything."

"That sounds like Mama," Emmy said as she saw the house for the first time. "Wow! Awesome! It's like a huge log cabin."

"Maria Catarina, you are here to relax and enjoy yourself, not to work." Karla pointed a finger at her older sister as they

229

walked into the main house.

Emmy smiled. *I can't believe it. Someone actually called Mama by her real name. Karla is actually telling Mama what she can and can't do. I never thought I'd see the day.*

Mama didn't say anything. *I may be on vacation, but that doesn't mean I can't help out.*

The kids checked out the huge main house.

"Kristen, come with me. I want to see the upstairs and pick out our room."

"Slow down, Em. We get first choice of rooms, so relax."

"Why do we get first choice?"

Kristen grinned. "Because I'm Daddy's princess and spoiled rotten."

"Must be nice." Emmy laughed.

Kristen's father got everyone's attention. "You may think I'm old-fashioned, but I don't care. I don't care what arrangements you have back home, but while you're staying here these are the rules. First, no unmarried couples can share a room." He noticed Kristen staring at him with her arms crossed over her chest.

"Oh, Daddy!" she sighed.

"Second... second... I don't have any other rule, except maybe this—don't get drunk."

Kristen thought her father meant Harrison so she said, "We're not going to share a room and none of us are really into drinking, except Emmy. She's always got a beer in her hand."

Tony and Derrick looked at Kristen and shook their heads.

Mr. Keasling thought about the graduation party where he saw Emmy holding a beer. *I didn't think she drank.* He glanced at Emmy. *She wouldn't lie to me. I think you're trying to pull a fast one, Kristen.*

Tony pulled Kristen aside later and reminded her, "You know her father is an alcoholic. You shouldn't have said that."

"Oh, crap! I wasn't thinking about her father. Is she upset?"

"I don't think so, but you should say something to her."

"I will later."

Most of the bedrooms had two beds. Tony and Derrick picked out a room, and Barry and Harrison found one to share.

230

Kristen and Harrison had made peace with one another, at least for this trip. Emmy and Kristen claimed the one with the best view of the mountains even though it was the smallest bedroom.

Emmy bounced on the king-size bed. "Kristen, look out the window."

"I admit it is quite a view, Em. Which side of the bed do you want?"

"It really doesn't matter to me."

"Then I'll take this side." Kristen knew it wouldn't matter because Emmy would roam all over the bed in her sleep.

Linda and Amber grabbed a room to share leaving two empty bedrooms for the rest of the family.

After unpacking, everybody headed downstairs to eat. The kids ordered pizzas because the cook didn't start until the next day. Emmy checked out the house as she wandered around.

"Krissy, look. There is a fireplace and a big screen TV."

"Yes, I can see, Em. There's a stereo system and..."

"Look out here!" Emmy hollered as she opened the patio door and walked outside. "There's a huge deck and a pool over there. There's a hot tub. Maybe we can use that at night."

Derrick joined Emmy and pointed. "There's a built-in grill over there and even though it looks like ceramic tile around the pool, I think it's concrete made to look that way. Should I throw you in the pool so you can see how warm the water is?"

Kristen walked up to Derrick and poked him in the ribs. "You better leave her alone or Amber might get jealous."

Emmy and Kristen eyed the heated swimming pool.

"I can't wait to use it," Kristen said.

Emmy looked at the guys, who had all stepped over to the pool. *I want to use the pool, too, but I don't want everyone to see me in my bikini.*

While they waited for the pizzas to arrive, they sat around the kitchen island and discussed ideas of what to do. Everyone agreed to put Derrick in charge of planning the various activities. The pizzas arrived and disappeared within twenty minutes.

The kids moved to the family room to watch a movie.

Derrick held up their choices. "We can either watch *I*

Know What You Did Last Summer, The Mask Of Zorro or *The Horse Whisperer.*"

Linda suggested, "Let's watch *The Horse Whisperer.* It's really good."

"No way! You've already seen it, and it sucks," Barry whined.

"No chick flicks," Tony said. "Let's watch the summer thing."

"You know it's a horror movie, right?" Kristen reminded him. "Emmy will have nightmares if she watches that."

Why did you say that, Krissy? Are you trying to embarrass me? You've been trying to make me look like a little kid ever since we got to the airport. Emmy bit her lip as she glared at Kristen.

"Has anyone seen *The Mask Of Zorro?*" Derrick asked. He looked at everyone.

"I've seen it, but I wouldn't mind seeing it again," Harrison said.

"Maybe tomorrow we can pick up some other DVDs in town, but I guess tonight's it's Zorro." Derrick popped in the DVD and turned on the TV.

Kristen pulled Emmy over to the black leather couch. "You can sit with me, Emmy."

Will you hold my hand in the scary parts? Emmy wondered.

Kristen patted a spot for Harrison and he dutifully sat on Kristen's other side.

"Do you mind if I sit on the floor in front of you, Em?" Tony asked as Barry and Linda claimed a large, overstuffed recliner.

"I don't mind as long as you don't tickle my knees," Emmy said.

Derrick and Amber lay next to each other on a big bearskin rug, and he started the DVD. By the time the movie ended, over two hours later, Emmy was tired.

"I'm going to bed. I can't stay awake any longer. Tony, would you carry my big suitcase upstairs. It's too heavy for me."

"Emmy, you know the rules," Barry said.

"I just want Tony to carry my suitcase."

"Maybe I should stay here, Em. We don't want to break the rules our first night here," Tony said.

"Fine." Emmy sighed. "Derrick, will you carry my suitcase for me?"

"I was only kidding, Em, I'll take your suitcase upstairs. Do you need help unpacking it?"

"No! I can do that by myself," Emmy said as she frowned.

Tony surprised her by kissing her cheek quickly in front of the other kids. They all hooped and hollered at them. Emmy felt her face turn red as she went upstairs with Tony. Tony set her suitcase on the bed and looked at Emmy.

"Thanks for helping with the suitcase, but I don't want you to kiss me anymore."

"I'm sorry. It was just a spur of the moment thing."

"Don't do it again. It really embarrassed me."

He came back downstairs a minute later, and no one said anything. Even Barry kept his mouth shut.

At midnight Kristen's mom came over to check on everybody.

"Where are Tony and Emmy? Don't tell me they are breaking the rules already."

"Mom, you don't have to worry about those two breaking the rules," Kristen said. *Emmy is as innocent as could be, and Tony's content to make sure she stays that way. At least I think that's the case.* "Tony's in the bathroom, and Emmy's in bed asleep already. She was tired and went to bed early. I think the trip stressed her out because she's never flown before."

"You all need to take it easy for a couple of days. Let your bodies adjust to the altitude," Karla reminded them.

At two in the morning Derrick turned off the TV, locked all the doors, shut off the lights and headed upstairs to bed.

Emmy woke up before Kristen, got dressed and wandered downstairs to look around. *I guess everyone else is still sleeping.* She thought until she walked into the kitchen and saw the cook.

"Good morning, young lady."

233

Emmy introduced herself, "Hi, I'm Emmy. I'm a friend of the Keasling kids."

"It's nice to meet you, Emmy. I'm Esperanza. Can I get you something for breakfast? We have a full refrigerator now."

Emmy giggled and then asked, "Could I have some eggs and maybe some bacon or sausage?"

"Of course you can, niña. I can make you an omelet if you would like."

"I would love an omelet, thanks, Esperanza." Emmy smiled. *This is like a restaurant, except I don't even have to pay.*

By eleven o'clock everybody was up and dressed. They gathered around the table in the breakfast area.

"What are we gonna do today?" Kristen asked as she buttered her wheat toast.

"Anyone have any suggestions?" Derrick asked. "I don't want to make all the decisions about what we do."

They talked while they ate and elected to stick together as a group today and go into town to check it out.

"Kristen, will you stay by me? I don't want Tony to pester me today. I told him he couldn't kiss me anymore. Let's walk around and window shop."

"Might as well hang with you. Harrison is content to be by himself reading his stupid book."

Tony stayed close to Derrick and Amber, since Emmy didn't appear to want him around. The women wanted to check out all the shops, which bored the guys to death. The whole group gravitated to the ski lift and took a ride to the top of Aspen mountain.

"Kristen, check out the view over here. Do you know the name of that mountain?" Emmy asked.

"I'm not sure. I know there is one called Snowmass, but I don't know if that's it. Derrick might know."

"It doesn't matter. I think everything looks so great with the snow on top."

When they got back into downtown Aspen, they walked around sightseeing some more. Emmy experienced some lightheadedness.

Kristen asked, "Are you all right, Emmy? You're walking around like you're drunk or something."

"Maybe I'm feeling the affects of the altitude like your mother warned us. I don't think the six-pack of beer I drank has anything to do with it." Emmy sounded a little sarcastic.

"Oh, Emmy, I'm sorry about what I said yesterday. It was thoughtless and uncalled for."

"Oh, it's all right."

"You didn't have anything to drink, did you?" Kristen asked.

"No, of course not. I'm not totally stupid," Emmy snapped.

"Well, do like Mom suggested and take it easy until you adjust more." Kristen sounded very patronizing.

What's up with you, Kristen? You're treating me like I'm twelve. Emmy wondered.

They ate lunch around two and then headed back to the house. Barry tossed a bunch of tourist information on the kitchen island for everyone to check out.

"Why don't you look through those, Derrick?" Harrison said. "We'll do whatever you suggest."

Derrick looked over the brochures. "I think we're all in agreement about going whitewater rafting and doing the mountain bike rides. We only have to figure out when to go."

"Will you be responsible for setting up those activities, please?" Kristen asked as she smiled at her brother.

"Yeah, I'll take care of the details since no one else will."

After dinner everybody wanted to use the pool and hot tub. As Emmy and Kristen were changing into their bathing suits, Emmy asked, "Does this bikini show too much?"

Kristen looked Emmy over. "The important parts are covered. Why?"

"I don't want to let the guys see something they shouldn't."

"Don't worry, Em. The guys will be staring at Amber and Linda and won't be paying any attention to you or me."

Emmy looked hurt by Kristen's comment. "I'm going to wear shorts until we get in the pool."

"Emmy, I didn't mean to hurt your feelings. You'll see what

235

I mean later." Kristen stared at Emmy. "Where did you get that bikini? The top looks like a small sports bra."

"I bought it at Frazier's Sporting Goods. I wanted to find one I wouldn't have to worry about coming undone," Emmy said and then giggled. "I tried on a string bikini first. It didn't cover much of anything. I might as well been naked."

"You're a goof, Em." Kristen laughed as she pictured her petite friend running around in a string bikini.

"I'm glad I bought this one. I heard Tony talking to Derrick about playing keep away. I want to have fun with the guys in the pool"

Emmy and Kristen joined the other kids by the pool. When Amber got out of the pool, Emmy saw exactly what Kristen meant. Amber looked like she could be a swimsuit model for Sports Illustrated and the bikini she wore didn't cover much.

"See?" Kristen nudged Emmy in the side.

"Wow! I didn't realize. She's always worn loose-fitting clothes whenever I've seen her."

Amber didn't pay any attention to the stares from the guys. Emmy snuck up behind Tony to tease him. "You better not be looking at what I think you're looking at, mister."

Tony turned around to face Emmy. "I was admiring the color of Amber's suit."

"How can you even tell what color it is? There isn't enough of it to see."

The guys jumped into the pool and tossed a volleyball around.

"Hey, Emmy, why don't you get in and play keep away with us?" Tony asked as he threw the ball at her.

"Okay." She caught the ball and jumped in at the deep end.

Tony took the ball away and then the guys made her chase the ball around the pool. She finally grabbed it. Barry was closest to her; he tried to take the ball away but couldn't.

"You better be careful where you grab me," Emmy warned Barry by nodding her head toward Linda. "She's watching your every move. It's a good thing Amber isn't in the pool."

"I wasn't touching you anywhere I shouldn't, Em." Barry

waved at Linda. "Hi, honey!"

Linda shook her head. *You're not ever gonna sleep with me again, Barry Newton.*

Emmy kept her arms wrapped tightly around the ball. Tony swam over, grabbed her around the waist and pulled her under the water, but she held on to the ball. They came back up for air, and Emmy looked like a drowned rat.

"Okay, you win, Emmy." Tony started to swim away.

Emmy took aim and threw the ball at him as hard as she could. Bullseye! She nailed him in the back of the head.

"You're gonna get it, Em." He quickly turned around and swam after her.

She shrieked and tried to swim away, but Tony caught her.

Kristen poked Derrick in the side as he climbed out of the pool. "Hey, would you look at those two. They're acting like kids. Oooh, did you see that? Tony tossed her in the air and she landed on her back."

Derrick winced. "That looks like it hurt."

The rest of the guys were ready to quit playing and got out of the pool.

Tony turned to look at Emmy. "Are you gonna stay in there all night?"

"I don't want you guys to see me in my bikini."

"Why didn't you say something. I'll get something to cover you. I'll be right back. Wait there while I get a towel."

"Thanks, Tony."

Tony headed over to the grill area and came back in a minute holding something behind his back. All the guys watched as Tony brought his hand out from behind his back.

"I got a towel for you, Emmy." He handed her a washcloth that wouldn't cover a baby's behind. Emmy looked up at Tony as he smiled at her.

"Harsh," Barry said.

Kristen and Linda smacked him. Emmy decided to get out of the pool holding Tony's towel in front of her bikini bottoms. She turned her back to the guys and shook her butt at them. The guys got a kick out of her antics and laughed hysterically.

"Way to shake that thing, Em," Barry yelled.

Derrick handed her a large beach towel. "Here, Emmy, maybe this will cover you better."

"Thanks for the towel, Derrick. At least you are a gentleman."

She wrapped up in the towel and smiled at the guys. Emmy didn't feel as self-conscious now, so she relaxed.

A few minutes later Tony asked, "Wanna try out the hot tub, Emmy?"

She saw Derrick and Amber in the tub. "I will if Kristen will."

Kristen joined them in the hot tub for a few minutes.

"I'm gonna get out and run up to the room. I'll want to grab a pair of shorts and a t-shirt. It will get cooler soon," Kristen said.

"Are you gonna leave me here?" Emmy grabbed Kristen's arm.

"Don't be a baby. You'll be fine, Em. Tony is with you." Kristen climbed out.

I'm not a baby, Kristen. Emmy looked at Tony and instinctively covered her chest with her arms.

Kristen ran up to the room and put on a pair of shorts. She grabbed a couple of t-shirts. One for Emmy in case she got chilled. When she returned, Emmy was out of the the hot tub and wearing her shorts.

"Do you need a shirt, Em?"

"Thanks, Kristen, you saved me a trip."

Emmy and Kristen noticed the guys staring at Amber again.

"Tony, are you still admiring the color of Amber's suit? At least close your mouth and stop drooling," Kristen teased.

"I was not drooling, and I think that color looks good on Amber."

"Yeah, sure. Come on, Em."

Kristen and Emmy walked over to the pool and sat on the edge with their feet in the water. Derrick wandered over and sat between them.

Emmy leaned against Derrick and whispered, "I didn't realize Amber was built like that. No wonder you like her better than me."

"Emmy, even though you aren't built like Amber, you are still the sweetest little girl I know," Derrick said.

Emmy frowned. "Thanks a lot." *Don't you start treating me like a kid, too.*

Kristen asked Derrick, "But are they real?"

Emmy and Kristen giggled.

"They are indeed real, and they are spectacular!" Derrick smiled as he remembered the *Seinfeld* episode. "Did I mention that Amber doesn't have any tan lines?"

"Maybe we don't either, Derrick," Kristen said.

"I know Emmy does because I saw them earlier."

Emmy turned red. Kristen smacked Derrick's arm and Emmy stuck her tongue out at him. Derrick placed his hands on their backs and pushed them into the pool. Tony and Barry heard the splash and ran over to see what happened.

"Emmy, why are you swimming with your clothes on?" Tony grinned.

Emmy splashed Tony. He reached out a hand to help Emmy and Kristen out of the water.

"We're going to get back at Derrick sometime when he's not expecting it. That's a promise," Kristen said.

Later, Emmy walked into the kitchen and saw Tony searching through the fridge. He stood up holding an apple. "Are you having fun, Emmy?"

"For sure! This place is beautiful. Are you doing all right? You probably wish Nikki was here. She looks more like Amber, if you know what I mean." Emmy grinned.

"You know I'm not dating her anymore. I know you wish Kenny was here with you."

Emmy grabbed a bottle of water. "He isn't, so I guess we should make the best of our vacation. We can be friends and have fun together. I wasn't expecting it when you kissed me yesterday."

"Sorry about that. I won't do it again." *I kissed your cheek. Why are you making it a big deal?*

"I'm going upstairs. I'm getting sleepy."

"See you in the morning, Em."

239

They looked at each other briefly before Emmy ran upstairs.

Alone in their room, Emmy asked Kristen, "Did you have much time to be with Harrison?"

"We had some time to ourselves, but we hardly even talked. He was more interested in reading a book, so I let him read while I listened to my iPod."

After a few moments of silence, Emmy asked Kristen, "Do you think Barry and Linda will follow the rules?"

Kristen grinned. "No way!"

Emmy laughed with Kristen.

"Were you surprised when you first saw Amber in her bikini?"

"Oh yeah. I had no idea. Why didn't you warn me, Krissy?"

Kristen began to mimic Derrick. "They are real, and they're spectacular."

Kristen looked down her pajama top as she and Emmy stood at the foot of the bed. Emmy laughed and did the same. She looked down her top and giggled, "At least they are real."

In their room Tony and Derrick asked the same question about Barry and Linda.

"How long do you think it will take them to break the rules?" Derrick asked Tony.

Tony thought about it before he answered. "Two days tops, maybe."

"I saw you looking at Amber."

"She sure is well built," Tony replied tactfully.

"Did I mention that she graduated as the valedictorian of her high school class, and she wants to be a doctor and do research on Parkinson's disease?"

"No, you never mentioned that before. Wow! What a combination of smarts and looks."

"You got that right!"

That night Harrison moved into one of the empty bedrooms because no other family members had shown up yet. He didn't want to share a room with Barry another night. Barry snored like a freight train.

In the morning Derrick, Tony and Kristen discussed putting together a pool to see how long Barry and Linda could go before they broke the rules.

"I think they will obey the rules, and behave for the whole time they are here." Emmy looked around at everyone.

Derrick said, "Emmy, you are the only person who thinks they will last more than a day."

Later, Barry learned about the wager. "I heard about your 'breaking the rules' pool. I want to let you know that Linda and I are determined to follow the rules like everybody else. If you want to put your money where your mouths are, I am willing to take your money."

The guys placed bets with Barry that he couldn't make it two weeks.

That morning Kristen took Emmy into town to do some shopping.

"Kristen, I can't believe the prices on this stuff. Look at this, eighty-five dollars for this top just because it says *Aspen* on it. I'm not wasting my money on this junk."

"It's not just junk, Emmy—it's designer junk! There's a big difference."

"Yeah! About seventy-five dollars worth of difference."

Emmy couldn't deal with the high prices, so she didn't buy anything except a sweatshirt for Kenny. For most of the day, everyone hung out at the house and chilled. Tomorrow they planned to go whitewater rafting.

Esperanza sang cheerfully in the kitchen as she made sandwiches and a salad for a late lunch. She also prepared some homemade salsa and tortilla chips. Everyone had a healthy appetite, especially Tony and Barry. Esperanza gazed with her mouth open as Tony shoveled in the food. After lunch most of the kids stayed around the pool. Amber drew lots of attention from Barry and Harrison. Kristen listened to her iPod and made sure she stayed out of the sun. With her fair skin, she would burn easily at this altitude. Derrick read a book for a class next semester. Linda sat by Barry and got after him for staring at Amber. Tony and Emmy had disappeared.

241

"Hey, Kristen, have you seen Tony and Emmy lately?" Barry asked.

"I think they're in the house. Why?"

"Maybe they are breaking the rules. You guys are so concerned about Linda and me when you should be thinking about those two."

"If you're so concerned, Barry, then let's go check."

Barry and Kristen walked in the house to look for Tony and Emmy. They checked the kitchen and were about to head upstairs when Kristen found them in the family room.

"Barry, be quiet and come here," Kristen whispered.

"Did you find them?"

"Yes, and you are right. They are sleeping together."

"Get out of town. For real?"

Kristen suppressed a giggle. "There's a camera in the kitchen. Go get it and be quiet."

Barry grabbed the camera and brought it to Kristen. "We will have some evidence to show your parents now. We can catch them in the act, so to speak."

"They're in the family room. I want to take a picture of them... sleeping... together."

"Whoa, Kristen. That's devious. Sounds more like something I would do." Barry grinned. "What are they really doing? I know they aren't... you know."

Kristen quietly walked over and snapped a couple of pictures of Tony and Emmy. He lay sprawled on his back on the couch—totally zonked. Emmy was in the recliner, curled up in a fetal position, sound asleep. Barry looked at Emmy, and then Kristen.

Kristen whispered, "Don't they look like a couple of little kids taking their afternoon nap?"

"Yeah, let's let them sleep. If we wake them they might be cranky later."

Chapter Twenty-Five

"Krissy! Wake up. We have to get ready to go rafting." Emmy bounded out of bed, glanced out the window at the snow-topped mountain and dug through her suitcase for her clothes.

"Why are you so bright-eyed this morning?" Kristen rolled onto her back and stretched her arms over her head.

Emmy jumped onto the bed with her feet tucked under her. "I can't wait to get to the river. I've never done anything like this."

Esperanza scurried about the kitchen as she made breakfast for everyone. Afterward they rode into town to meet the guides for the whitewater rafting trip. Tony helped the guides load up the rafts, and, as soon as the other customers arrived, they piled into the two large vans and headed out. They stopped briefly at the top of Independence Pass to take pictures.

"Derrick, will you take a picture of us?" Emmy asked.

Kristen handed her brother the camera, and she and Emmy stood in front of the elevation sign.

"Say cheese, or something equally stupid," Derrick said.

An hour later they arrived at their destination along the Arkansas River and prepared for the rafting trip. Tony helped Emmy with her bright orange life vest.

"Is that tight enough, Em?"

She looked up at Tony. "I can barely breathe. Is it supposed to be so tight?"

"I don't want it to fall off if you end up in the river."

"I don't plan on going for a swim." Emmy looked at Derrick and Amber.

Tony followed where her eyes were focused.

"I don't think Amber will fit," Emmy said and then giggled.

"Maybe there are different sizes for adults, Em. Yours is for a child. The other ones were too big."

She glared at him. *Why is everyone treating me like a child?*

"I'm kidding. Geez, will you lighten up?"

Eight people squeezed tightly together in the raft. Their guide took up his position at the back. This wasn't going to be an easy float down the river—they had to paddle. They would be on the river for six hours plus their lunch time.

The trip began easily through calm water, and they got used to paddling in response to their guide's commands. Soon they came to some rapids. Their raft shot through without any trouble.

Kristen reached out to touch the swirling river as a wave rose beside her. "I don't want to end up in the river. The water is cold since it comes out of the mountains."

Emmy checked her life jacket. "I don't want to end up in the river, either."

Later they came to the most difficult section. The raft bounced off a rock and ended up tilted almost straight down at one point. Barry lost his balance and bumped into Emmy.

"Tony!" Emmy screamed as she catapulted out of the raft. She immediately disappeared.

"Can you see her?" Derrick asked as his head swiveled back and forth.

"No, can you?" Tony answered. "Where the hell is she?"

"Emmy, where are you?" Kristen screamed. "I can't see her."

Everyone in the raft searched for a sign of Emmy as the raft was swept downriver by the strong current.

"I'm going to jump in," Tony shouted.

"No! Stay in the raft," the guide ordered. "If anyone has to go in after her, it will be me."

They kept searching. Thirty seconds later Derrick hollered, "There she is. I can see her."

"Where? I don't see her." Tony asked.

"Just ahead of us."

The guide saw Emmy's orange life vest and directed everyone to paddle as hard as they could. Slowly the raft edged closer to Emmy.

"Emmy! Can you hear us?" Tony yelled.

Eventually, the raft came close enough to enable Tony to reach out and grab the back of her life vest. He plucked her out of the river with one hand.

"Is she breathing? Do we have to administer mouth-to-mouth?" Barry asked.

"I don't know! I can't tell," Tony yelled. He turned Emmy over to face him.

She immediately vomited a gush of river water and coughed violently.

"Are you okay?" Kristen asked.

Emmy nodded her head and held out her arms. "I didn't lose the paddle."

"You are such a goof, Emmy." Kristen hugged her.

Tony wrapped his arms around her and kissed her cheek over and over. Emmy didn't complain this time.

"Your elbow is bleeding, Em," Derrick noticed.

She turned her arm to look. "I must have scraped it against a rock."

The guide opened the first aid kit and bandaged Emmy's elbow. He examined her for any other injuries. "It appears you were lucky. All I see is that scrape. You might have some bruising, but you're very fortunate."

"I've always been a strong swimmer, but I don't ever want to do that again."

The guide got them reorganized, and they continued.

"The water's not that cold, Kristen. You should try it."

"No thanks, Em. I'll stay right here if you don't mind."

The water was colder than Emmy let on because she was shivering. The guide dug out a blanket and handed it to Tony. Tony wrapped the blanket around Emmy and held her in his arms until they pulled up on a small beach.

They stopped for lunch, and, since Emmy appeared to have recovered, everyone teased her.

"I thought I would have to swim all the way back. It took you guys forever to catch up to me," Emmy said.

"We thought about it, but Kristen convinced us to let you back in the raft," Derrick teased.

The guide announced, "Lunch is ready. Everyone help yourself."

Kristen approached the guide a few minutes later. "This is really good."

"Thanks, my wife is responsible for the lunch. That's her over there with our son."

"Then I will tell her myself." Kristen walked on over.

Emmy sat on a large boulder next to the river and let the sun warm her as it dried her clothes. Tony joined her.

"Tony, watch that guy in the kayak."

"Where?"

"Over there. See how he goes under the water and flips right back up? That looks like fun. I'd like to try that someday."

"Yeah, it looks like fun all right." Tony didn't think he wanted to try it, but he didn't want Emmy to think he was afraid.

Lunch lasted for forty-five minutes, and they returned to their raft.

"We have more sections of rapids to negotiate, but none are as difficult as what we have already been through," the guide explained.

They sailed through the remaining stretches of rapids like veterans and after a couple miles of calm river, the trip ended. Nobody else was tossed out of the raft, and they returned to base camp, as they had dubbed the house.

Barry jumped out of the van and faced everyone. "Hey, guys, we *gotta* do that again."

"You just want to go again to watch Emmy get tossed out of the raft," Linda said as she scowled at him.

"I wouldn't have got tossed out if Barry hadn't lost his balance and hit me. I would have stayed in the raft while he went flying," Emmy replied.

Everybody teased her for landing in the river.

"Just wait until tomorrow. I'm going to beat all of you to the top of the mountain. Just watch. You'll be eating my dust."

They arranged to ride to the Maroon Bells on rented mountain bikes; Emmy intended to race the guys to the top, since she had adjusted to the altitude better than the other kids.

The next day they picked up their mountain bikes and helmets and got directions to the side road that led to the Bells. It was fifteen miles, almost all uphill.

246

Derrick suggested, "If this is going to be a race, why don't we give Emmy a head start. Does ten minutes sound fair?"

"I don't want one!" Emmy exclaimed. "I'm going to beat you guys up the mountain without any head start at all. I don't want any special treatment because I'm a girl."

Harrison swallowed his pride. "I know I won't be able to keep up with everyone, so I'm going to stay with the girls to keep them company. We'll see you at the top sometime today."

"That's a good idea, Harrison," Derrick said. "I did worry about the girls being left alone."

"Don't worry about us, Derrick. We can always turn back and go shopping. Can I have some money, please?"

"No way, Kristen."

The rest of the girls took off with no intention of racing to the top.

Barry walked up to Emmy and said, "There is no way you are going to beat me to the top. You might as well go with the other girls and give up now."

"That's mighty big talk for someone as out of shape as you, Barry. Do you want to make a little wager and put your money where your mouth is?"

"I was thinking of something other than money, Emmy. How about this? If I win, which I certainly will, I get to toss you into the pool in your clothes. If by chance some miracle happens and you win, then you can toss me into the pool. How's that?"

"I have a better idea. I saw a place in town that has a karaoke night. If I win, then you have to sing in front of all of us and the rest of the people in the bar."

"Fine. I accept the terms of the wager. I really shouldn't call it a bet because there is no chance of you winning, Emmy."

Emmy smiled. "We'll see, Barry. We'll just see."

The rest of the group took off. Emmy and Barry soon got ahead of the rest of the guys. Tony was a better athlete than any of them, but he also weighed much more. Soon they passed the three girls and Harrison.

Tony and Derrick continued to chase Emmy and Barry. Eventually, Tony's superior athletic ability began to show, and he began to close the gap to the front runners. Derrick drafted behind Tony to save energy and hung on with all he had. Tony caught Emmy and Barry and passed them with only a couple of miles to go. Derrick began to fade and fell behind the other riders. Barry kept his bike as close to Tony's as he could and managed to rest and recover a little. Emmy fell back twenty yards, then thirty yards.

"Emmy is toast!" Barry proclaimed to Tony. "Looks like it will be a two man race to the finish, Tony." Though Barry often rode his bicycle back home, this was his first time riding in the mountains.

Emmy dug into her reserves and didn't give up. She used the advantage of being able to see Barry and Tony to focus on the guys and slowly gained ground on them. Tony and Barry concentrated on each other so much, they forgot about Emmy. It took a few minutes, but she closed in on them. While Barry concentrated on Tony, Emmy passed them on the other side. They didn't even see her as she flew around them. Finally, Tony saw that Emmy had passed them.

"Holy Cow! Where did she come from, Barry?"

"I don't know. She must have gotten a ride or something. I thought we dropped her for good."

The last part of the climb to the parking lot got steeper and Barry really struggled to stay close to Tony. Tony dug deep into his reserves. He caught Emmy and passed her. Emmy didn't give up when Tony and Barry passed her again. Barry gave it all he had but suddenly hit his limit. He slowed dramatically as he watched Tony ride away. Emmy passed Barry. With only a hundred yards to go, Emmy caught Tony. Digging deep into her reserves she summoned one last burst of energy and passed him. She beat Tony to the finish line by five bike lengths. Tony finished second and Barry limped home in third place. After she passed him the last time, Barry had given up and walked his bike up the last steep section.

"Emmy, you did it. You beat us all. I'm so proud of you." Tony congratulated her with high-fives.

"I came so close to giving up when you passed me, but I couldn't let Barry win. I don't know where I got the energy to pass you the last time."

Tony asked, "Barry, are you all right?"

He coughed and waved his hand. "I'll be okay in a minute as soon as I stuff my lungs back in my chest. I don't know how you did it, Emmy, but you won fair and square. I guess I will have to practice my singing."

Derrick made the top after a few minutes, but it took the rest of the group another hour to reach the top. They finally made it, and they all took a short hike to the lake at the base of the Maroon Bells. After relaxing in the sun for an hour, they chose to head back down the mountain.

Barry touched Emmy's arm to get her attention. "Emmy, I want a rematch. I'll race you back down the mountain to the school that we passed."

"Okay, but I still won the bet. I'm still holding you to that."

Barry, Tony and Emmy took off down the mountain. It soon became apparent that nobody would catch Tony. His weight worked to his advantage now as gravity helped him easily make it down ahead of them. Emmy tried to keep up with Barry and managed to beat him at the end where the road took an uphill turn to go past the school.

"Yes! I beat you again, Barry."

"I think you cheated somehow, Emmy. I don't know how, but you cheated. You must have been using some kind of drug."

Emmy teased him for the rest of the day.

When Barry finally came down to breakfast the next morning, Derrick asked, "Why do you have such a stupid grin on your face?"

Barry confessed, "You win."

"Pay up, sucker." Derrick laughed as he held out his hand.

Barry asked, "Will you take a check?"

Linda eventually made it downstairs, and everybody stared at her with silly grins.

Linda smacked Barry on the shoulder. "Did you have to tell everybody!"

"I didn't tell everybody. I tried to keep it a secret."

"Liar! Liar!"

Kristen rolled her eyes. "Will you guys grow up? Stop teasing Linda."

"Barry and Linda are in love and need to show their affection. They can't just stop completely," Emmy said.

This caused the guys to start teasing Barry and Linda even more.

The Keaslings and Mama walked in the kitchen. "Are you guys enjoying Aspen so far?"

"Aspen is too boring, and there isn't anything to do," Derrick said.

The adults looked at Derrick with stunned expressions.

"I'm kidding. Everybody is having a good time."

"Mama, we had a bike race up to the Bells and guess who won?" Tony grinned.

"Who?"

"Emmy did. She beat everyone to the top."

Mama stood behind Emmy and patted her shoulders. "I figured Emmy would win. She is still a tomboy, and she doesn't weigh more than fifty pounds, so she didn't have as much to carry uphill as everyone else."

"Thank you, Mama. I weigh more than fifty pounds, but I won't tell how much more." Emmy asked Mama, "What have you been doing? Are you keeping busy, or are you just chilling? I hope you're not working too hard. This is supposed to be a vacation for you, too."

"I have been relaxing for the most part, but I would feel so guilty if I didn't do some work. Just don't tell Karla, okay."

"I'll never tell, Mama."

Later, everyone except Harrison used the pool. Harrison kept his nose in a book.

"Hey, you guys, there is this trail to a hidden lake up close to Independence Pass. Want to check it out?" Derrick asked as he looked at a trail map just after lunch.

After a bit of discussion, they decided to go for a hike that afternoon. They piled in the van and headed up the road. Tony and Derrick carried backpacks containing water and energy bars for everyone. Emmy started at the front of the line of hikers, and the tomboy in her and competitive nature of her personality took over.

She hurried along. *I'm going to prove I can hike as far and fast as the guys and outdo the girls. I'll show them that beating the guys up to the Bells was no fluke.*

The trail passed through a grove of quaking Aspen trees and a grassy meadow before becoming steeper and entering a spruce forest.

Soon Emmy and Tony disappeared out of the sight of the rest of the hikers. They waited for everyone at a fork in the trail to make sure nobody got lost—especially Barry and Linda. As they waited, Emmy stood on a rock with her back to Tony. "Will you catch me if I fall into you?"

"No, I'll just let you fall and hurt yourself," Tony teased.

Emmy looked back at Tony and let herself fall into his arms.

"Emmy! Don't do that," Tony scolded.

"I knew you would catch me. I want to do it again." Emmy sounded like a little kid.

She did it again, and Tony caught her. He was holding her in his arms as the rest of the group caught up to them.

Barry walked up to Tony and Emmy and grinned. "Hey, Emmy, you guys have to remember the rules. Just because we're out here on a mountain and not in the house doesn't mean you can flagrantly flaunt the rules."

Derrick joined in and said, "Now I know why you and Tony were trying to get so far ahead of the rest of us."

Tony didn't mind the teasing. "I was minding my own business, and Emmy just fell into my arms."

Emmy asked, "Are you finished acting like children? I love Kenny Colwell. Tony and I weren't doing anything."

"Then maybe he should move his hand." Kristen glared at Tony.

Emmy noticed the position of his hand. "Tony! Let go of me!" She squirmed out of his grasp as her face turned red.

That caused everybody to tease her even more. After the brief rest they continued their hike toward the lake. They passed through the spruce forest and into a small clearing.

Emmy looked up at the trail ahead and pointed. "Those look like some pretty steep switchbacks."

"Are you sure there's a lake up there, Derrick?" Barry asked. "I don't want to climb all the way up there and find some little puddle of water."

"I'm sure. It's called Grizzly Bear Lake."

"Do you think there might be bears up there?" Linda sounded concerned.

"If there are, Barry will chase them away. Remember how he protected us on our hike," Emmy said.

"A dog is one thing, but if we see a grizzly, it's every man for themselves," Barry said as his head swiveled around.

Emmy slugged Barry's arm, and then took the lead. "Come on. I want to see this lake."

Two minutes later Linda asked, "Are we there yet?"

Soon all the girls were asking, in whiny voices, "Are we there yet?"

When they finally got to the top of the switchbacks, the view made all the work worthwhile.

"Look at the water!" Emmy pointed. "It's as blue as the sky."

Derrick motioned toward the snow-covered mountain peaks. "The mountains reach to the heavens with jagged peaks like the teeth on a saw."

"What did you say? It sounded dorky." Kristen shielded her eyes from the sun.

"I read that in one of the travel brochures," Derrick admitted.

They spent two hours at the lake; all the couples had some time alone with each other. Emmy and Tony walked all the way around the lake before returning to the group.

Kristen asked them, "What were you two doing? You were gone for quite a while."

Emmy answered, "Nothing. I wanted to walk around the lake, but not by myself, so I asked Tony to go with me. How about you and Harrison? Is he still ignoring you?"

"We talked, but he doesn't express any interest in me anymore. I think he's sorry that he even came on the trip."

The downhill return hike flew by. When they got close to the van, Emmy jumped on Tony's back and got a ride to the end of the trail. She and Tony acted like little kids and Kristen smiled at her. After all, Emmy and Tony were the youngest, and Emmy often acted like a kid anyway. Kristen looked at Harrison and wished he wouldn't be so serious all the time.

Esperanza and her daughter, Cecile, prepared a traditional Mexican meal for dinner. Emmy surveyed the table and saw a large variety of dishes—stuffed poblanos, homemade tamales, pulled pork, shredded chicken, enchiladas and tortillas, beans and rice.

"Esperanza, everything looks so delicious. You must have been cooking all day," Emmy said. "Thank you so much."

"Cecile helped me, and it didn't take too long. I hope you enjoy it."

The conversation around the table became loud and boisterous as they recounted the day's adventure. Emmy received a good amount of teasing.

"Tony and I didn't even kiss, so get off my back," Emmy said in her defense.

Barry walked up behind Emmy and put his hands on her shoulders. He jumped back as Emmy turned and took a swipe at him.

Barry laughed. "You're expecting a lot if you want us to believe that story."

"Well, it's true," she replied softly as she mused about Kenny. *I would have kissed Kenny if he had been along,* she thought, but didn't dare say out loud.

After dinner Kristen asked Esperanza, "Would you mind baking a cake for Emmy? Tomorrow is her nineteenth birthday, and I want to have a little party for her because she's my best friend."

"It will be no trouble at all, Miss Kristen. Emmy is the little girl staying with you, right?"

"Yes," Kristen said. "What is it, Esperanza? You look confused."

253

"Did you say nineteen years old?" Esperanza asked.

Kristen understood now. "I know. Emmy looks so young, and she acts like she's twelve, but she's really going to be nineteen."

"When you get to be my age, it is hard to tell how old young people really are. I really thought she was about thirteen. Do you know what flavor of cake Emmy likes?"

"She loves chocolate cake and chocolate frosting."

"I will make a special cake for Miss Emmy."

"Thanks so much, Esperanza. I really appreciate it."

"Who wants to hear Barry sing?" Emmy asked as everyone, except Harrison, sat in the family room relaxing after stuffing their faces at dinner.

"Yeah, Barry, you have to pay up on the bet," Linda said. "I want everyone to hear how you sound when you sing in the shower."

"Fine. I'm ready to pay up." Barry put on a game face to hide his nervousness.

They headed into town to the Mollie Jerome Bar, and Barry signed up to sing. They didn't realize that all the other acts attended the Aspen School of Music and were actually quite talented. When it came Barry's turn to sing, the group yelled and hollered as loud as possible just to embarrass him.

"You can do it, Barry," Derrick hollered.

"Show 'em you're the boss," Tony yelled.

"Don't screw up," Emmy teased.

Barry managed to do an an adequate version of "Born To Run."

"Barry, that was almost all right. I didn't know you could sing," Emmy shouted as Barry returned to their table. *You were in the wrong key, but I've heard worse.*

"Neither did I." He wiped the sweat off of his face. "I was scared to death, so maybe that's why I sounded so good."

"Whoa, partner. Nobody said you sounded good. Emmy said you sounded almost all right. We thought you would sound like Tom Waits or Bob Dylan. Let's say you exceeded our lowly expectations and leave it at that," Derrick teased.

254

Kristen suggested, "Emmy, why don't you sing? I know they have 'I Will Be True To You' on the machine. I saw it."

"Yeah, Emmy, see if you can still sign up," Derricks urged.

Emmy checked with the person in charge. She turned and gave a thumbs up to her friends. She sang the Fridays At Five song that she helped write, and the whole place applauded.

The emcee took the mic and got everyone's attention. "I'm sure most of you know that last song as a Fridays At Five tune, but you just heard it sung by one of the original writers. Let's give her a big hand."

The crowd applauded again and Emmy covered her face with her hands.

"Don't be so shy, Em." Derrick moved her hands and stood her up. "You did a great job."

Emmy actually won a prize for third place—not bad considering the competition.

"I think they robbed you, Emmy. You should have won first place," Barry said. He adjusted his glasses and then high-fived her.

As they headed back to the house, Barry asked Tony, "Will you get mad if we go ahead and toss Emmy in the pool? We just want to tease her."

"Go ahead, Barry, but don't expect me to protect you after she gets out. She will probably get pretty mad at you."

They returned to the house and everyone headed out to the patio and pool after Linda suggested they watch the stars for awhile. Emmy had her back to them as Barry and Linda stealthily approached her. They grabbed her by the arms and legs.

"On the count of three, right?" They swung her back and forth as Emmy remained strangely and unexpectedly silent. "One! Two! Three!"

Only after they had tossed her into the air, did Emmy scream. She landed with a loud splash. She surfaced and hollered, "Barry Newton, I will kill you. Tony, grab him for me, please."

"You're on your own, Em. I promised Barry I would keep out of this."

Emmy swam over to the side of the pool.

"Here, Emmy, let me help you out. No hard feelings?"

"No, no hard feelings, Barry, just give me your hand."

He did, and Emmy hollered, "Big mistake, Barry!" as she grabbed his hand with both of hers, placed her feet against the side of the pool and pulled with all her might. Barry cartwheeled into the pool over the top of Emmy.

"Serves you right, you creep! I hope you drown!"

Tony stood by the edge of the pool and extended a hand to both of them to get out. Emmy tried to pull Tony into the pool but couldn't budge him.

"Emmy! Do you want my help or not?" Tony asked.

"Please help me, Tony,"

Tony pulled Emmy and Barry out of the pool. Emmy glared at Barry. She remembered when she was ten and punched him in the stomach. She thought about hitting him again as she nearly lost her temper. Tony sensed this because of the look on her face, so he grabbed her arms and held her.

"You're all wet, Em," Barry teased.

"Let me go, Tony. I'm gonna beat the crap out of him." Emmy squirmed as she tried to escape Tony's hold. She slipped on the wet surface and Tony almost fell on top of her. He regained his balance and held onto her until she calmed down.

"Are you all right now, Em? Is it safe to let you up?"

She frowned at Tony, but then nodded her head. Tony helped her up but didn't let go of her arms.

"You're a sore loser, Barry Newton." Emmy kicked at him but missed.

"Stop it, Emmy," Tony said sternly. "It's over." He turned her around and gazed into her eyes as she bit her lip.

"You can let me go now. I promise not to hurt him."

Tony let go and she faced Barry. "Sore loser," she repeated.

"I know, and you look like a drowned rat, Emmy." Barry kept his distance. "You're a good sport, Emmy. Linda would have killed me if I did that to her."

"Oh, just wait, Barry. I'm gonna get you back someday. I will wait for just the right time. But I will pay you back. You have to sleep sometime."

Chapter Twenty-Six

Emmy woke up on Thursday morning and stretched her arms above her head. She looked at Kristen, still sound asleep, *I wonder if Kristen will remember today is my birthday. I'm not gonna say anything and see what happens.*

Everyone woke up in groups of one or two at a time and kept Esperanza busy making breakfast and even a light lunch.

"We're sorry for making you cook so much," Kristen mentioned apologetically.

"It's okay. I don't mind. You kids are easy to cook for."

Emmy waited, but no one mentioned her birthday.

After lunch, Karla and Mama chased the guys out of the house. "You guys go into town and stay there until five o'clock. The girls want to have some time by themselves."

The boys grumbled but obeyed. Barry told the guys, "They are probably going to lay out by the pool and work on their tans."

"Yeah, so what, Barry?" Derrick grabbed his wallet, checked to see if he had some cash, then stuck it in his shorts.

"Don't you see?" Barry spun around to look at everyone. "They don't want us around so they can lay out in the sun without their bathing suits on. They will be naked all afternoon."

Derrick and Tony laughed at him.

"You're out of your mind, Barry," Derrick said.

"Come on. We can let the girls have an afternoon to themselves," Tony said. He wondered if Emmy would really do what Barry imagined.

Kristen and Emmy stayed by the pool all afternoon. Emmy wore her bikini and alternated working on her tan and swimming.

"Kristen, why don't you get in the pool with me?" Emmy asked.

"I'm sorry, but the chlorine in the pool ruins my hair. I'm just going to read." Kristen wore her bathing suit, but she had on a pair of shorts and a t-shirt. She was more concerned about getting sunburned since she was more fair-skinned than the other girls.

Emmy got out of the pool and walked over to the table where Kristen sat under the large umbrella. *Kristen, don't you remember that today is my birthday?* But Kristen still didn't mention anything about Emmy's special day as Amber came out to join them.

"Hi, Amber."

"Hi, Emmy. Hi, Kristen. Do you mind if I join you?"

"Of course not, pull up a lounger. The sun feels so good."

"We have the whole afternoon to ourselves," Amber mentioned casually.

"I wonder what the guys are doing?" Kristen asked.

Emmy thought about Kenny and wondered what he might be doing. *Surely, Kenny will remember my birthday even if no one else does.* She looked at Kristen and frowned.

Amber pulled a lounge chair to the other side of Emmy and removed her long t-shirt. Emmy had to look twice to make sure Amber had anything on at all. She had on the tiniest bikini bottom that Emmy had ever seen, but she was topless. Emmy looked at Kristen, and they both grinned.

Amber listened to her iPod and occasionally sang along to a song. She added sunscreen every twenty minutes and turned over more often than that.

Linda came out to join them and took her top off, also. "Aren't you guys going to take your suits off? The guys will be gone all afternoon. No one can see us back here."

Emmy and Kristen looked at each other. "No thanks, Linda. I think Emmy and I will keep our suits on for now," Kristen answered, then added, "Make sure you use plenty of sunscreen and keep adding it every fifteen or twenty minutes. You can burn a lot easier in this altitude."

Emmy took Kristen's advice and added more sunscreen to her arms and legs.

Kristen reminded her, "Put some on your face and neck, too."

Thirty minutes passed and Kristen had finished her book. She looked at Emmy. "I am going to take my top off for a while and lay on my stomach. Maybe I can get rid of the tanlines on my back." Kristen removed her shorts, t-shirt and her bikini top and lay on her belly. "Will you put some sunscreen on my back,

258

please?"

"Sure, Kristen."

Emmy reached over and put some lotion on Kristen's back for her. Emmy sat back on her lounger and lay on her belly. She undid her top and removed it. Emmy tried to put some lotion on her back.

Amber looked over and offered to help. "Do you need some help with that, Emmy?"

"Thanks, but I can get it."

"Don't be silly. Let me do that for you." Amber took the lotion and rubbed it on Emmy's back for her. "You have such soft skin, Emmy."

After lying on her stomach for ten minutes, Kristen turned over.

Emmy noticed. "Kristen! What are you doing?"

"What does it look like, Em? I'm working on my tan."

"What if the guys come back early?"

"Well, if they do, they won't be looking at me with Amber and Linda out here. Don't be so shy, Emmy. You look just fine."

Emmy looked at Amber and Linda. They were lying on their loungers with their eyes closed. Emmy turned over and smiled at Kristen.

"What are you thinking about, Emmy?" Kristen asked.

"What the guys would say if they came back right now." She wanted to ask Kristen why she had forgotten her birthday, but kept that thought to herself.

"I know what Barry would be doing, and I imagine he would not say a word. He would be too busy staring."

After about five minutes Emmy sat up. She reached under the lounger for the t-shirt she brought out with her. Emmy slipped it on as Kristen noticed.

"I don't want them to get sunburned," Emmy explained.

Kristen laughed and said, "You are too funny, Em."

Kristen noticed Linda and yelled, "Linda! Wake up. Did you forget to put more sunscreen on?"

Linda sat up. "I put some on a few minutes ago. Why?"

"Can't you feel how red your chest is?"

Linda touched her chest and winced.

"You need to cover up right now," Amber said. "Your breasts are gonna be a bit tender for a few days."

"Poor Barry," Kristen said.

The girls headed inside around four. Linda decided to shower and nearly screamed as the water hit her sunburned chest. Emmy got in the shower and winced as the warm water stung the sunburned skin under her arms.

The guys returned right at five, as hungry as could be. They ate dinner, and still no one mentioned Emmy's birthday. Emmy was near tears as she thought everyone had forgotten. At that instant Mama, Karla and Daniel walked into the dining room followed closely by Esperanza. Esperanza brought out the cake with the candles already lit.

Mama stood behind Emmy with her hands on Emmy's shoulders. "Happy birthday, Emmy!"

Emmy looked over her shoulder at Mama as the tears began to fall, "Oh, Mama, I thought everyone had forgotten my birthday. No one said a word about it all day."

Kristen hugged her, then everyone sang.

Derrick and Barry surprised Emmy when they brought out a couple of bags filled with gifts.

"When did you guys get these?"

"This afternoon," Derrick said. "Why do you think Mom made such a big deal about kicking us out of the house."

"Come on, Emmy! Open the presents," Barry shouted.

"Where should I start?" Derrick handed her a present and she opened it. "Wow! How did you guys know I liked this top?"

"Kristen told me you were checking it out the other day, but wouldn't spend the money on yourself," Derrick answered. "So, I bought it for you."

"Hey, I paid for half of it," Kristen reminded him.

Emmy opened all the gifts. Each couple had bought her a gift for her birthday. Even Barry and Linda got her a gift. They bought the latest Santana CD *Supernatural*. Harrison watched Emmy opening her gifts with a bored expression. Kristen gave up trying to get him to show some enthusiasm.

"We have one more gift for you, Emmy," Tony said. He handed it to her.

She looked at him and he grinned. She opened the gift and discovered a t-shirt inside with a picture of a girl on a bicycle on the front. On the back were the words "Maroon Bells Bike Race Champion" in large letters. Emmy laughed and teased Barry. "Too bad you can't wear this, Barry!"

"You know I let you win, Emmy."

"Right. That's why you looked like you were having a heart attack at the end."

The kids sat by the fireplace in the family room as the night began to cool off. Barry asked Linda, "What did you girls do all afternoon?"

"We worked on our tans for most of the afternoon. I told you that before. Why are you asking again?"

Barry looked at the guys with a look that said, "I told you so. We just wondered..."

"Okay, Barry, spit it out," Linda snarled at him.

"Did you keep your bathing suits on?"

Linda smacked his arm. "We were naked if you must know."

Amber laughed as she saw the expression on Barry's face. "Not naked, just topless," she said.

"All of you?" Derrick asked.

"Yes! All of us. Is there something wrong?" Linda grimaced as her bra irritated her sunburned chest.

The guys looked at Kristen and Emmy. Kristen smiled, but Emmy turned red. Derrick, Barry and Tony looked at Emmy's chest; this embarrassed her even more.

Barry asked, "Did you really go topless, Emmy?"

Kristen answered for Emmy. "We were mostly on our stomach but we turned over for a while. What's the big deal?"

Derrick answered, "Don't you know there are security cameras here?"

"What?" Linda and Kristen yelled.

"There are security cameras on the roof and all around the property. There is a room in the other house with a security

261

monitor. Everything is recorded."

Linda grinned at Derrick. "I don't care. Who's going to see the tapes anyway?"

"Maybe no one, except Mom and Dad might have seen the monitor. They check on us once in a while to make sure we're okay."

Kristen and Emmy looked at each other.

"Oh crap!" Kristen swore.

Emmy was too embarrassed for words.

"Emmy, are you all right?" Tony asked.

"Do you think Mama knows?"

Just then Mama walked in the family room. "I certainly do. Kristen and Emmy, you are both grounded."

"Mama!" Emmy and Kristen hollered.

"I'm kidding. Next time you should be more careful before you remove your tops."

Tony walked Emmy to her bedroom later that night and grinned as he looked at her chest.

"Are you trying to imagine what I look like topless, Tony Bertucci?"

"Guilty as charged."

"Maybe someday you will find out for yourself. Until then you will have to ask... Kristen."

Tony grinned, "I already did. All she said was something about real and spectacular."

They both turned their heads as they heard a loud cry from Linda's room.

Emmy and Tony laughed.

"Poor Barry. How will he survive?" Emmy shook her head.

Kristen's cell phone rang. She answered it and handed the phone to Emmy. "It's for you."

"For me? Who would call me on your phone?" Emmy took the phone and answered.

"Happy birthday, Emmy. Did you think I would forget?" Kenny asked.

"I thought maybe you did because you didn't call. Where are you?"

"San Diego. There are 20,000 people who want to say something to you."

Kenny held out his phone and right on cue 20,000 people screamed, "Happy birthday!"

"Did you hear that?"

"Yes, are you doing a show right now?"

"Yes, but we wanted to wish you a happy birthday. We are about to sing 'Sweet Girl' and I wanted to dedicate it to you. I love you, and I miss you so much!"

Emmy's eyes filled with tears, but she managed to say, "I love you, too."

"I'll talk to you later, Em. We gotta finish the show."

Emmy closed the phone and looked at Kristen. Kristen grinned at her.

Emmy wiped her tears away. "Did you know he was going to call?"

"Yes, he called me yesterday, and we set it up. He wanted to surprise you, and I couldn't say anything. He really loves you, Em. I know I have been trying to get you and Tony back together, but now I realize how much you and Kenny mean to each other."

Over the next two days, Derrick made trips to the airport as more cousins arrived. Julie and Jenny Keasling arrived from South Carolina. Julie was twenty-two and Jenny twenty-one. Both girls stood nearly six feet tall with long blonde hair and light blue eyes. Emmy thought they looked like twins. They definitely looked older than twenty-one.

Bobby and Brian were sons of Carmen Lombardi. Being older than any of the other cousins, they spent most of their time hanging out in bars in town.

Emmy mentioned to Kristen, "Those guys are scary looking. I know they are your cousins, but I'm afraid of them. Brian asked if I wanted to have a beer, and he leered at me. It was totally creepy."

"You don't have to be afraid of them, Em. All I would have to do is threaten to call Uncle Carmen, and they will leave you alone." Kristen didn't completely remove Emmy's fear.

Kristen spent most of the next couple of days with her cousins, whom she didn't often see. Emmy read books and worked on her tan by the pool. Tony hung out with Emmy to keep her company.

"Are you gonna sit there and stare at me all afternoon?" Emmy's frustrations surfaced on Saturday afternoon. "Go bother Barry and Linda."

"Sorry, Em. I'm bored so I thought I would hang out with you since Kristen is ignoring you. Barry and Linda went to town for dinner and a movie. I'm trying not to stare, but you do look good in a bikini."

"Will you go away for an hour so I can work on my tan? After that we can do something if you want."

"Yeah, whatever," Tony grumbled as he walked away. *Shoot! You don't have to be so mean, Em.*

Kristen thought that Harrison spent too much time with Julie and confronted him about it Sunday afternoon.

"Why are you paying so much attention to Julie? You are spending more time with her than with me. Why?"

"I'm not spending all my time with Julie. I still talk to you, and we have time to be together."

"Yeah, we spend time together. You stick your nose in a book while I listen to my iPod. I don't call that quality time together."

"What do you want me to do, Kristen? You won't kiss me, and you treat me like I have the plague. I thought we would spend our nights together." *That's the only reason I came. Your father ruined any chance at that with his stupid rule.*

"Maybe I don't let you kiss me because you are so busy kissing Julie, and I don't want to share my boyfriend that way."

"Well, maybe we shouldn't be boyfriend and girlfriend then!"

They argued and Kristen conceded that Harrison made a valid point.

That night Harrison, Brian, Bobby, Julie and Jenny went into town to a bar. Kristen waited on the couch downstairs for

Harrison to get back. He staggered in the house with an arm around Julie, kissing her. Kristen saw them, called Harrison a jerk and ran upstairs to her room.

"Wake up, Em! I need to talk to you."

"Kristen, what's wrong? Did Harrison do something?"

"I waited downstairs for him to get back. He went with the guys and Julie and Jenny to a bar in town, and he came back in the house holding Julie and kissing her. He saw me and didn't even stop kissing that, that..." Kristen couldn't even finish because of her anger. Emmy held her best friend while she alternately vented her anger and cried.

In the morning Harrison tried to convince Kristen that he did nothing wrong. "We went out for a few drinks and laughs. Nothing happened between me and Jenny."

"You're such an ass. You were kissing Julie when you came in the house. Does that mean you were kissing Jenny, too? Don't talk to me. I wish you didn't even exist."

"That's easily remedied. I'll call the airport and get a flight out of here today. You are being childish and immature. You need to grow up."

Kristen stayed angry with him and with her cousins, too. When Harrison left early on Tuesday, Kristen pretended it didn't matter.

"It's all right, Em. I don't care enough about him to even be upset anymore. I should have known the relationship wouldn't last."

"Well, at least you didn't sleep with him," Emmy joked.

Kristen managed to chuckle. *I did think about it.*

Bobby and Brian soon tired of Julie and Jenny and Aspen in general. They flew to Vegas. The sisters turned their sights on Tony. They flirted and competed with each other over him. Tony enjoyed the attention—to a degree. Julie and Jenny liked to spend their days in town shopping and managed to drag Tony along twice—two days too many, he learned.

"What are you doing in our room?" Emmy yelled while

265

holding a t-shirt in front of her chest.

Tony closed the bedroom door and leaned against it. "Sssh!" He put a finger to his mouth. "I'm hiding from those two crazy girls. They are driving me absolutely bonkers."

"Close your eyes so I can put this shirt on."

He did and listened for any sound in the hallway.

"Okay, you can open your eyes," Emmy said.

"Thanks, Em. Can I hide in here for a while? I don't want them to find me. They want to go shopping again."

"I thought you were enjoying their attention." Emmy sat on the edge of the bed.

He sat next to her. "Okay, I admit I did at first."

"They are gorgeous. They look like supermodels."

"Yeah, but they are.. what's the term?"

"High maintenance?"

"Yeah! That's it." Tony snapped his fingers. "All they want to do is go shopping and spend money."

"Did you spend your money on them?" Emmy asked.

"I bought lunch but nothing else. They made me carry their bags. I even had to sit and watch while they tried on designer outfits."

Emmy patted his thigh. "Poor baby."

"Quiet!" He put his hand over Emmy's mouth. "I can hear them in the hall."

Emmy moved his hand and stood up. "Maybe I should tell them where you are."

"No! Please, Em. Don't give me away," Tony begged.

Emmy grinned. "You owe me big time."

Tony stayed in the room for an hour.

"I think they're gone. Should I check?" Emmy asked.

"All right, but be careful."

Emmy slowly opened the door and peeked into the hallway. She quickly closed the door.

"What? Are they still there?" Tony asked. "What am I gonna do? I don't want to hurt Kristen's feelings, but her cousins are nutso."

"I'm kidding. They're gone. You can tell them I need to

266

spend more time with you if you want."

"Thanks, Em. I appreciate it."

Tony bumped into Julie and Jenny in the kitchen later and informed the sisters that he needed to spend more time with Kristen and Emmy. They didn't care and dragged him into town for dinner.

Emmy came downstairs at dinnertime and looked for Tony. She asked Esperanza if she had seen him.

"I saw him with those two sisters, Miss Emmy. I think they kidnapped him," Esperanza whispered as she grinned.

"Uh-oh," Emmy said. "I hope we don't have to pay too high of a ransom to get him back."

Three hours later Tony dashed into the house and spotted Emmy in the kitchen drinking a bottle of water. "Help me, Em!" He ducked behind the island and pulled Emmy down on top of him.

"Oh, Tony, we were so worried. We thought you had been kidnapped. How did you escape?"

"I told them I was going for a run." Tony stuck his head up high enough to look over the island, but quickly lowered it. "They forced me to take them out to dinner. Now they want me to share the hot tub with them. You have to protect me."

Emmy looked at him and giggled.

"What's wrong with using the hot tub?" Kristen overheard the conversation as she entered the kitchen. "And what are you doing down there?"

"They want me to share it with them... you know."

"No, what?" Emmy pulled him up.

Tony glanced back and forth between Emmy and Kristen. "They aren't going to wear their bathing suits and don't want me to wear one either."

Emmy and Kristen laughed.

"It's not funny!"

"It's hilarious," Kristen said.

Tony crossed his arms over his massive chest. "Go ahead and make fun."

Emmy bumped her hip against his. "Are you afraid?"

267

"I'm not afraid, but it's not right."

Julie and Jenny entered the kitchen and waved at Tony.

"Are you coming?" Julie drawled.

Kristen came to his rescue. "Daddy is coming over to use the pool. Would you like him to tell your father about this?"

"You're no fun, Kristen. We wouldn't hurt him," Jenny said.

"Come on, Jenny. We can see if Derrick is busy." Julie grabbed her sister and marched out of the room.

"Thanks, Krissy. I owe you." Tony wiped the sweat off of his brow.

Emmy hopped onto the island, giggled and then asked, "So do you want to use the hot tub with me and Kristen? We won't wear our bikinis."

"What's that?" Mr. Keasling asked as he walked into the room.

Emmy nearly fainted.

"Nothing, Daddy. Emmy was just teasing."

Two weeks passed quickly, and Barry and Linda needed to return home. They said goodbye to everyone, and Derrick dropped them off at the airport. Julie and Jenny decided to fly home the next day. Derrick willingly drove them to the airport. He returned to the house and plopped down on the couch. Emmy looked up from her recliner, closed her book and smiled.

"I know they're family, but being with those two for a week is worse than... than..."

"Being tortured?" Emmy asked.

"Yeah," he sighed. "No more trips to the airport for me. Amber and I are going to do some sightseeing. She would like to spend a couple of days in Denver. Would you be interested?"

"Thanks, but I would feel weird."

"I meant you and Kristen. Or maybe you and Tony."

Emmy shook her head. "You guys have fun. I'm fine hanging out here."

Tony, Kristen and Emmy rode mountain bikes to the ghost town of Ashcroft one afternoon. While they explored outside the old buildings, it began to rain. The temperature dropped, and the rain changed to snow flurries.

"I can't believe it! It was over eighty degrees when we left Aspen, and now it's snowing on us." Kristen looked up at the sky, letting the snowflakes land on her face.

They stood on the porch of the old hotel as they watched the snow falling.

"Too bad this hotel is closed. We could get a room and warm up," Tony commented innocently.

"And just how do you intend to warm us up?" Emmy asked with her hands on her hips and a gleam in her eye.

"I didn't mean it like that, Em." *God knows I wouldn't dare touch you like that.*

The girls giggled, but then started to get chilled.

"Tony, I'm cold," Kristen whimpered.

"Let me hold you. I'll keep you warm." Tony wrapped his arms around her.

"What about me?" Emmy asked.

"Come on, I can hold you, too. I've got long arms." Tony held Kristen and Emmy for a few minutes, then suddenly the snow stopped.

Tony laughed as he pointed toward the sun. "Just like Chicago weather. If you don't like it, just wait a minute and it will change."

Later that night, Emmy sat on the edge of the bed and watched as Kristen brushed her hair in front of the full-length mirror. "Do you think you and Harrison will get back together when school starts?"

Kristen paused and turned to face Emmy. "No way! I'm through with trying to find a guy to be serious about. From now on I'm not even going to think about men."

"Don't make promises you can't keep, Kristen," Emmy said.

"I can't believe we've been here for three weeks already," Emmy said as she packed her suitcase and took one last look at the mountains outside her window. "The time went by so fast."

269

"Come on, Em. We have to be at the airport in thirty minutes," Kristen said as she left the room.

"I'll be right down." Emmy looked around the room. "I guess I've got everything." She dragged her suitcase down the stairs.

"Derrick, would you put that in the van for Emmy?" Mrs. Keasling asked.

Emmy smiled at Derrick and then thanked the Keaslings. "I had the best time of my life. Thank you so much for letting me come along, Mrs. Keasling. I want to thank you, too, for everything, Mr. Keasling."

"Emmy, you are so welcome. We are glad you had a good time. I know how much you mean to Kristen. She would have been lost without you here."

Emmy sat by a window on the flight from Denver to Chicago. She squeezed Kristen's hand as they landed.

"You'll get used to flying, Em," Kristen said. "It's the safest way to travel."

"I doubt if I will have many chances to fly, but it wasn't too scary."

Emmy returned to her empty apartment. She listened to the sound of silence, since there weren't a dozen kids hanging around. She unpacked and wandered into the kitchen. She opened the fridge, grabbed a bottle of water and looked at her calendar. *Hmmm, July twenty-fourth.* She noticed a red circle around August eighth and counted the days. *Fifteen days until Kenny gets home. This will be a long two weeks.*

Chapter Twenty-Seven

Two hours after Emmy returned home from her vacation, Coventry Shield Healthcare called. They needed her to come back to work on Monday the twenty-sixth. She agreed immediately. She hung up her phone and checked her calendar. *This is perfect timing. Now I'll be able to register for three classes instead of two.*

Each day, after she returned to her apartment from work, she crossed one more date off on her calendar. She even worked on Saturday. She hadn't heard from Tony until Saturday night.

"Hey, Emmy, do you have plans for tonight?"

"Not really. What are you doing?" She plopped down on the couch and put her feet up.

"Nothing. Would you be interested in grabbing dinner and maybe hanging out?"

She bit her lip. "Would you mind if I say no? I've worked all week, and I'm kinda beat."

"No problem, Em. Just thought I'd ask."

She filled her day off with cleaning the apartment, doing the grocery shopping, paying her bills and other boring household chores. The second week proved to be even busier at work. She counted the days until finally the eighth arrived.

She called the Colwell home in the morning and reached Mrs. Colwell.

"Hi, it's Emmy. Do you know what time Kenny is supposed to get home by any chance?"

"He called and told his father to expect him home around five this afternoon. Would you like to be here to greet him?" Mrs. Colwell laughed as she asked such a silly question.

"I'll be there at four!" Emmy answered gleefully.

That afternoon Emmy paced around the Colwell's living room, occasionally looking out the front windows, as she waited for Kenny. He finally walked in the back door and hollered, "I'm home! Anybody here?"

Emmy turned and ran toward the kitchen. Kenny met her in the dining room and held out his arms. She nearly knocked him over as she ran into his outstretched arms. He kissed her, and they

271

held each other close as he spun around.

Mr. Colwell winked at his wife. "I guess we know who our son is most excited to see."

Kenny set Emmy down and gave his parents hugs. "I'm happy to see you guys, too. Emmy is younger and she runs faster."

"I was running to the kitchen to grab something to drink and ran into you accidentally. You just got in the way. It doesn't mean I'm happy you're home," Emmy teased.

They went back to the living room; Emmy sat on the couch with Kenny while his parents sat in their favorite chairs.

"We didn't even hear the limo in the driveway. You surprised us," Mom said.

Emmy added, "I kept looking out the window, but I never saw you."

"I had the driver pull into the alley because I figured you would be in the living room."

"Do you need help with your luggage?" Emmy asked. "Are you going to stay in the carriage house? I can help you carry your gear up the stairs."

Emmy didn't fool anyone. She wanted to have some time alone with Kenny in his apartment.

"I could use a hand, Em. Are you sure you don't mind?" Kenny grinned at his parents.

Emmy blushed as Kenny took her hand and led her out of the room. They ran out to the carriage house and carried his gear up the stairs and dropped it outside the door. Kenny unlocked the door and stepped inside. He flipped on a light and looked at the futon—still folded down as a bed. He grabbed Emmy and carried her to the futon and gently set her down. She scooted over to give him room. He lay beside her, and she pulled him close. They kissed for a moment, but then stopped.

"Did you miss me, Em?"

"Oh! Were you gone?" she asked and then giggled.

He kissed her again and ended up partly on top of her.

"I have to work in the morning, but I packed an overnight bag in case I ended up staying."

"What would your mother think if she knew you were

going to spend the night with me, young lady?" Kenny asked facetiously.

"I'm not sure. Will something happen to me if I spend the night with you?"

"Just because I love you so much, I promise that nothing will happen to you."

"But what if I want something to happen?" Emmy bit her lip.

"Okay, I'll kiss you. Is that all right?"

"You can kiss me all you want. I don't mind."

Kenny started to kiss her but tickled her instead.

She giggled and tried to get away, but he held her tight. When he stopped, she asked, "Are you going to treat me like a friend and keep tickling me?"

"No, I'm through tickling you. I don't want you to think of me as your friend." He kissed her one more time. They lay on their sides, and Emmy looked into his dark brown eyes.

"I missed you," Emmy said, and then grinned. "A little bit anyway. Now tell me about the tour."

Kenny talked about the tour as Emmy listened quietly.

"Now I want to hear all about your trip to Colorado. How did you and Tony get along?"

"We got along all right. We didn't fight or anything."

"Did he kiss you?"

"We kissed a couple times, but that's all." Emmy spent a few minutes telling Kenny about her adventures in Colorado. He laughed when he heard about her swim in the river.

She smacked his arm. "It's not funny. I could've drowned."

"I'm sorry, but the image of you in the river is funny. Weren't you wearing a life jacket?"

"Yes, but I still could have drowned."

Emmy continued and impressed him with her story about the mountain bike race and the night of karaoke. She told him about Kristen and Harrison fighting.

"After Harrison left, Tony spent a lot of time with Kristen. More than with me. He and Derrick both treated me like a kid sister most of the time. I guess I'll always be everyone's little

273

sister." She looked at Kenny, hoping he would do something to prove otherwise.

He looked at her and wiggled his eyebrows like Groucho Marx. "I know something I can do if you just say the magic word."

"Please!"

"Not that magic word."

"Then what?"

"I can't tell you! You're supposed to just say it, then this duck comes down... Oh, never mind. Have you ever heard of Groucho Marx?"

"Sure. He smoked cigars and wiggled his eyebrows like this." Emmy wiggled her eyebrows. "He's funny."

"He always tried to fool around with the leading lady."

"I don't want to be your little sister," Emmy whispered. "I want to be your leading lady."

"You are, Em," he replied as he moved closer and kissed her again.

"Emmy, are you all right?" her co-worker Tammy asked. "That's the third time today I have caught you staring out the window."

"I'm sorry. My mind is elsewhere. Kenny is home and..."

"Say no more. I understand." Tammy waved her hand.

"At least I get to see him every day after work. Last night we wrote a couple new songs."

"Really? I didn't know you were that into music."

Emmy nodded as she answered, "Wednesday we are going to church to sing for the teen group."

"That's great." Tammy placed a stack of files on Emmy's desk. "In the meantime, do you think you can put these files away?" Tammy laughed and her whole body shook.

On Saturday Emmy and Kenny had dinner at Ciao Bella with Kristen and her new friend, Joaquim Rafael—a model from Brazil. Kristen's vow to swear off men hadn't lasted long. Emmy glanced around the room from their corner table. She grinned because all the other women were sneaking glances at Joaquim.

274

When Joaquim excused himself for a moment, Emmy reached out and grabbed Kristen's hand. "Where did you meet him? He is absolutely gorgeous. That tan and that long hair and those deep brown eyes make me get all..."

"Emmy! Kenny is sitting right here."

"Oh, he knows I love him, but I still have eyes." Emmy turned to Kenny and kissed him to prove her point. "Anyway, how long have you been keeping him a secret?"

"We've known each other for six months. Don't get too excited, Em. He's only in the states two or three times a year. Most of the time he models in Brazil or Europe. We're friends, Em. Nothing more."

"Has he ever kissed you? That mouth of his..."

"He's never tried to kiss me."

"Oh, my God! He's not gay, is he?"

"No."

"Are you sure?"

"He does have a girlfriend back home."

"Ssssh, here he comes," Kenny warned them.

"I'm sorry, Krissy," Emmy said and then giggled as she mooned over Joaquim.

Kenny brought Emmy to church Sunday morning; after the service they ate dinner with his parents and Tom and Sherry. Emmy looked at the clock as she helped clear the table. *It's already two o'clock. Kenny will be gone in four hours. Where did this week go?*

After Tom and Sherry left, Kenny and Emmy changed into more casual clothes. Kenny took Emmy's hand and they walked out to the backyard. They sat on the rustic pine bench swing under the tall black maple tree.

Emmy leaned against his shoulder, looked up at him and sighed. "This is getting harder to do. Every time you go away, I miss you more and more."

"I know, Em. But you know this is my life. I'm never going to be a nine-to-five-Monday-through-Friday guy. There are going to be long periods when I'm gone. I will be home for Christmas.

275

We're taking a month-long break."

"I understand that, and it's okay."

"I love you, Em, and I know you love me..." Kenny paused.

"This better not be the part where you break up with me!" She sat straight up.

"No, but we do need to talk seriously about the next few years."

"Okay."

The refreshing breeze blew on their faces and Emmy bunched her hair into a bun.

"This is what I envision. You have to finish college and get your degree. I know that's important. Once you finish at Paul Frank, you should quit working and spend two years at North Park. I'd like for you to quit working now," he noticed the frown forming on her face, "but we won't get into that, yet. The band is going to be working hard to take advantage of our popularity. Who knows how long it will last, but I want to make enough money while I can to support me, and my family, for the rest of my life.

"This is the hard part, Em. I meet girls on the road and sometimes I go to dinner with them. Just for the company. I've never slept with them, and we don't even kiss, but I do like some companionship once in a while. I am a decadent rock star."

"You're the dorkiest rock star in the world," Emmy teased.

"It's not fair to you to sit at home and put your life on hold until I get back from a tour. I'm not saying I want you to start dating every good-looking guy you meet. Like Joaquim Rafael. But you should be able to go to dinner with a friend, or even a guy who might become a friend. Well, what do you have to say?"

She grinned. "Can I go to Brazil and look for Joaquim?"

"I'm serious, Em."

"So was I," she said before giggling.

"He is a very handsome man," Kenny admitted.

She scooted back on the bench and pulled her knees to her chest. "I have one question. How far into the future are you talking? Two years? Three? Ten? In ten years I want to be married and have kids. Will you be ready to settle down and raise a family and not be gone most of the year?"

276

"Yes, I want to have a family someday. I want to be able to support a family and not be on the road all the time. I think I will always want to be part of Fridays At Five, no matter what. We won't always be rock stars like U2 or the Stones."

"Somehow I can't picture you at age seventy prancing around a stage."

"Me neither. Do you understand what I'm saying?"

"I think so. You're telling me to have a life while you're gone, but to remember that you love me and somewhere down the road we might get married and have babies. Is that close?"

They both laughed.

"You are so smart."

"I'm only nineteen and you're forty-five," she teased. "And we're both too young to get married. Does that mean we can't..."

"Emmy! You better behave now."

"Will you promise to always tell me about girls you meet? I don't want there to be any secrets between us."

"I promise I will always be honest with you, but sometimes it's better to not ask the right, or wrong, questions."

"I would want to know, and I'd tell you."

"I don't know if I could take it knowing..."

"Are we talking about the same thing?" Emmy asked.

"I'm talking about financial and educational matters. What are you talking about, Em?"

"Yeah, those things. Long term investments and healthcare. Stuff like that."

They both knew they were talking about sex as he kissed her tenderly.

The four hours flew by; Kenny had to leave. They kissed and hugged, and then he was gone again. Emmy watched from the front sidewalk as the limo disappeared down the street and around the corner. She stood there for a few minutes as she thought about the next few years. She could not foresee a future without Kenny Colwell playing a major role in one way or another. But she wondered, could he see a future without her?

Chapter Twenty-Eight

"....and that is Touchdown Jesus," Tony informed Mama, Kristen and Emmy as he pointed to the large mural on the side of the Hesburgh Library. Tony was taking them on a tour of the Notre Dame campus on Saturday, August twenty-first—orientation day for freshmen. Mama took this opportunity to visit both Heather and Tony. Kristen and Emmy came along because Mama didn't like to drive that far by herself. Classes had not started yet, but football practice had.

"Do you know who your roommate is going to be?" Kristen asked.

"Yeah, I've known since the middle of summer. His name is John Randolph and he's from Defiance, Ohio. He plays football, too. We will be in Dillon Hall which is over that way. I'll take you by there later."

"Have you met him yet?" Emmy asked.

"Yeah, we met when practice started. This is John's second year at Notre Dame so he doesn't have to go through the same orientation as I do. If he did then I could introduce you guys, but I'm not sure where he is today."

Tony quickly adjusted to college life and developed a routine for studying. He learned to contend with a full load of classes and football practice. Tony earned a starting position for the season opener against Kansas on August twenty-eighth. The Fighting Irish beat the Jayhawks by a score of 48-13. Tony led the team with twelve tackles and caused a fumble. His roommate John played about half the time as a back-up tight end but didn't catch a pass. Emmy and Kristen watched the game with Mama at her house. Mama had a hard time watching because she worried about Tony getting hurt. Emmy yelled and screamed and kept jumping off the couch throughout the game—especially when Tony made a tackle.

Emmy was surprised to realize that she missed Tony and had been calling him once a week. She talked to him on Sunday afternoon, the day after their second game, which was in Ann

Arbor, Michigan, where they lost to the University of Michigan in a close game.

Tony asked, "Emmy, will you and Kristen come to the game against Michigan State? It's on the eighteenth."

"Let me see. The schedule is on the fridge. I think I can make it. Oh, no, I'm sorry I can't come that weekend. I was going to be rearranging my underwear drawer that day."

"Emmy!"

"I'm sorry, but having a neat and organized underwear drawer is important to me."

"Come on, Emmy. You've used that weird excuse before. It's so lame. If you are going to tease me, at least use a new line."

"Who said I'm teasing you?"

"You are teasing, aren't you?"

"Yes, you're such a dork. We'll come to a game sometime. I don't know which one yet. How do we get tickets?"

"Ask Mama if you can use the tickets I gave her. I know she will not come to the games because she gets too nervous. She's afraid I'm going to get hurt. She told Uncle Daniel and Aunt Karla they could use the tickets most of the time, but I'm sure they would let you and Kristen come to a game."

"Have you had any time to go out?" Emmy asked.

"What do you mean?"

"Go out on a date. I'm sure there are a lot of pretty girls there who would love to go on a date with you." Emmy reminded him of an earlier conversation. "You promised you wouldn't spend all your time studying and playing football. You need to have a social life, too."

"I thought you were kidding about that."

"You promised to go on three dates this semester. I'm going to hold you to that."

"Does it count if you and Kristen come to a game?"

"No! That's not a date, silly. You have to meet new girls."

"Yeah, well, I'll try."

Mama gave Emmy and Kristen her two tickets to the game after they came over to the house and whined about how much they missed Tony.

Emmy shrugged. "I don't understand it, Mama. I didn't think I would, but I actually miss him. It's like my big brother is gone. We want to surprise him by just showing up to see him."

"You girls can have the tickets. I don't like to watch football because it's too rough, and I'm afraid my baby will get hurt."

"Mama, do I have to remind you that Tony isn't a baby anymore, and he can take care of himself?"

"Tony will always be my baby no matter how big or grown-up he is. You will understand one day when you have babies." Mama gave Emmy a big hug. "Emmy honey, you are too skinny. You need to come over more often because I miss seeing you. You need to let me put some meat on those bones, or else you will get blown away by the wind."

Emmy rolled her eyes. "I will, I promise, and thanks again for the tickets. Tony will be so surprised to see us."

Emmy and Kristen planned to surprise Tony, but something came up to throw a monkey wrench into their plans.

Kristen called with bad news. "I absolutely have to finish this paper for my English 245 class."

"Are you sure you can't get out of it, Kristen? I really want you to go with me."

"I'll see what I can do, Emmy. You should ask Barry or Christopher or someone as a backup just in case I can't go."

"I could ask Barry, I suppose," Emmy said as she thought about Kristen's ex-boyfriend, Christopher Braun. *I'd rather go with Christopher, but I can't call him out of the blue. Kenny would understand if I go with Barry, but I'm not sure how he would feel about Christopher.*

Emmy called Barry. "I might have an extra ticket to the Notre Dame game. Would you be interested in going with me?"

"I'd love to, Em. When?"

"The game is Saturday afternoon."

"Shoot! I gotta work this Saturday."

"That's too bad. Maybe you can go to another game."

"I'd love to go see Tony play. Let me know if you ever have an extra ticket."

Emmy talked to Heather and explained that she might be coming alone.

"We can always sell the extra ticket, Emmy. That won't be a problem."

But then Kristen called her the day before the game with some good news, "I can go! I finished my paper and have the weekend free. Is it too late to change plans?"

"No, I still have your ticket."

At the game on Saturday Emmy and Kristen sat so high up in the stands they could almost touch the clouds.

"Can you see Tony on the sidelines, Kristen?"

"I think so, Emmy. All those players look so big. Tony doesn't stand out like he did in high school."

They kept looking. Kristen screamed and pointed. "There he is, Em. Number fifty-two!"

"I see him now!" Emmy was thrilled to see Tony in his uniform. He often shared his dream of playing football for The Fighting Irish with Emmy.

Right after the game, which the Irish won on a last minute field goal, Emmy and Kristen had no chance to even try and see Tony.

"Do you know how to get to Heather's apartment?" Emmy asked Kristen as they headed back to the car.

"I was there once, and I have the address and directions. It shouldn't be too difficult to find," Kristen said.

Because of the traffic, it took thirty minutes to get out of the parking lot, and another fifteen minutes to find Heather's apartment.

When they found the right street, Kristen checked the numbers. "There it is, Emmy! That building right there."

Emmy pulled into the parking lot. They entered the building and found the right apartment.

"Good! You found the place," Heather said as she let them in. "Tony is coming over for dinner as soon as he can, but he

281

doesn't know you and Kristen are here."

"Do you think he will be happy to see us?" Emmy asked.

"I know he will be thrilled to see you girls. He talks about you and Kristen all the time."

Tony finally got to Heather's place later that evening, and Kristen answered the door. Tony was surprised to see her, so he lifted her off her feet and hugged her.

Heather shook her head at Tony. "Will you put her down so we can eat, and say hi to Emmy while you're at it. She wants to talk to you, too."

"Hi, Emmy. This is a surprise. How are you and how's school going?"

"I'm fine and school is school," Emmy answered.

Kristen asked, "Why did you miss that tackle on number thirty-four in the third quarter? He faked you out of your jock on that play."

"If you really want to know, he happens to be an All-American running back, and he made a great move. I was supposed to have help on the left side on that play, but my teammate got taken out by a block."

"All right, you don't need to get so defensive. Get it, Emmy. Defensive. Tony plays defense."

"I get it, Kristen. I know more about football than you do. It was a zone read with Tony protecting the right side."

Kristen looked at Emmy like she was speaking Greek. "Whatever."

Emmy and Tony took a long time to eat dinner because they talked about the game the whole time. They rehashed every important play. Heather shook her head at them and moved her finger around her ear to indicate they were nuts.

"How long can you and Kristen stay?" Tony asked.

"We're staying overnight, but we have to get back home tomorrow."

Tony looked at Heather but didn't say a word.

"No!" Heather frowned at Tony. "Don't even ask."

"Ask what?" Emmy wanted to know.

"Nothing, Emmy." Heather would not let Tony spend the

282

night in her apartment with Emmy and Kristen there.

"Kristen, what are they talking about?" Emmy whispered.

"Heather is making sure Tony goes back to his dorm room because he can't sleep here. The couch is way too small and the alternative is the spare room."

"Why can't he sleep in the spare room?" Emmy asked.

"Because that's where you will be sleeping. Get it now?"

"Oh!" Emmy looked at Heather, and then blushed. "I wasn't even thinking about that. You guys must think I'm so stupid."

"No, we don't, Emmy. You're a little too naïve and innocent. You just don't think the same devious way we do," Kristen said.

Heather's apartment had two bedrooms and one bathroom. Mama slept in the spare one when she came to visit.

"Kristen, you can either share with Emmy or take the couch," Heather said. "The bed in the spare bedroom is small and squeaky and not much better than the couch. It doesn't matter to me. Just make yourselves at home. The blankets and sheets are in the hall closet if you want the couch. I'm going to bed soon. See you in the morning."

"I'll take the couch, Kristen. You can have the bed," Emmy said.

"No, I'll take the couch. You should use the bedroom."

Back and forth it went. Neither girl could make a decision. Heather and Tony had been watching and couldn't take anymore.

"All right, enough of this. I'm going to flip a coin. Kristen, call it in the air!" Tony said.

"Emmy, it's like the start of a football game. Should we shake hands first, Tony?" Kristen and Emmy giggled.

"Just call it, or I'm tossing you both out." Heather laughed while pointing at the door.

"Heads!" Kristen called.

"Heads!" Emmy called an instant later.

Tony rolled his eyes and Heather slapped her forehead.

"You both can't call heads. Only one of you can call it."

"Okay. You can call it," Emmy said to Kristen.

"No, you can call it, Em. I don't mind."

283

Heather stomped her foot. "Enough of this nonsense. Emmy, you are the visitor, call it."

Emmy grinned at Kristen. "I'm the visiting team, so I should be wearing a white jersey. I think I have one in my bag."

"Emmy!" Tony hollered loud enough to startle both Emmy and Kristen. "Just forget about your jersey and call it while it's in the air."

Emmy nodded.

Tony tossed the quarter in the air.

"Heads! No, wait. Tails! I call tails."

Everyone watched as the coin flipped over and over as it neared the ceiling. It fell in slow motion. Tony caught it in his hand, then slapped it onto his wrist. He covered it with his hand for a moment as Emmy and Kristen moved close to learn who had won.

Tony lifted his hand.

"It's heads! I win," Kristen informed Emmy. "I'll take the couch."

"But you won the toss. You should have the bed."

"I'll let you have the bed. I don't mind the couch."

Back and forth again. Heather threw her hands in the air. "I don't care if you two stand there all night trying to decide, I'm going to bed."

Tony hung around till close to midnight. He gave both girls hugs and then headed to his dorm.

"You can have the bed. I'll take the couch."

"No, I want the couch. You take the bed..."

Chapter Twenty-Nine

A few weeks later Emmy pulled the car into the driveway after work on Friday and saw LaRon Robinson shooting hoops alone. She joined him after changing into jeans and a sweatshirt. They shot baskets for a while, but then LaRon accidentally knocked her down as he jumped to get a rebound. She ended up in the grass by the fence. He came over to see if she was okay.

"I'm sorry, Emmy. I didn't mean to hurt you."

She smiled and said, "I'm okay. I tripped over my own feet, I think. How about a game of one-on-one? Think you can beat me, or do you want me to spot you some points?"

"Big talk for a little lady. I accept your challenge. Not that it really is much of a challenge."

Emmy explained the house rules to LaRon: "You can't block my shot if I'm outside the three point line. You can't foul me, but I can foul you if you are trying a layup."

"Fair enough," LaRon answered. He agreed, thinking she wouldn't be able to make many shots from there.

He could score on her at will, but she managed to keep the game close by hitting several three point shots. Emmy hung on his arm, shoved him and tried everything to stop LaRon from scoring, but he was so much taller and stronger than her. Emmy faked him out once and made a lay up. LaRon won, but Emmy impressed him by making the game as close as she did.

"Good game, LaRon, but I think you cheated! Want something to drink? I've got Coke and Dr Pepper and water."

"Sure! I'll take a Coke if you got it."

Emmy ran into her apartment and returned with two cans of pop. She grabbed two lawn chairs from the garage, and they sat facing each other making small talk.

"How is school going? You're a senior, right?"

"Yeah, this is my last year of high school. I'm going to the U of I down in Champaign. I got into the engineering school."

"Impressive! That's a tough school to get into. Do you have a girlfriend?" she asked. "You're a nice guy and not bad looking."

"Thanks, Emmy, I think. I don't have a steady girlfriend

yet, but I've gone out a few times with some of the girls from school."

Emmy smiled. *You're being modest. I bet the girls are all over you.* "I want a rematch. You were just lucky this time."

"Anytime you want, Emmy. I think I could beat you with one hand tied behind my back and blindfolded."

"Pretty strong trash talk for someone who almost got beat by a girl," Emmy said. "When is your next game? You are playing football this year, right?"

"Yeah, we're playing West Bartlett tomorrow. Wanna come and watch us sometime?"

"Maybe, I go to Roosevelt games when I can. Do you ever watch Notre Dame play?"

"Sometimes."

"I know the guy who plays middle linebacker. We used to date. His name is Tony Bertucci."

"I met him before when you first moved in." He took a long drink of his Coke. "I thought you were hooking up with Kenny Colwell. Did you guys break up?" *I remember how you acted with Tony and the other guy that day. They both treated you like they were more than just friends.*

"No, but he's on tour again. Notre Dame plays Arizona State tomorrow and I'm gonna watch the game. They should win."

"Let me know when you want that rematch and thanks for the Coke." LaRon finished his Coke and then hopped the fence to go back home.

Emmy sat on her lawn chair and thought about Kenny and Tony. Kenny wanted her to date other guys if she wanted, but he still loved her. She still loved him, but her feelings for Tony remained strong.

Kristen came over Saturday morning to spend the weekend with her. Emmy told her about a dream she remembered.

"You're just horny," Kristen laughed. "You need to stop thinking about sex so much."

"Stop it. I don't think about sex any more than you do," Emmy insisted.

Yes you do! You think about it as much as guys. "I would like to see you with Tony, but I understand your feelings about Kenny."

"Sometimes I wish I could just move away and start a brand new life."

"Emmy, don't move away. I would miss you too much. I mean, you would miss me. I wouldn't miss you at all. Besides, you would still miss the guys no matter where you live. You do realize that, don't you? Tony will only be in school for a few years, then things will be different."

"I know, but Kenny will be on the road... forever. That's his career." She paused and then added, "Don't worry, I'm not going anywhere, Kristen."

They watched the game that afternoon; Notre Dame blew out Arizona State by a score of 48-17. Tony again led the team in tackles. He intercepted a pass and almost ran it back for a touchdown, but he was tackled inside the five yard line.

That night they were sitting on Emmy's couch when Kristen called Tony. "Congratulations on the win. You had a lot of tackles. Too bad you are so slow though."

"What do you mean?" Tony sounded a bit agitated as he stood up from his desk and closed his Business 101 textbook.

"If I had intercepted that pass I would have run it all the way back," Kristen said.

"The guy who tackled me had the right angle." Tony looked at John and shook his head.

John laughed then asked, "Are you catching more flak?"

Tony nodded.

"Yeah. Whatever. Emmy wants to talk to you." Kristen handed the phone to Emmy, who was shaking her head.

"Talk to him, or I will go home."

Emmy stuck her tongue out at Kristen. "Hi, Tony. Good game. Too bad about the interception," Emmy said and then giggled.

"Are you going to give me a hard time about that, too?"

"No, sorry, I guess you can't help it that you're slow. Was that a lineman who caught and tackled you?"

287

"No, it was a wide receiver and he had the perfect angle." Tony was exasperated. "A lot of football is taking the correct angles to make tackles."

"I'm just busting your chops." Emmy grinned at Kristen who laughed about her choice of words. "Have you kept your promise and gone out with any new girls yet?"

Tony plopped onto his unmade bed. "No, I really don't want to waste time on a girl that I know I won't care about, and besides all my time is taken up with practice and schoolwork."

"But you promised," Emmy said. "That's an important part of college life. You need to socialize with new people."

"Fine, Emmy, I'll work on it, but only because you are insisting. You know it's the last thing on my priority list."

John laughed. "It's one of the top things on my to-do list."

"I'm sorry if I'm being emotional. I've been feeling a bit overwhelmed by work and school and keeping up with the apartment. I'm gonna ask Diane if she would move in with me. I doubt if she will, but I'm gonna ask anyway."

"What about asking Kristen?"

"I can't." Emmy turned her back to Kristen and then walked into the kitchen. "She would probably do it as a favor, but she is enjoying living on campus too much. Sometimes I wish I could share her dorm room with her instead of this place."

"What else is new?" Tony asked.

"Nothing much. LaRon was shooting hoops when I got home from work yesterday. We played a game of one-on-one and I scored a few times against him."

"Be careful. I wouldn't like it if you got hurt playing ball. Before I forget, I was going to ask you if you and Kristen can come to the game next Saturday. We're playing Southern Cal. Are you busy? Can you guys come?"

"I have to..."

"Don't give me that excuse about your underwear drawer."

Emmy giggled and then said, "I think we might be able to. It depends on whether Kristen gets her toenails done in time."

"That's lame, but at least that's a new excuse."

"We'll be there if it means that much to you."

288

Before she and Kristen headed to bed, Emmy called Diane.

"What's up, Em? It's kinda late." Diane didn't mince words.

"Would you consider moving in with me?"

"What? No way! I don't want to leave Craig. Why?"

"I'm lonely, and I need help with the rent. Please, just consider it. I don't want Grandma to keep giving me money. It wouldn't be like before because Mom won't be here to nag us."

"Emmy, you know I can't leave Craig. He needs me, and I don't think I could ever get used to living with you again."

"There is a spare bedroom, Diane. There's a decent bed in there now. You wouldn't have to share a room with me. I would even take the small bedroom," Emmy said.

"No, Emmy, I don't want to give you any false hope. I'm not going to leave Craig. Didn't Kenny offer to let you live in his apartment for free?"

"Yeah, but I can't do that."

"Why not? If you're not already sleeping with him, you will be soon enough."

"It's not that. I just can't move in with him, and that's all I can say."

"Well, I'm not moving in with you," Diane said.

"Okay, I understand."

Sunday turned out to be a beautiful, sunny fall day. Some of the leaves had turned colors, and some had already fallen. Emmy and Kristen were helping Mr. O'Brien rake up leaves in the afternoon when LaRon saw them and stopped over.

"Hi, Emmy. Wanna play some football? We need one more girl to even things up. Interested?"

"Yeah, maybe." She loved football and thought it would be fun. Emmy asked Kristen, "Wanna play football?"

"No, thanks. You can play if you want. I need to get back to the dorm. I've got to finish reading three chapters by tonight."

"Are you sure you don't mind?"

"I'm positive. Go ahead and play. Just don't get hurt. We're still going to the game next Saturday, right?"

"As far as I know. Mama has the tickets. I'll stop by and get

289

them during the week. Thanks for keeping me company."

Emmy gave Kristen a hug and then hollered at LaRon, "Give me a minute to change. Be right back."

She went inside and came back out a few minutes later after Kristen left. She walked with LaRon to the grade school down the street. She mentioned to LaRon, "My friend plays for Notre Dame. Have I ever told you that before?"

He rolled his eyes. "Every time I see you, that's all."

"I know I do. I'm just teasing." She poked him in the side.

When Emmy and LaRon got to the school, the other kids were already there throwing a football around. LaRon introduced her to them; she couldn't remember any of their names except for Shane Nolan and Shannon Stephenson. They chose up teams and played two-hand touch for awhile.

When they took a break, Shane asked LaRon, "Is that your girlfriend? She looks pretty young. Is she a good kisser?"

"She's not my girlfriend and don't ask such stupid questions. If her ex-boyfriend heard you talking like that about her, he would smash you into next year."

"Oooh, did we touch a sore spot?" Shane waved his hands. "We're really scared about her boyfriend. What is he, like a senior or something?"

"He plays football at Notre Dame and could pound you into the ground with one hand." LaRon shook a fist at Shane.

"Right! She has a boyfriend who plays for Notre Dame. Like we really believe that."

Meanwhile the girls pestered Emmy with questions.

"What grade are you?"

"Are you a freshman?"

"Is LaRon your boyfriend? Are your parents home? Do they have any beer in the house?"

Emmy didn't answer all their questions. "My parents aren't here right now." She exercised caution about letting anyone know she lived alone.

After playing for an hour, LaRon and Emmy lost interest. They walked back to LaRon's house. Shane and Shannon joined up with them in the front yard.

Shannon grabbed LaRon's arm. "I went to the game yesterday. That was a fantastic catch you made."

"Thanks. Too bad we got slaughtered." LaRon walked around the house to the backyard and everyone followed.

"Are your parents home? Got any beer in the house?" Shannon asked.

"They're home, but even if they weren't, I wouldn't let you have any beer."

"Spoil sport." Shannon bumped against LaRon and then turned to Emmy. "How about you? Sorry, I forgot your name."

"It's Emmy," LaRon said.

"Where do you live? I haven't seen you around before."

LaRon answered, "She lives next door to me and don't bother asking her for any beer."

"Can we have some pop at least?" Shane asked.

"All right, but I gotta finish some homework later." He pointed at the picnic table. "Have a seat, and I'll be right back."

LaRon went into the house and brought out four cans of pop. Emmy sat on the bench and Shane sat across from her. LaRon sat next to Emmy and Shannon sat on the edge of the table and started flirting with LaRon. Shane tried to engage Emmy in conversation. Emmy tried to ignore him. *He's rather crude, and Shannon seems like a slut.*

Shannon put a hand on LaRon's cheek. "Call me sometime if you want to go out again. We had a good time that night."

"Yeah, sure. I'll call you sometime."

Emmy looked at LaRon. He looked down at his feet.

Shannon waved goodbye as she and Shane left. "See you, Emmy. Maybe we'll run into each other at school."

Emmy waved back and laughed as Shane put a hand on Shannon's butt. Then she grinned at LaRon. "You and her, huh?"

"Aw! I only went out with her one time."

"I think she remembered it," Emmy teased. *I wonder what happened.*

LaRon tilted his head and looked at Emmy. "I made a mistake. I'm human."

"It happens." She patted his leg.

291

"It won't ever happen again. Not with her."

LaRon and Emmy talked for a time.

"Was that your stomach or mine?" Emmy asked as her stomach growled.

"I think it was yours, but I'm hungry, too. Wanna go grab a burger or something?"

"Sure." Emmy smiled at him. *You are younger than me, but that's all right. Maybe we could hang out as friends.*

"I'll drive. Just need to grab my keys and wallet." He ran into the house and quickly returned. "I know a great place that serves authentic Mexican. All right by you?"

"Perfect."

They talked about school while he drove. They placed their order and LaRon chose a table toward the back.

"Would you be interested in a real date, Emmy?" LaRon surprised her.

"I'm not like Shannon."

"I know. That's why I asked."

Emmy touched his hand. "Let me think about it. Work and school keep me pretty busy."

"Have you ever dated a guy like me?" He kept his voice low as he asked.

Emmy knew what he meant. "Sure! Tony is a jock, too."

They both laughed.

"So my color isn't an issue, huh?" LaRon asked.

"Actually, I've never given that much thought. I really haven't dated that many guys. Jocks, musicians or whatever." She finished her rice milk and went back to refill it.

LaRon watched. *She's tiny, but she has a good body. I don't know what to think about her. She could either be totally innocent, or she might have slept with all those guys she dated.*

Emmy sat back down. "I don't have an answer yet, but I'm sure we'll see each other around."

"I can be patient, Emmy," LaRon said as he smiled.

Chapter Thirty

Kristen Keasling called Emmy to talk about her second year at North Park College. "I'm enjoying my classes more this year. Did I tell you about my new roommate?"

"You mentioned you would have a different one this year." Emmy lay on her stomach in her bed while she read a textbook.

"Her name is Tess Easterly, and we are getting along great. We are almost exactly the same size, and we can share each other's clothes. We have similar ideas about men, too. Neither one of us wants to start a serious relationship yet, but we do enjoy dating different guys and having dinner at fancy restaurants."

"That goes without saying." Emmy laughed.

"What have you been doing besides working and going to school?"

"Nothing. That is my whole life. Work, school." Emmy sighed. "I can't wait for the weekend."

"Have you talked to Tony lately?"

"Not for a while. I did see LaRon again. We played one-on-one and then chilled. He asked me out."

"Really? Like on a real date?"

"Swear," Emmy said.

"What did you say?"

"I didn't say one way or the other."

"He's younger than Tony. Are you coming over on Friday?" Kristen asked.

"I am aware of his age, and, yes, I'm coming over after work. No class this Friday. Are you excited about going to the game?"

"Not as excited as you, but I do like the atmosphere. I hope the weather cooperates."

After finishing work on Friday, Emmy drove to North Park College to meet Kristen. She parked the car and made her way to Howe Hall. She saw some of the girls from Roosevelt High as they were rushing down the stairs. She knocked lightly on Kristen's door and waited.

"Come on in, Emmy. I'll be ready in a second," Kristen hollered.

Emmy entered and watched as Kristen pulled some clothes from her dresser and tossed them toward her bed. "What are you doing?" Emmy ducked out of the way of a flying pair of jeans.

"I'm looking for a certain pair of jeans."

Emmy counted six pairs of jeans already scattered about. *I've got two pair of jeans and one of them is about worn out.*

"Ah! Here they are." Kristen held up a pair of jeans.

Those look just the same as these other ones, Emmy stared at the jeans. "Will you spend the night at my place so we can leave early? I want to get there before the traffic is crazy."

"Yeah, I'll stay, but I need to stop at home first to grab some clean laundry."

"Is your mother still doing your laundry for you? God! You are such a princess."

Kristen grinned. "I know."

"Did I tell you about the scholarship I applied for?"

"Yes, did you get it? I hope so."

Emmy bit her lip. "No, I didn't."

"Oh, Em, I'm so sorry." Kristen hugged Emmy.

"I wish I could go to North Park with you, but I can't afford it yet, and I won't accept any financial assistance from anyone. I hope I can save enough money to spend my final two years there."

The subject came up again in the car as Emmy drove Kristen to her parents' house.

"My parents could help you with tuition and books and room and board and all that stuff. I'm sure they would."

"Kristen, that's a very generous offer, but I couldn't take money from them. I wouldn't feel right."

When they arrived Kristen saw her mother in the family room watching a rerun of *The Golden Girls*. Kristen talked to her mother about Emmy's situation while Emmy used the bathroom.

"We could help her if it means that much to you," Mrs. Keasling said.

"She's my best friend, Mom, and I wish we could go to college together. It would be so much fun."

"Yes, dear, we know. Maybe we can talk to her and come to an arrangement."

Kristen ran upstairs to her room to allow her mom time to talk to Emmy in private. Emmy came out of the bathroom and didn't see Kristen around.

"Emmy, could I talk to you for a minute?" Mrs. Keasling asked.

"Sure." Emmy wondered why.

"Emmy, we know how close you and Kristen are, and I understand you are putting yourself through school on your own. I respect that very much. I want you to know that we would like to help, if you would let us."

Emmy closed her eyes. *Kristen what did you tell your mother? You know how I feel.*

Mrs. Keasling continued, "Derrick has a full ride and Kristen has a partial scholarship. Would you allow us to help you so you and Kristen can both go to North Park?"

"Mrs. Keasling, that is so generous an offer. Believe me, I am grateful for your generosity, but I can't bring myself to accept your charity. I would rather work my way through school on my own, but I really appreciate the offer."

"I admire you for that, Emmy. Maybe we could work out an arrangement of some sort, so you wouldn't think of it as charity. Maybe an interest free loan."

"I don't want to take out any loans, Mrs. Keasling. I don't want to have student loans to pay for after I graduate. I want to be totally debt-free." Emmy shook her head, embarrassed to even be talking about this. "I applied for a scholarship, but I didn't get it. I could get some grant money, but it wouldn't be enough."

"Emmy, will you at least promise me that if you get in a bind, and are thinking about dropping out of school because of finances, you will let us help."

"Okay, I will promise you that I won't quit school because I don't have the money to continue."

"Good! We'll hold you to that, Emmy."

Emmy ran upstairs to join Kristen in her bedroom. "What did you say to your mother? She just offered to pay for North Park.

I felt like crawling in a hole." Emmy sat on the bed and watched as Kristen pulled more jeans out of her dresser.

"I told her about the scholarship, and how much I wished you could go to North Park with me. Which pair looks better?" Kristen held up more jeans.

"The one in your left hand." Emmy pointed. "You are still my best friend, and we can see each other on weekends, but I can't go to North Park just yet."

Kristen threw both pairs of jeans into the suitcase. "I know, Emmy. I thought it would be so great if we were at North Park together. We could be roommates." Kristen walked into her closet and looked for some tops.

"That would be perfect, but you know how I feel."

"I know, Em. You are stubborn and determined." Kristen grabbed several tops, walked over to the bed and tossed the clothes in her suitcase.

"Are you moving in with me?" Emmy grinned as she straightened out the clothes in Kristen's suitcase.

"No, this is what I need for school while my other stuff gets laundered." Kristen filled the large suitcase with other essentials. "That should last most of the week."

"Princess!" Emmy teased. *It must be nice to be able to afford all this.*

Kristen admired Emmy for putting herself through school without any help from anybody else. Emmy knew she would accept Kenny's offer to pay for her college before she would accept money from the Keaslings.

As she tossed and turned in the spare bedroom that night, Emmy thought about college. *Now that I know I'm not getting a scholarship, maybe I should think about Kenny's offer. I just can't let Krissy's parents pay for my college, but I could let Kenny.*

Emmy and Kristen hit the road on time in the morning—six a.m. Emmy drove and the traffic remained light until they got close to South Bend. They exited the tollway and took some local roads to get to Heather's apartment. They would leave the car there and walk to the stadium later. Tony knew they were coming and planned to meet them at Heather's after the game.

Heather let them in, but explained, "I've got a twelve hour shift at the hospital starting at ten. I'll give you my spare key so you can get in after the game. There's not much in the fridge, so you will need to order out. I do have stuff for lunch as long as you don't mind soup and sandwiches."

"That will be fine. We can order pizza for dinner."

When Heather left, Emmy and Kristen still had a couple of hours to kill before the game.

"Where do you think Tony is now?" Kristen asked.

"He told me they have a team mass at the Basilica of the Sacred Heart before every game, so that's probably where he is now."

"Why don't we leave now and check out the tailgating in the south parking lots?" Kristen suggested.

"Yeah, then we can watch the team walk to the stadium. Maybe we can get close enough to see Tony."

They walked to the parking lots south of the stadium and received several offers of food and beverages by scores of rowdy fans. They passed a van and four guys in Notre Dame sweatshirts whistled at them.

"Just keep walking, Em. Those guys are already drunk." Kristen kept her eyes straight ahead.

"Hey, sweetheart, come and have a beer with us. We've got plenty." One of them reached out and grabbed Emmy's arm. He pulled her towards the van.

"Let me go! I don't want a beer." Emmy tried to smack his hand away.

"Ah, come on. Just have one beer with me. I think you're kinda cute for a kid."

Kristen turned and and saw a guy with his hand on Emmy's arm. She watched as the guy moved his other hand to her bottom.

Emmy rammed her knee into the guy's crotch, and he fell like a tree. "I said I didn't want a beer, and I meant it!" she screamed.

The other guys backed away with their hands in the air.

"Okay, kid, we get the idea. Don't go postal on us."

Emmy and Kristen hurried away.

"Where did you learn to do that, Em?"

"Rory Porter showed me how to defend myself. I've never done that before, but it just kinda happened naturally. Did you see the look on that guy's face?"

They made their way to the library area and managed to get close enough to see the players as they walked to the stadium.

"Emmy! There he is." Kristen waved as she screamed. Both girls yelled, "Tony! Tony!" at the top of their lungs. He heard then turned to see them. He smiled and waved. The girls made their way into the stadium and were in their seats, above the clouds, in time to watch the marching band do their routine.

The girls didn't have a lot to cheer about as the first half ended with the Irish trailing 21-3. Southern Cal kicked a field goal early in the second half to go up 24-3. All of a sudden the threatening skies opened up, and it poured. The Irish fought back. The weather helped. It rained even harder, and the wind blew at gale-force speed every time the Trojans had the ball.

"Krissy, I think it must be the luck of the Irish."

"I thought I read somewhere that that meant bad luck."

Emmy raised her face into the rain. "No matter. I can sense the momentum is shifting."

Early in the fourth quarter, the Irish scored to cut the deficit to 24-16. With just over eight minutes to go, a field goal brought them within five points. With six and a half minutes left in the game, the Irish had the ball again.

"Isn't this so exciting, Krissy?" Emmy yelled at Kristen who huddled under her coat and didn't appear to be enjoying the game as much. They were both soaked to the skin.

"Can't think of anywhere else I'd rather be, Em."

"It's only rain. We'll dry off when we get back to Heather's."

The Irish moved the ball down the field to the eighteen yard line. The Irish quarterback Israel Steele dropped back to pass, but the Trojan defense smothered all his receivers. He took off up the middle and appeared ready to score when the USC free safety tackled him at the two yard line, and he fumbled. The ball trickled

298

into the end zone and a mad scramble for the ball ensued. After the officials pulled the players off the pile, John Randolph emerged with the ball. He held it up high, and the Irish moved ahead by a point. The two-point conversion failed, but the defense withstood the Trojans' last valiant attempt to score. Tony made a game-saving tackle on a fourth down play to seal the victory.

High up in the stands, Emmy and Kristen yelled and screamed as they jumped up and down in celebration.

"They did it! Can you believe it, Krissy?"

"Did you see who recovered the fumble?" Kristen asked.

"I couldn't tell, and I didn't hear who the announcer said. Tony will know. He'll tell us later."

Tony didn't arrive at Heather's apartment until till after ten o'clock.

"Where have you been?" Kristen asked when he finally arrived. "We about gave up on you."

"I was at the training center eating and celebrating with my teammates."

"Well, we ordered a pizza a couple of hours ago."

"I'm full..."

"Good, because Emmy ate the whole pizza herself. There's nothing left."

"I didn't eat it all. You had just as much," Emmy said. "Who recovered the fumble?"

"You won't believe this. It was my roommate, John. He wouldn't have been in on that play except that Denny O'Leary got his wind knocked out on the previous play. John entered the game as an extra blocker on their defensive end. He blocked him then ran downfield trying to get open and happened to be at the right place at the right time. I'll have to introduce him to you guys sometime. You would like him."

"I'm not interested in being *introduced* to a football player who lives three hours away," Kristen said.

Tony hung around for a while but needed to get back to his dorm. The girls spent the night and headed home early Sunday morning.

Chapter Thirty-One

"Bills! Bills! Bills! All I ever get are bills and junk," Emmy moaned as she checked her mail. "Whoa. What's this?" Emmy spied an envelope that looked interesting.

Emmy called Kristen. "I got an invitation to the wedding of two old friends from high school—Grady Harris and Maris Miller. Do you remember them?"

"I'm not sure. The names don't ring a bell."

"They were one year ahead of us in school. Well, it doesn't matter, but I got invited to their wedding. It's at a church in SoHam close to where my parents live, and I wanna go, but more importantly, I want you to go with me. It's on Saturday, November thirteenth. The reception is at the V.F.W. on Glenwood Street."

Kristen checked her schedule. "Emmy, you're going to be mad. I can't go. That's the same day as my Grandma and Grandpa Keasling's sixtieth wedding anniversary party, and I've got to be there for that or my parents will kill me. I'm sorry, Em. Why don't you go by yourself?"

"I don't want to go alone," Emmy whined.

"Don't start this again," Kristen said.

"What?"

"You didn't want to come to my graduation party unless you found a date."

"That was different. I'm not looking for a date to take me to the wedding," Emmy said. "Just someone to sit with and talk to."

"You could ask Tony since Kenny isn't home."

"He's probably got a game that day."

"Maybe not. They do have some open weekends on their calendar. It won't hurt to call."

"All right, I'll call him."

Emmy got off the phone and started to call Tony but changed her mind. Fifteen minutes later, she dialed his number.

"Hi, Tony, how are you? It's Emmy."

"Hi, Em. I'm doing great. How are you?"

"I'm okay. Say, I got invited to a wedding on the thirteenth of November and kinda wondered if you have a game that week."

Emmy sounded lame and kinda desperate.

Tony looked at his schedule. "We're in Pittsburgh that Saturday, Em, sorry."

"Oh, I understand. I should have checked the schedule before I asked. I forgot that I've got one on the fridge. I'm disappointed because I was hoping Kristen could go, but she can't. It's the same day as her grandparents' party."

"I gotta run. Thanks for calling and thinking of me. I'll talk to you later." Tony hung up; Emmy wondered if he was mad at her for bothering him, or if he had company—some female company.

Emmy called Kristen back right away but had to leave a message on her phone. Kristen returned the call a few minutes later. "Hey, Emmy, got your message about Tony not going. What about Linda? I suppose you could ask Barry if Linda can't go."

Emmy called Linda, but she couldn't go. She didn't bother to ask about Barry because Linda wouldn't let him go anyway. Emmy asked Diane if she would be interested in going, but she and Craig already had plans. She talked to Kristen again.

"Linda can't, or doesn't want to go, Not sure which. Diane can't go because she has plans. I'm running out of people to ask."

"There must be someone in this big old world willing to go on a date with you," Kristen teased.

"Very funny, Kristen." Emmy sounded annoyed.

"Wait! You said LaRon asked you out. A wedding would be a safe place for a first date."

"I can't go out with him." Emmy shook her head even though she was on the phone. "What time is your party?"

"Let me ask Mom. I'll call you right back, Em." Kristen called back a few minutes later. "The party starts at two, and will probably be done by five, six at the latest."

"Would you consider going to the reception with me? I know you can't make the wedding, but you could go to the reception."

"Sure. That will work. I'm sorry I didn't think of that before, Emmy."

"Good. Then it's all settled. It will be fun. You do remember Grady and Maris, right?"

301

"I remember them now. Both kinda chubby. They were in Derrick's class, right? I think he was friends with Grady."

"Yeah, Grady was always nice to me at a time when some of the other kids treated me like crap."

Emmy called Tony back. "Hey, it's me again. Are you mad at me for calling earlier?"

"No, sorry I had to get off the phone so quick earlier. I was kinda busy." Tony offered no other explanation.

"I wanted to tell you that Kristen is going to the reception with me. Her party will be over in time. I'll go by myself to the ceremony. Do you know Kristen's grandparents?"

"Duh! I used to go with Derrick and Kristen sometimes when they would see them. Anything else, Em?"

"No, I just wanted to tell you about Kristen."

"Okay, thanks for calling. I'll talk to you sometime."

Just before Tony hung up, Emmy thought she heard a girl talking in the background. *Good! Maybe he is finding the time for a social life.*

The day of the wedding finally arrived. Emmy woke up early and cleaned the apartment. She gathered her dirty clothes and walked over to see if Mrs. O'Brien was home.

"Good morning, Emmy dear. How are you?"

"I'm fine, Mrs. O'Brien. Would it be okay if I do some laundry this morning?"

"Of course it will be all right. I remember when the boys were in high school, and I was doing laundry every day. I'll make us some tea and we can talk. If you have time, I mean."

"I'm not busy this morning. I'll put this in the washer and come upstairs. I'll tell you my plans for this afternoon."

Emmy carried her laundry basket down the steep stairs into the unfinished part of the basement. *I'm grateful that you let me use the washer and dryer.* "Oooh, yuck! I hate these cobwebs." Emmy brushed one away from the counter where she sat her basket. *It's better than spending money at a laundromat.* She loaded the machine, turned the dial on the washer, pulled it out and ran upstairs to talk to Mrs. O'Brien.

302

Mrs. O'Brien pulled part of a cobweb from Emmy's hair. "I really need to get down there and clean out the mess. Those steps aren't easy for me."

"I could do it for you. You let me use your machines."

"That would be so sweet of you, dear."

Emmy sighed. *Great! What have I gotten myself into now.*

After her laundry was finished, she returned to her apartment and kept busy until she needed to get ready. She grabbed her new dress from the closet.

"I hope it looks as good today as it did at the store," she muttered. *I wouldn't have picked out one so short, Krissy. You talked me into buying it.* She showered, got dressed and looked in the mirror. *I guess it's not too short. Besides, I doubt if I see anyone I know.*

The ceremony started at three; Emmy wanted to stop by to see her parents beforehand. Her mother answered the door and Emmy hung her coat up in the small front closet.

"Emmy, you look so dressed-up. Where are you going?"

"Today is Grady and Maris' wedding. I told you about that last week. Hi, Daddy."

He grunted a hello but didn't get out of his recliner.

"I guess we forgot. Who are you going with?"

"I'm going to the ceremony by myself, but Kristen Keasling is going to the reception with me. It will be fun."

"I think Mrs. Sanders said they were going. Maris is her niece, if I remember right. You should look for them. Her son will be there. You should talk to him. Do you remember his name?"

"No, Mom, I don't know his name, but I will be polite if I see the Sanders family."

Emmy and Mom talked for ten minutes without arguing. Dad didn't say a word as he sucked on a beer.

Emmy checked the time. "I really need to get going. I'll call you this week."

"His name is Wayne, remember?"

"Oh, yeah, I remember now."

Emmy arrived at the church and waited in the back to see if she saw some of the kids from Roosevelt High. She hoped to see

303

someone to sit with, but she only recognized Mrs. Sanders from the neighborhood. *Wow! She's even wider than I remember. Shoot! Maybe she won't remember me.*

"Emily, is that you, dear? I didn't know you were coming. How are you, dear? Let me see you. You look very pretty. Is that a new dress?" *It's rather short, but I suppose that's fashionable.*

"Yes, Mrs. Sanders. How are you? Where is Mr. Sanders?"

"He's parking the car. He'll be right in. Wayne, come over here. Do you remember little Emily Colasanti?"

Wayne came over, smiled and pushed his glasses up. "Hello, Emmy. How are you?"

"I'm fine. How is school going?" *You're still as skinny as I remember. You take after your father.*

"I finished up at Paul Frank and now I'm working as a salesman at Ted Hamilton's Chevy. At least for now. Know anyone looking for a car?" He snorted as he laughed and pushed his glasses into place again.

"Emily, are you by yourself?" Mrs. Sanders asked.

She glanced around in near desperation for someone she knew. "Yes, Mrs. Sanders," she answered in resignation.

"You should sit with us. You and Wayne can catch up on things. Wayne, find seats for us while I wait for your father."

"Yes, Mother," he said.

Emmy didn't want to be rude, so she followed him. They found seats on the bride's side. Mr. and Mrs. Sanders joined them after a couple of minutes. Emmy sat on the far side away from the aisle so she didn't have to sit next to Mrs. Sanders.

"What have you been doing, Emily?"

"I'm working full-time and taking night classes at Paul Frank." She tugged down her dress because Wayne was staring at her legs. *Now I wish I hadn't worn such a short dress. Thanks ever so much, Kristen.*

"Do you still live at home or have you moved out? I never see you around the neighborhood anymore."

"I moved out after I graduated," Emmy said.

She's got great-looking legs, he thought. "Where do you live?" *She's not as tall as Diane, but she has certainly grown up*

304

since the first time I saw her.

Emmy didn't want to give Wayne her address. "I'm still in the area. Is that a new suit? It looks handsome." She changed the subject without him realizing.

"It's fairly new. I bought it for my grandfather's funeral."

"Oh, sorry. I didn't know." She glanced around the room.

"That's all right. Is that a new dress, Emily? You look pretty in it. I mean you would look pretty out of it, too."

Emmy jerked her head back to him with wide eyes. *Did you just say what I think you did?*

"I didn't mean it like that. I mean you look pretty in whatever clothes you are wearing, not just in that dress."

"Thank you. I understood what you meant." *Maybe I should go get my coat and use it to cover my legs. He's creeping me out with his staring.*

They ran out of things to talk about, so Emmy looked around again to see if she recognized anyone. She saw a group of guys she suspected were old high school friends of Grady's. She saw a couple of girls sitting four rows ahead of her who looked familiar, but couldn't remember their names. Then she remembered—Elaine Novicki and Cindy Mackens. The music started; Emmy watched as the bridesmaids walked down the aisle, and then Maris appeared.

"Doesn't Maris look so beautiful!" Emmy exclaimed as they stood up. *She's lost some weight.*

"She looks better than I remember," Wayne replied. "I haven't seen her for quite some time." *She's not as fat as she used to be.*

"So you're not really close then?" Emmy asked.

"Not really. My mom and her mom don't get along too well."

"I know what that's like."

Later, in the reception line, Emmy was standing with the Sanders family when Maris spotted her.

"Emmy! I'm so glad you could make it. It's good to see you again!"

Maris looked at Wayne. "Hi, Wayne, I'm glad you could be

305

here, too. Are you with Emmy? I didn't know you two were going out."

Wayne didn't say anything, and Emmy didn't have a chance to correct Maris because she was hugging Grady and didn't hear Maris' remark.

"You look very handsome today, Grady, and Maris is more beautiful than ever," Emmy said.

"Thanks, Emmy. I've been working out. Had to fit into this tux. You look great, too. I hope we get a chance to dance later."

"I would like that very much."

"Where are you going until the reception starts?" Wayne asked a few minutes later.

Emmy looked at her watch. "I'm supposed to meet my friend Kristen at six at the hall. I guess I have an hour to kill. I think I'll go to my parents' house and wait there. What are you going to do?"

"Nothing. I guess I'll just hang around here. Nowhere else to go."

Wayne had a sad look on his face, and, though Emmy didn't know why, she invited him along.

"Sure! That would be great," he answered.

"Right. Great," Emmy muttered. *This is going to be a nightmare. I just know it.*

Emmy and Wayne headed back to her parents' house. She didn't have a key, so she rang the bell. Mom let her in and saw Wayne with her.

"Wayne! It's so good to see you. How have you been? You look so handsome in your suit."

"I've been fine, Mrs. Colasanti. How are you?"

"Well, come on in. Have a seat on the couch with Emily. Tell me about the wedding. Did you sit together?"

"Mom! Geez. Where's Daddy?" Emmy kept her coat with her to cover her legs.

"He ran to the store to grab some dinner for us. I know you will have dinner at the reception. You can eat together and even dance. You will have so much fun, dear." Mom smiled. *Maybe you'll finally realize that Wayne isn't such a loser as Diane thinks.*

306

Emmy rolled her eyes. Mom continued to make a big deal about Wayne, as Emmy kept looking at the time.

"Oh, look. It's twenty to six. I should get going. I have to meet Kristen at six."

"Emily, it will only take five minutes to get there. You still have time. Don't be in such a hurry. I want to talk to Wayne." Mom smiled at him as Emmy rolled her eyes.

At ten till Emmy stood up. "I really have to go now. I'll talk to you later."

"It's been a pleasure to see you again, Mrs. Colasanti. I'll say hello to Mother for you." Wayne smiled.

Gag me! Emmy coughed.

"Bye, dear. Have a good time at the party with Wayne."

Emmy muttered under her breath. "I'm not going to be with Wayne, Mother."

When Emmy got to the V.F.W., she didn't see Kristen. *Where are you, Krissy? You promised you would be here.* At ten after Kristen finally arrived. "Oh, Kristen. I'm so relieved to see you." Emmy hugged Kristen as if she hadn't seen her for years.

"I'm glad to see you, too. How was the wedding and who is this with you?" Kristen removed her Ralph Lauren coat and hung it up.

"The wedding was fantastic—nice and short. This is Wayne Sanders. He lives by my parents. Wayne, this is my friend, Kristen Keasling."

Wayne and Kristen exchanged pleasantries.

"Maybe I will see you later. Kristen and I are going to find our table." Emmy and Kristen rushed off, leaving Wayne standing alone.

"Who was that guy, Emmy? He seems a little different maybe." Kristen laughed. "And suits like that haven't been fashionable for years. Derrick wouldn't be caught dead in one."

"That's putting it mildly. That's the guy Mom was always trying to set me up with. She is friends with his mother. They live in the neighborhood. Anyway, now you're here, and we're going to have fun." Emmy and Kristen found their seats, then headed to the bar.

"Two Cokes, please." Kristen smiled flirtatiously at the bartender. *Maybe I can talk you into letting me have some champagne later.*

They wandered around to see if they could find anyone from Roosevelt High they remembered. Emmy saw the group of guys she had seen at the ceremony. She recognized some of them as former football players. A couple of them smiled at her. Emmy hoped they would ask her to dance later. Kristen saw Elaine Novicki and Cindy Mackens on the other side of the room. They zigzagged through the crowd and talked to them for a few minutes. The bridal party arrived, and after a few minutes Emmy and Kristen managed to talk to Maris and Grady.

"How is Derrick?" Grady asked. "We've kinda lost track of each other."

"He's going to the University of Arizona. He wants to get into law school."

"By the way, Emmy, I told my mom that you were here with Wayne Sanders, and she moved him to your table. We would have had you together before if we had known, but Mom switched his seat so you can have dinner together."

Emmy appeared stunned as she looked at Maris.

"I'll talk to you guys later. I gotta go do my bride things." Maris waved as she flitted away.

Emmy looked at Kristen. "Oh, crap! Now what am I gonna do?"

"Come on, Emmy. How bad can it be? We simply have to sit at the table while we eat. After that you don't have to be around him if you don't want."

"Fine. Let's get it over with."

They went back to their table and discovered Wayne already there. He had a silly-looking grin on his face as he stood up.

"Emmy, isn't this great? We are at the same table. I told my mom, and she called your mom to tell her the good news."

"That's just perfect, Wayne." Emmy grimaced as she answered. She knew her mother would blow this all out of proportion.

308

Kristen came to the rescue by sitting between Emmy and Wayne. Kristen used her charm to keep Wayne occupied so he couldn't bother Emmy. After the meal, the toasts, and the first dances, Wayne hurried to the bar, ordered three Cokes and brought them back to the table.

"Thanks, Wayne."

"You're welcome, Emmy."

"How about some champagne the next round," Kristen hinted.

The DJ opened the dance floor to everyone, so Kristen pulled Wayne out to dance with him. After they returned to their seats, Kristen whispered to Emmy, "You should dance with Wayne at least once. He is pretty good. He surprised me, anyway."

"Kristen!"

"Go on! Just dance with him one time."

Emmy looked at the table where the football players had congregated. Two of them smiled at her, but they didn't show any interest in dancing. She danced with Wayne, and he surprised her as well.

"You're actually a good dancer, Wayne," Emmy said as she watched his moves.

"Thanks, I used to take lessons. Mom made me go, and now I get to cash in on the rewards. I get to dance with pretty girls like you and Kristen."

"Thank you so much for the compliment. Kristen is much prettier than me, though."

"I don't think so, Emmy. I think you're prettier than any girl here. In or out of that dress," he said.

"You've got a dry sense of humor. I like that, Wayne."

Later, Emmy had a chance to dance and talk with Grady Harris. "Do you remember when you were a senior, and I was at my first-ever school dance?"

"Kinda." Grady shrugged.

"Well, you were the first boy to ever dance with me. Other than Kenny, I mean."

"Really?"

"Yeah, I waited around all night, but no one ever asked me

309

to dance until you did. We danced, and you told me that you loved Maris, and I told you that she loved you, too."

"I remember that now."

"Now you guys are married."

After the song ended, Grady hugged Emmy. "I hope you will invite us to your wedding someday, Emmy."

"I will if I ever get married."

As Emmy returned to her table she walked past the football players. She smiled at them but then heard someone say, "That's Diane Colasanti's little sister."

"I remember Diane. She was sleeping around."

"I heard they were both kinda easy."

"Todd Delaney told me he did both of them."

"Yeah, I don't believe a word that sleazebag says. You know he got busted, right?"

"I heard he got caught with some jailbait."

"He could end up doing time and not in the juvenile center, either."

Emmy bit her lip and turned away without saying anything. She knew Todd from high school and had been the victim of his stalking. He spread sexual rumors about her before she met Tony. She stopped, gathered her courage, turned around and confronted the football players.

"I heard what you guys said about me. I want you to know that I never did anything with Delaney. He's a total ass."

The guys stared at Emmy with open mouths.

"And FYI, I'm not easy. Not that any of you will ever get a chance to find out."

She returned to her table with a bounce in her step. *It felt good to put those jerks in their place.* She found Wayne and Kristen in conversation. Although Wayne was not what anyone would call handsome, with his high forehead and weak chin, he was intelligent and charming—to a degree.

"Would you like to dance again, Emmy?"

"Yes. I'll dance with you."

When Maris came around to say goodbye, Emmy actually thanked her for switching Wayne to her table.

310

"I hope you had a good time, Emmy. Let's stay in touch."

"Yes, we should. Where are you guys gonna live?"

"We've got an apartment in Raynor Park. Not too far from where you used to live."

They hugged and Maris moved on. As Emmy and Kristen got ready to leave, Emmy noticed Wayne standing alone. "Do you need a ride home, Wayne?"

"I guess I could walk. My folks left early."

"Don't be silly. I'll give you a ride. Come on."

Emmy saw some of the football players again as she waited for Wayne to say good night to a couple of relatives. This time she didn't smile at them.

"I'll talk to you tomorrow, Kristen. I had a good time. I'm glad you were able to be here."

"It was fun, Em. Are you gonna give Wayne a lift home?"

"Yeah, he was going to walk."

Kristen smiled at Emmy.

"Don't even think like that, Kristen. I'm just giving him a ride home. We aren't going to become a couple no matter how much both our mothers wish it would happen."

Emmy gave Wayne a ride home, and they sat in her car talking for a few minutes. Emmy told him all about Kenny, since Wayne remembered him from the neighborhood.

"See ya, Wayne. I had fun dancing with you."

"Me, too. Can I call you sometime?"

"I don't think so, Wayne. I don't want to mislead you."

"I understand. Kenny sounds like a good guy. Good night, drive safely."

Emmy got home and discovered a message on the answering machine. She checked to see who had called. "I knew it!" She groaned as she listened to the message.

"Hi, dear. It's your mother. Call me tomorrow and let me know how your date with Wayne went. I hope you had a great time. Did he ask you out again?"

"Oh, for crying out loud, Mom. It wasn't a date!" Emmy threw her hands in the air in exasperation.

Chapter Thirty-Two

Mama called Emmy Wednesday evening. "Hi, Emmy, how have you been? I haven't seen you for a while."

"I'm okay. I've been busy with work and school. You know, the usual stuff," Emmy answered. "Are you okay, Mama? Do you miss Tony?"

"I'm feeling good, but I do miss him. It's so quiet in the house without him."

"I bet you're saving a fortune at the grocery store," Emmy said.

"I am." Mama laughed. "Karla called to inform me that she and Daniel won't need the tickets this weekend. They have to be in Denver. Would you and Kristen be interested in going? It's the last home game of the year."

"As far as I know, I don't have any plans. I'd like to go. I'll call Kristen and let you know."

Kristen had no plans, so on Friday Emmy and Kristen headed to South Bend. They didn't want to leave on Saturday because of the traffic.

Kristen watched as Emmy loaded a cassette into the player.

"What is that?"

"It's a cassette, duh."

"I know that, but it doesn't look like a real one."

"Since this car doesn't have a CD player, Kenny made me a cassette with both of their CDs on it. That way I can listen to their music in the car."

"Does his new car have a CD player?"

"Yeah, he waited until the '99s came out so he could get one with a CD player." Emmy tapped the steering wheel in time with the music.

While on the way, Emmy mentioned. "I talked to Heather, and she agreed to let us stay there."

"That's good. What would we have done if she wouldn't let us stay?"

Emmy thought about it for a moment. "I see what you're

getting at. All the hotel rooms would be taken because of the game."

"Ya think?"

Emmy made a face at Kristen.

"Hey!" Kristen pointed straight ahead. "Keep your eyes on the road, please. I do not want to crash."

"We could always crash with Tony and his roommate. I'm sure guys sneak girls into their rooms all the time," Emmy said.

"Somehow I can't see John and Tony sharing a bed."

Emmy grinned, "Then I guess we would have to..."

"I am not sleeping with a guy I have never even met!"

"I'm kidding. I'll sleep with John and you can share..."

"I'm gonna smack you as soon as we stop," Kristen warned.

"Oh, lighten up. I'm kidding." Emmy passed a van with a Notre Dame pennant in the window. "You can be so serious at times."

"You are up earlier than I expected," Heather said as Emmy and Kristen dragged themselves out of bed early the next morning.

Emmy opened the fridge and pulled out a half gallon of milk. "We want to do some tailgating."

"Do you know anyone who is going to be tailgating?" Heather asked.

"No, but we just have to smile and flirt with some guys, and they will feed us and give us something to drink." Emmy grinned, but she remembered what happened the last time.

"You better be careful, Em. Some of the guys might want something in return—something more than a smile."

"We will be all right. There are enough people around," Emmy said. *And I know better than to get to close to a bunch of drunks.*

Heather grabbed her car keys and purse. "I have to work. Can you fix your own breakfast?"

"I can, but I'm not sure about Krissy," Emmy teased.

"The spare key is on the counter. I'll be back later." Heather waved and then left.

"Are we going to get to the library early enough to watch

313

the players as they do their walk?" Kristen grabbed a box of cereal from the cupboard and filled a bowl. "How much milk do I add to this, Em?"

Emmy let her mouth fall open.

"I'm kidding. Now who's being all serious. Geez! Lighten up, Emmy." Kristen laughed but then poured too much milk into the bowl.

Emmy rolled her eyes. "Don't worry. We'll get there in time to see Tony."

"I just love the atmosphere and tradition on game day. It's so much more than at North Park," Kristen made sure Heather's apartment was locked as she and Emmy left.

"This is Notre Dame!" Emmy waved her arms as she spun in a circle. "Heisman trophy winners, national championships, all that great tradition. At North Park the students go nuts if they score a touchdown."

They walked to the south parking lot and within minutes met a group of guys and their girlfriends, who Emmy judged to be in their early thirties, willing to share their food and beer. Emmy had a taste for a beer, but thought about Randy Braun and her father for a moment. She chose bottled water, as did Kristen. They hung out for twenty minutes, and then headed over to the library in time to see the players.

"Isn't this exciting, Kristen?"

"I know. At least it's warmer and sunny today."

"There he is!" Emmy shouted. She waved her arms and jumped up and down to get his attention.

"Chill, Em. You're acting like a kid." Kristen waved but kept her feet on the ground.

The warm weather didn't help the Irish, and they lost to Boston College. After falling behind early, they mounted a late rally but fell short. With this loss there would not be a bowl game for Notre Dame this year.

Emmy kicked at a discarded beer can as she and Kristen walked back to Heather's place. "They should have won. They came so close. If that wide receiver hadn't dropped that one pass, they could have scored."

314

"You aren't going to start crying, are you?" Kristen put an arm around Emmy's shoulders.

"No, but I would if I was in the locker room."

"You better never be in the guys' locker room, Em."

"I meant if I was part of the team."

Kristen grinned. "Will you slug me if I ask you to lighten up?"

"Maybe," Emmy said. She kicked the beer can again and it hit the person in front of her.

He, and the guy walking beside him, stopped and turned around.

Emmy bit her lip as she looked up at the two guys towering above her and noticed their Notre Dame sweatshirts. "Sorry, I didn't meant to hit you. I'm sad because we lost."

"So are we." Ivan Kartelo smiled. He and the other guy turned around and started walking away.

"Those guys are tall enough to be basketball players," Emmy whispered to Kristen.

Ivan nudged Jere Macura. "Did you hear that? Maybe we should try out for the team."

Jere peeked over his shoulder. "The blonde is gorgeous, but her friend has to be in high school."

Tony made it to Heather's apartment by eight. Emmy let him in and tried to cheer him up, "If you win next week, your record will be six and six."

"Not exactly what we were shooting for at the beginning of the season."

"This is just your first season. Next year you guys will be better and maybe by your junior year you will win the national championship. You might even win the Heisman Trophy!"

"Middle linebackers don't win Heisman trophies," Tony said.

Emmy knew that nothing she said would make Tony any happier. After all, last year his team won the state championship. She decided to give him a hug and see if that helped. He held her close and didn't let her go.

"Tony, put Emmy down. You're going to break her ribs if

315

you squeeze her any harder," Heather warned.

He set Emmy down—embarrassed because of Heather's scolding. Tony gave Kristen a hug and a kiss on the cheek.

"Hi, Kristen. How's Derrick doing?"

"He's fine. School is going well, and he has a new girlfriend, but I don't remember her name, if he even mentioned it."

Tony reminded Emmy of a giant teddy bear. He played football with ferocity but was so gentle with Kristen and Heather. He treated Emmy a little rougher because she acted more like a tomboy. Emmy teased Tony about missing a tackle, and he chased her around the room. The chase ended quickly; she laughed as he lifted her up over his shoulder. He carried her around as if she were a little girl.

Heather scolded him, "Will you put her down before I have to smack you? She's not a toy. Behave like an adult for once, okay?"

Tony set Emmy down gently, "I'm sorry, Heather. I was just having fun. Emmy doesn't mind if I carry her around."

Heather patted him on the back. "It's okay. I know you miss her and just got carried away."

"Heather, I'm the one who almost got carried away." Emmy grinned, and they laughed.

Kristen rolled her eyes. "That was lame, Em."

Emmy could see how much Tony and Heather loved each other and that pleased her. It struck her as funny that Heather could get Tony to do whatever she wanted.

Tony looked at his watch, "It's already ten. I need to get back to study. John and I are gonna go to mass in the morning. Would you guys like to join us?" Tony asked.

"Are you trying to set me up with your roommate?" Kristen asked.

"Not necessarily. Maybe I'm trying to set Emmy up. Did you ever think of that?"

"I have a boyfriend!" Emmy reminded Tony—a little upset that he would even be thinking about John as a potential boyfriend for her. "What about you? Have you been dating anyone?"

"Not really. Football and studying take up all my time. Maybe next semester I'll think about seeing someone." Tony looked at Emmy and wondered if she and Kenny were still really in a relationship.

Emmy and Kristen decided to leave early in the morning. They skipped breakfast and hit the highway.

Tony called Heather and asked, "Is anyone going to join us for mass?"

"I will, but the girls took off already. They wanted to get back early for some reason. I'll meet you at nine."

"Did they say why they were leaving?"

"Not really. I think it was Emmy's idea. I think Kristen might have been willing to stay, but Emmy talked her into leaving."

"Do you think she got mad at me for wanting to introduce her to John?"

"Maybe. I thought you wanted to introduce him to Kristen." Heather poured some milk into her oatmeal.

"I guess I wanted him to meet both of them. I'll pick you up at eight thirty."

"I'll be ready."

Tony hung up and then slapped John on the back. "Sorry, buddy. Kristen and Emmy left already. Too bad. I think you would like both of them. They are both really pretty, but Kristen is taller. Emmy is tiny. I picked her up last night and carried her around like a sack of potatoes. I bet she doesn't weigh eighty pounds."

"You told me that you guys dated, right?"

"Yeah, we did."

"Why are you trying to set me up with her? I know you still have feelings for her."

"I care for her a lot, but like she's my cousin."

"I thought Kristen was your cousin, not Emmy?"

"Kristen is my cousin, and I love her. We've always been close. I kinda feel the same way about Emmy."

"If you say so." John shrugged as he stared at the picture of Tony and Emmy on top of the desk.

317

The Irish traveled to California to play the Stanford Cardinal in the final game of their season. Neither Tony nor John had ever been to California. Kristen came over to Emmy's place to watch the game.

"Come on, Krissy, they're ready to kickoff." Emmy bounced on the couch and waved for Kristen.

"I'll be right there. I'm just getting some water. Nothing happens right away."

The Irish kicked off and the Stanford player took the kick two yards into the end zone. He made two tacklers miss and broke into the open.

"No!" Emmy screamed. She watched in disbelief as the Stanford player ran the kick back for a touchdown.

Stanford kicked off and Layden Crowley ran the ball back to the fifteen yard line where he was nailed by a vicious tackle and fumbled. Stanford recovered and on the next play, scored another touchdown.

This is unbelievable! Emmy sat back against the couch with her arms over her chest and frowned.

Kristen hummed merrily as she walked into the room. She sat next to Emmy. "Did I miss anything?"

Emmy poked her in the side. "Do you see the score?"

Kristen looked at the TV. "Is that right? I thought they always started the game at zero to zero."

"They do!" Emmy yelled.

"I know they do. What happened, Em? I know how involved you get when you watch football."

Emmy explained how Stanford had scored.

"Are you trying to blame me for what happened?" Kristen asked. "Somehow I can't believe that simply because I was not here to watch the opening minute, it's my fault they are behind by fourteen points."

"I guess it's not your fault. There's still a lot of time left. I'm sure they can come back to win."

Notre Dame did come back and actually took the lead late in the third quarter.

"I knew they could do it," Emmy yelled as Layden

Crowley scored from the three yard line. "Now they just have to play good defense and hold them."

It was not to be, though.

"Get him!" Emmy yelled as the Stanford running back broke a tackle and headed to the end zone. "Shoot! Now Stanford is up by a point."

"Don't they have to kick the extra point first?" Kristen asked.

"Yeah, but those are almost always automatic."

The Stanford kicker, Mark Bisselli, almost proved Emmy wrong as his extra point try barely slipped inside the left upright. Notre Dame got the ball back, but three plays later, had to punt it away.

"Come on, Tony. You guys have to stop them." Emmy wrapped her arms around her football and squeezed it to her chest.

Kristen grinned. *You are something else, Em. I bet you are more excited than the players.*

In spite of Emmy's exhorting the Irish defense, and threatening the Cardinal offense, Stanford marched the ball down the field. Stanford scored again to go ahead 37-29.

"There's still time, Krissy. I know they can score," Emmy said.

Stanford kicked off, and Emmy jumped off the couch and began screaming and jumping up and down as Everett Stuhldreher ran the ball back to the fifty yard line.

"He should have gone all the way." Emmy pulled Kristen up and grabbed her hands. "There is still time. They have two minutes and one timeout left."

With only forty-five seconds left in the game, the Irish scored on a twenty yard pass from Israel Steele to tight end Denny O'Leary. The two-point conversion was successful, and Notre Dame tied the score.

"Are they going to try an onside kick, Em?" Kristen was almost as excited as Emmy by now.

"I think they might kick it deep and settle for overtime," Emmy explained.

Notre Dame kicker, Bobby Davis, sent the ball into the end

319

zone for a touchback. Tony and the Irish defense stopped the Stanford offense for no gain on the first two plays.

"It kinda looks like overtime," Emmy said.

However, a "roughing the passer" penalty gave Stanford a first down, and they continued the drive.

"That was a bad call." Kristen pointed at the TV during the instant replay. "Wasn't it, Em?"

Emmy shook her head. "No, I agree with the referee. I think it was a late hit." Emmy punched the couch. "They can't make dumb mistakes like that and expect to win."

A desperation heave down the field was caught by wide receiver Josh Walters, who scrambled out of bounds at the twenty-three yardline with two seconds remaining.

"I can't watch, Krissy," Emmy closed her eyes and said a prayer. "Tell me what happens."

"You have to watch, Em."

Emmy opened her eyes and watched as Stanford kicked a forty yard field goal, and the Irish fell.

"Are you all right, Em?" Kristen asked as Emmy's eyes filled with tears.

"It's just a stupid game," Emmy said as she cried.

It was quiet on the plane later that night as the disappointed team returned to South Bend.

Chapter Thirty-Three

With the football season now over, Tony caught up on all his studies and prepared for final exams. He crammed for hours and even pulled an allnighter. On December eighteenth the dorms closed. John Randolph headed home to Ohio. Tony stopped by Heather's apartment to take some Christmas gifts home for her. He made good time driving back to SoHam. He paused as he opened the back door and saw his mother in the kitchen. He could smell a ham in the oven and saw two pumpkin pies on the counter.

"Mama. I'm home!"

Mama turned to face him and smiled. Tony gave her a big hug as he lifted her off her feet.

"Put me down before you hurt yourself and keep your hands off those pies until after dinner."

Tony kissed her cheek. "Yes, Mama."

"Now tell me how your finals went. Do you think you passed everything?"

"I'm pretty sure I did all right on all my finals."

At about the same time, Kenny Colwell and the guys in Fridays At Five were getting ready for the last show before their holiday break. They were in New York City at Madison Square Garden. They would be heading home after the show on the bus this time. Since they had a month-long break, it was not as urgent to get home—at least according to Andy Walker. When they finished their soundcheck, Kenny called Emmy.

"Hey, Em. How are you. Are you getting anxious for Christmas?"

"I will be glad when it's here so I can relax for a few days. Is the show sold out tonight?"

"I believe it is."

"Must be nice to sell out the Garden. You guys might make it into the big time yet," she teased. "Do you know when you'll get home?"

"It won't be until sometime Sunday. Are you gonna be waiting for me?"

"I don't know. I really have a lot of work to do. I need to dust my lightbulbs and I have to repaint the ceiling in the bedroom closet. Plus, I have to rearrange the glasses in the kitchen cabinets." Emmy giggled and couldn't keep a straight face any longer. "I suppose if you really want me to come over for a few minutes, I will."

"I could always help you dust those lightbulbs, you know. I'm going to be home for a month."

"I'm going to sleep at home, but I think I'll go see your parents and go to church with them. Would it bother you if I was at church when you get home?"

"No, it will be afternoon before I get home. I wish we were flying, but Andy is being cheap!"

"You better be careful, or he'll get after you," Emmy said as she opened a cabinet and grabbed a roll of paper towels.

"He's standing right here. At least I'll be able to get some sleep on the bus."

Emmy could imagine Andy Walker standing there glaring at Kenny. Andy exercised great caution about how the band spent their money.

"Em, have you been dating anyone while I was gone? I hope you haven't been staying at home and cleaning house all the time."

"I haven't met anyone I wanted to date. How about you? Have you met any gorgeous women lately?"

"I've met plenty of them, but I haven't gone out with any of them. They're always around backstage before and after the shows so I talk to them, but that's all."

"Maybe we can go on a date when you get home?" Emmy asked.

Kenny teased her, "Oh, I don't know. I have to dust my..."

As soon as Emmy got off the phone with Kenny, it rang. She checked the caller ID. "Hey, Kristen, what's up?" Emmy set the roll of paper towels on the counter and put the cleaner under the sink.

"I've been trying to call you for an hour, she whined. "Who've you been talking to? Your mother?"

"Yeah, right. I was talking to Kenny. He'll be home tomorrow afternoon."

"Well, Mama called me. She told me I have to come over for dinner tonight and I have to bring you. Tony's home and she made a ton of food. I'll pick you up in twenty minutes so be ready."

"But, I have to..."

"No excuses. Just be ready, or I will drag you over there in whatever you're wearing. Derrick is home and he didn't bring a girlfriend with him for some reason."

"Does that mean I have to be Derrick's 'date' for the evening?"

"If you want to. He might like that. He might try to kiss you again," Kristen teased.

"Then forget it. I'm not kissing anyone tonight," Emmy answered and then thought about Tony. *I'm certainly not going to let Derrick kiss me, but what would I do if Tony tried? I might let him give me a quick kiss.*

Kristen read Emmy's mind as she asked, "What about Tony? What if he tries to kiss you?"

"I would probably let him kiss me, but he won't try. Remember he tried to set me up with his roommate the last time I saw him."

"Are you gonna be ready or not?" Kristen asked rather seriously.

"Yes, I'll take my weekly shower and even change my underwear. I might even wear deodorant."

"You are so gross. You should have been a boy." Kristen scowled as she hung up.

Kristen arrived twenty-five minutes later and walked up the steps to the porch. She tried the door; it was unlocked. "For crying out loud, Emmy." She muttered as she went in, walked up the stairs and right into the apartment.

"Em! Where are you?"

"In the bedroom. Come on in."

Kristen walked into Emmy's bedroom and saw that she was still getting dressed.

"Do you realize that I could have been a burglar and

323

walked in here and taken everything? You should keep your doors locked."

"I usually do, but I knew you were coming. Does this look all right?" Emmy asked as she held up a dress.

"You're going to wear a dress? I thought you would be wearing an old sweatshirt and those jeans of yours with the hole in the butt."

"There's no hole in the butt. Is there?"

"You better take a look. It might be time to replace those jeans. You've probably been wearing them since you were twelve."

"Have not. What about this dress?"

"It looks all right." Kristen walked into the living room and sat on the couch. "Don't take all night to decide what to wear."

Emmy laughed. "I don't do that. You do."

Emmy got dressed and wore the dress. In her jeans and top, Kristen looked more like a tomboy tonight than Emmy. They soon arrived at Mama's. Kristen walked in the back door and hollered, "Tony, where are you?"

"In the living room," he answered.

Kristen and Emmy walked through the kitchen and down the hall to the living room on the right. Tony slouched on the couch with Derrick. Mama sat in her chair going through the grocery ads. Both girls said "hi" to Mama and patted her shoulder.

Kristen turned to her brother and asked, "How did you get here so fast? When I left you were just getting in the shower."

"It doesn't take me two hours to get ready like it does you," Derrick said. "Hi, Emmy. You look so pretty. Is that a new dress?"

"Thank you, Derrick. It's not new, but I don't wear it often. It's good to see you again." Emmy turned to Tony and asked, "Hi, are you glad to be home and through with finals?"

"It was a rough couple of weeks. I had to get caught up on some classwork and study. It will be easier next semester."

"Don't you have spring football?"

"Yeah, but it only lasts about a month, and it's not as hard."

"How do you know? You haven't been through it yet."

"John went through it last year. This is his second year."
Why are you wearing a dress?

324

Mama got up. "I hope you kids are hungry because I made plenty of food."

"It smells so good in the kitchen, Mama. Do you need some help?" Emmy asked.

"Thank you, dear. You can help me in the kitchen. Tony, you and Kristen set the table. Derrick, would you see what everyone wants to drink and take care of that?"

"Yes, Mama!" everyone said.

After dinner, Mama started to clean up, but Emmy stopped her, "We can do that. Why don't you take it easy?"

"Are you sure?"

"Yes, we can clean up, and I know where everything goes so you don't have to worry."

"Then I'll go in the den and read. If you don't know where something goes, leave it on the counter, and I'll put it away before I go to bed."

"Everything tasted so delicious, Mama. Just like always."

"You are a sweetheart, thank you." Mama crushed Emmy to her chest.

Soon the kitchen was cleaned, the dishes were done and everything was put away. Emmy did most of the work, but everyone helped a little.

"What are we gonna do with the rest of the night?" Kristen asked. She stared at Derrick. *You're supposed to suggest leaving the house, doofus.*

"We could go to a movie," Derrick suggested. *See. I remembered, Kristen. Although I don't know why you're still playing matchmaker.*

"How about a game of Monopoly?" Tony recommended.

"Oh, no! 'Monotony' takes forever to play," Kristen complained. *Derrick, don't you dare agree to play that God-awful boring game.*

"Yeah, we haven't played that for a long time," Derrick said. "Okay with you, Em?"

"Sure, whatever you guys want to do," she answered absentmindedly as she thought about Kenny. *I wonder if they are on stage yet. I can't wait to see him.*

325

Kristen looked disappointed. *This isn't what I planned. I wanted to get Tony and Emmy out of the house so they could be together.* "Fine, but I get to be the shoe."

"Why do you always want to be the shoe? You are wacky, Kristen," Derrick teased.

She didn't answer—just made a face at Derrick.

Tony got the game from the bookcase in the living room. They moved to the dining room and set up the game.

"Should we play by real rules or house rules?" Derrick asked.

"What's the difference?" Emmy asked.

"If we play house rules then we throw money in the middle and whoever lands on free parking gets the cash."

"That's the way I've always played. I thought those were the rules."

Derrick explained the other house rules to Emmy—like not collecting rent if the next person rolls the dice before the owner of the property notices someone has landed on their property.

"We call it the 'Kristen rule' because she always forgets to collect her rent."

Kristen kept talking to Emmy and didn't pay close enough attention to the game, and the guys tried to take advantage when they landed on her properties. Emmy helped Kristen out by not rolling the dice until Kristen saw what had happened.

"That's mine! I own it. You owe me... eighteen dollars," Kristen hollered as she saw the battleship on Kentucky Ave.

"Emmy, why don't you roll the dice?" Derrick asked.

"We are looking out for each other. You guys try to get away without paying your rent."

Derrick played Monopoly the same way he played tennis—he was very competitive and hated to lose.

The game went on for an hour, and then Kristen landed on Marvin Gardens, which Derrick owned and on which he had placed a hotel.

"You owe me $1200, little sister. Pay up!" Derrick gloated because he knew she didn't have the money and had already mortgaged all of her properties except one. Kristen glared at her

326

brother as she handed over her property and what little cash she had.

"You guys need to team up so he doesn't win. He always wins," Kristen said. "I'm going to make some popcorn."

"Do you need any help?" Derrick asked.

"Ha! Ha! It's microwave popcorn."

Tony looked at his properties, then at Emmy's. He saw an opportunity.

"Em, I'll trade you Park Place for Tennessee and St. Charles Place."

"Why should I do that?" Emmy asked as she looked at her deeds.

"Then you'd have Park Place and Boardwalk. You could build hotels and make a lot of money."

"And you'd have all the yellow and pink ones. Give me your railroads, too."

"Deal!"

"No, Em, don't do it," Derrick groaned because now Tony would start building up his properties.

"It's my turn," Derrick rolled and landed on the Pennsylvania railroad. Emmy collected $200. Tony rolled and landed on a railroad.

"I like this." Emmy smiled as the guys landed on a railroad every turn. Soon she had enough cash to start building on Park Place and Boardwalk. The guys didn't worry because no one ever landed there.

"That will be $800!" Tony held out his hand as Emmy landed on New York Ave.

"Why?"

"Because there are four houses on it," Tony explained. *You're worse than playing with a child.*

"Hey! Don't yell at Emmy. She doesn't play this game like it's a matter of life and death like you dorks." Kristen grabbed a handful of popcorn.

Emmy looked at Tony and stuck out her tongue as she handed over the money. For the next four trips around the board, Emmy didn't land on any of the guys' properties. She even landed

327

on free parking and gained over $1500. She built up Park Place and Boardwalk slowly with money from her railroads.

"I hate those stinking railroads!" Derrick exclaimed as he smacked the table hard enough for the bowl of popcorn to jump and spill. "There must be ten of them on the board."

Tony ran into a streak of bad luck. He landed on three of Derrick's properties and was about bankrupt. The end for him came when he landed on Park Place and Boardwalk on consecutive turns.

"I don't believe this. Have you ever seen this happen before, Derrick?"

"Can't say that I have." Derrick grinned with confidence, assured of a win now.

"I believe you owe me $2000, please." Emmy grinned because she just bankrupted Tony. He turned over his property to her, and she paid the mortgage on all of them.

"Where did you get that much cash?" Derrick asked incredulously.

"I've been working on the railroads," Emmy sang sweetly.

The tide had turned, and twenty minutes later Derrick gave up. "Okay, Emmy, you win. I'm busted."

Emmy turned to Kristen, and they high-fived each other.

Tony shook his head. "I'd do that trade again. No one usually lands on those expensive places. How on earth did Emmy keep missing our properties. It was like she had loaded dice or something."

Kristen squeezed Emmy's hand as she grinned at Derrick. "I can't remember the last time anyone beat Derrick. Now he can't gloat so much."

Emmy looked at the guys. They were looking at the ceiling and whispering to each other.

"What are you guys planning?" Kristen asked. She knew something was up.

Tony smiled as he asked, "Em, do you remember when I hung you from the ceiling?"

She looked at Tony. Both he and Derrick were grinning. "Oh, no, you're not. I'm wearing a dress."

328

Emmy got up and moved toward the only door out of the dining room, but Derrick had it blocked. She ran around the table as Tony moved after her. Kristen tried to move Derrick out of the door but he grabbed onto the doorway and held tight.

Emmy and Tony chased each other back and forth. Tony laughed, but Emmy didn't.

"Leave me alone!" Emmy bumped into the China cabinet.

Tony edged closer. *Em, you usually like it when I tease you. Something is different tonight.*

"Mama! Come here quick," Kristen yelled.

Mama heard the commotion and got up to see what the ruckus was about.

"What are you doing to that child?" Mama had a difficult time trying not to laugh.

Emmy pointed at Tony. "He wants to hang me from the ceiling. Make him stop, Mama. I'm wearing a dress."

"You aren't really going to hang her from the ceiling again, are you, son?"

"I suppose not." Tony grinned at Emmy, and she slugged him in the arm—with some force.

"I'm never wearing a dress around you again, Anthony Bertucci!" Emmy screamed at him as she ran out of the room. Mama followed her.

Kristen watched and heard Emmy run up the stairs. A second later Kristen heard a door slam.

Tony looked at Derrick and shrugged his shoulders. "What was that all about?"

"Ya got me. She usually likes to be teased."

"Emmy's crying," Kristen shouted at the guys. "You went too far with your teasing. You better apologize to her. She wore a dress tonight just for you, you big dork." Kristen looked at Tony and Derrick and shook her head.

"Sorry, Kristen." Derrick turned to look at Tony.

"It must be that time of the month," Tony said.

By the time Kristen got upstairs, Mama had an arm around Emmy's shoulders as they sat on Heather's bed. Emmy was still crying.

"Are you all right, Em? I told those dorks they have to apologize for being jerks."

"I'm all right. I just got upset because he is treating me... never mind. I don't care anymore. I know now that's the way it will always be."

Mama dried her eyes with a Kleenex. "I'm sorry, Emmy. I thought you were letting Tony have some fun. I didn't realize you were upset."

"It's not your fault." Emmy paused and was able to smile. "I bet I would have looked pretty funny hanging from the ceiling tonight."

After a few minutes the girls came downstairs. Mama stayed upstairs and got ready for bed. Emmy walked into the living room. Tony stood up and approached her cautiously.

"I'm sorry, Emmy. I shouldn't have been teasing you so much. I got carried away."

"I'm sorry, too, Em. Will you give us another chance to be your friends?" Derrick asked.

"Yeah, you guys are still my friends. I should know better than to wear a dress when I come over here."

"It's still early. What are we gonna do now?" Derrick asked.

Emmy said, "I don't want to go anywhere else because I'm going to church with Kenny's parents in the morning."

"We can stay here and talk," Kristen suggested.

Tony looked up at the ceiling. "We might wake Mama up if we stay in here. Her bedroom is right above us. Let's go downstairs and play pool or watch a movie."

"Let's play pool. I want to beat Emmy at something tonight." Derrick grinned at her.

"You want to put some money on that, Mr. Keasling?" Emmy asked as she poked him in his side.

They went downstairs, and Tony uncovered the pool table. Tony's father bought it a few months before he died, so they had always taken good care of it. Tony and Emmy made up one team and Derrick teamed up with his sister. Since none of them had played in quite a while, they missed some easy shots. Eventually Emmy had a chance to win the game. The cue ball rested squarely in the middle of the table, and Emmy stretched as far as she could to reach the ball. The guys were standing behind her as she lined up her shot.

Kristen noticed Emmy's legs. "Will you two move down to the other end so Em can make this shot without you two looking at her legs."

The guys looked at Emmy and understood why Kristen wanted them to move.

"Sorry, Em," Derrick said as they moved to the sides of the table.

Emmy lined up the shot and hit the cue ball cleanly. It caressed the eight ball just right, headed to the corner pocket and... missed, leaving Derrick with an easy shot to win. He made the shot and high-fived Tony.

Kristen asked Emmy, "Did you miss that shot on purpose so we could win?"

"No way. I was trying to make it. I've never been very good at pool. I'm too short to reach some of the shots. I suck at bowling, too. I can never score above a hundred."

"Well, next time you come over here to play pool, make sure you aren't wearing a dress."

Emmy blushed. "Thanks, I didn't even think about that."

They hung out in the basement for another hour and then Kristen took Emmy home.

"Thanks for making me come with you, Krissy. I needed to have some fun."

"Thanks for beating Derrick at Monopoly. That was worth seeing. I'm sorry Tony treats you like... like... me, I guess."

"It's all right. I'm happy that we can at least be friends."

Chapter Thirty-Four

Emmy woke up at eight, got ready and headed over to the Colwell's home. She parked in the driveway and ran up to the back door. She was about to knock when Kenny opened the door. Emmy's face lit up when she saw him. She raised her arms and he hugged her, pulled her into the kitchen and spun her around. He kissed her cheek, her ear, her neck, then her lips.

"You told me you wouldn't be home until later. What happened?" Emmy asked as she removed her coat and hung it up by the back door.

"Andy pulled a fast one over on us. He kept telling us we had to take the bus home because it was too expensive to fly. All along he had a charter flight waiting at the airport."

"Remind me to give him a big kiss when I see him again."

"What's this about giving me a kiss?" Andy Walker asked as he walked into the kitchen.

Emmy ran over to him and kissed his cheek. "You are a teddy bear. You might act all tough and all, but inside you are a soft old teddy bear."

"Don't you ever tell anyone, or else you're fired," he said.

"But I don't work for you."

"If you ever do, then you're fired!" He hugged her for a moment.

She turned back to Kenny. "Do you have any luggage that needs to be taken upstairs to your apartment?" She grinned and then bit her lip.

"Sorry, Em, but I already took it upstairs. I might need some help unpacking it later."

"What time does church start?" Andy asked.

"We need to leave by ten," Mrs. Colwell answered as she pulled two pans out of the cabinet.

Emmy looked at Andy and asked, "Are you coming with us?"

"If it's all right with you, I will, princess."

Mrs. Colwell explained, "Andy's grandmother used to go to our church before she passed away. Every once in a while Andy

332

comes to church and sits in her pew."

"What was her name?" Emmy asked.

"Olive DelSasso. She was quite a character from what I've heard, let me tell you," Mrs. Colwell answered with a chuckle. "There are so many stories we could tell. I remember one time she stopped her car right in the middle of Jefferson Avenue and held up traffic because she got lost."

Emmy looked at Kenny and thought that name sounded familiar. "What's the name of that music shop where you guys get all your gear?"

"DelSasso Sound. Andy's uncle, Gregg DelSasso, owns it."

"I don't know your mother's name, Andy," Emmy said.

"Nola, Nola DelSasso."

They ate pancakes for breakfast and then headed to the church. Kenny and Emmy sat with Andy in his grandmother's pew. Kenny's parents sat on the other side of the sanctuary out of habit.

Andy pointed a to a small plaque on the arm of the pew. Kenny and Emmy leaned over and read the inscription. "This worship pew is dedicated to the memory of Olive DelSasso."

"I guess this pew really does belong to your grandma," Emmy whispered to Andy.

"I told you it did."

Andy noticed an elderly lady with pure white hair in the pew behind him. She smiled at him. After the service Andy turned to talk to her. Emmy stayed with Andy while Kenny left to talk to Ronnie Rojas.

"Hello, my name is Andy Walker. How are you today?"

"I'm doing all right for someone my age. I got out of bed this morning. At my age that's a blessing. Have you been here before?" she asked as she picked up her large purse.

"I've been here a few times over the years. My grandmother used to sit in this pew every Sunday. Her name was Olive DelSasso. Did you know her by chance?"

"I used to come to this church in my younger years—all the way through high school, but then I got married and moved to Tennessee. Olive and I were close friends in those days. She was Olive Haskins then."

"What is your name?" Andy asked politely.

"It's Selma Turner. Anyway, I remember that my best friend, Isabel Polmonari, used to call her Aunt Olive even though we were all the same age."

The mention of the name Isabel Polmonari caught Emmy's attention. "Isabel Polmonari—it's Sandusky now—is my grandma. I'm Emmy Colasanti. Are you still friends with her?"

"That was a long time ago, dearie. We lost touch over the years. I lived in Tennessee, then Arkansas. I moved back here a few months ago after my husband passed away. I'm not sure if she's still alive."

Emmy smiled and then said, "Oh, she's very much alive and lives here in SoHam when the weather is warm. She's in Florida right now."

Andy grasped the implications of this right away. "This is awesome, Emmy. We are related. We're third cousins, or something."

"Get out! That's not possible." Emmy looked at him and didn't understand.

So he explained the relationship. "Now do you see, Cousin Emmy?"

"I get it, Cousin Andy," she answered and gave him a high-five.

Kenny came back over and heard them calling each other cousin. "What's going on? Why are you two acting so weird? And why are you calling each other cousin all of a sudden?"

Andy said, "Emmy's grandmother is my grandmother's niece so we're cousins. Distant cousins, granted, but still cousins."

"You know if we trace our ancestry back far enough, we are all related," Kenny teased.

After visiting with Mrs. Turner, Emmy, Andy and Kenny found Kenny's parents and headed home. All during dinner Emmy and Andy called each other cousin just to annoy Kenny.

"Dinner was very good, Mrs. Colwell. It's not often I get a home-cooked meal like this. Thank you."

"You're welcome, Andy. You can always join us whenever you're in town."

"We will do the dishes and put everything away so you and Mr. Colwell can rest. Won't we, guys?" Emmy gave Kenny and Andy a look like Mama Bertucci would, and they both agreed at once.

"Yes, princess, whatever you say."

While working in the kitchen, Emmy asked, "When did your grandmother pass away, Andy?"

"January of 1980."

"That was before I was born!" Emmy exclaimed.

"It will be twenty years ago next month. I was still in high school in San Diego."

"Did you always live there?"

"Yep. Still got a lot of friends there."

After they finished cleaning up the kitchen, Andy told them, "I need to crash for a while. I didn't sleep all night on the plane like some guys. Is there a room upstairs I can use?"

"Sure, you can use my room or one of the guest rooms, it doesn't matter."

"I'll see you later then." Andy left the kitchen.

Emmy looked at Kenny and grinned. He grinned back and mentioned, "I still have to unpack my clothes. I might need some help."

"I think I can help a little!" Emmy giggled as Kenny took her hand. They grabbed their coats from the hooks by the back door and headed to the carriage house.

"Have a merry Christmas, Andy. Say hi to the family. Have fun in San Diego and Carolina, and I'll see you back here on the seventeenth," Kenny said as he dropped Andy off at Midway Airport on Tuesday morning.

"You enjoy your Christmas, too. Have fun with Emmy while you're home—not too much fun if you know what I mean. If you see the guys tell them to be ready for a hard two months of travel."

"We'll be ready," Kenny said.

Andy flew to South Carolina to spend the holidays with his brother Matt, Matt's wife Nina, and their two boys, Brent and

Blake, who were six and four-years-old. Andy had already purchased gifts for the boys and loved to spoil them.

Emmy now worked in the claims office at Coventry Shield Healthcare; that office didn't close down at Christmastime. It disappointed Emmy that she had to work while Kenny and Tony were home. Kenny made up for it by spending his evenings with her. He took her Christmas shopping, and she even let him buy a couple of gifts for her to give to her parents and Diane.

On Christmas Eve the office closed at noon, and the owners threw a party for everyone. Most of the employees did not have to return until January third, unfortunately Emmy was not among those lucky employees. Emmy's boss scheduled her to work Monday through Thursday, but then she would have a three-day weekend.

She hurried home after the party and changed clothes. She had an overnight bag ready in case she needed it. Kenny was picking her up, and they were going to see Kristen and Derrick. He walked into the apartment a few minutes after four.

"Hey, Em, I'm here. Where are you?"

"In the bedroom, making the bed."

He walked back to her bedroom and asked, "Are you ready? Did you get all the gifts wrapped?"

"They're all wrapped. Can you pull that corner up a little for me?"

He did, and Emmy inspected the result.

"When is the surprise inspection by your commanding officer? Will you receive demerits if the bed isn't perfect?"

Emmy made a face at him. "I want my bed to be made when I get back."

They arrived at the Keasling home. Kenny carried the large bag of gifts inside.

Derrick greeted them and then pointed upstairs. "Kristen is still getting ready."

"Thanks, I'll go hurry her along." Emmy ran upstairs.

"Merry Christmas! How are you, Kenny?" Derrick and

Kenny shook hands.

"Merry Christmas. I'm doing great. It's good to be home. How was school this semester?"

"Rough! I'm glad it's over."

Emmy and Kristen came downstairs and joined the guys. Tony, Heather and Mama arrived a few minutes after that. Mama immediately went to the kitchen.

"Do you need any help, Karla?" Mama asked.

"If I say no will you go sit down and rest?" Karla asked.

"No," Mama answered.

"Didn't think so. You might as well check the potatoes and gravy."

Thirty minutes later everyone gathered around the dining room table. Mr. Keasling carved the ham. Sweet potatoes topped with marshmallows and crushed nuts, garlic mashed potatoes, gravy, green beans with crispy onion rings—you name it, it was on the table. Round and round the different dishes passed from one person to the next as everyone filled their plates as they talked. Derrick, Tony and Kenny sat on one side of the table and started a contest to see who could eat the most in the shortest time. Tony had an advantage in size: he outweighed the other guys by eighty pounds.

Everyone left the table stuffed.

Tony patted his stomach and groaned. "I'm so full I may not eat for a week."

"Don't give me that. You'll be digging through the fridge in two hours looking for leftovers," Emmy said.

The women put the leftovers away and cleaned the kitchen while the men slouched on the couch and in recliners in the living room.

Then they gathered in the family room to open gifts. Emmy bought gifts for everyone this year and had one left over.

"I guess you can have this one, too, Kristen. I assumed Derrick would have someone with him."

"Thank you, Em." Kristen opened the gift and squealed in delight, "Oh, I just love Noa Noa! Where did you find it?"

Emmy grinned as she shrugged. "They had a big stack of it

337

at the Walmart for half price."

"I know better than that."

Kristen and Emmy put some of the perfume on to test it. The fragrance soon overwhelmed the guys. "Don't you like it?" Kristen asked Derrick and Tony.

"It's nice, but you must have put on half the bottle."

Later, Emmy walked into the kitchen and saw Tony looking for leftovers in the fridge.

"You had three helpings earlier, and you're hungry again. I can't believe it."

"I was looking for the pies. I know they're here somewhere. Do you know where they are, Em?"

"Not really. Did you look in the garage? They might have put them out there to hide them."

"You might be right. Let's go look."

Emmy followed Tony to the garage; they found four pies. They brought two into the house. Tony cut a slice for each of them.

"These are good. Did Mama make them?" Emmy asked.

"I think so. Do you remember the cookies Mama always makes for Christmas?"

"Yeah, those are delicious."

"Well, she made a box for you, Em. If you want to stop by tomorrow, or whenever you have time, you can have them."

"Thanks, maybe we can stop by for a few minutes tomorrow. We've got to see my parents in the morning. Then we're going to be at Kenny's house."

"I'll make sure no one eats them if you don't make it over for a few days."

Just then Mama walked into the kitchen and caught Tony and Emmy with a mouthful of cherry pie. "I see that you found our hiding place. You might as well bring the rest of the pies inside." Mama shook her head, but then laughed.

"Do you see what time it is?" Emmy nudged Kenny as they sat on the family room couch listening to Derrick talk about school.

"I'm ready to go if you are, Em," he whispered.

Emmy and Kenny told everyone good night and headed to

his place shortly after nine.

"Would it be all right if I sleep in the house? I know my mother will ask me where I slept."

Kenny rested his hands on her shoulders as he gazed into her eyes. "You just want to sleep in a comfortable bed and not on the old couch."

"Would you really make me sleep on the couch? Couldn't I use the futon?"

"No way! I get the futon."

"I'll see you in the morning then." She grinned as she kissed him.

Chapter Thirty-Five

Emmy awakened to the smell of bacon, eggs and coffee drifting upstairs from the kitchen. She stretched her arms over her head and could almost hear the bacon sizzling in the pan. She made her way downstairs and saw Kenny in front of the stove. She walked up behind him and wrapped her arms around his waist.

"This smells good."

"It's about done. Did you sleep all right, Em?"

"Okay, I kicked the comforter off the bed and got cold."

"You need to sleep in a sleeping bag because you always kick off the covers," Kenny said as his mother walked into the kitchen.

"Is the coffee ready?"

"Morning, Mom. It should be."

"Thanks for making breakfast. It smells delicious."

Mr. Colwell walked into the kitchen, kissed his wife and asked, "Do we have any hash browns?"

"I didn't make hash browns, but I fried up some sliced potatoes. They should be ready in five minutes or so."

Emmy set the table, and they ate together in the breakfast nook.

Thirty minutes later, Kenny patted his full stomach. "I'm stuffed. Are we gonna go over to your parents soon?"

"I suppose we might as well get it over with. Diane told me they dropped off her gifts last night. Craig didn't even go in."

"It'll be all right."

"Mom will probably ask you why we aren't married. Will that bother you?"

"Not at all. I'll tell her that I don't love you, and I'm never going to marry you."

"Not even if we have five kids?" Emmy grinned.

"Especially not if we have a bunch of rugrats."

Mom and Dad Colwell grinned at each other.

With the outside temperature in the upper thirties, they chose to walk over to Emmy's parents' house. They walked up the front sidewalk and steps, and Emmy rang the bell. Her mother

340

opened the door almost immediately.

"Emmy, it's so good to see you. Merry Christmas, baby. Merry Christmas to you, too, Kenny. Come on in." Mom's uncharacteristic cheerfulness made Emmy wonder if she and Kenny walked into the wrong house.

"Merry Christmas, Mom," Emmy said slowly. "How are you?"

"I'm doing fine," Mom answered and then shouted, "Ray, the kids are here. Come out and say hello."

Emmy's father walked out of the kitchen wearing an apron. He smiled as he approached Emmy.

What's going on? Emmy stood absolutely still.

"Give me a hug, Emily. It's so good to see you." He lifted Emmy off of her feet with his hug and then shook hands with Kenny. "I made some coffee earlier. Would you like a cup?"

"Sure, thanks." Kenny followed Mr. Colasanti to the kitchen, and he poured a cup of coffee for Kenny. "Milk or sugar?"

"Black is fine, thanks."

They joined Emmy and her mother in the living room.

"Kenny, sit down. We want to hear all about your tour."

Kenny looked at Emmy who raised her eyebrows and shrugged her shoulders. He spent a few minutes talking about the band and the tour.

Emmy remembered her news about cousin Andy; she asked her mother, "Did you know that you're related to Andy Walker?"

"Who?"

"Andy, the band's manager. He is a distant cousin. His mother was Grandma's cousin. That makes you and Andy second cousins."

Emmy explained the relationship and Mom remembered, "I think I might have met his mother once a long time ago. I think she moved away after she got married, and I just forgot about her."

"Do you remember your grandma's sister at all?"

"I suppose you mean my Grandma Polmonari's sister. I vaguely remember her, I think. Why are you asking?"

"Andy's grandmother's name was Olive and my middle name is Olivia. Did you name me after her?"

"No, we named you Emily Olivia after your father's great-grandmother. I can't even remember why. He never even met her."

"Oh, okay. We brought gifts for you and Daddy. Do you want to open them now?"

Emmy passed out the gifts for her parents. She and Kenny watched as they opened them.

"Thank you. These are pretty towels. I needed some more for the kitchen."

Her father opened a gift and smiled. "I know you didn't pick this out, Em. Thank you, Kenny. I needed a new socket wrench set. I don't know what happened to my old one."

Mom opened her other present. "Oh, Emmy, this is so beautiful."

"I thought you might like a necklace."

"You shouldn't have. This looks expensive."

"It's all right, Mom. Kenny paid for part of it."

Dad opened his other present and smiled, "You always get me a shirt. Thank you, sweetie. I wear out my shirts so fast."

Mom pulled out a card and handed it to Emmy. "We couldn't afford much this year. I hope you can buy yourself something you need."

"Thank you, Mom. I appreciate it." Emmy's eyes opened wide when she saw a fifty dollar bill in the card.

They stayed and visited with her parents for over an hour. No one argued or raised their voices—not even once. As they walked back to Kenny's house, Emmy asked him, "Who do you suppose those people are, and what have they done with my real parents?"

"Kinda spooky, huh? Like *Invasion of the Body Snatchers* or something."

"Yeah. Oh, I almost forgot. Do you think we could run over to see Mama Bertucci later? She makes cookies for Christmas, and she made some for me."

"We better go over and get them before Tony eats them."

Inside the Colasanti house Mom and Dad watched as Emmy and Kenny walked down the sidewalk.

"We did it! Emmy was here for over an hour, and we didn't

argue or raise our voices once. We acted like the parents from *Leave It To Beaver*. I'm going to call Diane and tell her we won the bet."

"She will have to talk to Emmy before she believes you. Are you really going to take the hundred bucks from her?" Dad walked into the kitchen to fix his eggnog and rum.

"Sure! She made the bet. I want some eggnog, too."

"She probably can't afford to pay it," Dad hollered.

"Then she shouldn't have made the bet," Mom yelled.

"You would take the last cent from her!" Dad sat down in his recliner and turned on the TV.

Mom glared at him. "Where's my eggnog?"

"Get it yourself," Dad said as everything returned to normal at the Colasanti house.

The huge pile of colorfully wrapped presents under the tree took almost an hour to open at the Colwell home. The second present Emmy opened was a computer mouse and keyboard.

"Thanks, Kenny. I'll need these if I ever get a computer." She looked at him and smiled.

He couldn't keep a straight face because he knew she knew he bought her a computer. "All right. You might as well open it now." He brought out a large box from the den and Emmy unwrapped it.

"Oh, Kenny, thank you. Now I can check emails without going to the library. Will you help me set it up later?"

"Okay, but it will only work in the carriage house apartment so you will have to move in."

Emmy kissed him. "Very funny. I do know a few things about computers."

After opening all the gifts, they enjoyed a light lunch, and then Kenny and Emmy left to see Mama Bertucci. Emmy knocked on the front door. Tony opened it with his mouth full of cookies and one more in his hand. He swallowed some of the cookies and managed to say, "Hi, guys, come on in."

Emmy frowned. "I hope you aren't stuffing your face with my cookies."

Mama walked out of the living room and hugged Emmy

343

first, and then she hugged Kenny. "He knows better than to eat the cookies I made for you, dear." Mama stared at Tony and frowned.

"They're not Emmy's, I swear!"

"Go get her cookies, and there better not be any missing, either," Mama said sternly. "Come in and sit with me. Tell me, how did the visit go with your parents?"

"Mama, it freaked me out!" Emmy exclaimed.

"I'm sorry. Did they argue again, dear?"

"No, just the opposite." Emmy waved her hands around for emphasis as she explained everything. "They didn't argue or yell at each other. They didn't get on my case about getting married, or anything else, really. I think they've been brainwashed."

"I'm happy for you. You are staying for dinner, right?" Mama didn't ask, but sort of commanded.

"If you insist, Mama."

Tony brought two tins of cookies in from the garage; Mama opened them to inspect the contents. "There are two lemon bars missing. Did you eat them?"

"I had to do a quality test to make sure they were good." Tony grinned as he sat next to Emmy on the couch.

"I guess it's all right that you had a couple cookies," Emmy said as she poked Tony in his side. "Kenny bought me a computer. Now I don't have to use one at the library. I can email Kenny and save on my phone bill. I can email you, too. It will be easier than trying to call each other."

Heather came downstairs and joined the others in the living room. Somehow the conversation turned to Emmy's childhood, so Kenny shared some embarrassing stories about her.

"I remember one time she got in trouble because of Barry. She rode her bike across Campbell Avenue, which was a big no-no, because Barry wanted to go to Darby's. Her father just happened to see her and took her bike away for a week. When she got it back she rode straight over to see Barry and punched him in the stomach."

"Did she really punch Barry in the stomach? Did he hit her back?" Heather asked.

Emmy nodded and grinned.

344

"She really did, and he couldn't hit her back because she's a girl."

Tony confessed to Kenny. "One day Mama saw me hanging Em from the ceiling and got after me."

"Really? You can hang her from the ceiling? I'd like to see that." Kenny looked at Em; she stuck her tongue out at him.

Tony stood up, grabbed her ankles and, as quick as a cat, had her feet on the ceiling.

"Put me down, you big ape!" Emmy hollered to no avail as she laughed.

Mama shook her head, and Tony deposited Emmy on the couch.

"I'm sure glad I'm not wearing a dress today," Emmy said as she poked Tony's chest.

Kenny put an arm around her shoulders and pulled her close. "How did that start?"

"She was at my house one day shortly after we met. She teased me about something. I can't remember what."

"I teased you about some school pictures of you from junior high."

"Yeah, right. You said I looked like a dork."

"No, you said that." Emmy corrected him. "I said you looked like a half-dork."

"Anyway, I surprised her by lifting her by the ankles and holding her feet to the ceiling. Mama walked in and got after me. I suppose I shouldn't do that anymore, huh?" Tony grinned at Emmy.

Heather added a story of her own. "The first time I met Emmy I thought she was a boy." Emmy turned red as she remembered that day. "She was outside playing in the snow with Tony, and Mama called them in to eat. He carried her over his shoulder and she had her hair tucked into her stocking cap. I thought she was Timmy from next door until she took off her cap. She still looked like a junior high kid."

"You still look very young, Em, but I'm sure glad you're not a boy." Kenny grinned at her.

They sat and talked for several minutes, and then Emmy looked out the window.

"Look, Tony, it's snowing! Can we go play in the snow?"

"If you promise not to throw snowballs at me."

"Why would I do that?" she asked with a mischievous grin.

"Because you are so devious."

"Come on, Kenny. Let's have some fun."

Kenny looked at Tony; they both smiled. Emmy didn't see the look in their eyes. Emmy and the guys went outside. Immediately, Emmy made a snowball and hit Tony in the back. She squealed like a little girl as he chased her around the yard until he caught her. He put her on his shoulder, carried her over to where Kenny had stockpiled a bunch of snowballs and put her down.

"It's payback time, Em."

She saw the snowballs and yelled, "No fair! Two against one isn't fair."

"We'll give you a five second head-start from... now!" Kenny counted very quickly. Emmy slipped in the snow as she tried to get away. Both guys pelted her with snowballs as she waved her arms to try to defend herself.

Mama and Heather stood by the front door and laughed as the guys kept hitting Emmy with snowballs.

"Mama!" she yelled. "Help me! These guys are ganging up on me."

She tried to scoop snow in her hands and toss it at the guys, but all she succeeded in doing was letting the wind blow the snow back in her face. Finally the guys stopped. Emmy lay on her back as Tony came over and tossed two handfuls of snow into the air above her. She delighted in letting the snow fall on her face as Tony stood over her.

"Do you remember the first time I ever brought you here, Emmy?"

"Of course I do. We had so much fun playing in the snow—making a snowman and having a snowball fight and I remember one other thing."

"What else do you remember, Em?"

She bit her lip as she answered, "It was the day I fell in love. I will never forget that day, Tony." She realized what she had said and quickly looked over at Kenny. *I hope you didn't hear that.*

Emmy and Kenny spent as much time together as they could during the week. Once again they went to the New Year's Eve party at the Keasling home. Tony came to the party alone, so Kenny and Emmy spent time with him to keep him company. When midnight arrived, Kenny kissed Emmy tenderly as he held her close. He let her go, and she looked at Tony. He smiled at her, and she gave him a quick kiss on the cheek.

"I'm not giving you a kiss." Kenny offered his hand and Tony shook it.

Emmy shook her head. "You guys are total dorks."

Kenny and Emmy stayed at the party until after one. They said goodbye to everyone and walked out to Kenny's car.

Emmy bit her lip as Kenny started the car. "It's kinda late to take me home. Maybe I should stay with you in the carriage house."

Kenny loved the way she did that whenever she became nervous. "I wasn't going to take you home, Em. Not tonight," he whispered.

Kenny pulled his car into the carriage house. He grabbed her overnight bag out of the backseat and carried it for her. She walked over to the stairs, stopped on the first step and turned to face him. She wrapped her arms around his neck and kissed him. *Maybe tonight will be the night.*

"Are we gonna sleep on the stairs, Em?" Kenny asked. She seized her overnight bag from his hand. His heart raced as he thought about whether it would be all right for them to share the futon.

"I'm not going to, but you might!" she squealed childishly. She raced up the stairs. Kenny watched from below. She used her key to open the door. Kenny followed slowly. His heart pounded.

"I'm going to get ready for bed." Emmy ran into the bathroom.

"Okay, Em," he answered as he stepped into the apartment. He looked at the futon and sighed, *One of these days I'm going to have to put in a real bedroom.*

He grabbed a pillow and blanket from the closet and tossed them on the old couch.

347

The first two weeks of January passed quickly. Emmy kept busy at work during the day and only saw Kenny at night. They went out to eat a couple of times. One night they even doubled with Tony and his 'date' for the evening, Kristen. Emmy went to church with Kenny both Sundays, and on the twelfth they sang for the Wednesday teen service.

Finally, the weekend Emmy had been dreading arrived. Tony needed to leave for school on Sunday afternoon, and the Fridays At Five tour resumed on Tuesday. On Saturday Kenny took Emmy, Kristen and Tony to dinner at Ciao Bella. They ordered appetizers, beverages and entrees. For the next hour Emmy listened as the other three talked.

Kenny finished his entree. "You've been awful quiet, Em. Even more than usual. Are you all right?"

"I'm fine. Just have stuff on my mind," she said as she fiddled with her pasta.

"Emmy, are you planning to take most of your entree home?" Tony asked.

"I'll probably end up doing that, but the food here is so good."

"One of these days you will be old enough and we can order a bottle of wine with our dinner," Kenny mentioned as he smiled at her.

"I'm not the only one here underage. Tony is even younger than me, remember?"

"I know. I was thinking about the future."

Upon leaving, Kenny left a large tip since they had tied up one of Mr. Sabatino's tables for so long on a Saturday night.

"Can we walk around the neighborhood for a while, Kenny? We come here to eat, but we never go anywhere else."

"How about it, guys? Are you up for a little sightseeing in this brisk night air?" Kenny asked Tony and Kristen. His breath hung in the air like a cloud.

"Sure, why not? Tony answered after Kristen nodded her head.

Kenny watched as Emmy pulled a stocking cap over her hair. He loved it when she had braids in her hair.

348

"What is it? Do I have something on my face?"

He gazed into her animated blue eyes as they dazzled him. "I was thinking about how amazing you are, and how much I love you."

He took her hand as they walked around the neighborhood. They passed several restaurants, taking in the music and the exotic aromas that drifted through the air. Kenny put his hands on her shoulders when Emmy stopped to peer in the windows of two art galleries. They passed a used bookstore and a home that had been turned into a dance studio.

Tony nudged Kristen and whispered as they watched Kenny and Emmy, "Have you ever seen her look so happy?"

"She does seem to be enjoying herself," Kristen answered with a trace of disappointment in her voice.

After church on Sunday, Emmy asked Kenny, "Do you mind if I go say goodbye to Tony?"

"Of course not. I'm assuming you want to go alone."

"You are so smart. Is that all right?"

"Sure. Just make sure you don't give him the same kind of kiss that I will get tomorrow."

"Oh, I wasn't going to kiss you goodbye tomorrow," Emmy teased.

Kenny swatted her bottom affectionately. "Do you really mean that?"

"You'll have to wait and see," she said.

Emmy drove over to see Tony and arrived in time for lunch. Mama made her sit down and eat. After lunch Emmy went upstairs with Tony to watch him finish packing. She sat on his bed and looked around the room at his posters of Dick Butkus and Mike Singletary.

"When do classes start?"

"Tuesday morning. I've got an extra class this semester, so I'll be busy even without football."

Tony stuffed one of his suitcases so full that he had trouble closing it. He looked at Emmy, picked her up and sat her down on the suitcase. "You weigh just enough to help me get this closed."

"I'm glad I'm fat enough to help."

Tony gazed into her eyes for a moment.

"You can move your hands now," she said.

"Sorry, Em. I lost track of what I was doing for a second." He closed the clasps and then lifted her off of the suitcase and set her back on the edge of the bed. "Sorry, I shouldn't pick you up like that."

She bit her lip. "It's all right."

Eventually, Tony had to leave. Heather was returning to South Bend with him since she had taken the bus to SoHam.

"It was good to have you two home for the holidays." Mama's eyes grew misty as she hugged them both.

Tony hugged Emmy, and she surprised him with a brief kiss. "Be good and go to class once in a while. Oh, make sure you go on a few dates, too."

"I will if you do the same when Kenny is gone. Maybe we could go to a basketball game this winter," Tony suggested.

"That would be cool. I could try and get a carload of kids to come."

"Sure. Why not?" Tony smiled halfheartedly. *I guess that would be better than nothing.*

Emmy and Mama waved as Tony backed out of the driveway. Heather waved goodbye as Tony honked the horn.

"I've got some leftovers for you to take home, child. You are too skinny."

"Oh, Mama! You always say that. Thanks for the food. I gotta run."

Emmy parked in the Colwell's long driveway. She heard Kenny playing his guitar as she got out of the car. She sprinted into the carriage house and up the stairs. He stopped playing and set his guitar down. "How did it go? Did you give him a kiss?"

"Maybe I did, and maybe I didn't," Emmy teased as she shed her coat and gloves. Kenny grabbed her and held her shoulders as she smiled at him. "I kissed him once like this." She kissed Kenny briefly.

"I suppose that's allowed." He grinned. "Will I get a different kind of kiss tomorrow?"

350

"I'm still not sure I'm going to kiss you at all."

He surprised her by picking her up, and dumping her on the futon. He got on the futon next to her and whispered, "Then I want my kiss now."

In the morning Emmy called the office to tell them she would be late. Andy Walker arrived at the Colwell home in a limo and waited inside the house.

"What are they doing? We need to shove off." Andy checked his Rolex again.

Mrs. Colwell smiled. "You must have been young once, Andy. Don't you remember?"

"I'll give you guys two more minutes," he hollered. "I remember all right."

Upstairs in his bedroom Kenny and Emmy laughed when they heard Andy. "Are you going to kiss me, Em? Did you decide yet?" Kenny asked softly as he held her in his arms. He could feel her trembling as the tears flowed down her face.

She lifted her head from his chest, put her arms around his neck and kissed him. "I tried not to cry, but I know I will miss you so much."

"I will miss you, too. You remember how to use your computer, right?"

"Yes, if I run into trouble, I will call Barry. He knows a lot about computers."

Kenny and Emmy came downstairs.

Andy saw the redness in her eyes from the tears, so he hugged her. "I'll take care of him, cuz. I'll make sure he emails you every day and calls you at least once a week." He kissed the top of her head, and then turned to Kenny. "Are you finally ready? Time is wasting! We've got to get this show on the road."

Emmy held Kenny's hand as they walked out to the limo. He kissed her once more then got in the limo with Andy. She waved goodbye as she stood with his parents.

Chapter Thirty-Six

Tony's spring break started on March eleventh, and he headed home since spring football practice didn't start until the twenty-first. North Park College's spring break began at the same time. Kristen was free, but bored. She called Tony and wanted to get together on Sunday. Tony agreed to meet her at his house at noon.

Kristen called Emmy and asked, "What are you doing tomorrow?"

"I'm going to church with the Colwells in the morning, but I've got nothing else planned. What are you doing?"

"I'm going to see Tony, and we're going to do something. Don't know what yet. Wanna join us?"

"Okay, I didn't know he was home."

"He got home earlier today. He's on break like me." Kristen paused for a moment. "Are you going to church with Kenny's parents every week? I've only seen you a few times since Tony went back to school."

"I'm making an effort to go with them, but I missed a couple weeks. Why?"

"No reason. See you tomorrow." Kristen ended the call and booted up her computer. She searched for information about Kenny's church and found an article from the SoHam newspaper. She read the entire article. *Doesn't sound too fanatical to me.*

Emmy drove over to the Bertucci house after church. Mama let her in and said, "Hello, Emmy. Kristen said you might stop by. How have you been?"

"Busy. Between school and work I don't have much spare time. I'm taking an extra class this semester. That's why I haven't stopped by. How have you been? Are you doing all right?"

"I had a cold and my back bothered me for a couple of days, but I'm all right. Tony and Kristen are downstairs. Go on down and join them. I should warn you though, a few of his friends are over. Do you remember Terry Pagonis from high school?"

"I know him because he played football."

"Nikki Foster is here, too."

"It's okay, Mama. Tony and I are just friends now."

"Of course you are, dear. I'm making lasagna for dinner if you can stay."

"I wouldn't miss an opportunity to have some of your lasagna. I'll talk to you later." Emmy gave Mama a hug before running downstairs.

Kristen saw her. "About time you got here, Emmy. How was church?"

"All right, I guess." Emmy looked around and recognized everybody. Tony and Terry played pool as the other kids talked about college life. Emmy figured out by listening that everyone lived in a dorm except for her. She talked to Nikki and learned more than she wished about Nikki's new boyfriend. The impromptu party broke up around four. Emmy and Kristen stayed to have dinner with Mama and Tony.

"Mama, the lasagna smells so good. Can I help with anything?" Emmy asked, while Tony and Kristen sat in the living room, sharing more stories about dorm life.

"I can handle it, dear. Why don't you sit and talk to Tony," Mama suggested.

Emmy joined Kristen on the couch. "Nikki looked prettier than ever, Tony,"

"I guess so. She's going to Northwestern and dating a guy in grad school."

"So she said. Did you ask her out for dinner?"

"I thought about it, but she seems pretty serious about that guy." *Maybe more serious than you are about Kenny.*

After dinner Emmy needed to get home. She got ready to leave, and Tony walked her to the door.

"Would you like to go to dinner tomorrow night, or maybe Tuesday?"

Emmy looked up at Tony and touched the small scar on his chin. "Do you mean like on a date or just as friends?"

"We could make it a date if you want. Would Kenny mind?"

"I might mind, but he has encouraged me to go out

353

occasionally while he's away on tour."

"Would you consider having dinner with me as fun?" Tony asked. "Or would it feel weird?"

"It would only be weird if you act like a dork," she teased. "Tuesday would be better for me. I have a class tomorrow night. Where do you want to go?"

"Would the Hungry Lion be all right?"

Emmy remembered the first time he took her to the Lion. "Sure, that's fine with me."

After work on Tuesday Emmy met Tony at his house, and he drove to The Hungry Lion. They talked about school, football and even Fridays At Five. Tony only teased her a few times, so Emmy thought of it as a pleasant evening.

Tony pulled into the driveway next to Emmy's car. "Do you have time to come in, Em?"

"I wish I could, but I need to get home. I've got some homework to finish." She found the car keys in her purse, unlocked the car and opened the door.

"Okay, I understand that. I had fun tonight, Em. I hope I didn't tease you too much."

"It was fun. Maybe we can do this again sometime." Emmy got in the car, closed the door, started the car and rolled down the window. *What exactly is going on, Tony? You treated me kinda like a girlfriend tonight. It was almost spooky.*

Tony put his hands on the window ledge and leaned over. "Do you have plans for Friday?"

"Class."

"Saturday?" *Maybe I shouldn't press my luck.*

"I don't think I have any plans for Saturday night. I'll have to clean the apartment and do laundry during the day."

He smiled at her. "I'll call you later in the week, and we can see how things are."

"All right. I'll see you later."

Emmy left; Tony didn't try to kiss her, although he did think about it.

Emmy checked the mail on Wednesday after work and opened a fancy envelope she figured must be a wedding invitation.

Oh, my God! Barry, it's about time. She kept reading. *Barry Newton and Linda Bailey, blah, blah, blah... getting married on May twelfth. That's strange. That's a Friday night.* She hadn't seen Barry or Linda since the vacation in Colorado.

Emmy called Linda later that night after class. "Hi, Linda, I got the invitation today. That's a Friday."

Linda explained, "We found this great place for the reception. Have you ever been to the Ingram Mansion?"

"I've never been there. That's that old place over by the Hill district, right?"

"Yes, and that was the only night we could get the place unless we waited for another six months. Barry didn't want to wait any longer so that's why the wedding is on a Friday."

Emmy knew Kenny would be on tour and not able to go to the wedding. She assumed Kristen and Derrick were going. She called Tony and, after making small talk for a couple of minutes, Emmy asked him about the wedding.

"It's on May twelfth, which is a Friday. Did you get an invitation?"

"Yes, I saw it in the mail today."

"Are you taking a date?" Emmy asked. "Kenny will be gone, and I thought if you weren't going with anyone, maybe we could go together."

"I'm sorry, Em, but I can't go. That's the last day of finals and I have two that afternoon. I wouldn't be able to make it to the ceremony and probably would miss most of the reception, too."

"Maybe I won't go to the reception then."

"Don't be silly. Of course you'll go. Barry and Linda are your friends. They would be so disappointed if you didn't show up. You've known Barry almost your whole life. Just go and have a good time."

"I don't think you or Kenny will ever be able to go to a wedding with me. Kenny is always on tour, and you're always busy with something. If it's not football, it's school or something. I want someone to spend some time with me."

355

Emmy ranted and raved about Kenny and Tony not being with her. She got so upset, she hung up on him. As soon as she hung up, Emmy regretted it and called Tony back to explain. "I'm sorry. It's that time."

"It's all right, Emmy. I understand. Do you still want to do something on Saturday?"

"Call me on Friday and I'll let you know how I feel, okay? I'm sorry I yelled at you." She hung up, walked into the bedroom and plopped onto the bed. *Why did you have to show up now?* She clutched her abdomen. *You're so irregular that I never know when you're gonna happen.*

Emmy wanted to go to the wedding but didn't want to go alone. She wanted a dance partner. She mentioned the wedding to her mom on the phone the next day.

"Barry and Linda are getting married, and Kenny can't go. I talked to Tony. He can't go because of finals."

"You mean Barry Newton from down the street?"

"Yes, Mom."

"We weren't invited. I thought we would have been invited. We've always been nice and neighborly to Mrs. Newton."

"It's a small wedding, Mom. They can't invite everyone."

"It doesn't matter. Since Kenny and Tony can't go, are you going alone?"

"Most likely."

"You could ask Wayne Sanders. You had a good time with him before."

"I was actually thinking about asking him. Not like as a date though, Mom. Just so you understand that. He likes to dance. Do you have their number?"

"I've got it somewhere."

Emmy called Wayne Sanders and told him about the wedding.

"I'd really like to go, Emmy, but I have to work until closing on Friday nights. I appreciate you asking though. We did have fun dancing. Maybe we could go dancing again."

"Sure, Wayne, I'll talk to you sometime. Take care."

Emmy didn't know who else to ask and asked Kristen. "Can you think of anybody who I could ask to go? I want to go with someone I know so I don't have to dance with strangers all night."

"There are lots of guys here at school. I'm sure one of them might be willing to go with you, Emmy."

"I don't want to go on a blind date. I might as well go by myself and take my chances at the reception."

Kristen had an invitation also and was wondering who she should invite. "I've got an idea!"

"What?"

"Let's go together. That way we don't have to worry about finding a guy. We could chill out and let our hair down."

"Kristen, you are so smart. I would have so much more fun with you than some guy from school that I don't really know. I guess there will plenty of guys to dance with."

"You could spent the night at my parents' house. It will be a blast," Kristen said.

"That would be fun. I've never spent the night at your house. It will be like a slumber party for the two of us. I can't wait. Do you think Derrick is going?"

"He will be here, and he's bringing his latest girlfriend. He broke up with Amber."

"Aw, too bad. I really liked Amber."

Tony called Emmy on Friday. She agreed to go out to dinner and a movie on Saturday. He took her to Ciao Bella for dinner, and then they saw *Reindeer Games* at the mall. As they were leaving the theater, Tony held her hand. She looked up at him and smiled. He hadn't teased her at all the entire evening. He took her home, walked her to the porch and kissed her cheek as he left.

He slapped his thigh as he walked back to his car. *I shouldn't have kissed her cheek. She's going to think I'm such a dork.*

Emmy stood inside the door and watched Tony leave. *Now I remember why I fell in love with him. He can be so charming when he wants. I wonder if he just kissed my cheek because of Kenny.*

357

Tony started up the car and waved to her. *I really like the way she dressed tonight. She looks so great in faded jeans and a white shirt.*

I bet he thinks I'm one of the guys again. I should have worn a skirt with this top instead of these old, worn-out jeans. Emmy mentally kicked herself.

The rest of March and the month of April were busy times for Emmy. She worked every weekday and went to class three nights a week. The other two nights she had to study. On the weekends she took care of the apartment, did the grocery shopping, laundry and everything else that she couldn't do during the week. She usually went to church with Kenny's parents. She talked to Kenny on Sunday afternoons, when possible, and they emailed each other during the week. Tony called her a couple of times; they emailed each other, too.

On April fifth Emmy called Grandma Isabel in Florida. "Happy Birthday, Grandma! How are you feeling?"

"I feel fine for a ninety-year-old lady."

"Are you doing anything special today?"

"I'm going out for lunch with some of my friends. I didn't want to make a big deal about today, but they insisted."

"It is a big deal, Grandma. Not everyone makes it to ninety."

"I'll think it's special if I live to be a hundred."

Emmy talked to Grandma Isabel for a few more minutes.

"I need to go, dear. My friends are on their way. Thank you for calling and remember that I love you, Emily."

"I love you, too, Grandma."

Grandma hung up and thought about her younger granddaughter. *You have always loved everyone, Emily. You're different from Diane in that respect.* Grandma chuckled. *And totally opposite from your mother. Patricia never loved anything or anyone—except herself.*

Chapter Thirty-Seven

Emmy stopped singing for a moment as she reached into the pocket of her jeans for her cell phone.

"Hey, Kristen, what's up?"

"Do you realize that Linda's wedding is next Friday? We need to go shopping. I don't have anything to wear."

"Oh, for crying out loud! You have a closet bigger than my whole apartment full of clothes. You are such a spoiled princess," Emmy teased as she used one hand to grab laundry out of the washer and toss it into the dryer.

"I know, but I hate to wear an old dress to a wedding. Can we go shopping this afternoon?"

"I guess so, but I'm not sure I can afford another new dress. I have some stuff here to finish first."

"I'll pick you up at noon. We'll do lunch and go shopping. Mom gave me some money, so I can buy new dresses for both of us and don't you dare argue with me. I'm buying today."

"You mean your mother is buying."

"Okay, if you want to get technical about it. What are you doing, anyway?"

"I'm in the O'Brien's basement doing laundry. I've been singing because I'm having so much fun."

"You're a goof."

"Can't you tell by now when I'm being sarcastic?"

Kristen arrived at noon. They wolfed down lunch at Burrito Palace, and then headed to the mall. Two hours later Kristen finally found a dress she liked. Emmy found one that she liked in ten minutes.

"I can't help it if it took me so long. I can't go to the kids department at Penney's and find one like you can."

"I didn't get this at Penney's," Emmy said. "I got it at Kids 'R Us."

"I want to make sure my dress fits right." Kristen shook her head at a high school kid holding a clipboard. "Those people are so annoying with their surveys."

Emmy laughed. "Maybe it's for that TV show. The one

359

where the emcee points to the board and says 'the survey said.'"

"Grandma Keasling watches that show religiously." Kristen stopped in front of a store and inspected the gowns in the window display. *Hmmm! That one is just my size and the color is perfect for my complexion. Maybe next time I'm here.* "You are still spending the night with me after the reception, right?"

"Yes, I am. Why? Don't you want me to stay now?" Emmy glanced at the Teens Forever window display. *I can't believe how much they're charging for jeans. What a rip!*

"You have to sleep in a guest bedroom. The last time I spend the night at your place, you kicked me so many times my legs were bruised."

"I did not."

"Did so. I should have taken pictures." Kristen abruptly turned and marched away. "Come on! Let's get home so I can try on my new dress again."

Emmy hurried to catch up. "Which one? You bought three."

Emmy took a personal day on Friday so she could go to the wedding. She got dressed, packed an overnight case, carried her new dress out to the car, and then headed over to Kristen's house. Kristen answered the door and took Emmy upstairs.

Emmy stood in the hallway at the top of the wide stairs and looked in both directions. "How many bedrooms are there up here? I guess I never paid any attention to that before."

"There are five bedrooms up here." She pointed to a set of double doors at the end of the hall. "That's Derrick's room. My parents used it originally. That's why it's so big."

"Is that why it has a private bathroom?"

"Well, all the bedrooms have a private bath. No, I take that back." Kristen pointed. "These two guest bedrooms have what Daddy calls a Jack and Jill bathroom. They share a bathroom and it's the only one with a door opening onto this hallway. You've been in my room before and the other bedroom is the same size. It was Derrick's originally." Kristen remembered the small house where Emmy grew up. "Daddy built this house with the intention of using the wing downstairs for Grandma and Grandpa."

360

"Did they live here?" Emmy remembered the time she saw Grandpa Lombardi at Kristen's high school graduation party.

"For a short time when we moved back here from West Bartlett. Grandpa didn't like staying here. He wanted to live in his own place. He was so stubborn."

"Tony once told me I was as stubborn as his grandfather."

They ate lunch and met Derrick's date, Haley Ferguson. Haley's red hair cascaded down her back and her oval face had more freckles than anyone Emmy had even seen. Emmy thought Haley looked pretty, but her quirky laugh made her seem a little ditsy compared to Amber.

"Do you and Emmy want a ride?" Derrick asked later. "Dad said I could use his car."

"He's letting you drive the Beamer! He never lets me drive it," Kristen complained.

Daniel Keasling had recently purchased a 2000 BMW 540i.

"He knows I can handle it," Derrick teased as he jiggled the keys.

"Come on, Em. Let's ride with Derrick and Haley. He can be the designated driver." Kristen grinned. "We can drink as much champagne as we want."

There are so many people sitting on Linda's side, but hardly anyone on Barry's side. Emmy realized as she and Kristen walked into St. Mark's Lutheran Church.

Kristen gazed at the flowers at the front of the small church. "I assumed you would sit on Barry's side, Emmy. You've known him a lot longer than you've known Linda."

"Good thinking, Krissy." Emmy glanced at one of the stained-glass windows and noticed a black cross inside a red heart with a white background shaped like a flower. "I've seen that symbol before. Do you know what it is?" she asked Derrick.

"That's called the Luther Rose," he answered. "Martin Luther used it as his seal, I think."

"You're so smart," Haley gushed while holding on to Derrick's arm. "I heard him make a speech on TV once."

Derrick grinned at Emmy, who rolled her eyes. *She's definitely not Amber.*

361

A few minutes later, Emmy caught Barry's attention as he waited at the front and made a face at him. He grinned at her and shook his head. After the short ceremony, he and Linda greeted them with hugs in the reception line.

"Why were you making faces at me, Em?"

"I remembered how you used to tease me when we were kids."

"Are you and Kristen coming to the reception together?" Barry asked as he shook hands with someone he didn't recognize.

"Yes!" they both answered.

"Oooh. Like a real date," Barry teased.

Emmy poked him in the ribs. "It's about time you made an honest woman of Linda."

"You know I wanted to get married right after high school, but Linda's parents wouldn't go for it."

Emmy thought they were really too young to be taking this big step at twenty years of age. She whispered softly, "Is she pregnant? Is that why you were in such a rush?"

Barry answered, "No, not yet. We're going to wait a few years to start a family."

At the reception Emmy and Kristen sat at the same table as Derrick and Haley along with two of Linda's older, single relatives. They introduced themselves, but neither Emmy nor Kristen could remember their names two minutes later. When the music started, Emmy and Kristen danced with several different guys. Sometimes they danced together. Emmy had a chance to dance with Derrick later, and he asked, "How are you and Kenny doing? I know you don't get to see him as much as you'd like."

Emmy bit her lip. "We're doing fine. I understand that music is his career. It's really the first love of his life."

"I'm sorry he's gone so much, Em. Maybe you could travel with him in the summer." He twirled her around and then put his hand on her back. "I know you're wondering about Amber."

Emmy nodded.

"She met an older man. I don't think it will last."

"So Haley is just a temporary replacement, huh?"

He laughed. "You could call her that."

Barry and Linda spent as much time as they could dancing but mingled with the non-dancing crowd, too. When Linda threw her bouquet, Emmy and Kristen both grabbed it. Kristen let Emmy have it, and they brought it over to the table to show Derrick and Haley.

Derrick smiled. "I guess this means you will be getting married to each other soon."

"Maybe we will." Kristen kissed Emmy on the cheek in front of everyone.

Shortly before Barry and Linda needed to leave, Emmy danced with Barry. She whispered in his ear, "Do you have anything special planned for tonight? Anything memorable?"

Barry embarrassed Emmy by whispering back, "It will be memorable because Linda and I are planning to do some things that you have never even thought of because you are such a sweet and innocent girl."

She looked at him, bit her lip and turned bright red.

They arrived back at the Keasling home shortly after midnight, walked into the family room and talked to Mr. and Mrs. Keasling.

"Here's the keys, Dad. Thanks for letting me use the car."

"You're welcome. How was the reception?"

Kristen plopped down onto the couch. "We shared our table with two of Linda's relatives. Total dorks!"

"Kristen! You shouldn't call them that," Mrs. Keasling said.

"Mom, you didn't see them. Emmy, am I right?"

Emmy nodded. "Total dorks, Mrs. Keasling. Kristen is not exaggerating in the least. They kept asking us to dance, but we wouldn't. They finally gave up and found a couple of women their own age. They were old. Late thirties at least."

Mr. Keasling lowered his head and peered over his reading glasses.

Emmy blushed. "Sorry, I didn't mean it like that."

Derrick put in his two cents, "I talked to them and thought they were rather articulate and very intelligent and handsome as well."

Emmy stared at Derrick as if he had gone nuts.

Kristen laughed. "I will take you to the psych ward now if you want since you are absolutely bonkers."

Haley grinned and giggled. She drank a lot of wine at the reception.

They headed upstairs, but before they changed out of their dress clothes, they gathered in Derrick's room.

This is such a cool room. Emmy ran a hand along the pale blue wall. *I bet it's bigger than my whole apartment.* She rubbed the cool leather on a couch at one end of the room.

Kristen waved. "Come over here, Em. We need to talk."

All three young women sat on Derrick's king-size bed to talk. The conversation soon turned to the subjects of sex and men. Derrick stood at the foot of his bed listening to them.

"I'm not listening to this."

"Good!" Kristen said. "You shouldn't be listening to us now anyway. This is girl talk. We might even want to talk about you so you should leave."

"In case you haven't noticed, Kristen dear, this is my room." Derrick waved his hand. "Why don't you leave instead?"

"Just go sit on the couch and watch TV while we talk about you." Kristen pointed.

Derrick shook his head, exhaled loudly and moved to the couch at the other end of his room. He turned on the TV out of habit. Kristen and Haley whispered to each other and began giggling.

A few minutes later Emmy got off the bed and walked over to the couch and sat with Derrick. He turned off the TV, and they talked about Kenny, Tony, school and life in general. She was about to tell him good night when he looked at her and smiled.

"What are you smiling about, Derrick?"

"It's raining."

"So? It rains a lot this time of year," she answered back.

Derrick reminded her of the day they went hiking and got caught in a downpour. Emmy thought about the time in the rain with Derrick.

"Why didn't you kiss me, or try to make out with me?"

364

"I wonder about that sometimes myself, Emmy." They looked at each other for a moment. "All right, I'll tell you. I really didn't like the way your hair looked and your legs are too short and your..."

"I get the picture, you stinker."

Emmy threatened to punch him where it would hurt if he kept teasing her. Derrick grabbed her hands to protect himself.

"I just couldn't, knowing I was leaving and wouldn't see you for such a long time. I like you too much to take advantage of you. I knew that you didn't have strong romantic feelings for me, and I didn't want to hurt you."

You're being sweet. I know you weren't attracted to me like your other girlfriends. Emmy kissed Derrick on the cheek. "You are my second most favorite boyfriend of all time."

Derrick feigned shock. "Who could you possibly like better than me?"

"There is only one boy I like better than you, but I can't remember his name right now." She leaned against his shoulder.

Derrick asked, "Is it Barry?"

She shook her head. "No, he's never been my boyfriend."

"Randy from high school?" Derrick put his arm around her shoulders.

"No, not him," Emmy said and then giggled. *Christopher maybe.*

"It must be Jayson Mathias then," Derrick said.

Emmy straightened up, made a face, stuck a finger down her throat and pretended to gag. "I remember his name now. It's Tony, you silly goof."

"Tony. I can't believe you like him better than Jayson."

"I know it's hard to believe. Jayson was such a classy guy, but I love Tony and you know that, so quit teasing me." She rested against him again.

Derrick looked at Emmy with surprise. She realized her *faux pas*. "I meant Kenny. I love *Kenny*!"

"I know you do, Em." He patted her leg.

"I love Tony, too. Just in a different way."

Derrick wondered how much wine or champagne Emmy

365

drank at the reception because she acted a little tipsy.

"Tony and I were talking on the phone a while back, and I hung up on him. He's probably still mad at me. I got mad at him because he couldn't be here tonight because of finals. Sometimes I get so frustrated with those guys."

"It's okay, Emmy. Kenny and Tony still love you even if you are a childish, immature, spoiled little brat."

Emmy hit him with a throw pillow from the couch.

"You know you still like Tony even if you got mad at him, don't you?"

"Yeah, I know I do."

Kristen was through talking to Haley, so she came over to the couch and sat next to Emmy.

"Are you ready to go to bed, Emmy? I am. Why don't you change and then join me in my room? I've got a king-size bed so maybe you won't kick me. We can talk about Derrick and make fun of him all night long."

"Okay, we can talk for a while, but then I'm going to sleep in the guest room. I don't want your legs to be all black and blue in the morning." Emmy jumped up and grinned. "Good night, Derrick. If your ears are burning later, it's because we are talking about you."

"Wait for me. I'm coming, too," Haley said and then giggled some more. "Good night, Derrick."

"Good night, Haley. I'll see you in the morning, okay?" Derrick gave Haley a kiss and a hug as Emmy and Kristen watched.

"You can let her go now, Derrick," Kristen said.

"Get out of here and let me sleep." Derrick shooed them out of his room. "Don't stay up too late and keep the noise down."

Haley went to her room. And, after changing her clothes, Emmy decided to stay with Kristen—at least for now.

"How much wine did you have?" Emmy asked.

"Two glasses. Not nearly as much as Haley," Kristen said. "Did you have any?"

"One glass and some champagne." Emmy put a finger to her mouth. "Or maybe two glasses and a glass or two of

366

champagne. I can't remember 'xactly."

"I saw you dancing with Derrick. Do you ever think about how things might have turned out if you two... kinda... you know?"

"You mean if he didn't think of me as your little friend? If he thought of me like Amber?" Emmy drew out her name.

"Yeah."

"Not really. He is very handsome and charming, but he didn't excite me like Kenny."

"Or Tony?" Kristen grinned.

"Tony never... Never mind. I don't want to talk about him."

The morning sun shone through the windows of Kristen's room. A gentle breeze stirred the trees, and birds sang their songs. Emmy and Kristen woke up gradually—a little earlier than they wanted.

Kristen felt a knee poking her in the back and a hand on top of her head. "Morning, Em. Are you awake?"

"Sorta. What time is it?"

"Just after seven."

"Why are we awake so early?"

"I don't know, but since we are let's go see if my lazy brother is awake yet."

"Why?" Emmy yawned.

"Because I want to see him. Don't you dare tell him, but I miss him when he's away at school."

Emmy rolled over onto her back. "I won't tell him if I can go back to sleep."

Kristen hopped out of bed. "Come on." Kristen took Emmy by the hand and pulled her out of bed. They went into Derrick's room and jumped on his bed to wake him up. Kristen sat next to Derrick, who lay on his stomach with his arms outstretched under the covers and a bit hungover.

"Wake up, lazy. Emmy and I want to play tennis."

"We do?" Emmy asked.

"Go away whoever you are." Derrick pushed Kristen.

"Come on, wake up! It's your favorite sister, and you need to get up."

Derrick groaned, hid under the covers and stuck his head under his pillow. Kristen poked him in the side, and he growled.

"You are in deep trouble, little sister. Leave me alone. I want to sleep."

Kristen laughed.

Haley woke up and wandered into Derrick's room because she heard the commotion. She looked half-asleep and fuzzy about what happened the night before because of the wine she'd consumed. The three young ladies sat on Derrick's bed and talked about the previous night. Haley put her hand on her stomach as nausea overtook her, and she ran into Derrick's bathroom. Kristen dragged the pillow and covers off of Derrick's head. He rolled over and sat up.

"I will tell Mom and Dad you were in bed with Haley last night unless you get your lazy butt out of bed and play tennis with both of us."

"I wasn't in bed with Haley," Derrick said.

"She was on your bed though."

"Yeah! Talking to you and Emmy."

"Let's not argue about semantics," Kristen said. "Get up."

Emmy sat on the other side of Derrick. She wondered if Derrick had slept with Haley.

"All right. I'll get up and play tennis, but first I'm going to bite your neck and turn you into a vampire."

Derrick moved toward Kristen, but she jumped off the bed and ran over to the couch as Derrick chased her. Derrick caught Kristen and grabbed her. He threw her over his shoulder and dumped her unceremoniously on the bed.

"Stop it, Derrick! I'm telling Dad."

"Go ahead. I didn't do anything wrong."

Derrick grabbed her legs with the intention of tickling the bottom of her feet. Just then Haley opened the bathroom door and Derrick stopped.

"What's going on out here?" Haley asked.

"Hide, Haley! Derrick has lost his mind and is attacking us. He thinks he's a vampire," Kristen warned.

Derrick chased Haley into the bathroom as she screamed.

While Derrick and Haley were in the bathroom, Emmy and Kristen looked at each other. Kristen got a mischievous look on her face.

"Come on."

"What are we doing, Kristen?"

"You'll see."

They moved to the bathroom door to listen to Derrick and Haley. They were leaning on the door trying to eavesdrop when the door opened suddenly. Emmy and Kristen lost their balance and fell into the bathroom on top of each other. Derrick looked at them and laughed. "What are you guys doing?"

"Nothing," they answered as they struggled to stand up and stop laughing.

"Scram and get dressed if you want to lose at tennis."

The three excited ladies ran out of Derrick's room laughing and giggling like little girls. Derrick shook his head.

Eventually, they all got dressed and went downstairs. They ate a quick breakfast, and then headed outside to play tennis. Emmy and Kristen made a better team than Derrick and Haley only because Haley had to be the worst tennis player in the world. Emmy and Kristen consoled her after the match.

"We're sorry you lost, Haley, but it's not your fault," Kristen said. "You can blame your partner."

"I don't mind that we lost. I did better than the last time. At least I hit the ball across the net a few times."

Emmy and Kristen teased Derrick mercilessly because they whipped his butt. Derrick accepted their teasing with a good nature. They knew he could have beaten them easily if he tried.

After lunch Emmy told Kristen, "I think this has been the most fun I've ever had at a wedding."

"Are you thinking of simply the wedding and reception, or are you including last night in Derrick's room and this morning, too?"

"I guess I am thinking about the whole thing. The wedding, reception and last night with you." Emmy hugged Kristen. "I've got to call Tony and tell him how sorry I am for acting like a spoiled brat."

"He's not still mad at you. Stop living in the past. I think

369

you're using that as an excuse to call him."

"No. I'm not," Emmy professed, even though Kristen knew better.

Emmy drove home and called Tony as soon as she dropped her overnight bag in her bedroom. "I'm sorry I acted so immature about everything. How did finals go? Did you pass everything?"

Tony didn't catch the first part of Emmy's conversation. He assumed Brenda Rollins was calling, but then he recognized Emmy's voice.

"Hi, Em. I think I did. Finals were challenging, but I'm pretty certain I did well on them. I'm really sorry I couldn't be there with you."

"I know how important school is, and I'm really sorry I acted like a spoiled brat."

"It's all right, Emmy. I know why you acted that way." They kept talking, and Tony mentioned, "I've signed up for summer school. It starts in the middle of June. Until then I'll be working for a landscaping company for a few weeks in Ohio with John. After that I am going on vacation with Mama and Uncle Carmen and Aunt Sharon. I'll only have a few free days before summer school starts. I do hope I can see you before I have to start classes. I want to talk to you about the future."

"Okay, I'll talk to you sometime after you get home." The disappointment was evident in her voice because she wouldn't see him much and maybe even not at all. She wondered, *What did you mean by the future. I hope I can see you once or twice at least.*

She knew Kenny would only be home for a few days here and there over the summer. The tour and recording sessions in Los Angeles would keep him busy for some time. She saw Kenny on May twenty-ninth—his mother's fiftieth birthday, when he made it home for the day. They didn't have a chance to be alone because the Colwell house was filled with people celebrating the event. They kept in touch using email and she kept busy at work to take her mind off both guys. She forgot that Tony was even coming home at all.

370

Chapter Thirty-Eight

Emmy stood in the produce aisle of the Sainsbury's grocery store holding a green pepper in each hand, trying to decide which one looked better when a grocery cart bumped into her from behind. She frowned as she wondered why some idiot couldn't see her standing there.

"For crying out loud, can't you..."

She turned around to see who had bumped into her; her frown slowly changed to a smile. She looked at the large young man behind the shopping cart next to a lady who must be his mother and dropped both green peppers.

"Hi, I'm not sure if you remember me or not," Tony said.

She decided to tease him back by pretending she didn't recognize him. "You do look familiar for some reason, but I can't quite remember why."

She both laughed and cried at the same time as Tony looked at her with a huge smile on his face. The memory of a little boy flashed through Emmy's mind, but it only lasted for an instant.

He grinned and explained, "My name is Tony Bertucci, and you once went on a date with me."

Emmy put a finger to her mouth and tilted her head. "You took me on a date once. Hmmmm, I don't recall ever going on a date with anyone who looked like you."

She lifted her arms, and he hugged her as Mama smiled.

"Now I vaguely remember you. When did you get home, and how did you find me?"

She asked him a dozen more questions all as fast as she could possibly talk—which was pretty fast.

"Slow down, Emmy, and I'll tell you as we finish shopping."

She reminisced about how polite and sweet he treated her on their first date and also how shy he acted. She remembered when he kissed her, and she fell in love with him... and a thousand other thoughts flashed through her mind in an instant.

"It's just a coincidence that we ran into you here. I was going to call Kristen and see if we could all get together tonight or tomorrow."

"How long will you be in town?"

"Just three nights, Em, then I gotta go back."

"Do you want to go out for dinner tonight?" Emmy asked. *Whoa! Did I just ask him out on a date?*

"I would like that very much except Mama has requested I eat dinner with her tonight." Tony didn't say anything else about dinner.

Mama stepped in and asked, "Would you be able to join us for dinner, Emmy? I'm making lasagna, and I know you like that."

"I'd love to come over for lasagna. I'll be there as soon as I can get home, put these groceries away and freshen up."

Tony said, "I'll go with you and help you with your groceries. Will that be okay with you, Mama?"

"Yes, I can finish my shopping alone. I'll start dinner, and you can help me finish if you want, Emmy."

"Is it all right if I come over?" Tony asked Emmy as he leaned down and picked up the green peppers.

"I don't mind," Emmy answered. *I hope the apartment is clean. Did I even make my bed and pick up my dirty clothes?*

After checking out, Tony helped Emmy get her groceries into the car.

"Thanks." Emmy closed the trunk. "You really surprised me. I never expected to see you or Mama in the store."

"Mama saw you before I did." Tony folded his large frame into the front seat.

Emmy reached down for the lever. "You can slide the seat back a little."

Tony moved the seat all the way back, and they headed to Emmy's place. As she drove she thought about how Tony's father had died so many years ago and how Mama had raised three kids all by herself. Emmy quickly put the groceries away while Tony sat on the couch.

"I'm ready to go." She ran through the living room and into her bedroom. She looked in the mirror. *I guess I look all right.* But then she noticed a stain on her t-shirt. *Shoot! I need to change. I can't believe I went shopping in this.* She grabbed a top from the closet and quickly removed the t-shirt and put on a clean shirt. She walked back into the living room. "Now I'm really ready. Why didn't you tell me I had a stain on my t-shirt?"

He shrugged. "Sorry, Em. I didn't notice it."

Mama opened the fridge just as Emmy and Tony walked into the kitchen. Mama gave her a big hug and scolded her, though she smiled after doing it.

"You need to come and see me more often. If you don't, I will have to come to your apartment and visit you. Look at you. You are still too skinny. Don't you ever eat anything, dear?"

"I'm sorry I haven't kept in touch. I've been so busy with work and my classes."

"I want you to eat an extra helping of lasagna."

Emmy grinned. "If you insist."

After dinner Emmy sat in the living room with Mama and Tony. They talked about school and spring football. Then Mama excused herself and went upstairs to her bedroom. Tony and Emmy sat on the couch and talked for another hour.

Emmy looked at the antique clock on the wall. "I really need to get home. I've got to be at work early tomorrow for a training session, but I have Friday off. Will you let me pick the place we go tomorrow night? I want to try this new restaurant that is supposed to be good and not cost an arm and a leg."

"We can go wherever you want. All I want is to see you."

"Should I see if Kristen wants to join us?"

Tony shook his head no.

Tony arrived at Emmy's apartment the next evening wearing a suit and tie. He rang the bell and tried to stretch his collar.

Emmy ran down the stairs and opened the door. "Wow! Aren't you dressed to kill. I better change into something nicer than these old things."

"You look nice, Emmy. I think you look good in jeans."

"I can't go wearing these old faded jeans with you in a suit. It'll only take a couple minutes. Promise! Come upstairs and make yourself at home."

373

Tony sat on the couch while Emmy changed. She changed into one of her best dresses and came out to the living room to show Tony. She modeled her dress for him and curtsied like a princess.

"Emmy, you look positively gorgeous in that dress. Is it new?"

"I've had it for a while. Actually, this is the dress I wore to Barry and Linda's wedding and reception."

"Now I really wish I had been there with you."

They left for the restaurant. They were checking out a new place by the mall called the Texas Steakhouse. Tony ordered a Porterhouse steak and inhaled it, along with a baked potato and his salad. Emmy needed a box to take most of her salmon and baked sweet potato home. Tony told her about finals, his work landscaping with John Randolph and his vacation in the upper peninsula of Michigan.

"Uncle Carmen has this huge house on the lake. We went fishing every day."

"What did Mama do?" Emmy asked.

"She and Aunt Sharon actually came fishing with us a few times."

"For real? I can't see Mama doing that."

"She used to go fishing quite often as a young girl. You'd never know it now, but she used to do everything her brothers did. After Aunt Karla was born, she had to help Grandma take care of her."

I bet that's when she became the person she is today, Emmy thought.

Tony talked more about Mama as Emmy listened attentively. Tony fascinated Emmy with previously unheard stories of his mother's childhood. Stories Tony first heard from his grandmother. After dinner Tony brought Emmy back to her apartment, and they sat on opposite ends of the couch.

"How is work going? Anything new? Did you get a big raise or a promotion yet?"

"Work is all right, but I might have a good line on a new job. One that pays so much better. Tony, I'm really sorry I got upset

374

with you about finals and the wedding and everything. I acted like a spoiled baby."

"Em, that was a long time ago. I'm not upset about that. It never really bothered me. You shouldn't worry about that."

He pulled her next to him and tickled her until she complained. "Okay already, enough." She looked into his eyes very seriously. "You can't tickle me anymore because it is immature and we are too old for that kind of childish behavior."

"Do you want me to kiss you?"

She giggled and then said, "No way. I don't want to kiss you because boys are smelly and gross."

Tony arched his eyebrows. He had seen her act this way with Kenny, but never with him. He decided to play along. "I don't really want to kiss you because you are a girl and girls are icky."

They teased each other for a few minutes while acting like little kids.

"Are you a good football player, or did you sit on the bench for the whole season?" Emmy knew the answer, but simply wanted to tease him.

"I was the starting middle linebacker and I made the most tackles on the team."

"Whoopty-doo, doesn't say much for the rest of your team, does it?"

"You're gonna get it, Missy."

After they stopped teasing each other, Emmy asked Tony, "Why don't you take off this jacket and tie? You'll be more comfortable that way."

So he did.

"I plan to graduate in three years with my degree. That is why I'm working so hard and going to summer school. After I graduate I hope to play in the NFL for a few years, then start my own business."

"Wow, you've got everything figured out. Are you going to get married and have a family? Do you already have names picked out for your kids?"

"Yes, I plan on getting married, and I want lots of kids, but I don't have any names picked out yet."

375

"I was just kidding. Do you already have a girl picked out to marry?"

"I think I do, but..." Tony paused.

"Well, do I know her? Did you meet her at Notre Dame? Are you gonna tell me her name? What if I don't approve of her? Does she know how to cook? Will she make a good mother? Does her family have lots of money? Is she good in bed?" Emmy chuckled, then laughed as Tony's expression showed more exasperation as her questions became more facetious.

"I don't have a girl picked out yet. I just know what my dreams are."

They sat quietly for a moment.

"Can I have a Coke or something, Em?" Tony asked as his nervousness built.

"Sure, I'm sorry I didn't offer you something to drink before."

She got some pop for them and sat down on the couch facing him with her feet tucked under her. She put a blanket over her legs.

"Now tell me more about your future plans."

They continued talking, and Tony outlined his plans for the future in more detail. Emmy listened but teased him a little.

Then Emmy sat up straight and flipped a few strands of hair out of her face. "I want to talk to you about something important and no teasing or joking. This is serious, okay."

"What is it, Em?"

She scooted closer with the blanket still covering her legs. Tony looked at her body, and then into her eyes.

"Do you remember the day in high school when you were talking to me and Todd Delaney started bothering me and you made him stop?"

"I remember. Is he bothering you again?"

"No, thank God! He's not bothering me, but a few months ago he got arrested for assaulting a girl. My mother happened to see in the paper last week that he had been sentenced to prison. I'm so grateful that it wasn't me. I wanted to thank you for protecting me that day. That's all."

376

She leaned forward to kiss him quickly on the cheek, but he turned his head. She kissed his mouth, and he kissed her back. She moved closer to him and reached out her arms. He held her tightly to his chest as he thought about how Emmy could have been the victim of Todd Delaney.

They didn't say anything for a moment. Then Tony touched her side.

"That tickles. Stop it!"

"Can't I tickle you a little bit?"

"No. I already told you. No more tickling." Emmy didn't move his hand away.

Tony kept tickling her as she giggled so hard. Emmy didn't resist as he held her, then moved her onto his lap. He could almost wrap his large hands around her slim waist. She spun her legs and sat on his lap with her back to him. She leaned back against him. He stopped tickling her and put his left arm around her waist. She relaxed on his lap, and he held her close. They sat that way for a couple of minutes and talked softly to each other. She cherished the safety and security of his embrace.

Tony moved his arms to allow Emmy to get off of his lap. She sat facing him again. "Do you remember when I tried to seduce you in high school?" Emmy asked softly.

"Is that what you were trying to do? I didn't realize it," Tony answered with a chuckle.

"I tried, but I didn't really know how, and you wouldn't even make out with me."

"I remember. It was one of the most difficult things I've ever had to do."

"What do you mean?" Emmy tilted her head. "You didn't do anything."

"I know. That made it so difficult. I always thought you were the most beautiful girl in school from the first time I laid eyes on you. It took me two years to muster enough courage to talk to you."

"Courage!? Kristen had to drag you up to me and you said, 'Hi, your hair looks nice,' and then you ran away without telling me your name. Courage, my butt. I had to drag your name out of you after you chased away that jerk."

"What Todd did to you upset me so much. He tried to ruin your reputation and make you look like a slut. I wanted to hurt him somehow."

Emmy smiled and her eyes filled with tears as she remembered how Todd treated her. Tony didn't say anything for a moment.

"Can you stay longer? Or do you need to get home right away?"

Tony thought about her question. He knew from talking to Kristen that she really loved Kenny Colwell. He wondered if something had happened between them. "I really should go. I have to get up early. I have to read five chapters before the first class."

Emmy moved the blanket aside and rose from the couch. They stood facing each other. Tony touched the side of her face gently, and then brushed her hair lightly. He grabbed his jacket and tie. Emmy walked him downstairs and out to his car while holding onto his arm.

"Call me as soon as you are finished studying and I will come right over. We should do something together."

"Okay, Em. I had a good time tonight."

"You mean you enjoyed inhaling that steak!" Emmy exclaimed.

Tony laughed as he patted his stomach. "It did taste pretty good. I'll call you tomorrow."

The next morning Emmy worked outside with Mrs. O'Brien on the flower gardens and didn't hear her phone ring. When she went back inside, she noticed that Tony left a message.

"Hey, Emmy, I just finished studying. It's a little after noon. Come on over whenever you want."

She called him back, "I'll be over as soon as I can. I was outside when you called. See ya soon."

Emmy jumped in the shower and got ready. *Where are my good jeans? They're more comfortable than the fancy dress I wore last night.* She found her jeans and a new t-shirt to wear. She put a purple ribbon in her hair, checked herself in the mirror and then drove over to see Tony.

Mama hugged her. "Emmy, you are too skinny."

"Mama, you told me that just the other day. I can't gain weight overnight."

"We have some leftover lasagna for lunch."

"I love leftover lasagna. It always tastes even better the next day. Are you trying to fatten me up?" She smiled at Mama.

Tony asked, "What do you want to do this afternoon? We can do anything you want."

"Can we go over to the baseball field and watch a game? I noticed a game getting started when I drove past. I think that would be fun. You can buy me a hot dog and pop and we can sit in the sun and work on our tans."

"That sounds okay to me. Do you want to go with us, Mama?" Tony asked.

"Thanks for asking, but I'm going to work around the house, watch some TV, and take a nap."

During the game Emmy yelled and screamed at both teams and at the umpires, one of whom happened to be her former teacher and one of Tony's football coaches from high school. Mr. Niles came over to talk to Tony between one of the innings.

He pointed and shook a finger at Emmy. "Tony, you better control Miss Colasanti, or else I will toss her out of the game."

"I'll try, Coach, but I'm afraid she is absolutely uncontrollable."

Coach Niles laughed. "It's good to see you kids again. I watched your games, Tony. You are getting better every year."

"Thanks, Coach. It's good to see you again. I'll try to keep her under control, but it's not easy."

"I'm sorry you are having such a hard time seeing today, Mr. Niles," Emmy said and Mr. Niles laughed.

After the game Tony and Emmy went for an hour-long walk. They didn't want to waste such a beautiful day by staying indoors. They got back to find Mama fixing a big meal for dinner.

"I made all your favorites, and you better eat something. Whatever is left is going home with you anyway."

"Thank you, Mama. You are such a generous person."

After dinner Emmy and Tony helped Mama with the dishes and cleaned up the kitchen. They watched television with Mama until her bedtime.

Mama asked, "Are you going to spend the night, sweetie?"

Emmy looked at Tony to see if he wanted her to stay.

"Yes, she's going to stay," Tony answered Mama's question.

"I did pack an overnight bag just in case. It's in the car. I'll go get it. Be right back." Emmy ran out to the car.

Mama looked at Tony but didn't say anything.

Tony said, "I know, Mama, Emmy will sleep in Heather's room. I promise."

Emmy came back in and kissed Mama good night and went back to the couch with Tony.

"I'm not really tired yet. Why don't we go for another walk? It's such a pleasant night."

They went outside and walked around the neighborhood.

"Kenny wants me to quit working and go to North Park with Kristen."

Tony ducked under a branch. "Are you gonna do it?"

"I'm thinking about it. I could finish college quicker that way, then we could be together."

Tony looked at her. "You're talking about you and Kenny, right? Do you love him?"

"You know I do, but it's so difficult with him gone all the time."

"I know it is. The sooner you finish school, the quicker you can be together." The conversation was definitely not going the way Tony had hoped. They stopped under a streetlight. He turned to her and looked into her innocent blue eyes. They sparkled and danced. They always did when she talked about Kenny.

They crossed the street and continued walking. She asked, "Do you ever wish things were different between us? Do you ever regret that we broke up? Could you ever love me more than football?"

"More than football? Let me think about that." Tony thought for a moment and then grinned.

She stopped abruptly and faced him with her hands on her

380

hips as she waited for his answer.

"Yes, Emmy, I could love you even more than football. If I had to choose right now between you and never even touching a football again, I would choose you in a heartbeat."

"That's a crock!" Emmy laughed. "I know you're just kidding. I wouldn't ever make you give up football if we were together just like I would never make Kenny give up his music. Just as long as he loves me more."

Emmy smiled. She took Tony, and herself, by surprise as she wrapped her arms around his neck and kissed him. Just as a passing car illuminated them in its headlights.

"Did I shock you by kissing you like that. I just got carried away. I'm sorry."

"It's all right as long as you don't do it again," Tony told her, though he didn't mean it. "You know you can't spend the night in my room, don't you?"

She smacked his arm, "Duh! I know. I wouldn't want to break Mama's rules."

When they were ready to return home, she jumped on Tony's back; he took her for a piggy back ride all the way home. She giggled like a little girl as Tony carried her.

They went upstairs, and Emmy got ready for bed. She used the bathroom and then bumped into Tony in the hallway.

"Sorry, Em. Do you need anything? An extra blanket or...?"

"I'm fine, and I don't think I will get too cold."

"If you do, I am just..."

"I know where your room is. Good night, and I'll see you in the morning."

"I didn't mean it like that. I meant if you needed... Never mind. Night, Em."

Mama heard them in the hallway. Mama smiled as she thought of her late husband and how proud he would be of his family.

Chapter Thirty-Nine

"Anything special you want to do today?" Tony asked Emmy as they had breakfast Saturday morning.

"Let's go to the zoo. We've never done that together, and I haven't been there for so many years." Emmy poured more syrup over her pancakes. "Let me call Kristen and see if she wants to go with us. Do you want to go, Mama?"

Mama stood at the stove and flipped the pancakes over. "Oh, Emmy, that would be too much walking for me. You go with Tony and have fun."

"Tony, do you mind if I see if Kristen wants to come along?"

"I don't mind. We can leave her there with her relatives in the monkey house."

"She's your cousin, so I guess if she's a monkey you are a baboon." Emmy took another bite of pancakes. "What are you doing?"

Emmy squealed as Tony hopped around scratching his armpits while he made noises like a monkey. He moved closer and tried to kiss her and lick her face.

"Yuck! Stop it, you dork. Mama's watching."

"Mama doesn't care if I kiss you."

"Mama! Make him stop. He's acting so weird."

"That's how he normally acts, Emmy. You should know that by now." Mama shook her head as Tony grabbed a banana from the bowl on the table.

"Whew! I'm glad I got that out of my system. I feel much better now."

Emmy shook her head and laughed. "You're such a lovable dork."

Emmy called Kristen after helping with the breakfast dishes. "Today you are going to do what I ask."

"Why? What time is it, Emmy? It's Saturday. I want to sleep until noon."

"You can't. Get your butt out of bed and get dressed. You're coming to the zoo with me and Tony. He's driving."

Kristen sat up in bed. "With Tony? You're going to the zoo with him?"

"Yes. Don't make a big deal out of it. Don't go back to sleep, or else I'll drag you out of bed in your jammies."

"Give me an hour." Kristen tossed the covers aside.

"Emmy, look at this one. Doesn't it look just like Tony?" Kristen watched a chimpanzee as it scratched its back.

"You're gonna get it, Kristen." Tony grabbed her around the waist. "I'm gonna toss you in the water with the alligators."

"Tony, please don't do that. It might give the gators a bellyache," Emmy said.

Kristen pushed Tony away. "Thanks for sticking up for me, Emmy. I guess I know who your best friend is now."

"Kristen, you'll always be my best friend. Tony is simply a casual acquaintance at best."

"Now I am gonna toss you both to the gators," Tony said as he placed an arm around each of them.

"You better not. Can't you read the signs? They say 'please don't feed the animals.'"

"Who's got the map?" Emmy asked. "I want to make sure we see everything."

"I've got it in my back pocket," Tony said.

"I absolutely have to see the dolphin show. What time does it start?" Emmy pulled the map out of his back pocket and smacked his rear.

"We could go to the two o'clock show. That would give us time to see all the stuff along here." Tony showed the girls what he meant on the map.

"Where is the snake house? I want to see all the snakes and lizards and things," Emmy said.

"Oooh! Gross! I don't want to see that. I get creeped out just thinking about snakes." Kristen shuddered at the thought of being close to a snake even if it was in a cage.

"You're such a princess, Kristen."

"And you are a tomboy who probably played with snakes when you were a kid," Kristen retorted.

"What do you mean? She's still a kid," Tony teased.

They stayed at the zoo until it closed at five and then stopped at Darby's to eat. After hanging out at Darby's for two hours, they drove over to Roosevelt High. Emmy saw lights on at the ball diamond.

"Hey, there's a baseball game. You wanna watch?" Emmy asked Kristen.

"We can for a few minutes, but baseball is boring," Kristen answered.

Tony parked the car, and they walked over to the field. Kristen scanned the bleachers for someone she knew. Emmy watched the action on the field. Tony stopped walking and Emmy bumped into him.

"Sorry, Tony. I should watch where I'm walking."

"There's some kids we know over there." Kristen pointed to the top of the bleachers at the far end.

Thwack! Emmy heard the sound of the ball hitting the bat and caught the flight of the ball as it soared high into the sky. The catcher tore his mask off, tossed it out of the way and sprinted in her direction.

"Look out!" Kristen screamed and covered her head with her hands.

The catcher reached out a hand to keep from running into the chain-link fence as he kept his eyes on the ball. The spinning ball came down on her side of the fence and Emmy caught it.

"Hey, nice catch," the catcher said.

Emmy nonchalantly flipped the ball to him. "What? You think girls can't catch a baseball."

It was after nine o'clock when they dropped Kristen off at her house.

"Thanks for the ride. I had fun." Kristen grinned at Emmy. "Don't let him stay too long tonight, Em."

"We'll have to do it again when they have the snakes out of their cages," Emmy teased.

Kristen hopped out and ran inside.

Emmy thought about what Kristen said. *Why would I let Tony stay at all. What did you mean?*

Tony drove to Emmy's apartment and pulled into the

384

driveway. She started to get out of the car, but he stopped her. He held onto her arm. "Emmy, there's something I want to tell you."

"What? Are you going to tease me about being a tomboy again because I caught that baseball?"

"No, this is serious."

"Yeah, right." She laughed. "You're never serious with me."

Tony looked at her and sighed. "I miss you so much, and I need you to be a part of my life. I'll do whatever it takes for that to happen if you'll just give me a chance."

"Oh, Tony, I miss you, too. You know I want you to be a part of my life. You are as important to me as Kristen. I want us to be good friends."

"No! No!" Tony shook his head violently. "That's not what I mean, Em. I want to be more than your friend. You are my whole life. Without you, I'm empty and lost. I know I screwed up in the past, but I'm different now. I can treat you the way I should have before we broke up."

Emmy didn't know what to say. For fifteen seconds there was absolute silence in the car. To Tony, eternity wouldn't last as long.

"Are you gonna say something, Em?"

She couldn't even look at him as she shook her head.

Finally, Tony whispered, "Emmy, I love you."

"I love you, too, but I really love Kenny. You can come inside and talk to me if you want."

"Are you sure?"

"Just to talk." Emmy bit her lip. *Did Kristen know about this? Is that what she meant about staying too long?*

They sat on the couch and talked for over an hour, though there were many periods of awkward silence. Then Tony asked, "Are you still going to wait until you're married?"

She knew exactly what he meant but didn't answer him.

When she didn't respond, he continued, "I guess I shouldn't ask you that. I'm sorry. It's none of my business."

You're right. It isn't any of your business. She looked at him then stood up. "I need to get to bed. You can crash in the spare room if you don't want to go home. There is an extra blanket in the dresser if you need it. I'll show you where I keep the towels and stuff in the morning if you're still here."

"Night, Em. Can I give you a good night kiss?" Tony asked as he got up and moved close to her.

"I don't think you should. I'll see you tomorrow." She put a hand on his chest to keep him away—as if that would stop him if he were really determined to kiss her.

Tony spent the night at her apartment but slept in the spare room. Emmy lay on her back and struggled to fall asleep because she couldn't stop thinking about what Tony said.

Crap! Why now? God! Tony, your timing couldn't be any worse. I know I love you, but maybe not the way I used to. Emmy thought as she buried her head under her pillow for a moment. *What if I do though? Oh, Kenny, why aren't you here tonight instead of Tony? Why did I tell him he could crash here?*

Tony also had trouble falling asleep. Twice he got up and thought about walking through the living room to her bedroom. Both times he stopped as his conscience got the better of him.

Maybe she really wants me to come to her room. She might be waiting for me right now. If I don't make a move, she will think I'm a wimp. On the other hand if she doesn't want me... I might ruin everything if I try to force her. She will think I'm worse than Todd Delaney. I should have just gone home. Kristen, I never should have listened to you.

Emmy woke up first and got dressed. She put on a pair of baby blue shorts and a white t-shirt with a purple Fridays At Five logo on the front. She brushed her hair and used a piece of purple ribbon to tie her hair in a ponytail. She tiptoed quietly through the living room on her way to the bathroom. She paused in the kitchen. *Should I let him sleep? I should take him home so I can get my stuff done.* She opened the fridge, looked for something to drink and grabbed a bottle of apple juice. She drank it straight from the bottle and then put it back. *I should see if he's awake.* She avoided the spot in the living room floor that creaked. She knocked lightly on the door of the spare bedroom and opened it. The door squeaked like a nail on a blackboard. *Shoot! That's enough to wake the dead.*

"Are you awake? Are you decent?"

"Yeah, I was just laying here and thinking." He turned on his side and propped himself up on his elbow.

"Oh, I'm sorry I disturbed you. Did you get a headache from thinking too much?"

"Very funny, Em!"

"I'll take you home whenever you're ready."

"Give me a few minutes." He moved his feet to the floor and sat up. "Are we going to talk about last night?"

"What about it? We didn't do anything." She glanced at his boxers and t-shirt.

"I meant what I said. You know. About how I feel." He tossed the sheet back and sat on the edge of the bed.

"Did you really say that? I thought it was a dream." She bit her lip because her attempt at humor fell flat.

"I meant every word. We have to talk about it sometime."

"I know, but I can't just now." She turned to walk away.

Tony jumped out of bed and caught up to her. He tenderly placed his hands on her shoulders.

"Don't, Tony," she cried.

"Don't what? I didn't do anything."

"I can't talk about it. Let's just go to your house."

"Give me a minute to throw on my clothes." He sighed. *What can I do to convince her that I really meant what I said?*

Neither one spoke for a several minutes on the way back to Tony's. Emmy stared at the road. Tony stared out the window. The radio was turned off. Tony rolled down his window.

Finally, Emmy asked, "Do you think Mama will be upset that you didn't come home last night? I'm sure she knows where you were."

"I don't know." He turned to look at her. "I don't think she'll be mad. I think she will understand."

"She might swat my butt," Emmy joked.

Tony laughed. "Mine, too."

Emmy grinned, but then thought about her mother. *Mom would smack me and probably lock me in my room.*

387

Emmy and Tony walked into the house together. Mama didn't ask him where he had been—she simply knew.

"Are you all right, Emmy?"

"I'm fine, Mama. Tony slept in the spare bedroom so nothing happened. Well, some stuff did happen, just not that. We talked about everything though."

Tony shook his head. *No, we didn't! You won't talk about the most important thing.*

Emmy looked up at Tony and bit her lip. *I know what you're thinking and you're right.*

Mama made breakfast while Emmy watched Tony finish packing. He had to leave for Notre Dame today. He carried his large suitcases downstairs and out to the car.

"I'm sorry that I kinda fibbed to Mama," Emmy apologized as she lifted a small suitcase into the trunk.

"Yeah, it's all right." Tony slammed the trunk and walked away. *I didn't expect you to say anything in front of her.*

"You're mad at me."

He snorted. "Whatever gave you that idea, Emmy?"

"Breakfast is ready," Mama said. "Sit down and eat, Emmy."

"I'm sorry, Mama, but I don't have an appetite right now. My stomach is in knots."

"Try to eat a little, honey. I could make some tea if that would help." Mama squeezed Emmy's shoulders.

"No thanks, Mama." Emmy sat down across from Tony. She watched him eat and neither one spoke.

Tony finished eating and placed his plate in the sink. "Thanks for breakfast. I need to get going."

Emmy walked outside with Tony and Mama. Tony approached Emmy cautiously. Since she didn't back away, he kissed her cheek before getting into the car.

"I will see you soon, Emmy. Don't cry. I'll call you when I get to school."

"I'm not going to cry," Emmy said cheerfully, and she almost believed it.

"Drive safely, son."

"I will, Mama. I love you!"

"I love you, too, son."

They watched and waved as Tony backed the car out of the driveway and drove away. Mama held Emmy close and kissed the top of her head.

"Now come inside, and I will pack up some food for you to take home. You need some meat on those bones. You are too skinny."

"Yes, Mama," Emmy whispered.

They turned and walked back to the house. Emmy hung onto Mama's arm. She glanced back at the driveway, wishing Tony's car were still there.

Mama pulled casserole dishes out of the refrigerator for Emmy to take home. "I made some of this yesterday morning, but most of it I made last night." She filled up a large box with food as Emmy stood beside her and watched.

"How will I ever eat all of this? Oooh! I love your baked beans." Emmy forced a grin, but then she whimpered.

Mama turned and looked at Emmy. Emmy shifted her weight back and forth from one foot to the other. She bit her bottom lip to keep it from quivering. Mama knew she needed to cheer her up somehow.

"What's wrong, baby?"

"I don't know what to do, Mama. I love Kenny, but I think maybe I still love Tony, too. What am I gonna do? How will I ever choose between them? I know one of them will be hurt no matter who I choose."

Mama put a hand on Emmy's cheek and wiped away a tear. "When the time is right your heart will tell you who to choose." Mama hugged the girl she loved as a daughter. "You aren't the only girl who has gone through this, sweetie. When I was a young teenager, feelings about boys confused me, too. For a time I struggled with the very thing you are now."

"Really?"

Mama nodded her head, and then asked, "Have I ever told you how I met Peter Bertucci?"

"No, you never have." Emmy's eyes lit up.

"Have a seat at the table, and I'll tell you a story about how I met the love of my life."

Mama sat at the kitchen table and closed her eyes for a moment. Emmy sat across from Mama and tucked her feet under her. Emmy put her elbows on the table and her chin in her hands. Emmy's bright blue eyes sparkled with excitement now as Mama began her story.

"I was fifteen years old and going to church with my family. We sat in our pew, and I turned and looked over my shoulder and there he was..."